Counter Hex

by

Margarita Gakis

Fable Press

This is a work of fiction. Names, characters, places and events portrayed in this book are either products of the author's imagination or are used fictitiously. Any character resemblance to actual persons, living or dead, is entirely coincidental.

Counter Hex
Book 2 of *Covencraft*

Published by Fable Press
FablePress.com

Cover by Steven Novak

ISBN: 978-1-939897-12-1

First Edition: June 2014

To Donna - Your enthusiasm for my work, both in progress and finished, warms my heart! The care, consideration and attention you exhibit humbles me. ONE HUNDRED AND FIDDY PERCENT!

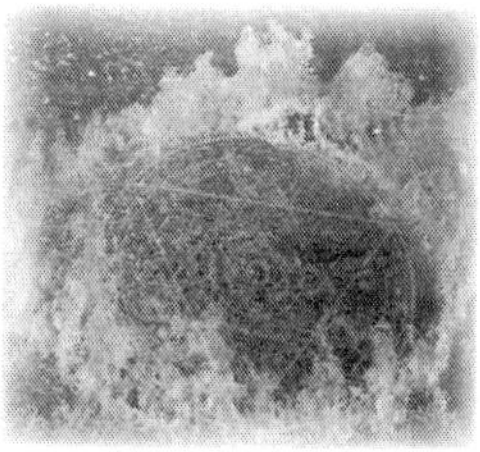

CHAPTER 1

Jade trudged through the hip-deep sewer water, her face a rictus of displeasure and disgust.

"'Join Counter-Magic,' they said. 'It will be fun,' they said," she muttered to herself.

The radio transmitter in her ear squawked and she winced at the volume, but with her hands encased in thick rubber gloves, she lacked the dexterity to adjust it.

"I believe we said it would be interesting. I don't recall a promise of 'fun.'"

"It was *implied*! The fun was implied!" she said back.

Josef chuckled in her ear and although she was up to her waist in muck and grime, she still found the sound warm and inviting. "Think of it as an adventure."

"I can't hear you over the sound of how much this sucks!"

He laughed again, his deep-timbered voice in her ear. "Ah yes, the glamorous life of a Counter-Magic Agent."

Glamorous was about the furthest thing from what it was.

Not two days after Jade made her decision to stay at the Coven, Paris informed her that Josef from Counter-Magic had asked if Jade would be willing to join his department. Paris told Jade it was Counter-Magic's job to seek out bad or tainted magic and contain it. Whether that meant counter-hexing or nullifying a spell, or perhaps using a specially sanctioned hex to clarify and cleanse magic was up for debate - each case was assessed individually. Working under Josef's direction, the department stabilized the use of magic within the immediate Coven area and outside the city if necessary. To Jade, it sounded like it would be intriguing, fun and full of problem-solving.

Also, at the time, she didn't have anything to do on a day-to-day basis and the boredom was killing her.

She'd met Josef once before. He'd attended the ceremony where Paris stripped the power of a witch that had tried to get a demon to kill Jade.

Good times. Fond memories. If she kept a journal, the entire thing would have been filed under,

"Shit that went down and nearly killed me, Volume 3."

Volumes 1 and 2 were already taken up by her childhood, thanks.

Josef reminded her of a fit Gepetto, or maybe a Patrick Stewart type. Older, in good physical shape, striking, white hair. He exuded a casual confidence that she found soothing and calming. When Paris had said that Josef wanted her for his department Jade had been surprised and blurted out, "Why?"

It turned out, Josef told Paris he thought Jade's magic would be a powerful addition to his department. The fact that Jade was learning demon magic, and was the only witch in the Coven to do so, was a big selling point. Most witches couldn't or wouldn't touch demon magic. Some wouldn't even speak of it whereas Jade plunged herself headfirst into it. It also helped that she seemed to have a knack for it.

Jade also thought demon magic was fun, but she kept that little tidbit to herself. She'd brought it up once to Callie and the look on her face had been a mixture of horror, worry and apprehension. Jade spent the rest of the afternoon trying to take it back and convince Callie that she hadn't really meant it and Jade was only learning the basics. Honestly. Pinky swear.

Since then, the only person Jade discussed demon magic with was Paris and even he, with all his power as Coven Leader, got a little chalk-faced at times.

Before she said yes to Josef's offer to work for him, Jade thought she'd asked Paris and Josef the right kinds of questions about Counter-Magic. She asked what she would have to do and they answered that she would work on magic gone awry and learn how to counteract it. Jade asked if she would work in the Coven, and they said mostly, yes. She asked how much it paid and Paris explained that her salary was based on her experience, but she would also receive a stipend for hazard pay. He then he quoted her a number that was well over what she'd been making back in the regular world as a statistician. Jade couldn't say yes fast enough after hearing that number.

Now, trudging through the city's underground sewers in hip-high rubber wading pants, trying valiantly to keep the spell that blocked scent from her nostrils working, and trying really hard at not thinking about what she was slogging through, she realized should've asked for more money.

"You guys totally save this stuff for the rookies, don't you?"

"Yep," Josef said, unapologetic over their two-way radio. "I'll be honest, this happens at least once or twice a year. Some younger witches get overeager and try combining stuff they don't really know about and then, not knowing any better, they flush it down the toilet. We try to educate them about it in school, get them while they're young, but..."

"But it only makes some kids want to try it themselves," said Jade, her lips curling in disgust as something unidentifiable floated by. Yuck.

"You got it. You're the third witch I've had to send down into the sewers this year. It's been a busy one."

"Ugh. When I get out of here, I want to see those kids. I want to see the whites of their beady little eyes and I'm going to tell them exactly what will happen to them if they try this again."

Josef laughed again in her ear. "We try not to scare the younger witches, Jade. It's bad for PR."

"I don't give a shit about PR," she said back, balancing on her booted tiptoes as she had to wiggle through a tight spot in the sewers. "Despite the head lamp you gave me, it's dark down here. Despite the anti-aroma spell you taught me, it stinks. Despite the rubber pants I'm wearing, I can feel the yuck seeping into my pores. I will not be clean again until I can take a full hazmat decontamination shower, complete with radiation scrub down and high-pressured hoses. I'm going to put the fear of me in those kids. I'll do classroom visits, I will let myself be surrounded by those little knee-high rug rats with their sticky fingers and grabby hands. I will let them know the horror that will be visited upon them if I have to come down into this sewer again."

Jade reached a junction point and, based on the map that Josef had made her memorize before coming down, she knew she needed to boost herself up and over the access point and then head left. She should almost be at the blockage point. There was some weird magic vibes coming from the area, but even Josef, after all his years, was stumped as to why the system was blocked. Still, it was deemed an easy and safe enough task for Jade to attempt. Her first Counter-Magic assignment.

Yay.

She placed both hands on the low stone ledge, the light from her headlamp illuminating far, far too much of the thick soupy water and its contents for her liking. She pushed up hard, feeling her wrist twinge painfully. Dr. Gellar had only taken her cast off last Tuesday after Jade had broken her wrist dealing with what she liked to call 'her little demon problem.' After being in a cast for four weeks, Jade found her bones weak and unstable - as though both she and her wrist didn't really trust each other yet.

With some really awkward shimmying and hefting, she was up and over the access point, splashing down with a wet thump on the other side. She grimaced. She was pretty sure things were landing in her hair. Even with her ponytail secured up high on her head, it still wasn't safe from sewer goop. She flapped her hands in what could only be considered a childish manner. It was so gross. *She* was so gross.

"You should nearly be at the confluent point," Josef's voice said in her ear. "Just up ahead and to your right."

She waded deeper into the area and was about to give a snarky retort when she froze. Something down here was *shifting*.

Keeping her head, and by extension the headlamp, still, she moved her eyes around. "Josef? Does something live down here?"

"What? No," came the immediate reply. "It's the sewer. Nothing lives down there. We've had an anti-vermin hex on it for ages. It's well maintained every year."

She heard something again - a wet, slithery sound and this time she couldn't stop herself from wildly moving her head, shining her light in all directions. She thought she saw something, at the far end of the tunnel, to her right, exactly where Josef was sending her.

"Is this some kind of hazing thing?" she questioned, taking slow steps forward. The weight of the water and sludge made her progress lurching and inefficient. If she needed to run away, she was going to be slow - like a shopping cart in a snowy parking lot. Up ahead, she thought she saw movement, but the bouncing light of her headlamp was too murky in the dark depths. She couldn't be sure.

"What are you talking about?"

Jade narrowed her eyes, trying to see better in the dark. "Something's down here."

Josef paused a little too long for her liking. When he spoke, it was with the practiced tone of a man who was used to having his word obeyed. "Okay, Jade. I want you go back the way you came. We'll reconvene at the mouth of the sewer and suit up some more senior witches to go in."

Jade felt a rush of relief that he believed her. "So you're not hazing me, hey?"

"Definitely not. Come back out of there, Jade."

She paused for a second longer, still trying to squint into the hazy dark.

Something pink and quick snapped out of the blackness and hit her lamp, knocking it off her head. She squawked in surprise and flailed backward. She hit the wall of the sewer, her cheek pressing against it - slimy, wet and slippery. She squealed again, pushing herself away just as Josef was barking questions in her ear. Something brushed by her leg and she jerked. Turned around in the dark, and without her lamp, she didn't know which way to go. She forced herself to stop moving and to take a deep breath. She tasted sewer gas and sludge and she realized in her panic, she'd lost control on the aroma-blocking spell. She panted slightly, the rush of adrenaline making her heart race. She could vaguely see the muddled light of her lamp, a few feet away, underwater, illuminating the area around itself with a sickly glow.

She really wished she hadn't seen into the water. Gross.

Josef was still talking in her ear and she managed to take a deep breath and then answer him. "I'm fine, I'm okay. Something… something hit my lamp and I lost it. Can I use a fire spell down here for light?"

"No," came the sharp reply. Immediate, brokering no argument. "Absolutely not. You're in a contained area tied to the city's water supply and there's already a mixture of magic about. We can't add to it. Can you get to your lamp?"

She made a face. She could. But it was under water. There was *no way* it was going back on her head. Still, she guessed she could hold it up to get out.

"Yeah. Yeah, I can get it."

"Do that. Come out. We'll go back in."

A hissing sound right behind her made her freeze. Her eyes widened and she started to turn slowly. There was as scrabbling and scraping sound that made her blood run cold. She could feel sweat breaking out on her upper lip. Whatever was down there with her was right behind her. Despite what Josef had warned, she readied a fire spell. They could deal with the fall out of whatever happened. She wasn't about to get eaten alive without even trying to defend herself.

She swiveled her neck first, then her shoulders, and then the rest of her body, causing a soft wave in the water. She heard the hissing sound again and then another sound. A kind of whimper.

She could just barely make out the rough outline of something. It was the size of a big dog - a husky or maybe a retriever. It didn't move as Jade stared at it, but she heard the strange, high-pitched whine again. Intrigued, she moved closer.

"What are you?" she whispered.

"Jade? What are you doing? What's happening?"

"Yeah," she muttered, not really paying attention. "Hang on," she said absently, moving closer to the odd shape. Suddenly a pair of reflective eyes opened, their silver-green staring back at her grey ones.

"Holy shit!"

"Are you okay?" Josef asked.

Jade's eyes were adjusting quickly in the darkened sewer and she could make out more as she got closer. The silver-green eyes blinked at her. She jerked back when the creature lurched and moved. She heard the distinctive shuffling, shifting, scraping sound again and then the whining sound. Now, in front of it, she thought she could finally make out more of its features and its situation.

It was stuck.

"Remember all those urban legends about alligators in the sewer?" Jade asked Josef.

There was a pause and then Josef answered. "You're joking."

"'fraid not. Big guy too. I think he's stuck." Jade peered closer and the large eyes blinked at her, staring up like they had found salvation. She felt kind of bad for it all of a sudden. Stuck down in the sewer, in the dark. No way out. She held up her hands in front of it in a non-threatening manner, like she would with a strange dog. It blinked again and watched carefully as she moved one hand forward and then pet it on the head. It closed its eyes and gave a low, sad sound.

It was the saddest fucking thing she'd seen all week.

"We've got some witches suiting up to help you and…" Josef paused and she heard him talking to someone else, "some people from the city."

A pink tongue, unusually long and slender, popped out and licked at her other glove. It must have been what knocked her lamp off her head. It poked at her gloved hand and she could feel the strength in the muscle.

"Okay, I'll… just wait here, I guess," Jade replied.

"You can come out. The team knows where they're going."

Jade looked down at the monstrous lizard and felt bad about leaving it alone in the dark again. She pet it soundly on the head and it made a strange sort of 'whirring' sound. Jade thought it might be purring.

"Nah. I'm good."

*

Getting the half-lizard, half-'whatever' out had been like watching something be birthed. It was messy with a lot of grunting and it felt a little bit disturbing. At the end, it was topped off by profound relief.

It took three extra Counter-Magic agents and Jade to break up the solidified muck that had trapped their curious amphibian. They pulled, clawed and heaved until finally, with a wet 'plop,' the lizard fell out of the drainage pipe and into the water where it splashed and flailed like a toddler without water wings. It tried to climb up Jade, its sharp, piercing claws puncturing her rubber wading boots, causing them flood with soupy sewer water. It didn't stop until it clawed its way up her torso, clinging to her like a scared cat in a room full of rockers.

"Aw, Jade," said Daniel, one of her fellow agents, "you look positively maternal."

"Bite me," she retorted, trying not to make any sudden movements while clutching awkwardly at the… thing. She thought she maybe knew how it felt; Jade couldn't swim herself and the lizard-thing was heavy and muscular, ready to sink like a stone. From what she could tell, it didn't have webbed feet or fins.

It felt like it weighed about sixty or seventy pounds and Jade doubted she would've been able to hold it if not for part of its body still being submerged and buoyed by the water. She looked up and around the cavern, more lit now with the addition of several other witches and their headlamps. She could see a jutted edge that ran along the interior and she would have bet her morning cup of coffee that the creature had been keeping to the high ground.

Daniel wasn't even trying not to laugh as he unfolded a tarp from his kit bag and made a kind of hammock swing with another one of the witches. Jade hefted the creature in her arms a bit, settling its weight as Daniel and the other witches worked on the carry-sling.

Jade considered herself 'friendly acquaintances' with Daniel, Henri's boyfriend, ever since she started working and jogging with him. The day after her brief introduction to the office of Counter-Magic, they spied each other running in the local nature reserve. She jerked her head once in greeting, he jerked his head back. The next day, she found him waiting at the parking lot when she pulled in, doing calisthenics until she arrived. They had a comfortable, no-talking running routine, only broken up by one of them picking the music for the entire run and blasting it through their MP3 player.

When the call came in about the blocked sewer drain, it was Daniel she heard stage whisper, "Get the rookie!" He'd had a shit-eating grin on too - all perfect teeth and eye-crinkles.

Jade was going to make tomorrow's run *hard* on him. She was already composing her list of upbeat, bubble-gum, dancey pop. It was the exact music she knew he hated. She might even throw in "It's Raining Men," just to be a brat.

Once the sling was ready, one of the counter-magic guys, whose name she didn't know, got spat on by the lizard when he tried to grab it away from Jade. She managed to shift herself over to the sling and once she bent over a bit to lay it down, it seemed to get the idea and pushed off her, landing in the hammock. They ended up sort of ferrying it out like a beached mermaid. It helped that Jade was tall. Her five-foot ten-inch height was on par or close to the male witches they'd sent in, making the sling pretty even as they carried it. The creature lay heavy in the sling, paddling its taloned feet idly as they maneuvered their way back out of the sewer. It started hissing and spitting whenever it lost sight (or maybe smell) of Jade. Daniel guffawed when Jade moved herself closer to the thing and it calmed down again. She didn't think its eyesight was too good. At least not once they were outside in the bright light of day. As they stepped out into the sunlight, it hissed loudly once and then a weird, dome-like Elizabethan collar snapped up and over its head, like a strange lizard-parasol. Jade saw Daniel flinch when it happened and she smirked, making a point to catch his eye to let him know she'd seen it and wouldn't let him forget it.

Scaredy cat, she mouthed. He stuck his tongue out at her.

Josef stepped forward to get a closer look at both Jade and the creature. "You're bleeding a bit," he said, gesturing to Jade's torso with a frown.

"I'm also covered in sewer-sludge and my wading boots are full of water. I'll likely be dead from dysentery by morning."

Daniel held his hand up to his chest in mock sorrow. "Ah, Jade. We hardly knew you."

"Funny." Her face was deadpan as she pulled her ruined shirt away from her torso and inspected the claw marks on her chest by poking her nose into her shirt.

She'd live.

"I'll escort the…" Josef trailed off.

"Lizard thing?" Jade prompted helpfully, shucking muck off her gloves one at a time.

"Yes," Josef said. "I'll take it back to the Coven and get a vet or a cryptozoologist or a -"

"Priest?" interrupted Daniel as he and Jade shared a laugh while Josef gave them a chiding look and chose to ignore Daniel's comment.

"Good work, Jade," Josef said and she felt a surprising rush of warmth at his tone. "I'll see you back at the Coven."

They loaded the lizard into the back of one of the city sewer trucks that the Coven had borrowed for the trip. As the truck pulled away, Daniel and Jade winced at the ear-splitting howl the lizard let out.

"I think it likes you," Daniel joked.

"My milkshake brings all the boys to the yard."

Daniel made to slap her on the back, but then stopped at the last moment, wrinkling his nose. Water was leaking out of the puncture wounds the lizard had left in her boots and Jade was standing in a little puddle of her own making. "Come on, we'll get you off to the medlab. I'm sure Gellar will want to give you a tetanus shot. Or twelve."

"And a decontamination shower, I hope," Jade said, unhooking the straps of her boots and then wiggling out of them. She knocked them over, spilling the water and sludge out. Daniel stared singing softly, 'Tip me over and pour me out,' from "I'm a Little Tea Pot."

She glared at him. He grinned his shit-eating grin at her again.

"Welcome to Counter-Magic, Jade."

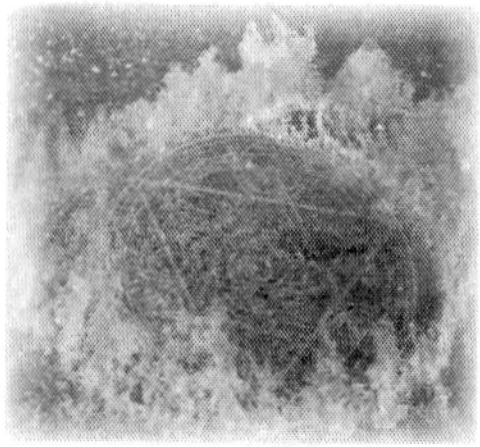

CHAPTER 2

Jade ducked into one of the bathrooms in the medlab before Gellar could see the mud, sewage, blood and just general disgusting mess she was. She'd mostly finished dripping and sloshing on the ride back, but she still left wet, ugly boot prints from her waders. One of the more senior witches cast a spell to keep her from trailing too much muck and gunk as she moved, but it would have taken extra magic to make her completely drip-free and Jade hadn't been comfortable letting someone else do magic on her. Since she didn't know any spells of her own yet for it, she was left with the mess. The small bathroom in medlab was equipped with a utilitarian shower and Jade stripped off her clothes, bundling them up, tossing them with a wet plop into the bag for medical laundry.

If they couldn't disinfect and clean them, no one could.

She took the hottest shower she could stand, using one of the antibacterial bars of soap like it was going out of style. The claw marks and small wounds from the lizard burned and stung under the assault of the water and soap, but it was a good hurt - the kind that let you know things were getting cleaned up and cleared out. Jade stayed under the spray longer than she usually did, taking time to clean under her nails, in between her toes and wash her hair three times.

She could still smell sewer-stench. It had probably invaded her soft palate and nasal cavity and would linger for days. She toweled off and snatched a set of scrubs, piles of which seemed to be ever-present in the medlab. Jade managed to slick her wet hair back in a dripping ponytail that left a cold, wet patch between her shoulder blades.

This was the second time she'd filched a pair of scrubs from the medlab. She resolved not to feel bad until her total reached five. She rolled her eyes at herself. Given her history, she'd reach that total soon enough. Dr. Gellar was waiting for her, nearly tapping her foot with impatience when Jade stepped out of the bathroom in a cloud of steam and fog.

"Did you think you could avoid an exam?" Gellar asked with a smile. Despite the fact that she *was* a doctor and most of the time Jade saw her it was because Jade was hurt or in pain, she liked Gellar. She was friendly, but not falsely so, and she seemed to genuinely care for her patients.

"Trust me, you didn't want to see me before I showered."

Gellar's smile widened. "I heard. Sewer detail. And Josef phoned in to say you had some small wounds."

"I was going to tell you."

Gellar motioned her into a small examining room and shut the door for privacy. She tutted as she saw Jade's wounds and went to work on cleaning them. One needed three small stitches and Gellar looked horrified when Jade said it wasn't worth freezing the area and to stitch it up without anesthetic.

"I will do no such thing," Gellar said. "I don't tell you how to cast spells and you don't tell me how to treat you."

Jade frowned. "I just meant it would be faster."

Gellar sighed. "I don't even want to guess at the kind of medical treatment you've had in the past if you're so keen to get out of here that you'd rather me sew you up without anesthetic."

"It's three little stitches!" Jade wasn't sure what the big deal was.

Gellar mumbled something to herself about hacks, charlatans and gluttons for punishment as she prepped a needle and her suture supplies. She also poked her head out and asked one of her assistants to grab a tetanus shot and two other things Jade couldn't pronounce.

Jade still smelled sewer. She surreptitiously sniffed her arm while Gellar prepared her items. She got a strong whiff of the medical soap, a little bit of detergent from the scrubs and eau de sewer stench. Hmmm. Possibly still just in her nose though. Tough to say.

Gellar was quick. Ten minutes, four bandages, three stitches and three burning shots in her upper arm later, Jade was hopping off the table, wanting to curl her toes up and away from the cold floor. She wondered if Gellar knew where she could borrow some shoes.

"You have to stay put for fifteen minutes in the medlab so we can be sure you haven't had a bad reaction to the shots. Also, you'll have to come back in five days and I'll take those stitches out," Gellar said as she opened the door to the little room.

Paris was waiting outside the door, his sharp blue eyes frowning a bit when he saw Jade and heard the tail end of Gellar's words.

"I was under the impression you weren't injured," he said, his crisp British accent perfectly enunciating the consonants. He always looked impeccable in his usual outfit of tailored slacks and a dress shirt - not a strand of dark hair out of place. Standing in front of him while she was wearing med-lab scrubs made her slouch, trying to make herself not as noticeable. With only a few inches difference in their height, she wasn't quite successful.

Jade rolled her eyes. "I'm not injured." She waved a hand. "Couple scratches."

Gellar pointed her finger at Jade. "Scratches that I want to keep an eye on. You were in a sewer with open wounds. Any redness, swelling, lines radiating out or undue pain, you come in. Immediately."

"Sure," Jade said with a shrug moving to step by her. Gellar blocked her way.

"I mean it."

She leveled Jade with a look and Jade was unprepared and confused at the level of concern and care. "Okay. I will," she said, a little nervous. Gellar pursed her lips and stepped out of Jade's way.

"Keep your bandages dry. Change them tomorrow." She made a flourish gesture with her hands towards Paris. "She's all yours," she said to him.

Paris' lips curled into a bit of a smile. "I heard you had an interesting day. I thought perhaps you might appreciate a ride home since Josef is tied up with your discovery." He sniffed the air a bit. "What's that smell?"

"Ugh, I *knew* I stunk like sewer! It's embedded in my skin, I swear." Jade plucked at the scrubs she was wearing and gave her own little unhappy sniff. "Plus, I don't have any shoes."

He looked down at her bare feet and she immediately curled her toes and pointed her feet a bit inward awkwardly. Feet were ugly. It's why people wore shoes.

"We can stop by the dungeon and see Callie. Perhaps she has something for you to borrow?"

Jade looked sideways at him. "Have you looked at her feet? Ever? She has tiny perfect Cinderella feet. She wears a size six and half. I wear a *nine* and a half." She sighed. "I think I have my extra runners in the gym lockers. I can scoot down there and get them."

"What happened to what you were wearing for your assignment?"

She started making her way out of the medlab, trying not to feel like she was stuck in one of those nightmares she had where she showed up in public places with no shoes on. "With any luck, my clothes are being sent into an autoclave as we speak. Maybe I'll get the pants back. Being in your coven is turning out to be a little hard on the wardrobe."

Paris followed her out of the medlab and toward the grand staircase that led down to the lower floor. The locker rooms were on the main floor with the gymnasium being an entirely separate building they'd constructed as an add-on to the Covenstead. The original Covenstead, built over 500 years ago, hadn't really had a need for one. Jade had almost gone to the locker room when she arrived back from the sewer instead of the medlab, but since she was certain she didn't have a change of clothes in her locker and she absolutely wasn't going to change back into her sewer infested ones, the medlab with its handy scrubs had seemed like the better choice.

As she and Paris made their way down, she tried not to let the sideways glances and surreptitious glares annoy her. Although she'd agreed to join the Coven and had made some (dare she say it) friends, it didn't mean that she'd been as easily accepted in the general coven fold as Callie had made it seem she would be when Jade had first been asked to join. Jade wasn't a born witch - something that had never happened before. Witches were always born into covens, with at least one witch parent, until Jade was discovered. So far she was the only one - an anomaly. Jade also had a lot of power - untrained and unbridled power that she was still learning to control. All that on its own would have been enough to make other witches suspicious. The *piece de resistance* had been when Jade had been attacked by not one, but two demons. It ended up one of them had been called by a witch who worked in the Covenstead. Out of that, Jade had ended up learning demon magic, a skill she was still pursuing, unabashedly.

Add it all up, and she made most people in the Coven nervous. Really nervous. Drug dealer trying to cross an international border nervous.

It didn't matter, Jade told herself. She didn't need everyone to like her.

Paris interrupted her surly thoughts. "Josef is dealing with a local vet and is consulting a herpetologist online to see if they can determine just what exactly you managed to find down there."

"Herpte-what?"

"Herpetologist. Reptile and amphibian specialist," he said, clarifying.

She made a face at the thought of studying that her whole life and then considered his tone. "Why do you make it sound like it was my fault? It's not like I put it down there."

He smiled a little at her. "No, but trouble does seem to have a way of… finding you."

She pointed her finger at him. "That's victim blaming. It could have been anyone that waded in there and found the creepy lizard thing."

"But it wasn't anyone. It was you," Paris said pointedly, raising an eyebrow at her. She was about to mouth off some more when a shout from the stairs below caught her attention.

"Here she is! Our resident crocodile princess!"

Jade rolled her eyes at Henri's enthusiastic greeting, hopping the rest of the way down the large staircase to meet him at his desk.

"Daniel filled you in?" she said ruefully. It had been too much to hope that Daniel wouldn't tell his boyfriend the whole story.

Henri laughed. "Oh my god, yes! My only regret is that there aren't pictures of you and that… thing. Whatever it is. I hear they are still trying to figure it out." He wrinkled his nose a bit. "You know you still smell like sewer, right?"

Jade huffed. "Yes," she said, just barely managing to get the words out from in between her gritted teeth.

He held up his hands in defense. "Just checking. Hey, if you can't rely on your friends to say you stink, then who can you rely on?"

"I'm starting to see why it is that I never had friends before," she said dryly and Henri smirked and bounced on his toes.

He gave her the once over, taking in her bare feet. "Do you need shoes?"

"Yeah, I think I have a spare set in my locker I can grab."

"I have some runners here. I was breaking in a new pair of dress shoes last week. You can borrow them. I don't need them back right away."

Jade felt embarrassed by the quick and easy gesture. She shifted from one bare foot to the other while Henri, not waiting for a response, immediately dug into one of his desk's drawers and pulled out a pair of sneakers.

"Um, thanks." She took them and fiddled with them for a moment before undoing the laces and stuffing her feet in.

Henri smiled. "No problem. By the way, I was going to text you. Callie and I are going shopping this weekend for our outfits for the Coven Ball. You in?"

She looked at him blankly. "I don't know what that is."

Henri looked from her to Paris and then back again expectantly. "You didn't get your invite? They went via email."

Jade shrugged. "Nope, sorry." She turned to look at Paris, his familiar, 'I'm perplexed' frown on his face.

"I'll have my assistant follow up with HR to see why you didn't get it."

"Details," Henri said, flapping his hand. "So, shopping is a 'yes' then since you probably don't have anything to wear? It's in ten days so we have to go this weekend."

"Uhhhhh, yes," Jade hedged. She wasn't actually committing to going to any kind of coven party thing without more information, but she liked hanging out with Callie and Henri. Even if she wasn't shopping for herself, she would still like to hang out with them.

Paris and Jade left with Henri promising to text Jade with the details for shopping as soon as they were firmed up. Her feet flopped in Henri's runners, untied and loose, as they left the Covenstead main entrance. Jade noticed a few witches giving her a wide berth. Whether it was from the lingering stench that hung on her from the sewer or just the usual avoidance she was becoming accustomed to, she couldn't say.

Once in Paris' car, she felt more on even ground, watching the sights of the city pass her by outside the window as he drove. Before coming to the Coven, she couldn't remember the last time she'd been a passenger in someone else's car. This morning she'd been picked up by Josef to take her to the sewer assignment and before that, she'd been hitching rides with Callie, Henri or Paris. She'd even taken public transit a few times.

She missed her car.

She missed a lot of her stuff if she was honest with herself. Jade had been putting off going back to her apartment, the one she had before coming to live at the Coven. She wasn't looking forward to closing it out, breaking the lease and moving the rest of her life out here. She'd made the decision to join the Coven and she was… well, maybe not happy, but definitely satisfied with that decision.

She didn't know if she was ready to let go of her old life yet either. She was reaching the point, however, where it was getting ridiculous. Her rent for the apartment was due. Jade had already paid one month to have it sitting empty and continuing to do so was just fiscally foolish. Her car was gathering dust back in the apartment building parkade, her clothes getting musty in the closet. A sigh escaped her lips.

"Rough day?" Paris inquired, his tone slightly teasing and she knew it would likely be a long, long while before she lived down her sewer trip.

Jade thought briefly about telling him what she was thinking about her apartment - about shutting it down and packing it all up. What came out of her mouth instead was, "Yeah."

"Well, since you had to tackle sewer duty and were injured in the process-"

"I'm not really injured, I'm just kind of banged up a bit," Jade said.

"It's certainly enough to warrant the rest of the day off. Josef won't expect you back at work today."

"Nice!" Jade fist pumped a bit. Although she was still new and her job wasn't hard, it was still pretty sweet to get the rest of the day off. She was already envisioning her sofa, a blanket, some TV watching and maybe some reading. With a fresh pot of coffee. Mmmm.

"However, I did have something planned for tomorrow, if you agree."

She shifted a bit in the passenger seat to face him better. "Um, okay. What's up?"

"You recall Hannah, yes?" Paris asked simply.

"Yeah. Oldest witch in the coven. She works for the Council, right? She holds a seat there and represents you guys with the other supernaturals? Well, us guys, I guess."

"Yes. I believe I mentioned she has a particular skill with tarot cards and that it's customary for everyone at the Coven to have their cards read by Hannah at some point. She's invited us over tomorrow to have your cards read."

"I thought she didn't live here," Jade said.

"She keeps a house here although it remains empty most of the time. She lives closer to the Supernatural Council headquarters for convenience sake."

She tapped her finger on the car door. "What will I have to do?"

Paris shrugged slightly while driving. "Nothing really. Hannah wishes to read your cards. It's a way for her to get to know you better. She can pick up pieces of your past, your history, your magic."

Jade felt a bit of fear curl in her stomach at Paris' words. Her past. Her history. She feigned mild disinterest, doodling a bit with her fingers on the window. "What kind of stuff does she usually see?"

"I'm not sure. Readings are between Hannah and the particular witch at the time."

"So, she doesn't tell you what she sees."

"No," Paris answered and then his eyes flicked over to her and back to the road again. "If you're worried about that, no. She won't tell me what she sees about you. She won't tell anyone." Paris paused. "You needn't be afraid."

"I'm not," she said automatically.

"Good," Paris replied smoothly. He pulled the car up in front of the little cottage she'd just barely started to think of as her own. "I'll make arrangements with you tomorrow once I firm up a time with Hannah."

Jade hesitated, hand on the handle of the car door, ready to escape. "What if I change my mind, once we get there?"

"I'm not going to force you to do anything you don't want, Jade. Hannah won't either."

She felt better at the assurance and she nodded a bit. "Okay. Call me, I guess. Or I'll see you at the coven tomorrow."

"Good work today."

Jade felt uncomfortable at the praise and squirmed a bit, using the motion to get up and out of the car. "Thanks." Before he could say anything else, she slammed the door shut and escaped up her walkway to her cottage. She heard his car idle there for a moment, waiting for her to get inside before he drove off.

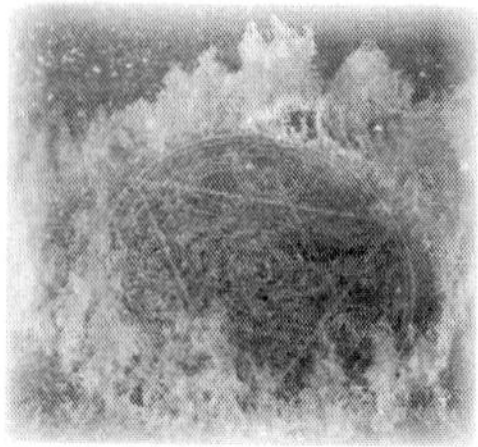

CHAPTER 3

Jade's cottage was small but homey. Even though it had come pre-furnished by the Coven and she hadn't had a say in the furniture and decorations, she still found it soothing and familiar. Comfy couch, afghan thrown over the back, lamps with 40-watt bulbs and worn end tables made the space soft and welcoming. Coming back after a day at the Coven felt almost like coming home sometimes, instead of feeling like she was coming back to a hotel - a place where all her things were, but not a place she felt totally comfortable.

Jade didn't have keys on her, but she didn't use the traditional lock on the door anyway. Since Jade had learned a little bit of demon magic, she felt more secure using a minor spell she'd found that locked her door and kept anyone she didn't want out. She'd tried it out one day, asking both Henri and Callie to open the door after she'd hexed it. They both found themselves reluctant to even approach her walkway leading to the door. Jade had also noticed since she started hexing the door, the mail man left her pile of fliers and notices on the bottom step, not even getting within a few feet of her spell work. Satisfied it worked, she continued to use it. The most convenient part was that the hex continually recognized her and let her through without any further magic.

She kicked off Henri's shoes and stared longingly at the kitchen for a moment before deciding that another shower was definitely in order before she ate. She trudged up the stairs and immediately headed into the small ensuite bathroom that jutted off her bedroom. She pulled her ponytail down and examined the small patch of hair at the front of her skull that was growing a bit faster than the rest. After her run in with the demon when she first joined the Coven, Gellar had to shave a small area to stitch up a cut. When Callie had kept seeing the small, stubbly patch day after day, she asked Jade why she didn't charm it to grow faster.

Jade hadn't even realized it was an option.

Callie had pointed her in the direction of a few spells and Jade managed to work one of them, but she ended up with a patch of hair that grew a little faster than the rest. Callie seemed to think it would even out on its own and advised leaving it instead of trying to counter-hex it and start over again. Like a blister or hangnail, Jade couldn't stop checking in on it and poking at it, frowning every time she had to trim the section to match the rest of her haircut.

She turned the shower water on and took her small scissors out, fiddling at making the ends of her hair even while she waited for the water to heat up. Heedless of Gellar's words, Jade ripped off her bandages. She'd had enough stitches in her lifetime that she wasn't concerned about getting the small wounds wet.

She just needed to feel *clean*.

While she'd appreciated the anti-bacterial and stinging antiseptic quality of the soap at the medlab, she was infinitely more grateful for her own sweet-smelling body wash and loofah. There was something so comforting about being in your own shower, surrounded by your own things.

Or at least travel sized containers of your own things. She really needed to go back to her apartment and get her stuff. She was almost out of body wash.

Project 'Get Her Stuff and Commit to Moving to the Coven' needed to commence sooner rather than later. If Josef didn't have any other sewer assignments for the rookie of the group, maybe Jade could go back tomorrow, pack her things, load up the car and start processing the paperwork that it would take to shut down her life there.

While she knew it was the right decision, she still felt a melancholy weight settle in her stomach at the thought. Jade didn't consider herself particularly attached to the apartment or her job, but it had been the last place she'd seen Lily.

She closed her eyes, willing the thought away. She didn't need concrete walls or steel girders or really crappy hallway carpet to remind her of Lily. It was just a building, just an apartment, just a place that housed things, she told herself. It didn't mean anything.

Jade avoided looking in the mirror when she got out of the shower. She towel dried her hair and secured it back in another ponytail, not once looking up at her foggy, waterlogged reflection. She had things to do, plans to make. But first, lunch.

She padded down the stairs, making her way to the kitchen when she heard a strange scrabbling, scratching sound at her front door. Frowning, she stepped over to it and swung the door open.

The lizard-creature from her morning romp in the sewer bolted past her like a dart. She shrieked in surprise and then raced after it. It leapt up the stairs, quick and nimble and she barely caught sight of it racing into her bedroom and then diving under her bed.

"No! Hell no!" she shouted as she ran after it. She skidded to a stop in her bedroom and then hunkered down on her knees, peering under the bed. Sliver-green reflective eyes blinked back at her.

"Get back out here! What are you doing? Ugh, you can't be here! Aren't you supposed to be in quarantine or being dissected or something?"

It blinked its strange, luminescent eyes at her and didn't move.

"You've got to be kidding me! How did you even get here?" Jade reached a hand under her bed, trying to snatch an arm or a claw. It scooted back farther, out of her reach.

"You can't stay here."

More blinking - the silver-green orbs watching her carefully.

"I mean it. I don't keep… lizard-things. Or pets. It's bad enough buying groceries for myself."

It made a soft of huffing sound and tried to move back further, but encountered the wall. She thought maybe it scared itself a bit because it started slightly like it was going to come back toward her, but then stopped and blinked at her again.

"I'm serious. You probably eat fish or cats or small children. I don't know. But I'm not getting any of those things for you."

It gave off a quiet, whining sound that was just…

She rolled her eyes. Pathetic. It was pathetic.

"That's not fair," Jade said, a complaining tone marring her voice. "I barely just moved in here myself. I don't even know if there's a pet policy. And even if there is it probably doesn't apply to lizards."

Its pink tongue darted out and licked her outstretched hand quickly. It felt like nubbly sandpaper - rough, but not too unpleasant.

It was a High Noon standoff. Lizard-thing vs. Jade. They watched each other, neither blinking. After a few seconds, it made a low, 'pffffft' sound and then licked her again.

Dammit. She thought she might like it a bit. It was ugly and strange, but it looked at her like it knew and liked her.

Jade rocked back a bit on her heels, moving away from the bed slightly. "I'm not going to feed you. If you managed to survive in the sewer, you can manage to find your own… whatever it is you eat around here."

She heard it move under the bed. She couldn't be sure, but it sounded like it was coming closer to her.

Jade shuffled further back, scooting on her butt. "And no accidents in the house or you're gone. I'll hex the place against you."

One clawed, scaled foot peeked out from under the bed. It was the first good look she'd gotten at it. In the sewer, it had been too dark and once outside, her own eyes had still been adjusting as it had been taken away. It had a four-pronged foot - each toe had a sleek, sharp black claw. She absently fingered one of the puncture marks on her shoulder. She could easily see how it had been able to pierce her skin so quickly. She waited a minute and heard it shift again, its strange lizard snout coming out from under the bed. It was triangular, but blunted, like a bearded dragon. It was more a pale lemon-lime than the green she had first thought it was. It was textured and scaly, but more like a fish than a lizard. Slightly iridescent, it glimmered a bit in the light when she moved her head to get a better look. Jade shifted back again, giving it more space. It didn't come all the way out, but stretched its odd neck until the rest of its head was visible. It rested its chin on the floor and stared up at her with soulful eyes. They were uniformly one color with a vertical oval pupil that was wholly black. It had strong ridges encircling its eye sockets, giving it a hooded, haunted look.

She crossed her arms over her chest. "I'm calling you Bruce. Bruce Banner. You can't stop me."

Its tongue flicked out again, this time tapping her on the knee.

"Fine," Jade said emphatically. "You can stay."

It looked like she now had a pet.

*

Paris returned to the Coven after dropping Jade off and headed directly to the lab where Josef was working on dissecting the unknown creature. He liked to tell himself he wasn't going so that he could check up on Jade's mission and ask how she was fitting into the Coven.

Except he was.

He walked into the lab and was confused to see Josef crouched underneath a shelving unit. A look off to the right showed three Counter-Magic agents working some kind of locator spell. From the looks on their faces, they weren't having any luck. An unknown woman, presumably the veterinarian was reviewing a set of x-rays on a light table.

Josef crawled out from under the table and stood, catching sight of Paris as he did.

"Problem?" Paris asked.

Josef looked grim. "It appears our unknown lizard has escaped."

"How?"

Josef jerked a thumb toward his three agents. "It seems these gentleman can't keep track of one little lizard."

"It was very fast," one of the young men piped up. "And it had sharp claws." The other two nodded along quickly, one clutching his arm. Paris frowned, turning back to Josef.

"Is this a serious breach?"

Josef sighed and glanced over at the women. "Our vet says probably not."

"Probably," Paris repeated.

"Well," Josef drawled. "It doesn't seem like it's your average kind of lizard. From what we can tell, it started out that way. But somehow it ended up down in the sewer and started eating all the magical odds and ends it could find. From that, it grew and changed. Now it doesn't fit any kind of classification. From the tests we could run before Larry, Curly and

Moe," he cast a disparaging look at the young agents and they had the grace to look sheepish, "lost it, it appears to be smarter than your average reptile. It's got higher cognitive reasoning and may even be emotionally intelligent."

"But you don't know for certain," Paris said.

"Not until we get it back."

"Can you track it?"

Josef looked at the young men and one of them cleared his throat. He smoothed back his pristine hair cut in a nervous gesture before he spoke.

"We *were* tracking it, but it's like… well… it appears to have disappeared."

Paris raised an eyebrow at the young man. "Disappeared. You managed to find it in the sewer, but now you can't."

"We don't know if it can cloak itself or if it found some kind of magic dead-zone to hole up in."

"Is this a coven security matter?" Paris questioned Josef, but the older man shook his head.

"I don't think it's dangerous, if that's what you're asking. It was down there for years and we only found it because it got stuck and blocked a valve. While it was here, it didn't seem aggressive. More…" Josef sighed, thinking for a moment. "To tell you the truth, once we got it away from Jade, it seemed a little sad."

Paris blinked twice. "Sad."

Josef nodded. "I think it was stuck and she found it, helped it out and it… I don't know. It liked her or something. All I know is when we drove away from her it howled like a lost dog and I swear the thing was moping even as we ran tests." Josef shook his head in amusement. "This is one for the books for sure. That witch is something else."

"That's the primary reason I came to see you. To ask you about her," Paris said, casting a sideways glance at the other agents and then corralling Josef off to one side. He hesitated briefly before asking what was on his mind. "How is she doing?"

"In Counter-Magic? Good. She shows up on time, puts the work in, pays attention. She's got an attitude on her, but she tries."

"And the other agents, other witches?" Paris felt his heart sink a bit at the careful hesitation on Josef's face.

"She's only been here a short time. Less than two weeks in the actual department."

"That's not an answer."

"I know," replied Josef, gathering his thoughts. "The other agents are wary of her. Most of the Coven, actually."

"That's what I was concerned about." Paris turned to look at the triumvirate of counter-agents still trying to work their locator spell on the lizard. They were in each other's space, crowding one another casually in an easy manner. One said something and another one laughed and then poked him in the shoulder. They had a camaraderie.

Paris had yet to see Jade have that same camaraderie with others in the Coven. She was friends with Callie and Henri, and by extension, the men they were both seeing - Nick and Daniel. He was hesitant to put himself on the short list of her friends as he was the leader of the Coven and always felt like he maintained a slight distance. He did think they had a rapport and she certainly seemed comfortable around him, but Paris hadn't noticed her making any other relationships in the Coven. In fact, he'd noticed the distance the rest of the Coven members seemed to enforce around her. They physically kept away from her, glancing sideways with wary, watchful eyes. Jade was the first non-coven born witch they knew of. On top of that, everyone knew she'd been the target of a demon attack. In a strange way, Jade bore the negative backlash from the attack on her life more so than the man who had sent a demon after her. Matthew had been well-liked around the Coven - quiet, mousy, from a good coven family. Most witches agreed that Matthew dealing with a demon to take Jade's power was wrong, but it still seemed that he was the more sympathetic party of the entire mess. Having lost an eye by Jade's magic and becoming permanently disfigured only seemed to increase support for him. He was currently ensconced in a psychiatric facility for supernaturals and Paris knew several witches from the Coven were trying to get in to visit him, whereas people weren't exactly lining up to welcome Jade to the Coven.

"She's different," Josef said, interrupting Paris' thoughts.

"She's still one of us," Paris countered.

Josef paused, weighing his words. "People will come around. She's not the easiest person to get to know, but she works hard and she's good at magic. Besides, it's not as though she doesn't have any friends."

Paris couldn't help but feel they were discussing Jade like a grade-school child on the playground. "True enough. I was merely… concerned."

Josef clapped him on the shoulder. "You're being a good Coven Leader, like your mother before you."

Paris managed a thin, wane smile at the words as he inclined his head as a form of goodbye, taking his leave of Josef. That was a whole separate issue he was dealing with - his mother.

If he'd been asked two months ago if his mother had ever dealt in demon magic he would have laughed at the very thought. However, after Jade discovered three demon grimoires belonging to Paris' mother, filled with demon magic and hexes, he'd started re-examining every moment, every memory, every small detail he could think of about her. He was only able to read through the grimoires for short spans of time, finding they made his eyes burn and his head ache. Her handwriting, as well as her magic, was unmistakable. Any hope Paris had harbored that the books weren't hers, despite being found in his house and with a letter to him from his mother, died as soon as he started studying them in earnest. They were clearly hers. He'd only made it through half of the first volume, but it was saturated with her essence. It was taking him considerable time to unravel the complicated and tangled demon spells she'd constructed.

Jade seemed to have an easier time with demon magic. Whether it was because she had a natural aptitude or had been touched by demon magic when Matthew set one after her, Paris was uncertain.

He tried hard not to wonder if there was any other reason Jade was so adept.

While Paris was only halfway through one volume, having only short bursts of time to work on it, Jade appeared to be gaining familiarity with the other two volumes. She claimed many of the spells were still a mystery to her, but she'd had more luck deciphering some of the easier ones. She could also read the books for longer, not getting a headache as quickly as Paris did. Paris also reviewed the demon grimoire next to his mother's other spell books, trying to establish when she might have started it, or when demon magic was introduced into her repertoire. He couldn't help but think if he could somehow figure out *why* she started using demon magic, then perhaps it would all make more sense.

He was no closer to figuring out the 'why' of it than he had been when he first found out.

The other issue he was facing was that, somehow, word of the demon grimoires had gotten out, not only to his Coven, but to others. Paris had already denied several requests from other covens to examine the books. Demon magic, though taboo, was a bit of a fascination. People wanted to see them, to read them, to study them. Paris fought back a shudder at the thought of those books ever making it into the hands of the general witch populace. He'd only just begun to examine one himself and had no idea what he might find. Given the headaches he suffered while reading them, Paris could only assume the very pages themselves were imbued with magic and he could admit he was very afraid at what might happen if others started reading them. For now, he felt relatively safe knowing that he kept one book safe, at his house, while Jade had the other two. His very worry about Jade not having many friends and acquaintances was the same thing that made him believe the books were safe with her. She wouldn't be inviting people over and having them lying about. If the grimoires got out, if witches started trying their hand at demon magic, Paris didn't want to think about what could happen. While Jade was new with magic, he couldn't deny her affinity with the demon spells and the healthy dose of common sense and street smarts she possessed. He felt the books, and the magic, were safe with her.

He had to push his thoughts aside once he was back in his Coven office. The demands of his job didn't leave much room for rumination and musing. Paris found the rest of his day eaten up by minutiae - responding to correspondence, a quick phone call with other Coven Leaders and then a follow up video conference with the werewolves to ensure they weren't experiencing any bleed-over magic like they had been when Jade first arrived at the Coven. Satisfied the werewolves were unaffected and stable, he continued on with his other coven business.

A knock at his office door pulled him out of his thoughts. "Enter."

"Is this area off limits now that I have my own coven?"

Surprise flooded Paris and he stood up immediately. "Veronica, what are you doing here?" He hadn't seen Veronica in person in over a year and half. His eyes flickered down to his email quickly to see if he missed a message from her indicating she was coming by. She was Coven Leader at another Coven only a short drive away, perhaps a couple of hours. However, given how busy they both seemed to be, they didn't often get the chance to see one another in person. He thought their last email exchange had been a couple weeks ago and didn't recall anything about a visit then. She looked impeccable as always -

well put together in a smart suit, her honey-blonde hair pulled away from her delicate features. She walked easily over the carpet in her heels, coming around his desk and giving him a hug. She felt like he remembered - soft, fragrant, and warm. He sometimes wondered why they'd ever stopped seeing each other.

"I thought I'd come by and visit. I hear you've got a new witch and she's not coven-born. You had to know you'd draw attention." Veronica kissed him quickly on the cheek, brushing away a smudge of lipstick as she did. She pulled back and he ended up cupping her elbows slightly. Up close, her features seemed a bit pinched and tight - as though she hadn't been sleeping well. Paris supposed that was to be expected. Running a Coven was quite an undertaking and while Veronica certainly had the aptitude for it, her magic wasn't nearly as strong as most Coven Leaders. Veronica had always gotten things by hard work and tenacity - making up for what she lacked in magic.

"It's always a welcome surprise to see you," Paris said. He gestured over to the Queen Anne chairs by the fireplace in his office. "Why don't you sit and I'll have some tea sent up. We can catch up a bit."

Veronica's hand was warm and solid on his arm as she spoke. "That sounds lovely, Paris." She headed over to the chairs while Paris sent a quick message to his assistant, asking for a tray to be brought up before he joined Veronica at the hearth. She'd kicked her shoes off and tucked her feet up underneath her while still managing to sit straight up, appearing somewhat regal.

"So, how long are you here for?" he asked.

Veronica pushed a stray bit of hair back behind her ear. "Oh, you know I hadn't really firmed up any details. I thought I'd come by, see how your new witch was doing, get all the gossip. Maybe stay for your Coven Ball?"

Paris nodded. "Of course. How are things at your Coven?"

Veronica waived a hand in dismissal. "I'm sure it's the same all over. Every department wants more funds and each one has an argument why they are the most deserving."

Paris huffed, nodding his head slightly in agreement. "That certainly sounds familiar."

Veronica leaned forward a bit and tapped her hand on his arm. "Let's not talk about work. We get enough of it during the day. Tell me, how have you been?"

"Rather the same, I suppose. I'm afraid I don't have much to talk about if we're taking business off the table." Running the Coven didn't leave him with much time for anything else.

Veronica made a low sort of 'hmm'-ing sound. "And you've got a new witch, born outside a coven. That's certainly new."

"Yes, her name is Jade," Paris said. "To be honest, getting her here and convincing her to stay was problematic." Paris had the quick, biting thought that if Jade were there, she would screech in outrage at his simple explanation.

Veronica's perfectly groomed eyebrows went up. "Really? She was already using power before you located her, correct?" At Paris' nod, she continued. "I would have imagined she would have been thrilled to find an explanation and to be around other witches."

"I think Jade is accustomed to being on her own. She wasn't quite ready to join in with a full Coven. Of course, there was also the business with Matthew."

Veronica's eyes darkened and she nodded in sympathy, placing her hand back on Paris' arm and resting it there. "I heard. I'm so sorry about that. I can't imagine that breaking a witch's power, even one as relatively weak as Matthew, was an easy task."

"No, certainly not." Paris took a breath in. "All that to say, it's been difficult getting Jade settled."

They were momentarily interrupted by a knock on the door and Paris rose to answer it. He took the tray of tea from his assistant and brought it back over to the fireplace, handing Veronica her tea, plain, before adding a liberal amount of sugar to his.

"Paris, I don't like to gossip, but I'm afraid I also heard another rumor," Veronica said, her voice low and quiet as she sipped her tea.

"I'm almost afraid to ask. Nothing travels as fast, as far-"

"-or as false as Coven gossip," Veronica finished the familiar saying for him, with a smile. Her smile faded and she settled her teacup and saucer in her lap. "I'm sorry if this crass or blunt, but if possible I like to dispel rumors. Certainly one of this size and nature." She paused and Paris had a feeling he knew what she was going to say before she spoke. "I've heard that your mother dealt in demon magic and, in fact, had several demon grimoires."

There it was. It's not that Paris was a secret keeper by nature, but he was certainly circumspect. He had to admit there was a large part of him that hoped word of his mother's demon grimoires would never get out. But, as with most coven matters, it seemed that had been a foolhardy thought.

"I'm afraid it's true. We did find some grimoires of hers that were hidden and they do contain demon magic." If Paris thought it would get easier to say with time, he was wrong. It did not. Veronica's face was a mask - as though she was hiding her true expression and he wondered what that meant.

She swallowed another sip of tea before speaking. "I'm stunned," she said honestly. "I remember growing up here with your mother as Coven leader and I never felt anything in her magic that even hinted at using demon spells."

"Nor I." Paris stared at the tea in his cup as if it were a scrying surface and could give him the answers that he needed.

"What's in those books, Paris?" Veronica asked. "Are they dangerous?"

"To be honest, I'm not entirely sure of their contents. I can't read them for very long. They cause headaches and blurred vision. Jade is having better luck than I am."

"Jade has seen the books?"

"Yes. She's proved to be quite adept at using demon magic."

"Really," Veronica said, her tone low and soft. "I assume you're keeping these grimoires safe?"

"I've got one at my house, in the same spot all three remained for years undiscovered. I'm certain no one else can find them. The location was charmed by my mother to be a hiding spot for them and wouldn't be easy to find without someone knowing what they were looking for."

Veronica made a low 'hmmm'ing sound. "And the other two?"

"With Jade. She's able to work her way through them faster and has shown more of an interest in them than in other magic."

Veronica frowned. "Paris, I admit that has me concerned. She's new and she's essentially unknown to us. Is it wise for her to have those books? To be using those books? Shouldn't you keep all three together, with you?"

"I trust Jade," Paris said simply. It was the truth. He did trust her. While she certainly had an interest in the books and demon magic, Paris had never once gotten the sense from her that it was a malicious or cruel interest. It was more like watching someone figure out a new and complex toy. Jade liked poking things, and the demon books were her new shiny gizmo.

"Well, I certainly have to make an effort to meet her if she's inspired such faith in you already." Veronica smiled over the rim of her teacup. She placed it down on the small side table next to one of the chairs. She brushed her hands together and smoothed her skirt before folding her hands in her lap. "Well, I should leave you to your work. I'm sure we'll have time to catch up while I'm here."

Paris stood as Veronica did, reaching out to help her to her feet. She slid her cool fingers into his hand and gripped lightly, using him for a bit of balance as she got her shoes back on.

"I'm afraid my trip was very ill-planned. I haven't even got a place to stay yet," Veronica said.

"I can have my assistant book you a hotel room, if you like."

Veronica smiled and again her face looked a little drawn and tight. He wondered if running her Coven was taking a bit more of a toll on her than he'd previously thought.

"That would be lovely, thank you."

*

Googling how to take care of a lizard had been a bust, mostly because Jade couldn't figure out what the heck Bruce was. He didn't match any of the pictures that she found. He looked most like a Bearded Dragon, but he was way too big and a bit more lemon-green than they appeared to be. He had a collar like an Australian Lizard, but again, he was just too big for that. The Collard Lizard was closest in color to Bruce, but too small. Other than alligators and crocodiles, she really couldn't find anything close to his size. Jade had made a dinner of some baked chicken and potatoes and despite her earlier assertion that she wouldn't feed Bruce, she'd felt bad and ended up giving him a fair portion of both. He seemed to enjoy it and was now looking content, sleeping in front of the fireplace while Jade worked on her computer. She eyeballed him and tried again to match up his appearance with something, anything on the web.

Nada.

Maybe she should give the herpetologist a call. But, that would entail admitting she had a seventy-pound, possibly contraband, lizard in her house. Feeling bored with her Google searches, she flipped her tabs over to Netflix and called up a season of a crime show she'd been meaning to watch. Turning off all the lights, she settled in to watch.

Three hours into watching and Jade knew it was either time to go to bed or to declare it an official TV marathon and watch all of season 1 in one shot, tomorrow at work be damned. One in the morning - decision time. The room was dark except for the glowing of her laptop. She really should get one of those cords to hook it up to her TV. She couldn't keep acting like a college student and watch all her stuff on a tiny screen. Her finger was wavering on the button to start another episode when Bruce leapt up from his prone position on the floor. His claws skittered on the hardwood as he flipped up to his feet. His collar flushed out like a large fan, circling his head. He pointed his body toward the door and hissed - a low, drawn out sound that made the hair on the back of Jade's neck rise. He skittered over to the front door, stopping only once he was right in front of it. He hissed again and another sound came from his throat, a kind of growl.

Did this mean he had to go out? Or had just gone totally feral? Maybe it hadn't been the brightest idea she'd ever had to let an unknown creature stay in her house without telling someone. She closed the lid of her laptop, finding the 'click' it made in the darkened room louder and sharper than usual.

"Bruce?" she said quietly. "Do you want to go outside?"

He hissed at the door again and Jade got slowly to her feet, nervous to approach him. He seemed bigger and meaner in the near-darkness. Jade gently touched one of the puncture marks that Bruce's claws had already left - stitched up by Gellar. She didn't think Bruce would hurt her, but she was still wary as she approached.

She opened the front door and he shot out like a gun from a bullet - disappearing into the shrubbery around the house. With the winter approaching, the leaves had started to desiccate and fall off, making all of Bruce's footfalls loud and crunchy. There was a far amount of rustling from where he vanished into the dark. Jade squinted, trying to make anything out, crossing her arms over her chest to ward against the chill that moved into the doorway from outside.

"Bruce?" she called quietly. The rustling stopped and Jade thought the silence that followed it was worse than the ruckus had been before.

"Bruce?" she said again, this time a little lower, more like a hiss.

There was a sharp rustle and he trotted out from the hedges, a mess of dead leaves coming with him. His tail swished as he walked, throwing up more debris as he came up the steps to the house, glanced once at her and then went back inside. He scuttled up the stairs and she rushed to lock the door and follow after him, not wanting him to jump all over her bed.

Jade caught up with him just as he was fixing to jump up, back end wagging a bit as he moved to make the jump.

"Hey! Not after you've been outside."

He gave her an affronted look and then made a 'pffffft' sound, settling beside her bed.

"What was that all about, buddy? Were you catching mice or was that a lizard potty break?"

He blinked up at her, his pink tongue coming out like a dart to lick over his snout and then disappear back in his mouth.

"Silence is golden, hey?" She sighed. "You better not wake me up at three to go back outside. The answer will be 'no'." It was time for her to go to bed anyway and it seemed he'd gotten his little run out of his system.

Another 'pffft' sound escaped him and she felt like they understood one another.

"All right, then. Goodnight."

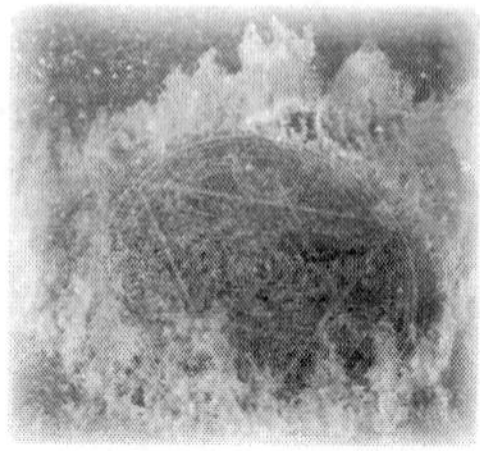

CHAPTER 4

Jade slept hard that night. She woke up the next morning feeling every stretch and strain her muscles had gone through in the sewer the day before. In the in-between state where sleep and awake were simultaneous, her alarm confused her at first, making her wonder what the hell the sound was before she reached out a hand and slapped it off.

She had a long, solid weight pressed up against her side. She cracked one eye open and spied Bruce stretched along the length of her, pressing against her like a wolf in the wild. She shimmied her hip a bit to disturb him, hoping to wiggle him off. His eyes slid open and immediately focused on her accusingly.

"It's my bed."

He didn't move except to close his eyes.

Jade huffed and tossed the covers back, burying him underneath. He seemed clean enough. Given that he lived in a sewer for god only knows how long, he didn't have a stench about him. He must be light on his feet for his size because she didn't recall waking up in the night when he jumped on the bed.

Jade still wasn't going to feed him. Mice or pellets or whatever he ate, Bruce was on his own.

She scrounged up a running outfit, set the coffee up to brew so it would be ready when she got back, and was out the door. She took the back alleys to an access point in the nature preserve close by. Sure enough, as she hopped over the token chain link fence with its "Do Not Litter - Be like the forest! GREEN!" signage, she spied Daniel's car coming down the road. She dropped down from the fence and trotted over, catching up just as Daniel got out.

Jade jerked her chin at him. He jerked his back. Morning greeting ritual complete. This early and before any coffee, it was all that could be hoped for.

She pressed play on her iPod, firing up the playlist she made the night before. The grimace on Daniel's face as he heard the opening strains to Scissor Sisters was more than worth it.

"I claim cruel and unusual punishment," he said, his voice low and gravelly from the early morning.

"You 'rookied' me into going down into a sewer with an oversized magical lizard," Jade retorted back, falling easily into a light jog next to him. "You deserve this, the Village People, some remixed Barry Manilow and Shakira."

Daniel groaned and lengthened his stride a bit as they hit the first tree on the path. "Why do you even have that music at all?"

"It's a guilty pleasure."

They fell into their usual routine of running with the only sound the pounding of feet on the pathway and the upbeat, peppy tunes coming from her iPod.

Jade couldn't say she liked running. She didn't actively hate it, but she didn't exactly enjoy it either. It was a means to an end. It kept her fit and meant she could fit into her jeans on a regular basis, so she did it. She tried to let the rhythm calm her brain and get her to the 'sweet-spot' where she wasn't thinking about how much her legs were burning or how hard it was to breathe, but instead just focused on the sound of her inhaling and exhaling, the pulse of her feet and the feel of the air brushing by her face.

It reminded her of how she used to feel around Lily.

They wound up back at the parking lot soon enough and as usual Daniel offered her a ride home. It was almost longer to drive than it was to walk back, but after her run she never felt like hopping the chain-link fence again - legs too rubbery and well used. Daniel dropped her off with a promise to see her later at the Coven for more of her training.

Letting herself back into her cottage, she peered around the door looking for Bruce but he was nowhere to be seen. Feeling foolish, she even called out for him, but heard no response. She felt a little sad and melancholy at his absence. Jade shook her head at herself and continued on with her morning routine to get to work.

Once at the Coven, Jade was met with the impressive bureaucratic red-tape that apparently couldn't be avoided even when working for a bunch of witches.

"What do you mean 'file a report'?" she asked, staring up at Josef.

Josef smiled down at her. "Ah yes, the second most glorious part of Counter-Magic - the paperwork.

We need you to fill in a Field Consultation Form, a Contact with Unknown Entity/Creature Form and then your General Report on yesterday's trip to the sewer."

"Is this some kind of hazing thing?"

Josef laughed at her expression. "Nope, just your everyday bureaucracy."

"Ugh." Jade sighed booting up her computer. She looked forlornly at the small travel cup of coffee she'd brought from home. She was going to need a bigger mug. "I thought being a witch was going to be way cooler than this."

"Well, if you get your paperwork in on time, maybe I'll teach you a new spell. Got any you want to learn?"

She did have quite a few. "There's maybe one on transfiguration that I'd like to learn," she said, trying to look nonchalant.

Josef laughed again. "Well, you like to shoot for the stars, don't you? All right, do you paperwork and I'll take a look at the spell you want to learn. If I think it's not too hard, we'll give it a try."

Happy like a child promised an ice cream after school, Jade went back to her computer and started her paperwork.

*

After a morning of slogging through paperwork, Paris thought if he left early he could grab something for lunch on his way to his meeting with the local vampires, be back by six, have time to grab a bite to eat, and then take Jade to Hannah's by seven. He sent an email quickly to Jade asking her to be ready by six-forty-five. He received a smart-alec response back that she would be ready at six-forty-five but if he showed up his customary ten to fifteen minutes early, he could wait. Outside. In the car.

He considered a childish response of reminding her he was the most powerful witch in the Coven (Hannah excluded) but refrained. When his phone range moments later, he almost thought it would be Jade, iterating her email for him to be on time and not early, and he was surprised to hear Veronica's voice on the line.

"Settling in?" he asked, updating his calendar to indicate he'd be busy this afternoon.

She laughed a bit in his ear. "The more things change, the more they stay the same. Did you know that they closed the bakery on third?"

Paris sighed. Sadly, he did know. They'd made the best éclairs in the city. "Yes, about six months ago. Retirement." Paris' sweet-tooth hadn't been the same since that bakery closed.

"I was going to pop by and get you some of those chocolate things you like, but there's a cell phone shop there now. The horror."

He laughed at her dry tone. "Well, I appreciate the thought, at any rate."

"Listen, how about I take you to lunch? Tell me they haven't closed the Italian place downtown? I may cry if they have."

"No, it's still open, but I'm afraid I'll have to pass on lunch. I've got a meeting with the vampires and was planning on picking something up on the way."

"Heavy hangs the head that wears the crown," Veronica mused. "How about dinner?"

"I'm afraid that's booked up too, I'm taking Jade to see Hannah tonight to have her cards read."

"Oh, she hasn't had them done yet?"

"It was too crazy when she first arrived. Although she hasn't said so explicitly, I think Hannah made a special trip back to the Coven to do it." Paris paused, hearing the silence on the phone. "I'm sorry, I'm not able to make it today."

"Well," Veronica said. "No matter. Perhaps tomorrow." He could hear the false lightness in her tone and wondered if there were problems at her Coven that she wanted or needed to talk to him about. "The Italian place and I won't take no for an answer."

"All right. Dinner tomorrow it is."

"Wonderful. I'll see you then."

They made short work of their goodbyes and Paris admitted he was a little distracted as he did, already focusing on the next thing in his inbox.

By the time the meeting with the vampires wrapped up later that afternoon, Paris had a bit more time than he thought before he needed to pick up Jade to take her to Hannah's. He briefly considered calling Jade and asking if she had plans for dinner, but the last time he'd taken her out, she managed to convince him to eat at a fast-food chain. He didn't think he was up to another visit and he couldn't think of anywhere else she might like to go, given her propensity for casual dining. He'd have to find some place in town that wasn't a burger joint, but wasn't so fancy that she'd scowl upon seeing it.

Paris was outside Jade's cottage at twenty to seven and was surprised when her door swung open and she came out. She poked her head back inside quickly, as though she were checking something and then shut the door quickly, hopping down the steps to his car, sliding her arms into a bright blue fall jacket as she did.

"You're not going to berate me for being five minutes early?" he asked as she slid into the passenger seat.

"I'll give you a free pass this time since it's only five minutes," she replied cheekily, settling her jacket around her. "So!" she clapped her hands together. "Off to Miss Cleo for tarot card reading?"

"If you mean Hannah, then yes," Paris replied smoothly as he drove.

"Aaaaand," Jade said, stretching out the vowel, "what's the word on the lizard thing?"

"Interestingly enough, the word is 'escape.'"

"Oh yeah?" Jade questioned. "You guys worried?"

Paris made a slight see-saw motion with his head. "I suppose not. It doesn't appear that the creature is dangerous. It will likely return to the sewer, I imagine. We'll have to add some sort of community learning about letting pets loose and not properly cleaning up magical leftovers, I suppose."

Jade nodded and out of the corner of his eye, he could see her tapping her fingers against her knee. "So no full scale manhunt or anything."

"Are you concerned? Did you think the creature was dangerous?"

"No, just," she waved a hand casually, "curious."

Paris glanced quickly over at her, but only saw the back of her head and a bit of the side of her face as she stared out the passenger window.

He stopped at a red light and took the opportunity to face her again. "If you are concerned, I hope you would tell me."

Jade turned to look at him, her cool grey eyes open and almost childlike. She shrugged. "Not concerned."

He saw the light turn green out of the corner of his eye and had to look away, back to the road.

Hannah lived in an older part of town where the trees were so large and full that in the summer they sometimes appeared to be touching each other across the road, creating a lush canopy effect. Now, in late fall, bordering on early winter, the sidewalks and streets were littered with crunchy, dry leaves. Paris saw a few people, witches and mundanes alike, trying to rake them into massive piles. There were the requisite children tossing and throwing leaves about, generally making more work than helping.

"How come they're raking?" Jade asked. "Why not just woo-woo the leaves away?"

"It's a nature thing. It's good for witches to be involved in tasks and chores that put them in connection with nature. It's beneficial to touch things of the earth, work with our hands. It keeps our magic clean and grounded."

"Ugh, does that mean I have to rake my own yard?"

Paris smiled. "Yes. I believe you'll find a small shed in the back with all the tools you need. It will help you with your earth magic as well. You're weak on it. And water."

"Water is hard," she protested. "It's all-" she made a circling motion with her hands. "It makes me feel like I can't breathe."

He felt his own eyebrows go up. "Truly? You never mentioned that before."

"Is that weird?"

He hedged. For all her bluster, he'd come to realize that Jade was sensitive about fitting in and being considered on par with other witches. "Some witches have a hard time with one or two of the elements," he said, hoping that would be a good enough answer to assuage her.

She groaned. "It's weird. I knew it."

Clearly he had to work on his soothing skills if she was able to so easily read him. "You'll get there, Jade." He turned off the main road, down a small side street and then down Hannah's partially obscured driveway. Hannah had several large trees on her property and he could see the neighborhood children had been hard at work collecting leaves into several haphazard piles. Hannah would often treat them to cinnamon hot chocolate for their labor, or perhaps even work a few minor spells for harmless but spectacular fireworks in exchange. Their parents were happy to get them out of the house and working, and the kids couldn't wait to light the fireworks up. Hannah always charmed them with safety-hexes to keep anyone from getting burnt or injured. When Hannah wasn't in town, Paris thought she might have a service that came by to take care of her property. He'd never seen it look anything less than impeccable.

Hannah's house, like the neighborhood, was old. The dark wood planks of her front step sagged from years of use and the chains of the small swing she had on her front porch groaned and clinked in the wind. If he was being honest, it was the perfect Hallows' Eve house, Paris thought. It had a slightly dark, ominous look, although everyone in the neighborhood knew Hannah too well to be put off by it.

Jade, however, didn't know Hannah yet and as Paris parked the car in front of the house, he could see Jade hesitating as she got out of the car. He tried to see it through her eyes and not as a regular visitor. It was reminiscent of a two-story farm house - wider than it was deep. The charcoal grey of the house was worn lighter in areas. Hannah's summer gardening was pulled out and the flowerbeds were stark and empty in the waning dusk light. Some old leaves spun and cracked as the wind caught them and Paris saw Jade's fingers twitch by her side.

"As I mentioned, there's nothing to fear. I'm sure it looks quite ominous, but it's perfectly safe."

She turned and looked at him with doubt in her eyes. "This is the beginning of every slasher-horror flick I've ever seen. 'Come on into the creep-tastic house! Nothing bad will happen to you. Totally safe!'"

"I can assure you are totally safe."

Jade started slightly at Hannah's voice and even Paris looked up quickly. He'd been so focused on Jade he hadn't heard Hannah open the door.

Paris was always surprised by how small Hannah was. He supposed in his mind he was a perpetual child looking up at her and his mother crafting spells, working hexes and incantations. She had also been such a grounding force for him since he became Coven Leader, that he often forgot she was hardly five-foot-two. Her hair was the same perfectly polished sliver it always was, pulled back into a strange and intricate knot. Her exotic, violet eyes crinkled at the corners as she smiled at them.

"Jade," Hannah said, her voice like soft honey. "I've looked forward to meeting you in person."

Jade shot a sideways look at Paris and he had the distinct impression that she was about to bolt. Paris stepped up toward the doorway and bent over slightly to give Hannah a hug and kiss on the cheek.

"Hello, Hannah. It's good to see you."

"You as well," Hannah said. She turned and looked back at Jade expectantly. "Come closer, dear. I won't bite."

Paris could see the way Jade straightened her shoulders, as if screwing her courage to the sticking plate before coming up the steps and facing Hannah.

"Hi," Jade said flatly.

Hannah had to tip her head back to look at Jade. "My, you are something, aren't you," Hannah murmured. She reached out to clasp Jade's hands and Jade flinched back, snatching her hands out of Hannah's grasp. Paris knew Hannah well enough to see the slight disappointment in her eyes.

"Please, come in," Hannah said, sweeping an arm wide in welcome.

Paris gestured for Jade to go before him and she raised her eyebrows and then jerked her thumb to indicate he should go first. He frowned and inclined his head to indicate she would go first and he would follow. Jade shook her head and crossed her arms, turning her face away from him. He sighed. It was clear she wasn't going to budge. He capitulated and stepped in first, fearful for a moment that she wouldn't follow and would perhaps bolt for the car and lock herself inside like a four-year old.

He was relieved when he heard the floorboards creaking behind him indicating she'd followed. Paris caught her gaze out of the corner of his eye as Jade sidled up beside him.

"I thought perhaps we could take some tea in the dining room," Hannah said from up ahead and Jade turned to him and made a face.

'*Tea?*' she mouthed. He gave her his best, most serious '*I am the Coven Leader*' look. She rolled her eyes and huffed, but she didn't run back out the door so he considered it a win.

They followed Hannah to her pristinely arranged dining room where the fine china and teapot were already set out, along with some small macaroons and sugar cookies. Paris stepped forward quickly to reach Hannah's chair before she could and pulled it out for her, tucking it back in close to the table. He turned to do the same thing for Jade and found her already seated and snatching some macaroons off the tiered tray.

"Paris, would you?" Hannah pointed at the teapot and Paris found himself serving the two women. "So, Jade, how do you find coven life so far?"

Jade swallowed her cookie and wiped away a few errant crumbs from her lips. "Um, it's okay."

Hannah paused waiting for Jade to elaborate and when she didn't, Hannah's eyes flicked quickly to Paris who managed a small shrug.

"I hear Josef has taken you into Counter-Magic?"

"Yep." Jade picked up the teacup that Paris had filled for her and sniffed it a bit. She took a small sip and seemed to enjoy it, taking another sip right after.

Hannah spared another glance toward Paris and then back to Jade. "And you're enjoying the work so far? Learning magic?" Hannah prompted, obviously hoping for a longer, more detailed response.

Jade looked up over the rim of her teacup, first at Hannah, then at Paris and then back to Hannah again. "Yep," she repeated.

Hannah nodded. "Good, I'm glad."

Silence descended on the dining room; the kind that was pressing and awkward, begging for someone to jump in with an inane remark or ridiculous factoid of life just to break up the quiet.

"Jade had quite an interesting day with Counter-Magic yesterday," Paris said, hoping that all those years of service as Coven Leader would do well now in brokering some conversation.

"Did you, my dear?" asked Hannah, eyes alight.

Jade shrugged. "Um. I guess. There was a sewer. And a lizard thing. Everyone seemed to think that was out of the ordinary. I'm pretty sure I'll smell like sewer for a week."

Paris could see Hannah's shoulders visibly relax as Jade finally opened up a bit and spoke. "Ah the city sewers. I think they send the rookie down every time there's a problem."

Jade huffed a bit in laughter as she snatched another macaroon and bit into it. "So I gathered."

The conversation was a bit easier after that with Hannah inquiring which spells Jade was working on and Jade reporting back like a dutiful child on a break from school.

"You've been doing quite well on your fire spells and most of your air spells, but need some work on earth and water," Paris added at the end, addressing Jade directly. She rolled her eyes at him.

"Yeah, I know, English. You keep giving me homework."

"You keep not doing it."

"I like reading the demon magic books better," she protested and he had to stifle his initial reaction. Although he knew she was studying them and in fact, he was helping her, he still had the knee-jerk reaction to demon magic he'd always had. *Stop. No. Don't. Wrong.*

"Be that as it may," Paris said, keeping his tone even and smooth, "You should still focus on your other magic. You'll likely have more use for it than you will of the demon texts."

"Statistically speaking, the odds aren't in your favor. I've been here, what, less than two months? And I've already had to contend with two demons."

"Those were quite unusual circumstances."

Jade smirked. "Trouble always finds me," she said, tossing his words from earlier back at him.

Hannah immediately rapped her knuckles on the table hard and loud. Jade raised her eyebrows.

"I'm a superstitious sort," Hannah said. "Now, if you would be so kind, my dear, to wait for me in the sitting room." Hannah gestured to a set of closed, sliding oak doors behind Jade, where the sitting room branched off of the more spacious dining room. "I have a quick business matter to discuss with Paris and then I'll be along to read your cards."

Jade's eyes flicked once to Paris and then back again to Hannah before she grabbed two more cookies off the tray and then pushed her chair back. She placed the cookies comically in her mouth while she tucked her chair back under the table. She glanced at them sideways as she made her way to the sitting room, clearly suspicious about what they would be discussing. Paris gave her what he hoped was a reassuring nod. She stuffed a cookie in her mouth by way of acknowledgement and slid the sitting room doors shut with a thud.

"I'm sure her ear is pressed up against that wood," Paris said eyeing the door.

Hannah gave a small laugh. "Although I hardly wish to discuss state secrets with you, it's charmed to be sound proof." She took a sip of her tea. "So, tell me, how is young Jade settling in."

Paris held back a smile. To Hannah, all the Coven members were young and she often referred to them as though they were still children. Well, he supposed, if he lived to be as old as Hannah, perhaps he would too. He measured his words carefully before speaking. "She's… settling."

"Settling like a brick wall that we'll be seeing cracks in sometime?"

"I don't know," Paris answered honestly. "It's difficult to tell if she's aware of the distance the other coven members have afforded her or not."

"But you've noticed," Hannah prompted.

He took a drink of his tea, wishing he'd added more sugar and wondering if he could snatch another two cubes to assuage his sweet tooth. "Yes. Myself and Josef at the very least. I could check with Callie as well."

"Jade hasn't mentioned it at all?"

Paris turned and looked at the heavy oak doors, behind which Jade sat waiting. "No. But I don't get the feeling that she would bring it up with me even if she had noticed. Or if she'd bring it up with anyone at all."

Hannah made a low 'hmm' sound as she sipped from her china cup. "I admit, I'm curious to see what the cards have to say about her."

"You've done some readings on her before," Paris replied, "to help us find her in the first place."

"Yes, but this is the first time she'll be touching the cards and I'll be doing a reading for her with her present. I'm curious. I've done some poking around in the Council archives and I have made some casual inquiries to other covens. I wanted to know if there was any mention in the history books of something of this nature happening before - a witch born outside a coven to a mortal body."

When Hannah paused, Paris found himself inching slightly forward. "And?"

"And nothing, I'm afraid." Hannah set her cup down and nibbled at one of the cookies she's set out. "She's drawn attention."

Paris straightened up in his seat. "What sort of attention? Another demon?" he asked immediately.

"Nothing so dire this time. I meant from other covens. Word has traveled and witches are a curious sort. I suspect we'll be seeing a few more visitors to the Coven in coming weeks. Most likely at the Coven Ball, I would imagine. It will give them a reason to come and have a look-see."

"She's not an animal in a zoo."

Hannah patted him on the hand affectionately. "And we won't let anyone treat her that way. Don't get your English up, it's just simple curiosity." She brushed her hands together as if dusting them off. "Well, sitting here eating macaroons isn't going to answer any questions."

Paris stood up hastily and tried to make it to Hannah's chair to pull it back for her before she could stand, but she beat him to it. "You'll have to be faster next time," she said with a wink. "Help yourself to more tea." She opened the sugar cube container and plucked out two more, dunking them in Paris' tea with a smirk. He never could hide anything from her. "If you run out of sugar cubes you know where to find them in the kitchen."

"Thank you, Hannah," he replied wryly, stirring what was sure to be a now perfectly sweet cup of tea. He watched Hannah pull back the oak doors and caught a glimpse of Jade sitting in one of the large chairs in the room, seemingly engrossed on her smart phone. She looked up as Hannah came in and then looked past Hannah to catch Paris' eye. He raised his teacup at her in a quick salute before Hannah shut the doors, blocking them from sight.

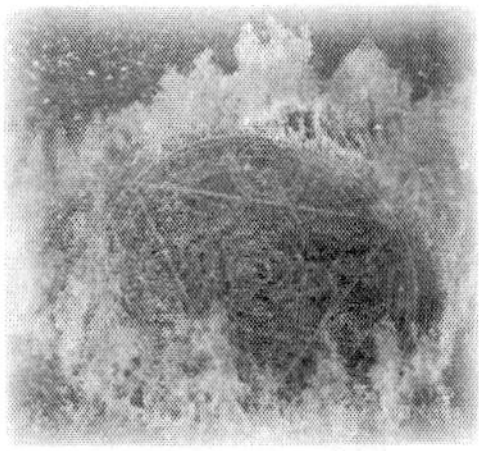

CHAPTER 5

When Hannah looked at her, Jade couldn't help but feel like she was being measured against some invisible stick with strange markings that made no sense. She was never quite sure if Hannah's expression meant Jade was measuring up or found sorely lacking. She wondered if Hannah was ever tempted to use that phrase that southerners were so fond of, 'Bless her heart' - usually reserved for someone terminally stupid but relatively harmless in the grand scheme of things. Jade shifted uncomfortably and tried not to use her tongue to poke at the small rock of cookie dough stuck behind one of her molars.

"Just us girls now," Hannah said with a smile.

Jade curled her lips in what she hoped was at least a weak approximation of a grin. Hannah took a seat at the small writing desk that Jade sat opposite. Jade had kind of sunk into the large over-stuffed chair and she tried to leverage herself upright a bit to seem more engaged. It wasn't quite comfortable, but she perched on the edge of the chair and then rested her elbows on the small desk.

"So, tarot cards?" she questioned. Hannah smiled and drew three decks of cards out of the drawers. They were larger than regular playing cards and seemed a bit thicker too. Jade found herself inexplicably drawn to one of the sets with bright colored flowers on the backs of the cards, showcased against a matte black background. She reached out and touched the corner of the cards, her eyes running over the pinks, greens and oranges of the flowers.

Hannah pulled the other two decks away and put them back in the drawer. "You chose quickly."

Jade snatched her fingers back. "I didn't know I was picking," she said, her tone sounding a little petulant even to her own ears.

"There's no right or wrong answer, Jade," Hannah said. She pushed the cards toward Jade. "Would you shuffle them for me, please?"

Jade shrugged as she shuffled the cards. Hannah smiled at her.

"What?" Jade asked sharply.

"You say a lot with your shoulders, and your eyes," Hannah replied and again Jade pictured some invisible stick being held against her.

"Most people do." Jade shuffled the cards carefully, not wanting to bend or split them. Her fingers itched to split the deck in two, slap both sides down on the table and fan the two halves together, but that always left decks bent and soft. It was perfect when they were your own cards, but she didn't want to do that to someone else's. She settled for pulling them apart and feeding them back together.

"So, are you the most powerful witch in the Coven?" Jade asked.

Hannah tapped a finger on the table and Jade set the cards down. "Is that what Paris told you?"

"He said you worked for the Supernatural Council and I know he asks you stuff when he doesn't know, so I kind of figured."

Hannah picked up the cards and clasped them close to her heart for a moment, eyes closed, like she was saying a prayer over them or something. She opened her eyes again and started laying out cards, face down, on the table.

"I've known Paris since he was a child. I'm happy to assist him when I can."

"Hmm. That's not really an answer," replied Jade.

"No. It isn't."

Jade did a quick count of the cards Hannah was laying out, getting to twenty-one before Hannah started flipping a few over. She studied each one as she turned it, tapping against one or two thoughtfully. They meant nothing to Jade. She had a book on tarot cards in her study materials, but had passed it over in favor of continuing on with the demon books. Looking at the strange pictures of swords, cups, staves, knights, skeletons and what looked like some bad-ass women, she was wishing she'd paid more attention.

Hannah's eyebrows drew together in concentration and by the time she flipped over five cards, she looked confused. Jade found herself leaning further away from the table.

"Jade, what were you thinking when you were shuffling?" Hannah asked.

Taken aback by the question, Jade had to think about it. "Uh, I dunno. Nothing. Um. The Coven. Trying not to bend the cards."

"Were you thinking of someone? Someone close to you?"

Jade shook her head. "No. I don't really, I mean um, there's no one… Just the cards."

Hannah flipped over another two cards, frowned deeper and then looked up at Jade. Jade pushed back into the chair at the searching look Hannah gave her.

"May I hold your hand?" Hannah asked.

"Why?"

"Sometimes it helps me interpret what I'm reading. Your cards are disjointed and it's almost as though… it's as if they tell two stories and I can't separate them."

Jade had been reaching her hand out toward Hannah and then pulled it back quickly at her words. "Can you read minds?" she asked sharply. It seemed like a ridiculous question, but for all Jade knew, it was a part of magic and tarot card reading.

Hannah smiled assuringly. "No, my dear. It simply helps me isolate your energy and get a better sense of the cards."

Jade slid her hand slowly across the cool, slick wood of the table. Hannah's fingers slipped around hers, dry and warm. Looking down at the chapped, dry skin of her knuckles, Jade had the stupid thought that she wished she'd put hand cream on that day. She didn't feel anything 'magic-weird' when Hannah touched her, but Jade still felt like a tightly coiled spring, waiting to let loose and bolt away. Hannah stared at her intently and then back down at the cards. With her other hand, she turned another card over.

"Your past is dark. Murky. It's like… looking through water. So much water."

The words made Jade feel sick and she yanked her hand back. Hannah looked up, startled. "What? What is it?"

Jade shook her head. "Nothing. I don't know why I did that," she blurted, wishing she wasn't saying the words out loud even as she spoke them.

Hannah stared at her as though waiting for Jade to say more. Jade resolutely met her gaze and stayed still.

"These are the cards of your past," Hannah said, pointing to the ones she had flipped over. She continued to stare and although her gaze wasn't mean or harsh, Jade definitely got the impression that Hannah wanted her to speak. It was the kind of prompting, pensive look that Jade was sure had worked on people all over the Coven. Jade nonchalantly scratched at her ear and shrugged.

"Okay," she said, giving Hannah the same look right back. This wasn't her first rodeo with people who wanted to be chatty.

Hannah's eyes softened a bit and she seemed to relent as she moved onto to the cards that were still face down. "We can revisit that again at another time, I suppose." She flipped over the next three cards. "Your present is a bit clearer." Jade leaned forward a bit. "Learning, small sacrifice, all the things you are doing now. But…" Hannah turned over another card. "Separate. Apart." She looked back up at Jade. "Tell me, dear, do you not feel as though you belong here?"

"Why?" Jade asked immediately. "Is that what the cards say? That I don't belong?"

"Not at all. The cards are a reflection of you. They say you feel as though you don't belong."

Jade didn't have an answer for that. Belonging was a touchy-feely kind of thing and Jade worked hard to avoid things like that. You couldn't really measure it or quantify it, so in the grand scheme of things, what did it matter? "I guess I belong here as much as anywhere else."

"That's not really an answer."

"No, it isn't," Jade replied, echoing Hannah's words from earlier with a bit of a smirk and what she knew as probably a bratty expression.

Hannah tipped her head a bit as though in acknowledgement. Jade kind of liked her. She was sassy. Her eyes darted over the cards as she turned them over, moving them around at times, as though trying out different combinations.

Jade pointed to a card of a man in a white robe. "What's that mean?"

"That is the white knight. The card of salvation."

"I don't need to be saved."

"I never said it was you that needed saving. Perhaps you will save someone."

Jade shifted, uncomfortable. She didn't really think of herself as the saving type. "What about that card?" asked Jade, pointing to an intricate card featuring black birds and swords.

Hannah shuffled the card around some, laying it against some of the cards that were already flipped over and then putting it down and flipping over a few more. "I'm not sure," she finally answered. "I don't know what it means."

"I thought this is what you did. Like not all the time, but, you know, on the regular."

"I am sorry, Jade," said Hannah with a genuine tone of regret. "I've never had a reading that was so … your cards…" Hannah shook her head. "Your cards do not tell a story."

"Huh?"

"Most witches, when they come here, their cards tell me a story. Some details are vague, some answers left out, but there is a general sense of linear time about their readings. Your cards…" she trailed off again. "You're cards are scattered. Almost random. Pieces and chunks and it doesn't make sense when I put it together."

Jade chewed the inside of her lip. It didn't matter, she told herself. She was no worse off than she had been when she arrived. It didn't matter that the cards didn't make sense. It wasn't like they were going to tell her future anyway.

"'s'fine," Jade mumbled, sitting back in her seat. "It's not like I was hanging around waiting to find out what they said."

"I assure you, I've been doing this a long time. This has…"

"Never happened before," finished Jade for her. "I told you, it's fine. I'm in the same boat I've always been. Nobody knows what tomorrow will bring."

Hannah nodded with the air of someone distracted. She pulled out the deck again and placed three more cards on the table.

"Jade, dear, have you had any problems using your magic?" Hannah asked as she reviewed the cards.

"Uh, no," replied Jade, trying to think. "I mean, I don't think so. I've been doing my lessons and sometimes things go -" she made a see-saw motion with her hand. "But Paris says that's pretty normal. Why?"

Hannah looked up at Jade and then down at the deck of cards in her hand. As if making a quick decision, she handed the deck back to Jade. "Could you shuffle them again, thinking about your magic and lay out three cards of your choosing, from anywhere in the deck?"

The cards were warm from having been in Hannah's hands and Jade shuffled them quickly, trying to think about her magic. She made a move to pick a card and then started wondering if she should be waiting to feel a tingle or something. She decided she was probably over-thinking it and just snapped three cards from the top of the deck, placing the rest back on the table. Hannah leaned forward and turned them over quickly, looking from them to Jade and back again.

"Does it say that I'm not doing it right?" Jade couldn't help herself but ask.

"No," Hannah said lowly. She took the bulk of the deck and slipped three more cards out. "It implies that I am not."

Jade wasn't sure what to make of the statement. Before she could ask any questions, Hannah was up from her chair and pulling open the sliding doors.

"Paris," Hannah said sharply, "I need your help."

Paris was up from his chair like he'd been shot, coming quickly to the side room. "What's the matter?"

Hannah pointed toward the table. "I need you to pick up those cards, shuffle them and deal out three."

Paris immediately stilled. "I don't deal with tarot cards, Hannah. You know that."

Hannah pursed her lips together. "I wouldn't ask if it wasn't important."

Jade felt like an entire conversation was going on between them silently as she watched. Paris stared at Hannah, she stared back. He ground his jaw, she squared her shoulders. For a moment, it looked like both of them were getting ready to do battle.

"Hannah," Paris began.

Hannah reached out and touched Paris' arm. "Please, Paris. I promise I'm not trying to read you or your future. Just these three cards."

Paris' lips tightened and he came over to the desk where Jade still sat. He glanced down at the cards on the table and Jade had the sudden urge to cover them up, like a journal laid out forgotten on a bed, discovered by an unexpected visitor. He didn't seem to stop and really look at the cards, though, only reaching past her to grab the deck.

"What do you need me to think about?" he asked.

"Your magic," Hannah replied.

Paris looked surprised, but merely nodded and then started shuffling in stiff, economical movements. After a few seconds, he stopped and fed out three cards from the deck, face up. He set the deck down and Jade saw him brush his hands off on his pants, like they had been made dirty by the cards. Hannah leaned over his cards, frowning.

"Have you felt anything strange or different about your magic lately?" she asked. He seemed surprised, his eyebrows coming up slightly and then drawing together.

"No."

"What about the Coven in general? Anything different?"

Again he thought about it for a moment, shaking his head. "No," he said, slower this time. "But now that you mention it…" his voice trailed off and they both stared into the distance for a moment.

"There's something off," Hannah said.

Paris nodded. "It's like it's dulled or fuzzy."

"Yes. There's a feeling about the Coven like it's muted. I hadn't noticed it until I was reading Jade's cards."

They both turned to look at Jade at the same time. "What?" Jade asked.

Paris reached a hand out, like he was going to touch her and Jade leaned back away from it. "Your magic is … still sharp. Bright."

"Okay," Jade said with a shrug. "So what?"

"So whatever has happened, you are unaffected," Hannah finished.

Jade fought the urge to shrug again. She didn't know what any of it meant. "Okay. So I'm not affected. I don't understand what the problem is. Is this unusual?"

"Yes," Hannah said.

"What have you been working on in your spare time? Any of the demon books? Demon spells?" Paris asked.

Jade felt something cold and slimy in her gut. "Hey, if something weird is going on, I didn't do it."

"No one is saying you did it on purpose, my dear," Hannah began, her voice taking on a soothing tone that made the hairs on the back of Jade's neck go stiff. "But sometimes when you're new and dealing with magic that you don't understand-"

"No," Jade cut her off. "I'm careful. I may be new, but I'm not stupid. I don't do any spells unless I understand them. Not even if they look fun. And I haven't done anything lately."

"It may have taken a day or so for it to manifest. I'd like to take a look at what you've been working on," Paris said. Jade huffed wryly at the way he dodged everything she'd said. He didn't believe her.

"Fine." Jade crossed her arms over her chest. She wanted to tell him to go fuck himself, but she kind of needed a ride back to her cottage and had the feeling that if she said what she really thought, he'd take away all her grimoires. "It's all at my place."

Hannah reached out a hand and rested it on Paris' arm again. "Why don't you take Jade home and look at what she's been working on? I'll do some scrying and additional card reading to see if I can find anything else out. We can meet at the Covenstead to review tomorrow. Jade, you could join us." Hannah said the last bit directed toward Jade, a small smile on her face as though she could smooth over any hurt feelings.

Jade looked back at her coolly. "Sure," she said flatly. "Is that it for my tarot card reading?"

"Yes, dear," Hannah said. "I'm sorry I couldn't tell you more."

Jade pushed back from the table and stood up, feeling a little sick. She probably shouldn't have eaten so many macaroons. "I told you it's fine." She jerked a thumb toward the front of the house. "I'm gonna go wait in the car." Paris nodded once at her before she stepped past him and then made her way outside.

The air was cool and sharp with the spicy scent that sometimes came out at night. She crossed her arms over her chest again and breathed deeply. Jade knew, no matter what anyone thought, she hadn't done any magic that would have affected the entire coven.

Okay, she was pretty sure. Maybe not 100% sure, but reasonably sure. She kicked at a rock with her toe. Besides, even if she had done something like that, it was hardly her fault. If there was even the possibility that she could have that kind of effect on the entire coven, they shouldn't have let her have those books in the first place.

Right? Right.

In her mind, she ran over the pages of the demon grimoire she'd been reading through. She didn't recall anything that could have affected the Coven's magic. It had all been half-spells and partial anecdotes of dealing with demons. A binding spell that looked interesting. There'd been one or two spells on opening and closing portals to the demon dimension that Jade had been particularly interested in. Her only experience with demons had left her feeling cagey and nervous about their ability to cross over if sufficiently motivated. She got the impression that opening a portal from the demon dimension was hard work for the demons unless they were called by someone on this side. Jade had been interested in knowing how to close a portal once opened. She didn't want to be surprised by any more demons, not after last time. If they could open doors, Jade wanted to know how to shut them. The spells were half-complete with some notes in the margins from Paris' mother, Sakkara, about possible ways to finish them. Jade toed at the ground as she thought about everything she'd read. She hadn't said anything out loud, had she? She recalled reading over the half spells in the grimoire and making notes, but she didn't call on any of her magic to do it. Unless she'd done it unknowingly. She groaned inwardly. If she *had* somehow done something to the magic of the Coven, Paris would never let her look at those books again without him present.

Jade heard Hannah's front door open behind her and turned to see Paris coming down the front steps.

"If it's all right with you, I'd like to head back to your place and take a look at the books," Paris said, using a wide sweeping arm to herd her toward the car. He kept his distance though and she appreciated that he seemed to have picked up on her aversion to being touched. He hardly ever invaded her personal space or crowded her. She didn't mind when women did it. Women were different. They mostly had a way of coming into your personal space that didn't feel like they were trying to piss all over your territory or trying to crowd you out. Jade felt different about men crowding her. Paris seemed to be careful about how he approached her and on the rare occasions he had come into her large personal bubble, she didn't get a pushy or overbearing vibe from him. She never felt like he was trying to prove anything or that he was oblivious to the fact that it was her space. Jade got back in the car and slumped down in the seat.

"So, like, what are the chances that I *did* do something? I'm not saying I did," she said, rushing to clarify, "but, you know. Statistically speaking, what are the numbers?"

Paris focused on driving while he spoke. "I'm not quite sure, to be honest. As we've discussed before, you're powerful and you seem to have a knack for some things. But a spell of this magnitude, if it were indeed affecting the entire coven, would have been quite a feat to pull off. Especially if you did it while unaware. It would be equivalent to catching lightning in a bottle."

"So, doable but damn unlikely?" she hedged, feeling a little bit better about the whole thing.

"Just so. Jade," said Paris, his eyes darting off to the side to look at her briefly and then back at the road. "I don't want you to think we're immediately suspicious of you for any undue reasons. You're quite powerful and you're untrained. If you did do something, I've no doubt it was an accident and certainly not malicious."

"It's fine. I get it," she said quickly, not looking at him. "I do. New girl comes to the Coven, figures out demon magic. Who knows what she'll do? I'm not mad." It was *mostly* the truth. She wasn't mad. But she still felt defensive and put out. Out of the corner of her eye she could see him setting his shoulders, like he was getting ready to assuage her and keep doing it until she really believed him. "So," she said quickly, cutting anything he could say off. "Your magic's busted?"

"I wouldn't put it like that, but there's definitely something off about it."

"You can feel the whole Coven?" Jade asked, thinking about how Hannah had asked him to check in with the Coven's magic.

"Yes. We're all tied to each other after a fashion. Your magic is still quite new to you so you probably don't feel as attached to us yet. As Coven Leader, I'm more tuned to the Coven as a whole. It's like white noise. It's there, but I don't always notice it unless I'm paying attention. You could probably learn to sense it as well. You're certainly strong enough. Perhaps once you've been here longer, I can help you with that."

Jade made a noncommittal 'hmm' sound.

"Coming to the Coven Ball will also help you feel more connected to us," Paris added.

"I'm getting that eau de desperation again, English," she said, recalling when he'd first tried to get her to come to the Coven. She'd gotten the sense then, rightly so, that he was afraid she wouldn't come back with him. She didn't know it at the time, but if she had said no, it meant he would have to try to break her magic. Jade had watched him break another witch at the Coven, Matthew, the witch who had tried to steal Jade's power. She wasn't sorry she watched because she felt like she needed to see it, but Jade still remembered how much Matthew had screamed. She got an earnest feeling from Paris now; he was trying so hard to make sure she felt included. Jade waved a hand at him. "I already joined your coven. You don't have to keep selling it to me."

"That's not what I'm trying to do, Jade. I just want to ensure that you feel welcome here. This is your home now."

"Yeah." She winced. Even she could hear the reservation in her voice.

As Paris pulled the car up in front of her little cottage, she sat up straight, remembering her lizard 'friend,' Bruce. Crap. Jade hadn't seen him since yesterday. If he was back and Paris found Bruce in her cottage, he'd take him away. Or give her shit for it. Neither was appealing.

"Problem?" Paris asked and Jade realized he'd parked the car and was wondering why she hadn't gotten out.

"Uh. No. Nope," she said quickly, getting out of the car. She said a silent prayer in her head that Bruce would stay out of sight. Or maybe he wouldn't even be in the house. Jade had left one of the windows open in the living room for him and she'd kind of hoped he'd come back and find his way inside. Now she was just hoping he stayed missing until Paris left.

Not sensing Paris behind her as she approached the front door, she turned and looked back for him. He was standing a few feet from the house with a somewhat distasteful look on his face.

"What is that?" he asked, gesturing widely with his hand toward the front of her house.

"What? Oh, that's my demon lock. Sorry." She had to close her eyes for a moment to recall the spell to add someone to the magic and then had to concentrate, feeling the demon lock shift and whirr as she adjusted it to let Paris in. In her mind, she imagined it like a puzzle box - intricate and interlocked, each piece fitting in with the one next to it. She pulled it apart and unlocked the bits and bobbles of it until she felt it fall apart. She opened her eyes and waved him up.

"It's open now."

He raised an eyebrow at her. "Seems like a lot of work when you could just use a key."

"No one can get by the demon lock. I found it in the demon grimoires. It was very specific. Only my magic can break it unless someone knows the exact counter-spell. Keys can be copied. Locks can be picked," she said with a shrug. "Besides, I don't have to unlock it for myself. It knows me."

"What about when people come over?" he asked, crossing the threshold to her place.

She glanced sideways at him. "Who would come over? That's the first time I've had to unlock it in two weeks."

Paris seemed troubled by that, but didn't say anything further. She kicked her shoes off and tried to circumspectly look around for any and all large lizards that may be inhabiting the premise. She didn't see Bruce. So far, so good.

"Demon books are in the kitchen," Jade said, jerking her thumb over her shoulder. Paris nodded and then followed after her. She had her books spread out on the kitchen table and Paris immediately sat down and started perusing what she'd been working on. There was a plate with some toast crumbs and a smudge of peanut butter on the table, as well as three coffee mugs. She moved forward awkwardly and gathered the dishes up, loading them in the dishwasher. Paris rested one of his hands on the table and then pulled it back slowly, staring at the smear of peanut butter and raspberry jam that was now smushed into the heel of his palm.

"Oh, shit, sorry about that," Jade blurted, wetting a paper towel for him. Paris took it gingerly from her and he wiped his hand off and then swiped at the table. He checked the table and his hands once more before he started flipping the pages of the books she was working on. Her eyes kept darting toward the ceiling, wondering if Bruce was maybe upstairs or somewhere else in the house. She should go check. Paris looked like he wasn't in any kind of a hurry, carefully flipping through pages, stopping to read spells as he went.

"Um, I'm just gonna go change my clothes," she lied quickly. "I feel like I still smell like sewer, so, you know, um make yourself comfortable. Start a pot of coffee, whatever."

Paris looked up and started to stand. "Is your coffee in the pantry?"

"Oh God, I don't keep anything in the pantry. Not since the whole 'demon portal' thing," she replied. Even after the whole incident with the two demons ended, she still got a hinky vibe from the pantry and avoided it in general. When she'd gone through the whole process of warding her house, she'd thought long and hard about what to do with the pantry. After a few sleepless nights, she decided not to ward it. She'd never told Paris that and so far, he hadn't seemed to notice. "I don't want my food sitting in there. Gross."

He stared blankly at her for a moment. "It's quite safe now, but if you're concerned, I can check it again for you. With the additional demon magic we've been learning I'm sure we can fix it."

"You can 'fix' it a hundred times, I'm still not putting anything in there," Jade replied. "So! Coffee's next to the fridge, don't be shy with the beans, I like it dark. Like my heart."

Paris blinked again at her and she managed what she was sure came across as some kind of bizarre smile before she took off for her bedroom upstairs. Coming up the stairs she could just barely see the door to her bedroom ajar and she paused for a moment. It looked like there were clothes strewn on the floor. Okay, she knew she was messy, but she wasn't *that* messy. Bruce must have tossed her things around. For what reason, she wasn't sure. She crept forward quietly and pushed the door open.

No lizard to be seen.

Movement from the corner of her eye made her turn her head and she caught sight of a tail swishing back and forth from the closet.

"Bruce!" she hissed. The tail stopped and disappeared into the closet to be replaced seconds later by the blunted snout of the lizard-thing. Jade stepped over to the closet and peeked inside. "Where have you been? I was worried about you." Bruce stared up at her, motionless like she was some kind of predator. She sighed. Okay, so it might have been hard to tell by her hissing tone that she'd been worried. Jade relaxed her shoulders and unclenched her fists. Bruce had made himself a little nest of her clothes - it looked like her workout pants from yesterday, her running top (also from yesterday), some socks and a pillowcase. He blinked up at her with his large, reflective orbs.

She couldn't even be mad at him. When she was feeling scared, anxious or just low, she liked to crawl into the closet to sleep too. Seeing Bruce centered in a pile of her clothing, looking like he'd been napping while she was gone… "Yeah," she muttered. "I can relate."

He moved forward a bit and butted her with his solid head, making the 'pfffttt' sound again.

She patted him on the head and was rewarded with another 'pffffttt' sound. "Thanks, buddy. I'm glad to see you again, too."

*

Paris was beginning to get the first twinges of a 'demon headache' - the kind he got from reading his mother's demon grimoires - when his phone buzzed in his pocket. He took a quick glance at the caller ID that indicated it was Callie.

Callie started talking as soon as he answered. "Is your magic weird? Mine's weird. I tried to do a locator spell to find Stuart and I ended up finding four lost socks and a hair pick."

"Yes, Hannah noticed something was off while she was reading Jade's cards. From what I can tell, there's something affecting all the magic of the Coven."

Callie paused for a moment and Paris could almost hear her chewing her hangnails. "Did Jade do something?" she asked, her voice a little slow and hesitant.

"Not that I can tell so far. Her magic, however, appears to be unaffected."

"Oh crap," Callie said flatly. "That's gonna look horrible if it gets out. But," she continued on, her voice taking on an undaunted tone, "you don't think she did anything," Callie clarified.

He flipped over another page of the grimoire, his mother's handwriting starting to swim before his eyes. He couldn't manage much more reading tonight. That was the problem with the demon grimoires. Well, one of the problems, not the least of which being that they were tainted magic. "As I said, it doesn't look like it so far. Did you find Stuart?" Paris inquired regarding Callie's fat feline.

"Ugh, yes," she said emphatically. "He was in the neighbor's garbage can. They had salmon last

night. I think at this point I owe them a new can. He keeps destroying their lids."

"He's quite persistent and surprisingly agile for a cat of his size," Paris said offhandedly, turning another page.

"He's not fat! I keep telling everyone! He was the biggest in his litter."

"Mm-hmm." Paris rubbed his eyes. He pushed the book away from him slightly and closed it. He wished he hadn't touched his eyes. His mother's demon grimoires always made his hands feel a little greasy and soiled. Additionally, he thought he might still have some peanut butter on his hand from earlier. "Has anyone else complained about their magic, that you know of?"

"No, but I can ask around discretely, if you like,"

"Please. Do your best to be discrete, but at this point, if you've noticed it casting just a regular locator spell and Hannah and I have noticed it…" he sighed, trailing off. "I can't expect the rest of the Coven to remain unaware for long."

"Will do." Again, Paris swore he could hear her worrying her cuticles. "Um, so did you or Hannah have any idea why Jade's magic was unaffected?"

"We didn't really get a chance to get into too much discussion, but I would hazard a guess that it either has to do with how much of it she has or the fact that she's different from us."

"Because she wasn't born in a coven."

"Exactly. And she's still essentially untrained. She's learning, yes, but a lot of what she knows is just beginner magic. Her magic hasn't fully integrated into the Coven's magic yet either, I don't think," Paris added. All the witches in a coven tended to be 'in tune' with one another - sort of like a symphony of instruments. Each witch had their own tone, timbre and pitch unique to themselves, but still in harmony with the rest of the coven. As children learned, they 'tuned' their magic to work within their coven - adding to the blended balance.

Jade was still rather like a new tuba - out of synch and tune with everyone else, belting out notes without knowing how to make herself fit in.

Now that he thought about it, it was an apt description for her personality as well as her magic.

"You're friendly with Jade, correct?" he asked Callie.

"Yeah. I like her. She's fun," Callie said easily. "Why?"

Paris pushed himself back from the table a bit and peered around the corner to ensure Jade wasn't on her way downstairs in case she overheard. "I've just been concerned. I don't know that she's fitting in around the Coven and to be frank, I've no idea what to do about it."

"Hmm," said Callie. "Well, I don't know if you can do anything about it. I mean, she's an adult, Paris and so is most of the Coven. It's not like you can just… order people to hang out with her. Even if you could, I doubt she'd appreciate it."

"No, I suppose you're right."

"I get that you feel responsible because you're the leader and you invited her here, but at the end of the day, it's her choice to make friends and engage with people and I don't think you have any control over that." Callie paused for a moment letting her words sink in. "Give it time. She's new and she's…

well, I get the impression she hasn't had the easiest time with people in the past."

Paris thought about what little he did know about Jade and about what he'd learned about her life before she came to the Coven. She'd had a job, but no serious attachments or commitments - going to and from work with little deviation from her routine. Perhaps she was one of those people who didn't need social attachments as much as others did. He made a mental note to look a little further into her history to see if it offered any more information.

Callie continued. "I think you're underestimating the connections she *has* made here. Henri and I go for coffee and lunch with her separately and together a lot, and she goes running with Daniel. Henri says he's never managed to have a running partner for longer than a week before."

"So you think she's fitting in."

"I think she's doing okay, but even if she wasn't fitting in, like I said, I don't think there's anything you can do about. And if you did try to do something, she'd likely kick you in the kneecaps."

He huffed in laughter at that, taking Callie's tone to heart. "All right, I won't interfere."

"Henri says we're going shopping this weekend for stuff for the Coven Ball. I'll try to talk to her then. But I think it will be okay."

Callie's advice reminded him why they'd been friends since they were children. She was good at parsing things out and making him relax about worries that were generally out of his control. Being groomed to be Coven Leader from such a young age had made him hyperaware of his surroundings and ingrained the desire to always 'fix' or 'handle' things that didn't necessarily require his attention. Callie had a way of getting him to see that quickly. Usually without coming to blows.

"Okay, I'm going to poke around about people's magic and maybe try a few more minor spells of my own to see if I can figure out any useful information."

"Thank you," Paris said. "Hannah is also doing some work and hopefully we can get this sorted out quickly, before it becomes too much of a problem."

He hung up with Callie's promise to come by his office tomorrow morning ringing in his ears. He heard the shower turn on upstairs and glanced sideways at the coffee pot. If Jade came down and there wasn't coffee, Paris would likely get an earful. He had to stand next to the pantry as he worked and as soon as he did, he got a sense of 'wrongness'. He tentatively loosened his hold on his magic, letting it brush up against the pantry. It was akin to reaching into a toilet tank. The brain kept saying it was clean, but the hand screamed otherwise. He snatched his magic back. Paris wondered if it was just the consequence of demon magic - perhaps once a space had been used as a portal, as Jade's pantry had been, it would forever carry a taint. He'd have to keep looking in his mother's grimoires and see if there was anything about a lingering effect.

While the coffee was brewing he heard a strange thud from upstairs and was about to call out to see if everything was all right when he heard Jade's elephant footsteps coming down the stairs. He knew she could be quiet when she wanted to, but she clearly felt comfortable enough in her cottage to be as loud as she liked. It wasn't much, but he supposed it was something to show she was settling in.

Jade entered the kitchen in yoga pants and one of her graphic t-shirts. He didn't understand most of the clothing she wore and this was no exception. There was some kind of chemical compound detailed on the front and he frowned at it, wondering what it meant.

"Eyes are up here, English," Jade said. Her grey eyes stared at him coldly.

Paris started as he realized he'd effectively been staring at her chest. "My apologies. I was… your shirt…" he made a vague pointing notion, not letting his eyes wander down again.

She glanced down. "Oh yeah," she said with a smile. "That's the compound for caffeine. Cool, huh?"

He nodded once, not sure what the appropriate response was.

"So," she continued. "Have I broken the Coven or what?" She made a waving motion toward the grimoires on the table.

Paris turned back toward them, grateful for the shift in conversation. "As far as I can tell, no. It wasn't you."

"Oh thank *fuck*," Jade replied, sagging slightly. "I was starting to question I really knew anything if I'd somehow managed to break the Coven without even realizing it."

"Well, while it's good news for you, it's bad news for me. Or rather, the Coven."

"Puts you back at square one?"

"Just so," he said, nodding slightly. He pushed the demon grimoires away from him a bit as he sat down, still feeling a lingering, grimy feeling on his hands. "I'll call in the department heads tomorrow and see if anyone is working on anything large or unusual. There's always Research and Development. They might have done something untoward in their work."

"What are the chances it's another demon?" Jade asked as she stepped over to the coffee put, pulled a mug down from the cupboard and started pouring.

"Contrary to your experiences when you first arrived here, we don't have a problem with demons. They stay in their dimension and we stay in ours."

She shrugged. "So you think, anyway."

"I assure you, what happened to you with Matthew making a demon deal and then with…" Paris made a vague gesture that he hoped conveyed the demon Seth who had taken an interest in Jade. Paris disliked saying his name, especially when surrounded by demon grimoires. Seth was the kind of demon that would stretch the rules as far as he could. If he could make it seem like Paris or Jade called him forth, into their dimension, he would. Jade nodded, understanding his reluctance. He continued, "Those things are not common. I'll certainly look into it, but I'm fairly confident it's not demon magic."

Jade sipped her coffee and shifted a bit on her feet. "Um, do you want me to look into it? I'm better at the demon stuff than you are."

Paris hated to admit she was right. Not because he had any problem with Jade being better at something than him, but because it highlighted her acuity with demon magic. She was astoundingly good at it and could read the demon grimoires for longer than he could. He wasn't sure what it meant, but it made him uneasy to say the least.

"For now, no. Although I appreciate the offer."

She shrugged again. "Suit yourself." She took another sip of her coffee. "So what's with this mixer?"

Paris had no clue what she was talking about. "I'm sorry?"

Jade waved her hand. "The mixer. The Coven Ball thing. What's that all about?"

"It's a social event organized by the Coven for the Coven. It promotes togetherness and familiarity. Gives the Coven a chance to socialize outside of work."

Jade snorted into her coffee a bit. "Jeez you sound like you rehearsed that from a brochure. Don't make it sound too great or anything."

He frowned. "It's generally a nice event."

"Oh my god, stop. You're making it sound worse." She fiddled with her cup. "So, everyone has to go?"

"Generally speaking, attendance is not mandatory, but most people choose to go. I had hoped to present you formally to the coven."

"You'd hoped to what now?" Jade asked back quickly, eyes narrowing.

"When a witch comes of age, there's a ceremony of sort for family and friends. An introduction of the new witch into the Coven proper as a functioning member of the whole. It's a good way for our children to feel like they've finally achieved a certain status."

"I'm not a child. I pay utilities and have to clean out the fridge and take stuff in for dry-cleaning. Full-on adult. Have been for a few years now."

Paris nodded in agreement. "Yes, but you've not yet had a chance to be introduced to the Coven as a whole."

"Getting almost killed by one of your members and bickering with a demon was introduction enough, thank you."

He studied her carefully. She'd begun to inch away from him as though the very thought of being formally presented to the Coven, or being considered part of the Coven was anathema to her. Paris didn't want to push, but he couldn't help but feel like this would be an important step for her in belonging.

"Please consider it," he asked. "It's ceremonial and has no impact on your power or your magic, but I do think it would be a good gesture. For the Coven and for you."

Jade shrugged noncommittally and Paris felt his own shoulders sag. He didn't think he'd get more from her tonight and decided he should cut his losses.

"Let me know. I won't bring it up again." The silence hung between them for a moment as he gave her the chance to speak, but she remained silent. "All right. I'll leave you to your studies," he said, indicating the grimoires. He felt his nose wrinkle slightly in distaste at the books. "While I don't believe your work has anything to do with our Coven magic problem, please continue to be careful."

"Sure," she said causally.

Paris made his way out of her kitchen, pausing at the front door when he heard a loud thump, like before, from upstairs. He glanced sharply at the ceiling. "What was that?"

"Uh, window. Open."

"It's fairly cold outside."

"I like the fresh air. Okay! See you tomorrow!"

Jade swung the door open and made a sweeping gesture to usher him out.

"Good night, Jade."

"Yep, 'night."

He saw her looking up the stairs with a resigned scowl on her face before she shut the door on him.

*

When her alarm went off the next morning, Jade again woke up with Bruce pressed against her back, almost pushing her from her side to her stomach. She slapped her alarm and then nudged her body backwards, trying to get Bruce to move over a couple inches.

He didn't budge. Jade pushed back a bit more, rolling a bit onto her back and over top of him. One of his feet came out and kicked her in the kidney. It wasn't hard, but it was definitely a 'stop moving' kind of kick.

Great. Her bed was taken over by a giant lizard.

Rolling out of the other side, she grabbed her running clothes and dressed quickly. She set the coffee pot up and then headed out to meet Daniel. She deiced to give him a break today and left her MP3 player at home, figuring yesterday's run with pop tunes was enough punishment.

By the time she was back, sweaty and feeling a little gross, Bruce was sleeping on the heat vent in the foyer, his serpentine-like belly pressed up against the grate.

"You're gonna burn yourself," she said disapprovingly. He flicked his tongue at her and settled back down. The house was chilly with the windows she'd left open for him. She'd have to think of a better solution. So far, it seemed it was working. She hadn't yet found any lizard-messes about (and god, she didn't even want to think about what that might entail), but it wasn't a permanent solution with winter coming up. Maybe she could get a doggy-door installed or 'magic' the door to let Bruce in and out.

Such was her life these days - worrying about how she was going to let a seventy-pound lizard in and out of her house easily.

Jade shook her head at Bruce, rolling her eyes slightly. Fine. If he wanted to scald his belly, he could have at it. She headed for the kitchen for coffee. She'd finish going through her routine - having a cup or two, shower, getting ready - and then head to the Coven.

She paused as soon as she stepped foot in the kitchen, her eyes immediately drawn to the pantry.

"Seth," she muttered.

The pantry door swung open slowly and she wanted to bolt from fear as well as roll her eyes again at his theatrics.

"Hello, possum. Miss me?"

CHAPTER 6

Seth looked the same as the last time Jade saw him. He was unbelievably good looking - dark hair, dark eyes, but he was too slick looking, too... slippery. She guessed it had to do with his demon nature, but she wasn't about to ask. Dressed in dark jeans and a grey Henley, he looked so regular and casual. If she passed him on the street, she would've been hard pressed to identify him for what he was. Except for his eyes. They were black obsidian; glittering like an oil slick on a sunny day. He must have his power dialed down. Sometimes, Jade couldn't look at him without getting sick and dizzy. Seth had some kind of ability to turn his 'otherness' down lower, so Jade could look at him without feeling like she was about to tip over.

Seth showing up in her pantry wasn't exactly a surprise. After the last time they talked Jade knew she hadn't seen the last of him. Seth wanted her to make a deal with him and Jade had the feeling he'd keep showing up until she did. She was prepared to keep saying no; no matter what carrots he dangled in front of her. Even if they had to do with Lily.

She forced her shoulders down and back - she tended to hunch them up and forward when she was scared. She grabbed a mug from the cupboard and poured herself a cup of coffee, keeping her movements methodical, even and slow. Next was creamer from the fridge and then she stirred her drink as though she didn't have a care in the world.

"A little help here, possum. I seemed to be trapped in your pantry."

"I know," Jade replied, feigning the casualness she didn't feel. "It's the only part of the house I didn't ward." She turned back to face him, feeling fortified by her coffee cup, holding it in front her like a shield.

The door to the pantry was open, Seth standing just inside, leaning against the jamb. "Afraid you would miss me?"

"More like, I figured you'd show up again and at least this way, I've a good guess of where it'll be."

"Ah, the devil you know." He smiled, dark eyes shining. "You do remember anytime you want to see me, all you have to do is call."

"I left the pantry unwarded so I would know where you would show up, not because I wanted to see you again."

"Me thinks the lady doth protest too much." When he smiled, his teeth were like sharp, pointed pickets, lined up in his mouth - hard and dangerous.

"Why are you here?" Jade asked, trying not to let Seth get a rise out of her. That's what he wanted, to keep her off balance - probably in the hopes that it would eventually lead to her making a deal with him. She wasn't going to let that happen.

"Once again, I'm here to offer you a bit of goodwill, possum. I can't help but feel like we got off on the wrong foot."

"You came into my bedroom in the middle of the night and threatened me."

"I offered you information," Seth countered. "There was another demon after you, one called by a witch in your Coven and I graciously offered to give you details."

Jade rolled her eyes so hard they almost hurt. "You wanted a deal."

"Still do," Seth admitted showing off his teeth again. "That's why I'm here *again*, out of the goodness of my cold, black heart to tell you there's trickery afoot, possum. Trickery afoot."

Jade wanted to ask him if this was about Coven magic being compromised, weakened, or whatever was wrong with it, but she always felt like Seth was fishing for information at the same time he was offering it. She hated to think that she would let something slip that he didn't already know. He paused waiting for her to say something and she had to nearly grind her teeth together to fight the urge to speak.

He smiled again at her silence, lips curling and eyes lighting up. "Clever possum. You're quite good at this. Are you sure you haven't dealt with demons before?"

"There've been a few bottom feeders in my life. You're kind of all the same."

Seth held up a hand against his chest in mock affront. "You wound me."

"Are you going to continue to posture and grandstand? I've gotta get ready for work." Jade jerked her head toward the kitchen door.

"Very well, possum. Have you noticed something amiss in the Coven's magic?"

"Maybe," Jade hedged. "So what?"

"Well, *maybe*," Seth said, matching her tone, "I know something about it."

You sure didn't waste any time coming to talk to me about it, thought Jade. As far as Jade knew, something had been wrong with Coven magic only since last night. It made her nerves tingle to see how fast Seth showed up at her door. Well, in her pantry. Whatever.

"And you think it's worth a deal."

Seth shrugged, casually tapping at the doorjamb with the tip of one of his fingers. "You'll have to make one to find out."

"No dice," Jade said, shrugging one shoulder.

"I could be persuaded to add in some extras. Maybe some information about Lily?"

Jade felt a stone sink in her gut. If there was one thing that always got to her, it was Lily - even just the mention of her name. She forced herself to take a measured breath before she spoke. "You keep playing that card and I've yet to hear anything worthwhile."

"I can't play my biggest card without something from you first."

"Then I guess we're at a draw," Jade replied. She told herself Seth didn't know anything about Lily. No one did, no one but Jade. People may know her name and know that she was someone from Jade's past, but that was it. No one knew anything else. No one knew the truth.

Seth made a low, quiet 'hmm'ing sound that made the hairs on the back of Jade's neck stand up and prickle. "You know, you're not my only iron in the fire, possum. It could be that I end up growing tired of playing these games with you and move on to greener pastures."

"If you want to threaten me, you shouldn't make it sound like something I actually want."

Seth stared hard at her, his obsidian eyes glittering. Sometimes Jade thought they moved, like liquid held back by a thin meniscus. "You're dying to ask me questions, aren't you?"

"You tried this game once already and I did just fine without your help last time."

She saw something flicker in his eyes. "Tell me, how are the scars healing? Demon wounds often get infected. All sorts of nasty things like to hide out in our claws."

It made her want to run upstairs, grab some peroxide and start swabbing at her healing wounds. She stayed still by reminding herself that Dr. Gellar was quite good at her job. The stitches were out now and Jade's skin appeared to be on the mend with no sepsis in sight.

Still… hell, she should take a bleach shower just to be on the safe side. Demons, sewers… blergh. A tickety-tack sound on the linoleum broke through her thoughts and she saw Seth's eyes go wide with humor.

"What is that? Possum, have you gotten yourself a pet?"

Out of the corner of her eye, Jade could see Bruce waddling into the room. He took one look at Seth and his lizard-Elizabethan collar flipped up, a hissing sound emanating from him. Seth laughed and Bruce scurried forward, stopping just outside the pantry, spitting and snapping at the demon.

Seth laughed. "Oh my, you are entertaining. Wherever did you get such a creature?" He eyed Bruce thoughtfully and then sniffed the air a bit. "Is that the distinct aroma of magic and… sewer, I detect? What a horrid little thing."

"Hey, you shut up about Bruce," Jade said before she could stop herself. It was one thing to come in here and insult or taunt Jade, but it was another thing to do it to Bruce, who clearly didn't realize he was totally out of his element and probably thought he was protecting her.

Seth chuckled "Apologies, possum. I didn't mean to offend your little… whatever he is." Seth pulled himself upright and ran a hand through his hair. "Well, I'll leave you to it. Remember, if you want to see me, I'm just a word away. Just say my name, with intent, and I'll hear you."

Like hot waves of air rising from heated asphalt, he shimmered and shifted, his shape disappearing from sight, leaving her blinking and wondering just when exactly he faded to nothingness.

Bruce spat and hissed at the pantry and then turned and looked at her accusingly, as if Jade were somehow to blame.

"Look, if I ward the pantry, he'll just pick somewhere else to show up."

Bruce flicked his long tongue out at her.

"He will! And he'll do it in front of a bunch of people. They already don't like me."

Bruce made a 'pffffft' sound and Jade sighed. She saw some stray crumbs on the counter and on a whim, she swiped them to the floor where Bruce happily scurried over and started flicking them up with his long, sticky tongue.

"Now I'm fighting with a lizard." She swallowed down a big gulp of her coffee, glancing at the time on the microwave.

She was late for work. Great.

*

Jade caught the third bus after her normal one and arrived at the Covenstead a full forty-five minutes later than usual. She hated public transit. As if she didn't already feel grungy and grimy from the sewer and then Seth, she had public transportation to add on top of that. She missed her car. She really need to go back to her apartment, shut the whole thing down and officially move to the Coven. Jade would then have her stuff, have her car… and be fully committed to coven life.

That part was still a bit of a stickler for her.

Henri eyeballed her from his reception desk and then pointed at his watch.

"I know," Jade scowled. Based on her appearance, she had nothing to indicate why she was late. She was in her standard 'uniform' of jeans and a graphic tee, hair in a ponytail, long enough that the ends of it touched the top of her spine. She didn't even really do her makeup - just some mascara to frame her eyes. With her pale grey irises, she found if she didn't at least wear mascara, everything tended to be overshadowed by contrast between her eye color and black pupils. One thing she didn't miss about having a 'normal' job was the wardrobe. Most of the other witches did tend to favor business-casual, but since Jade didn't see it written down anywhere she pushed the 'casual' side of that equation.

She dropped Henri's borrowed running shoes, tucked into a grocery bag, onto his desk. He snatched them easily and slipped them into a drawer under his desk.

"I know you were up running with Daniel. Why so late?"

She waved a hand in a vague gesture. "Just, ugh, one of those mornings." Jade didn't want to tell Henri about Seth. She didn't want to tell *anyone* about Seth. She knew she was already *persona non grata* at the Coven, or *persona non* whatever-was-Latin-for "we don't like you and think you consort with demons and demon magic."

It wasn't consorting per se. More like she routinely got stalked by them. She didn't seek it out. Except for demon magic, but that was because it was really cool and more interesting than regular magic. Still, discretion was the better part of valor. Or so she heard.

Henri eyed her critically, his gaze going up and down her and then settling just off to one side and she knew he was reading her aura. He was really good at it and based on the look he was giving her now, hers must be screaming like a polygraph.

She debated telling him the truth, but one glance around let her know there were too many other Coven members about, some of them already giving her a 'look.' Jade's gaze settled on a trio of witches, two men and a woman, who were coming down the large Covenstead staircase, chatting quietly to each other while gazing sideways at her. Henri followed her gaze and made a sound.

"Ugh, don't mind them. Everyone's a bit tetchy today. There's something wrong with our magic. Have you noticed?"

The trio watched her all the way down the stairs, stopping only when they headed for the cafeteria. "No," she mumbled. "I mean, not really. Mine seems fine." She kept her voice low.

"Yeah? Does Paris know that?" Henri asked and she felt relief not hearing any maliciousness in his tone.

"Uh, yeah. He was with me last night when he started figuring this all out."

Henri grinned and leaned forward over his desk. "Last night? Do tell."

Jade rolled her eyes. "Getting my tarot cards read, Henri."

"Is that what the kids are calling it these days?" He smirked and then winked at her.

"Anyway," she drawled, loud and long. "It was Hannah who mentioned it first. I guess my magic's not affected. But, you know, don't tell anyone," she added. That was the last thing she needed - the rest of the Coven finding out that on top of her affinity with demon magic, while everyone else's magic was 'broken,' hers was working just fine.

"No worries. So, this means you and Daniel will probably be busy in Counter-Magic. If people's magic is going wonky…"

"I guess. They're still putting me through my paces. Checking my spells, getting me to recite herb combinations. Counter some minor spells they toss my way for practice or testing. 's pretty boring."

"Not every day can be a glorious day in the sewers."

"Don't remind me." Jade made a face and then spared a thought for how Bruce would fare in her house today. She made sure to close her bedroom door and after seeing the way Bruce eyeballed a pair of her pumps, she put all her shoes up high or in the closet. Maybe she should tell Paris she had the lizard - just so they didn't waste any Coven resources looking for him. "Uh, is Paris around?"

"He's usually the first one here. Sometimes, I think he sleeps here, standing up, like a horse, so he still looks completely unwrinkled the next day."

Jade's shoulders shook in laughter along with Henri. She could picture it perfectly.

"But," continued Henri, "I just sent some visitors up. A couple of other Coven heads have come for a visit - staying for our Coven Ball, looking around. You know, diplomatic shindig."

Jade made a face. "Is that a good idea with all of our magic wonky? Does it look bad?"

Henri waved a hand. "These things happen. Well, not exactly these things. I mean, I've never heard of the entire Coven being affected before, but magic's natural and like nature, sometimes there are weird events. I'm sure it will all get worked out. Besides, it's not like we're enemies with other covens. They're witches, we're witches. There's enough magic for everyone."

It seemed weird to Jade. She kind of thought of the Coven like its own little country and other covens as little sovereign nations themselves. The idea that there wouldn't at least be *some* friction felt idyllic and almost… fairy-tale-like.

Then again, she was definitely a cynic. If she was dying of thirst in the desert and a glass of liquid appeared from her, she'd guess 'poison' before she guessed 'water.'

"So, shopping this weekend," Henri continued and Jade had to shake her head a bit to clear it. "I figure we'll start around ten-ish and then break for lunch and then continue on and then dinner out?"

"Jesus, how long can it take to find some outfits?"

"Oh my god, this is the event of the season. You can't just show up in any old thing. You have to look fantastic."

Jade raised one of her eyebrows at him. "I see most of these people every day and I'm pretty sure most of them saw me yesterday covered in sewer gunk. Who exactly am I trying to impress here?"

Henri rolled his eyes. "Just trust me on this. We need the whole day."

"I don't know, that seems like a lot of shopping. It's still a week away, right? I could probably order something online and have it shipped and still be in time."

"Absolutely not!" Henri exclaimed. "No, no, no, no! You have to try it on and Callie and I will coordinate."

It sounded like a lot of work and Jade made a face. Henri flapped his hands at her.

"You just… focus on magic and things you do well and leave shopping to me and Callie."

Jade wanted to stay and hash it out with Henri, ensuring she wouldn't have to endure a marathon shopping spree on the weekend, but she was running late. Henri made a shooing motion at her as his phone started ringing and he picked it up. She mouthed a 'bye' at him and then headed up the staircase to the third floor, where the Counter-Magic offices were located.

Josef raised his eyebrows at her as she entered and she gave him a sheepish grin.

"Are we cutting into your grand schedule, Jade? So glad you could finally join us."

She felt her face flush and wanted to immediately go on the offensive. How would he like it if a demon showed up in his pantry at seven in the morning for a quick chat? Would he still be able to make it on time for work? But that would entail letting the entire office know about Seth and she wasn't ready to go down that route. Instead she nodded tersely, and took a seat at the little cubicle they had set aside for her. Daniel gave her an inquiring look and she shook her head at him.

"What did I miss?" she asked under her breath, speaking out of the side of her mouth to Daniel.

"Something's up with Coven magic. We have a bunch of service calls today for Counter-Hexes, but we all have to be tested first to see how many of us are affected and to what degree."

Great. So, her hope of keeping secret the fact she was unaffected just sailed out the window. Josef directed them all to the medlab not two minutes later, where Dr. Gellar was set up with the same apparatus Jade had first seen when she arrived at the Coven. To Jade's knowledge, it was akin to getting an EEG - there were electrodes hooked up to the brain and equipment monitoring the results. She wasn't sure of the exact science of it - what it measured or how - but she knew when she arrived at the Coven, they had taken a baseline reading of her. It stood to reason that Gellar would be testing them again to see how far off their baseline they were. The science behind it was something Jade was interested in and she wondered if she could ask Gellar about it sometime. Obviously there was a measurable quality and quantity to magic - that's what the machine was for. But knowing that there was something wrong with the Coven magic and being able to sense or measure that was intriguing. How easy or complex was it to quantify magic in scientific terms? Could they use the results of their tests today to determine how to counteract whatever was going on with the Coven's magic? Would Gellar know the answers to those questions, not being a witch herself?

Jade felt a sharp poke in her side and turned an accusing eye to Daniel. He smirked. "You're up," he said, gesturing toward the chair with the electrodes. "Newbies first."

She could feel the eyes of the other Counter-Magic members as she stepped forward to the chair. She wondered if there was any kind of patient confidentiality she could invoke or if that would just look strange and cause more of a spectacle. There were nine other witches she worked with in Counter-Magic, including Daniel. She felt uncomfortable at the thought of having her power tested with them all watching. She was working on her control and her skill, but she was more than well aware that she didn't have the same level of training or experience as well… everyone else in the Coven. While Jade had worked some spells in the Counter-Magic offices, she never had to do anything with everyone watching. Her molars ground together, giving off a slight squeaking and groaning sound in her ear as she stepped up to the chair. Should she tell Gellar that as of last night, she appeared to be unaffected? Maybe she wasn't anymore. Maybe whatever was wrong with everyone else's magic in the Coven was now wrong with hers as well.

Jade wasn't sure what she wanted - to be unaffected and have her magic intact, or to be like everyone else and have there be something wrong.

Gellar smiled at Jade as she sat down. "How are you stitches doing?" she asked conversationally. Gellar, along with an assistant, a young man whose name Jade didn't know, started hooking up the electrodes.

"Fine," Jade answered, her tone short.

"No redness? Doesn't appear to be infected?"

"Nope. I'm good."

"Excellent. Now, we're going to put you through the same tests we used when you first arrived. Fire, water, earth and picking a charmed element. I'm going to measure your results and then use your baseline tests as a comparison. I should be able to then determine to what extent your magic has been affected."

No one else seemed interested in Gellar's spiel, so Jade guessed it was solely for her benefit.

Jade nodded tersely and then a question came to mind. "What about when you had Paris push my magic?"

Gellar nodded in understanding - during Jade's initial testing upon her arrival at the Coven, the end of her test had consisted of Paris trying to overwhelm Jade's magic with his own. Paris had explained it was a way of measuring power - one witch's magic was used to glamour over another. The amount of time the witch being tested managed to hold out determined their power level.

Not only had Jade held out against Paris' magic, she'd managed to push him back - something no one had managed to do before.

"No need for that just yet," said Gellar. "We know how strong you are and, based on what Paris and Hannah have told me about what's happening to Coven magic, it's being warped in a way. I want to run additional tests on the Coven members, but power testing requires several of the stronger witches of the Coven, Paris included, to be available. We're making arrangements, but scheduling is a nightmare."

It amused Jade that with all the magic and power in the Coven, things often still boiled down to the mundane aspects of life - time and availability. Gellar stepped back, ready to start the testing and Jade spared a glance over at the other witches. Gellar came closer again, fiddling with one of the electrodes. She bent low toward Jade.

"If you like, I can clear the room," she offered, her voice soft and quiet.

"No, it's fine," Jade replied, immediately regretting it. Gellar nodded once and moved away again.

"All right, Jade. Your testing was only a few weeks ago, so you probably remember the routine. Let's start with fire."

The word hadn't even died from Gellar's lips and a huge fireball erupted in front of Jade, causing everyone in the room, including the doctor and her assistant, to take a step back. Jade felt the heat of embarrassment and the flames from her magic lick at her face. She hadn't meant to do it so quickly, nor make it so big. She was nervous, and control was something she knew she wasn't good at. She tried to dial the orange-red sphere down a bit, make it less hot, less fierce, but all that happened was she extinguished it entirely. She heard a few titters from the group and from the corner of her eye she could see Daniel trying to give her an encouraging smile. She resolutely didn't look over.

"Okay!" Gellar said brightly, completely ignoring how badly Jade did. "Let's move onto charmed objects."

*

Paris didn't see anything out of the ordinary as he reviewed the scans of witches Dr. Gellar provided. Other than the obvious - no one's magic was working correctly. Except for Jade's. Gellar had forwarded along Jade's results when her testing was done and they were almost exactly the same as they had been when she was first tested. This told Paris two things: one, Jade was completely unaffected; and two, she hadn't learned much control since joining the Coven. He should be spending more time with her, working on her spells, putting her through some meditation exercises. He found it hard to remember that while she had a natural ability, she completely lacked any formal training. In a way, she was like a music prodigy - she could pick up the instrument and play, but was likely sloppy on technique and lacking musical theory.

There was a quick knock at his door and before he had time to reply, it was already swinging open.

“I knew I’d find you already neck-deep in work this morning.” Veronica came in holding a tray of three coffees and Paris frowned for a moment before she spoke again.

“Look who I ran into outside.” She turned back to the door and Paris found himself mirroring her expectant look. A man walked in, perhaps slightly younger than Paris, closer to Jade’s mid-twenties. He had sandy blond hair and dark brown eyes. Paris felt a moment of memory lapse when he didn’t recognize him, before he felt the surge of familiarity.

“Paris,” Veronica intoned, “you remember Dex, leader of the Fourth Coven, two counties over.”

Dex came closer, coming around to stand behind Veronica and holding his hand out. “Paris, good to see you again.”

Paris shook his hand firmly. “You too,” he said with a grin. “How long has it been?”

“If you can’t remember, then too long,” Dex replied with a smile. “Running a coven doesn’t leave us with much time to socialize, does it?”

“Certainly not,” said Paris. He gestured over to the Queen Anne chairs by the fireplace in his office. “Why don’t you both have a seat?”

Veronica and Dex headed over to the chairs while Paris managed to pull his office chair out from behind his desk, pushing it through the soft, plush carpet and over to the sitting area. He sent a quick message to his assistant, asking for a tray to be brought up and then joined Dex and Veronica at the hearth.

“Dex, I’m afraid you’ve come at a bit of a bad time, we’re having a problem with our magic at the moment.”

"I had wondered what was happening," Veronica said, a slight frown marring her features. "I felt as though something were amiss this morning, but I wasn't sure if it was just me. Then Dex mentioned it as well."

"Have you been in contact with your own covens? Are they affected?" Paris asked immediately, not sure if he was hoping they had been affected or not.

Veronica nodded. "Yes, but so far nothing. Just Dex and myself."

"So it seems to be localized here then," said Paris, adding it to the mental list he was keeping. "I'm not sure if that's good or bad news. I had thought about calling around to some other Covens or perhaps driving over to see if it's localized here or not."

"That might not be a good idea," Dex said. "At least, not until you get more information. What if it's like a sickness and you end up spreading it?"

"True enough," Paris agreed. "I suppose at this point the best course of action is to gather more information. So, Dex, I know Veronica stopped by to find out a bit more about Jade and catch up with us. What brings you by?"

Dex smiled. "I admit, the same thing. Wanting to meet your new witch. Quite a rarity."

Veronica leaned forward into Paris' space. "You know, why don't you and I stay here and see what we can figure out about this magic problem. Dex can go see Jade, and I can meet her later. That way she won't have two people bombarding her at once."

"I'm sure she'd appreciate that. Coven life has been a big adjustment for her," Paris said. "She's down in Counter-Magic this morning and could probably take a break." While Paris wasn't sure Jade would appreciate meeting too many new people, it would be good for her to meet witches from outside the Coven. Perhaps she'd get a better sense of what being a witch meant.

Dex stood back up, smoothing out his shirt. "Sounds good. Paris," he said with a smile. "Good to see you again."

"You as well."

Veronica waited for Dex to leave the room, watching him go, before turning back to Paris. "So, what have you got so far on this trouble with your magic?"

*

Back in the Counter-Magic offices after her testing, Jade tried to focus on the problem in front of her. The rest of testing had progressed about the same as her fire spell - embarrassing and public.

This was exactly why she didn't like to hang out with people. When you fucked up on your own, there was nobody but you to see it. Get too cozy with people and you were bound to make an idiot out of yourself in front of them.

No one else had managed to nearly singe off the eyebrows of half the people in the room except for Jade. Fantastic. Although, there were a few green flames, sludgy water spells and one person managed to melt the coins used in the charmed objects test. Unlike Jade's error with her fire, however, from the way their magic felt, it was clear that it was being affected by whatever was wrong with the Coven.

Daniel had said that Jade's magic felt 'clean,' whereas everyone else's magic had a sort of dullness or taint to it.

When Jade asked if everyone would have felt that, Daniel hesitated and Jade didn't need him to answer. It was a given now that at least the Counter-Magic Department knew her magic was unaffected. She found herself on the receiving end of a few more hairy eyeballs as they headed back to their offices.

Josef pulled her aside and gave her some workbooks to slog through. Jade liked to call them Magic Train problems. They reminded her of math problems in school; *If Train A leaves the station going 50 miles an hour and Train B leaves two hours later going 60 miles an hour, how long until Train B overtakes Train A?* Only now, the problems read like: *If Thomas works a level 2 water spell with only incantations and Yolanda arrives 4 hours later to find the area flooded, should she use runes, incantation or herb magic to counteract the spell? What is her best choice to counteract the damage done by the spell?*

As Jade understood it, part of Counter-Magic was simply becoming familiar with a lot of magic. The best witches in the department weren't the strongest witches. The best witches were the ones that worked with magic regularly enough to be familiar with most of the spells that often went awry. Jade's brain worked well with written and visual input. As long as she kept reading, kept ingesting data, kept learning, she knew she could become one of the best Counter-Magic witches in the Coven.

It was just really boring at the moment. She sighed and resisted the urge to rub at her eyes; she'd just make a mess of her mascara.

She felt a strange sensation in her hip and it took her a second to realize it was her phone buzzing at her.

COFFEE??!!!??

She smiled and started typing back a caps-locked 'A THOUSAND TIMES, YES,' to Henri, including Callie on the text message as well. Callie responded back that she'd grab them a seat in the cafeteria and see them in five. The dungeon where Callie worked was closest to the cafeteria, even though she had to come up the stairs to get there. Callie hated when Jade called it the dungeon, declaring it hadn't been used for that purpose in years and was now simply 'The Library.' It didn't matter what you called it or how many books and candelabra Callie brought in - it was still a former dungeon, left over from when the Covenstead was built. Stone walls, chilled and damp atmosphere, dark corners.

Although if you needed a quiet spot to read, you really couldn't beat it.

The cafeteria, on the other hand, had clearly been some kind of receiving hall or ballroom. It was on the main floor and Jade thought the Coven must have had some extra windows put in because it was more open and airy than she would have expected of a building so old. It had regular cafeteria-style seating - round tables for groups and some smaller ones off to the side - as well as food service. The coffee was quite good, which was a relief. There were no coffee shops close to the Covenstead, not without a car - a thing Jade sorely lacked at the moment.

Jade grabbed her purse and raised an eyebrow at Daniel, miming drinking coffee with one hand. He was taking down an incident report of another magic spell gone awry and she drifted closer to catch sight of the notes he was making. She caught the words 'lingering stench,' 'gelatinous substance,' and 'impervious to soap and cleaning supplies,' before she hightailed it out of there. The last thing she needed was for Daniel to decide he needed 'the rookie,' namely her, to go into another situation that would require a full decontamination shower afterward. She started reading a reply text from Henri, a rant about someone coming to his desk to ask him a 'quick question.' It had the classic typos of someone who was trying to type out a message while hiding their hands under their desk and Jade guffawed out loud at the notion that Henri would 'bee free minuets.'

Just outside the office, she collided with something, someone, hard and sharp, dropping her phone and cursing loudly when the casing broke off in pieces.

"Sorry."

Jade crouched on the ground, gathering up the two halves of her protective case and exhaled in relief when she saw her phone was still working. "I wasn't looking," she replied, snapping the case back on and then standing up to face the person she ran into.

He was taller than her, by quite a bit, which was always surprising to her. At five-foot ten, she was used to seeing people at a certain level and this guy was easily six-foot-two or maybe three. Blond hair, brown eyes, he smiled at her like people who know they are good looking do - confident and casual, knowing their looks make a statement.

He was in her space, crowding close to her, and yeah, she'd run into him, but people normally take a step back after something like that. Jade eyed him warily. He was outright staring at her and it buried the needle on her creep-o-meter.

"Again, apologies," he said, as though she hadn't heard him the first time.

"Yeah, like I said, I wasn't looking, soooo... my bad."

He frowned at her a bit - the kind of look you give someone when you're expecting some kind of input from them - a word or some kind of sign. She frowned right back and then made a move to go past him. He stepped to block her, smiling again. He was the kind of guy who was probably used to his looks getting him out of a lot trouble.

"I'm Dex." He said it like it was meaningful or important.

She half-shrugged her shoulders. "I'm late," she said briskly, moving again to step past him, faking him out by jerking to the left and when he moved that way, she swept around his right side and started down the hall.

"You don't know of me?"

Jade shot him a sideways look. "Should I?" God, he was already on her nerves. Probably one of those guys who thought his reputation preceded him or something. Whatever.

"I'm visiting from one of the other covens. Actually, I was hoping to get a chance to meet with you."

Jade could hear him falling into step beside her, but she didn't turn around. "Why?" she asked, her eyes darting sideways slightly again.

"First witch born outside a coven? Working demon magic to boot? You're quite the rarity."

She stopped and hitched her purse up on her shoulder. Yeah, she was just a special snowflake. His tone was full of charm and she had an image in her head of a snake oil salesman. “So what?”

“So, I’d like to get to know you better.”

“Again, why?”

He shrugged. “I just want to be friendly. Find out if you’re happy here or maybe if you’d like to join another coven.”

“Who are you?” she asked, eyes narrowing.

“I’m Coven Leader, two counties over. Thought I’d pop by for your Coven Ball and meet you.”

“Are you here to poach me? Sway me to another coven with the promise of what? Fame? Money?” She started down the grand Covenstead staircase, ponytail swinging as she went.

Dex smiled again, teeth white and perfect, like dominoes lined up, ready to fall. Like Seth. Jade hated creepy smiles. “Nothing quite so nefarious. You’re a suspicious one, aren’t you?”

“Strange men walking up to me asking to get to know me better? It’s weird.”

“Surely it’s not that weird. You’re an attractive woman.”

Ugh. God save her from men who thought she should be immediately flattered because they said something about her looks. Her looks were just her looks. You couldn’t help how you were born looking and wanting to get to know someone solely based on their looks was just… the opposite of flattering. It made her edgy and nervous.

“Have coffee with me,” he cajoled.

She was sure the face she was making was the same one she made when she got the first whiff of sewer water the other day. "No, thanks."

"Come on, it's just coffee."

Her creep-o-meter went off again. She'd said no, and that was the end of that. "I'm late. Excuse me." She made it down the flights of stairs, noting as she came around the corner to the main area that Henri wasn't at his desk. He must not have been as long as he thought and was already on his way to the cafeteria.

Dex was keeping pace beside her. "So, you're working in Counter-Magic."

She made a face. "Read that off the sign on the door?"

He chuckled a bit. "Yes, but I also heard it from Paris."

That sounded… strange. Paris wasn't the type to gossip or share information casually. It probably meant that Dex had asked about her specifically. Even creepier. She passed Henri's desk and headed down the hallway to the cafeteria.

"You like it?" Dex questioned, slightly trailing after her. Damn, she hated the tall ones. They could easily keep up with her stride.

"Like what?"

"Counter-Magic," he offered.

She turned slightly, staring at him unblinking. Jade didn't like his smile with its perfect Californian proportions.

"I guess. Look, it was nice to meet you or whatever. I'm not currently shopping around for a new coven. I'm still trying to figure this one out. So thanks, but no thanks."

Finally at the cafeteria, Jade hit the right-side double door hard, causing it to swing open with a crack. She could leave Dex behind now and he could just… flitter away or whatever it was that really plastic looking people did. She headed straight for the self-serve coffee bar, reading the signs as she approached. Flavored, flavored, flavored… she wasn't opposed to flavored coffee, but Chocolate-Raspberry was a definite 'no.' Maybe she'd do half Pecan Vanilla and half Espresso roast.

"Ah, nice to see the coffee selection is decent."

"Oh my god, learn social cues!" she exclaimed, seeing Dex approach her out of the corner of her eye.

Dex smiled at Jade as though she amused him, grabbing a cup and starting to fill it with Hawaiian Islands Blend. She snatched a paper tumbler off the stack and started her own. Do not engage. That was the key. She just had to ignore him long enough and he would go away.

If not, she was pulling out her fire spells. He may be a witch, a Coven Leader, but she'd managed to best Paris. Okay, so it was just the once and she hadn't really known what she was doing at the time, but still. She felt sure she could handle this Ken-doll.

At the condiment stand, while Jade tried to sort out which container was half and half and which was skim milk, Dex saddled up to her, standing too close to her personal bubble. She had a large personal bubble. He was in it and she didn't like it.

"I bet I know most of the people in this cafeteria."

She sighed loudly and put as much aggravation and distaste as she could into it.

"I probably even know the people you're here to meet. Now, who could it be? Who would you make friends with here?" Dex's voice trailed off as he started looking around the cafeteria and Jade had a sudden horrible thought about whom he could possibly be friendly with.

"Dex!"

Jade cringed at the cheery sound of Callie's voice carrying across the cafeteria. Callie happily jogged up to meet Dex, her face bright with a smile, her blonde hair flapping behind her like a curtain of fine silk. Callie launched herself at Dex and he caught her with a laugh, hugging her fondly. Jade's shoulder blades twitched, an uncomfortable sensation that made her flex her scapula, pulling her shoulders back and cracking her neck a bit. She looked up from her coffee to see Dex watching her even as he hugged Callie.

"It's so good to see you!"

"You too," Dex said with a smile. Jade wanted to roll her eyes but refrained. It was a feat of Herculean strength.

"Oh, you've met Jade?" Callie asked, stepping back from the hug, but still staying well within Dex's personal space.

"I was just getting to know her," Dex said, casting his eyes toward Jade. She stirred her coffee as viciously as you could with a plastic stir-stick.

"You two know each other, I take it," Jade said, popping her stir-stick into her mouth and chewing on it.

"Oh sure! We go way back. He's at his own coven now. For…" Callie trailed off and looked at Dex, her nose wrinkling slightly as she thought.

"Seven years, just about," Dex said and Callie nodded with a smile.

"We were thick as thieves when we were younger," Callie enthused, smiling fondly at Dex. "Oh! I heard Veronica's here too?"

"She is, she's just wrapping up some business with Paris and then she might join us," Dex answered.

Callie turned to Jade. "Veronica's another Coven Leader that used to live here."

Jade managed a small smile. "You guys got a lot of those, huh?"

Callie shrugged. "I guess so. You know, it's not so common for one Coven to have so many powerful witches, there must have be something in the water here!"

"What are you working on these days?" Dex asked Callie, steering the conversation away from himself.

"The Library of course," Callie said easily. Callie loved her library. It was hard not to get caught up with her when she started getting all fond about old-book-smell and how beautiful ancient paper was. While Jade had been interested in the demon grimoires for their spells, Callie had wanted to see them for their book bindings and paper - also checking out the ink weight and calligraphy used in the illustrations and markings. Jade had no doubt the grimoires would end up under Callie's lock and key someday - safely catalogued in her library.

"Come sit with us," Callie cajoled. "Henri, Jade and I were just about to have a coffee break. Do you have time?"

"For you, of course." Dex held his elbow out for Callie and she threaded her own arm through it, turning to head back to the table where Henri was waiting. Just as Dex turned, he winked at Jade, probably hoping to come across as charming and suave.

She thought it looked smarmy and gross. Jade shoved the plastic stir-stick back in her mouth and kept chewing on it. She'd been looking forward to her coffee break with Callie and Henri and now she kind of wished she'd stayed in Counter-Magic, even if Daniel was going to send her back into another sewer.

*

Coffee with Dex was just about as far from a relaxing break as Jade expected it to be. Henri and Callie regaled the table with stories from the Coven's past - laughing and joking, chatting about people they knew. Dex appeared to be a gracious guest, letting Callie and Henri drive the conversation, but Jade didn't like the vibes she got off him. Jade only perked up a bit when they mentioned that right after Paris became Coven Leader he managed to blow out all the windows in the Covenstead with a spell meant to push a heavy rain storm a bit farther south to have the brunt of it pass over the nature preserve.

"Glass! Glass everywhere," Callie explained. "Now some of our older windows were stained glass," Callie said, leaning in to give Jade a bit more context. "And there was this one that had a … well, it was almost… you know, it was a little-"

"It looked like two swans fucking with a stag looking on taking notes," Henri butted in and Jade nearly choked on her coffee. "It did!" Henri exclaimed. "It was supposed to be some kind of homage to nature and the swans and the forest, but honestly, those swans were doing dirty things to each other and the stag was *interested*, if you know what I mean."

Callie laughed, making a loud snorting sound. For such a delicate looking woman, she could snort like a bull charging a red cape when she laughed.

"I maintain, to this day," Callie finally managed, poking at the table with one of her fingers, "that Paris did that on purpose. He'd always hated that window."

"It was an expensive mistake," Dex added. Some of Jade's interest and mirth died when Dex entered the tale. "Didn't it cost nearly $50,000 to replace all those windows?"

Callie nodded, sipping her coffee. "Oh my god, yes! It was such a disaster. You might be interested, Jade, to know that Counter-Magic keeps them charmed now to keep them from shattering like that again."

Jade nodded but crumpled a bit on the inside. Another thing she hadn't known. She questioned if she was ever going to be able fit in with people who had so much shared history with each other.

Jade felt a touch at her knee and she looked down to see that Dex's chair had moved a little bit closer to her than it had been before. She pushed her own back and got to her feet.

"Speaking of Counter-Magic, I should probably get back."

Dex turned slightly in his seat to look up at her. "I expect your department will see a rise in calls if magic is being affected across the Coven."

Jade narrowed her eyes at Dex. "I guess."

"Paris talked to you?" Callie asked, resting her hand on Dex's arm.

Dex nodded. "He mentioned it yes. He wanted Veronica and I to be on the lookout for any magic shifts or changes in our own Covens. So far our Covens report back as unaffected."

"What about your own magic?" Jade asked instantly.

Dex quirked his lips. "I confess, I do find it affected. It started sometime last night, I think. It's like… an inkdrop in a bucket of water - swirling around and changing the color."

Jade shrugged one shoulder. "Maybe you should go home. You might find that once you leave, your magic will improve."

Callie looked at Jade quickly, eyebrows coming together in a frown at Jade's tone.

"I thought about it and discussed it with Paris and Veronica, but since we don't know the cause, we all agreed it might be best if we stay here. If we're somehow infected, we could potentially be bringing that problem back to our Covens. As long as they report no issues, I'm happier staying here until it's resolved."

Jade faked a smile, but by the looks on Henri and Callie's faces, she didn't fake it well.

"How is your magic?" Dex asked, his eyes settling on Jade. His gaze made her twitchy.

Jade thought about lying, but knowing that the entire Counter-Magic Department had been there for her test, decided against it. "Unaffected," she said flatly.

Dex's eyebrows went up. "Well, that's a lucky break. Any thoughts on why?"

"As you said, just lucky, I guess."

She saw one of his fingers tapping against the side of his coffee cup. Jade felt like she was in a Mexican stand-off. He was clearly trying to get her to talk more, and she wasn't biting.

"It could be because Jade is so new to the Coven," Callie broke in. "Or maybe it has to do with her being born outside it." Dex didn't take his eyes from Jade as Callie spoke, only leaning over slightly as she talked.

"Lucky indeed for you."

Something in his tone, in his posture, in his face made the hair on the back of her neck itch. Jade's eyes shifted quickly to Henri and Callie, but neither one of them seemed at all perturbed by Dex. Seriously? This guy was their friend? No one found him creepy but Jade? She knew her creep-o-meter was more sensitive than others, but *come on*.

"Callie, Henri, thanks for the coffee break," Jade said. "Dex." She added nothing past his name, leaving it hanging awkwardly in the air. As she started walking out of the cafeteria, she heard Callie explaining to Dex that Jade just took a while to warm up to people and not to take it personally. Jade wanted to march right back and tell Callie she didn't need to explain her behavior to anyone and that if Jade wanted to dislike someone, it was her choice and no one else had to give two shits about it. Looking over her shoulder and seeing Callie's big eyes so genuine and wide made Jade feel churlish and childish. Callie was just being herself - kind, generous and open.

Pretty much the opposite of Jade. Callie was more like Lily. It was probably one of the reasons why Jade liked Callie so much.

Now she just felt maudlin on top of feeling a little left out and segregated. So, just your average weekday morning.

She knew she should head back to Counter-Magic - she'd been away far longer than she could reasonably justify as a coffee break - but instead she found herself taking a right at the top of the third floor landing instead of a left.

Paris' assistant, Suki, wasn't at her desk. Jade was starting to wonder if Suki was just a disembodied voice that was able to use the telephone, keep Paris organized, and interact with members of the Coven and the Supernatural community at large, all without ever being seen. Jade had yet to meet Suki in person, but saw her name on emails and correspondence from Paris, and had even spoken to her on the phone once. Jade mentioned it once to Callie and Henri and they laughed - of course they had seen Suki. She was just a busy woman and her job generally left her in a mad rush to get things done.

Jade reserved the right to consider the possibility that Suki was incorporeal until she managed to put her own eyes on the woman.

With Suki not being at her desk, Jade went straight to Paris' office door, knocked once and entered without waiting for an answer. She stopped short when she stepped in. Paris looked up from his desk, an expectant look on his face. Beside him was one of the most beautiful women Jade had ever seen. Blonde hair, green eyes, perfect features. She was like one of those really fancy cats. Jade didn't know what they were called, but they were the kind you would see in pictures with royalty, looking better than all the humans surrounding them. Jade heard a quote once that cats used to be worshipped as royalty - and cats remembered that. The unknown woman had that same sort of presence - like Jade was in the midst of some kind of reagent. She was standing next to Paris as he sat, right in his space, her hand on the back of his chair, her body bent in half as she leaned over to look at something on his computer. She was pristinely dressed - sharp, crisp white shirt tucked perfectly into a navy pencil skirt, her honey blonde hair in some kind of upswept do. Her green eyes settled on Jade and she smiled.

Even her lipstick was perfect.

Jade felt shleppy in her jeans and t-shirt tee, ponytail and tennis shoes. Despite her earlier thoughts that morning, she wished she wasn't putting so much 'casual' in 'casual wear.'

"You must be Jade," the woman said, standing upright, her hand never leaving the back of Paris' chair. "I'm Veronica."

Jade's eyes darted to Paris quickly and then back to Veronica. Paris stood. "My apologies, I should have introduced you. Jade, as stated, this is Veronica, one of our other Coven Leaders. Veronica, as you have correctly guessed, this is Jade."

Veronica came out from around the desk and Jade's eyes flicked down to Veronica's feet and yes, she was wearing three-inch heels and walking perfectly in them. Veronica held out her hand and Jade took it, returning the firm, yet not overbearing grip.

"It's so nice to meet you," Veronica said. She cupped the bottom of Jade's hand while she shook it, her hands soft and warm.

"I didn't know you were busy, sorry," Jade muttered looking at Paris and wanting to kick herself. She looked back at Veronica. "I mean, it's nice to meet you as well. Sorry for interrupting."

Veronica stepped back out of Jade's space and leaned against Paris' desk casually, almost sitting on it. She waved a hand dismissively, perfectly French-manicured nails glinting in the light from the bay window. "I'm glad you did. I wanted to meet you." She crossed her arms over her chest. Her white shirt fit her perfectly - not stretching or pulling awkwardly as she moved. Jade had never managed to be comfortable in a shirt like that. She'd always felt constrained and bound. Although Veronica's shirt looked like it cost more than Jade had ever spent on an entire outfit, so that likely had something to do with it.

"Is something wrong?" asked Paris, taking his seat again.

Jade pulled her eyes from Veronica back to him. "No, I was just…" she took a breath. "I was just wondering what was going on with the Coven's magic and if you'd found anything out."

"Veronica and I were just discussing that. Unfortunately, I don't have any real news. Has something happened?"

Looking between Veronica and Paris, Jade thought they matched - like a tea set or a collection of paintings. Veronica looked totally at ease in Paris' office with its large bay windows, plush carpet and sweeping desk. Jade hadn't even wanted to sit down the first time she came in; she felt too overwhelmed. Veronica clearly felt at home enough to nearly perch on the desk casually, unaffected by the space.

Jade shook her head. "No. I was just curious."

Paris' eyes searched her, narrowing slightly at the corners and Jade took a step back. She should leave. She shouldn't have come here and barged in like she had any right to the space.

"I should get back to Counter-Magic."

Veronica checked her watch. "I'll walk you out. I'm afraid I must be going as well." She pushed herself off of Paris' desk and then stepped back around, picking up her purse from the floor next to his chair. "I've got a dial-in meeting for my Coven."

"Do you need a place to work?" asked Paris. Jade felt like she was intruding on their conversation, but since Veronica had indicated she would walk Jade out, she felt like she couldn't leave until Veronica did.

"Callie has a spot for me in the dungeon." Veronica leaned over and kissed Paris on the cheek, thumbing away the slight stain of lipstick she left behind. Paris had casually tipped his head to the side to let her, unsurprised, as though this were a common occurrence.

Jade couldn't take her eyes off the small smudge of color that stayed on his cheek, even as Veronica straightened and came around his desk.

"Tell me Jade, are you looking forward to the Coven Ball?" Veronica asked, linking her arm through Jade's easily. Jade flinched slightly at how close she was but couldn't step back without physically pulling her arm away. Jade turned away from Paris and followed Veronica's steps across the soft plush carpet toward the door. In her heels, Veronica was about an inch taller than Jade and it felt strange and unnatural to have to look up to her. Women were generally shorter than her. First Dex and now Veronica. She straightened her spine.

"I guess," Jade answered. "I'm not really sure what to expect."

"It's a wonderful event. Although my magic's affected by whatever's going on here, I can't be sorry about being here for the Coven Ball. Did you know I grew up here?"

"I don't remember if Callie mentioned it."

"Are you friends with Callie?" Veronica asked. They passed by a few other witches from the Coven and Jade noted that while some of them were the ones that had been giving her the cold shoulder and sideways glances before, they all had smiles and waves for Veronica.

"Yeah, I guess so."

"I miss hanging out with her. I don't get much time for socializing and phone calls anymore. So, how are you finding Coven life? I admit, I was curious to meet you and may have traded on my history with the Coven to come here and see you."

"Yeah, I get that feeling a lot."

"We're a nosy crowd, aren't we?" Veronica said, leaning in slightly into Jade's space. A cloying, crowded feeling settled on Jade's shoulders and she pulled away from Veronica firmly.

"That's one way of putting it."

Veronica laughed, a low, easy sound. "We're sort of like a small, isolated town in some ways - living in each other's back pockets." Veronica had a slow gait and Jade wanted to rush ahead at her normal speed and just leave her behind. Thankfully, they'd reached the junction of the hall that would lead her back to Counter-Magic.

"Yeah. I'm heading this way. I guess you'll be heading down to the library to work now."

Veronica smiled, warm and perfect. Despite the color she'd left on Paris' cheek, (something that Jade couldn't stop thinking about), her lipstick still looked pristine. "I hope to speak with you again. I'm really interested in your insights on Coven life and maybe any ideas you might have on how we do things."

Jade could feel her eyebrows doing that thing they tended to do when she was unimpressed with something. She could train herself out of the habit, but found her eyebrows did a lot of good communicating for her and generally made it less necessary for her to speak when she didn't want to. "Mm-hmm."

Before Jade could turn and leave, Veronica reached out and squeezed Jade's bicep lightly. "It was good to meet you."

Jade looked down at Veronica's hand and then back up into her grass-green eyes. "Yeah. Sure." She felt like she could still feel the imprint of Veronica's hand on her arm the entire way back to Counter-Magic. Daniel pointedly looked at his watch when Jade sat back down at her desk and she mouthed the word, 'Sorry,' at him as she booted up her computer and opened up her spell books again. He gave her a quick concerned look and she got the feeling he was about to say something more, when Josef announced that Jade was in charge of the incoming email box and needed to start logging the incoming incidents.

Total rookie job.

Jade logged onto the shared server and started reading through the inbox, sighing at the contents. She was going to need some kind of classification system to track the incoming emails and figure out how she wanted to rank or file them. She tightened her ponytail and opened a spreadsheet. She paused to brush her hand over her t-shirt and arm to erase the phantom feeling of Veronica's touch, rubbing her skin roughly until she couldn't feel the lingering sensation of the other witch anymore.

*

If asked, most people would hazard a guess that being Coven Leader meant that Paris' day was full of important meetings, life-changing decisions, power lunches and discussions over drinks.

Sadly, the reality was generally exactly like what he was doing now - reading reports, trying to pull together a rather large amount of disparate data to form a cohesive picture. After meeting with Dex and Veronica in the morning, he'd met with the Coven's department heads to discuss the current issue as well as get their input and feedback.

Research and Development emphatically denied they had anything to do with the current state of Coven magic, either as a department or as individuals. Paris read through the Department Head's last report and pulled up the master list of their active projects. He was slowly working his way through all the spells, making notes on anything that seemed powerful enough to affect the entire Coven or seemed out of the ordinary. While he'd read the reports at the time they were due, he'd certainly never paid as much attention to them as he did now.

Hannah was seated in one of the Queen Anne chairs in his office going through the logs for Counter-Magic over the last six months. She was also looking for anything out of sorts or perhaps a number of things that, in combination, may be responsible.

Supernatural Relations and Defense reported no strange or unusual activity over the last six months, but Paris still needed to work through their material as well. He'd checked in with the nearest werewolf pack again, and despite them usually being sensitive to anything amiss or out of sorts with the Coven's magic, they reported no ill effects as of yet.

Paris hadn't heard anything from the Fae, and Mother Nature willing, it would stay that way. The last thing he wanted to do was pick up the phone and have displeased Fae on the other end. Or course if the Fae were displeased, Paris would likely find himself sucked into an alternate reality or suddenly turned into a unicorn or perhaps torn limb from limb with no warning whatsoever. The Fae were unpredictable. No news was always good news.

The morning hadn't been too bad but, shortly after lunch, Counter-Magic started logging more incidents. By late afternoon, there were a reported fifty-six occurrences of magic not working. Locator spells were going bad and retrieving strange and unusual items - a mother looking for a missing socks came up with a French horn, a horseshoe and a thimble. A teen looking for her dog ended up finding her father who was having an affair (that must have been one hell of an incident report). A witch with a green thumb using a spell to put his garden to sleep for the winter instead ended up with four new peony plants and six zucchinis. There didn't appear to be any rhyme or reason when the magic went wrong - it was random. By the end of the day, the hotline was reporting steady incoming calls, with a second line needing to be added.

But whatever was affecting the Coven's magic was only affecting spellcraft. Witches themselves didn't seem to be reporting any symptoms or ailments - only when they used magic. Dex and Veronica received reports from their Covens, both still unaffected.

As if reading his thoughts, Hannah spoke up from her chair.

"I see Veronica's in town."

Paris made some notes in the margin of the report he was reading, trying to figure out if he could discern some kind of pattern. If he could, he might be able to counteract some of the effects. "Yes. Dex as well. It's been a while since they visited."

"Has it?"

Something about Hannah's tone caused Paris to look up at her. She was tucked into the chair, feet folded beneath her demurely, her stocking-clad feet just barely poking out from underneath her black slacks. She favored jewel tones and wore a deep red jacket that contrasted sharply with the dark leather of the chair.

"They're generally quite busy with their own Covens," Paris offered.

Hannah made a vague sound of agreement, turning pages and settling into the read the top page of a report.

"You did say you thought we'd be seeing some visitors interested in Jade. Given her anomalous origin, it only makes sense that Dex and Veronica would want to meet her. Also, attending another Coven's Ball is always an option for anyone."

Hannah made another sub-vocal sound and nodded her head slightly. Paris frowned. There were times he wished he could forgo politeness and just demand that Hannah speak up if she had something to say. Unfortunately, experience had taught him that demanding answers from Hannah would only lead to a vicious tongue-lashing and her disapproval. Despite his age, he tried to avoid both as well as he could.

"Did they ask to meet Jade?" Hannah finally questioned.

"Yes. I believe Dex went to see her at Counter-Magic and then she happened to stop by while Veronica was in my office."

Hannah nodded her head slightly. Paris drummed his fingers on the desk watching her.

"It's hardly surprising." He felt the need to justify Dex and Veronica's actions and he wasn't quite sure why.

"No, no, you're absolutely correct."

Hannah continued to read the reports on her lap, focused and intent while Paris felt his center of attention had shifted. He was just getting his stream of focus back when Hannah spoke again.

"What have you decided upon for Jade's talisman?"

Paris froze, fingers mid-air above his keyboard. "Bullocks."

Hannah finally turned to face him. "You forgot." Her tone was decidedly unimpressed.

"I'm running a coven," Paris defended. "One that is under some kind of magical...," at a loss for a word, he ended up grasping for the first thing that came to mind, "whammy. I did not forget, I simply... haven't addressed it yet."

"The Coven Ball is a week away, and as her mentor it is your responsibility to charm a talisman for her. A suitable, specific talisman as a show of her formal entrance into the Coven and a sign of her importance to us all."

"Yes, yes," Paris replied tersely, pinching the bridge of his nose. "I know. I hardly need a reminder of it."

"Clearly, you do, if you've so easily left it...unaddressed." Hannah stressed the last word, eyes narrowing.

Paris sighed. Witches had been getting talismans from their Coven mentors for years. Hannah was right, it *was* a sign of their formal introduction into Coven magic. Children would receive one when they were in their late teens or early twenties. It was a gesture indicating they were no longer to be thought of as children, but instead were now functioning members of the Coven, able to perform their own magic. It was also an affectionate gesture between mentor and witchling - a sort of rite of passage. While Paris had been prepared to present Jade to the Coven formally at the ball, he'd completely neglected - *forgotten* - to secure her a talisman.

"I still have a week."

"If you want to put a good charm on it, you've less than that. If you put anything less than a three-day charm on that talisman, I'll..." Hannah paused and Paris could see the wheels of her brain turning as she thought up a suitable threat. "I'll bind your spell for heating up your tea."

"With the Coven's magic not working, you may end up merely finding my lost socks."

Her eyes narrowed and she pointed a finger at him. "I'm sure I've got enough juice to make it work, despite the problems with the Coven."

"I use that spell all the time. It would take a significant amount of magic," he said, his voice carrying a warning tone. Hannah would have to cast her net wide to catch every instance of him using it, and given his power level, it would take a hefty spell to bind him.

"Yes, and I've got magic to burn. A three-day charm at least. Unless you think she's not worth it?"

Checkmate. Goddamn she was shrewd. "Of course not, Hannah."

"Good." Hannah shifted slightly, settling herself back down in her chair. "I expect you to tell me all about it next Friday, a full day before the Coven Ball."

"Of course."

She huffed, a smile curling her lips. "It consistently amazes me how your English accent can make anything sound charming and pleasing when I've no doubt what you really want to tell me is to mind my own damn business and stop hen-pecking you"

He smiled back at her. "I wouldn't dare think any such thing."

Hannah laughed again. "I'm fairly certain that was the English equivalent of, 'You're damn right, you old witch.'" She winked at him and he felt about ten years old. She flipped through a few more pages of the report she was reading and then sighed. "I don't have anything useful from these reports. I wanted to try scrying tonight, but I'm leery of what might happen with the mirror."

"I know. I'm worried about similar things. Most of the Coven uses magic in small doses - to find missing objects, personal spells, a little psychometry here and there - nothing big. I was hoping I wouldn't have to put out any bans or limitations on magic, but given that we don't know what's wrong with the Coven magic, nor can we predict what will happen, I think I'll have to. I hope no one will be foolish enough to try any larger spells."

Hannah regarded him carefully for a moment. "You could try to bind the Coven magic to a lower level. As Coven Leader, that spell is within your power."

Paris grimaced. "I thought of that too, but I can't be sure what would happen. My own magic is affected by whatever's wrong. I can feel it almost constantly now. Like a heavy, damp mold hanging over us."

"You're not as affected as the rest of the Coven yet, I don't think," Hannah replied. "You may still be able to get away with it."

Paris didn't like the thought of attempting any sort of binding spell on the Coven when he wasn't sure of his magic. He'd always had control over his spells and bindings - perhaps he was even a bit prideful of his precision and his ability to work meticulous magic. The thought of performing a Coven-wide spell, a binding spell, while he was anything less than absolutely sure of his power left a bad taste in his mouth. If something were to go wrong, he could damage the Coven's magic indefinitely. Even if they were then able to reverse or fix whatever was wrong with it, there was no guarantee that his binding spell could be undone. The Coven's magic was a like a tuning fork at a certain pitch and as Coven Leader, his binding spell would have the ability to warp that fine, clear instrument, damaging it forever.

"I don't know, Hannah," Paris hedged, his voice low. "It's a big risk."

Hannah shifted slightly in her chair, turning more toward him. "What about Jade?"

Paris blinked, surprised by the question. "What about her?"

"Her magic is unaffected. With your guidance, she may be able to cast a Coven-wide spell."

Paris took a deep breath, mulling it over. "She certainly has the power, but… her magic is still volatile."

"That's where your guidance would come in."

Paris thought carefully about how to phrase his next words. "I'm fairly certain that guiding Jade in that manner would be akin to trying to lead a hungry wolf by holding a raw steak in front of it as bait. I may end up getting the wolf where I want it to go, but I'll lose both my hands in the process."

"She trusts you," Hannah said confidently, as though there were no doubt about the statement.

"I'm glad you think so. Sometimes I rather get the feeling she trusts me about as far as she could toss me."

Hannah nodded at first and then said, "She's strong. She could probably toss you quite far." She waited for Paris to acknowledge her with a small smile before continuing. "Think on it, but don't think too long. Whatever's affecting the Coven seems to be getting worse. You may only have a small window of time to act."

Nothing like an ominous, murky deadline looming. Paris hoped whatever was wrong with the Coven's magic would be resolved quickly and painlessly without his interference. At the same time, he was also aware that wishing for a solution didn't make it so.

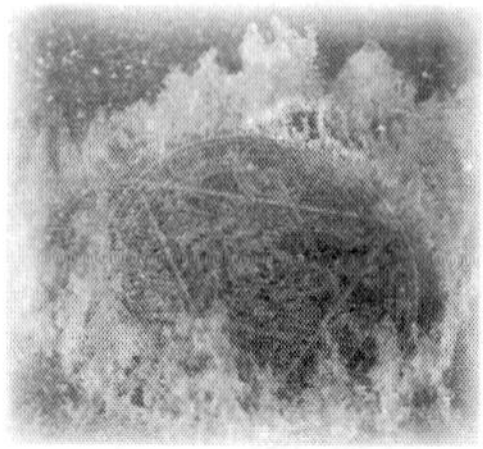

CHAPTER 7

Jade pulled her ponytail tighter, checking her makeup in the mirror. She looked at Bruce's reflection, his lizard-eyes watching her. Over the last two days, Jade had discovered he liked to follow her around everywhere. She didn't know if he was lonely, liked her or was just bored. He flicked his tongue out, making the now-familiar 'pfffttt' sound. He was seated in the tub, his serpentine belly pressed against the cool enamel.

"Just shopping today," she said. She'd gotten in the bad habit of talking to him as though they were really having a conversation. "God I hope it doesn't go on too long. I've got about a two-hour maximum for shopping malls."

He made another 'pffffft' sound, his long claws clacking on the surface of the tub as he shifted.

"Right? Like what could you possibly do in all that time? Look at some dresses, try some on, pick one. Should be a snap."

His tail swished back and forth, running up and over the edge of the tub.

"Today, you and I are going to try to something new, Bruce," she announced, turning to face him. "I found a demon spell to make glass permeable so your window is closed, but you should still be able to get through." Jade had tossed through some apples, a can of soup and a book - all made it through without any incidents. She hadn't yet convinced Bruce to give it a go. She tried to lead him there, but short of putting a leash on him, she wasn't sure how to go about it. Biting the bullet, she'd climbed out it herself and back in, but he just flicked his tongue at her and stared at her like she was crazy. She clapped her hands once. "So! In and out privileges granted. But you know, if there's an accident today I won't hold it against you since it's new."

Bruce blinked at her and then swished his tail again. She supposed that was as close to an affirmation as she was going to get.

Jade heard the beep-beep of car horn and checked the time - Callie and Henri were here to pick her up. God she missed having her own car. She really needed to just woman up and finalize her move to the Coven - cancel her lease, move her shit and get her car. She'd been just about to do it too. Last night, she'd reviewed her online banking accounts and saw that the automatic withdrawal for her rent was due in five days. If she took the train back to the city now, she could have all her stuff packed up and break her lease - paying the penalty instead of her rent and break even.

Instead, she'd closed her laptop and texted Henri and Callie that she would be ready to go shopping.

She must be crazy if she was picking shopping over anything else.

With one last look at Bruce (crossing her fingers that he'd figure the window out), Jade was out the front door and then sliding into the passenger seat of Henri's car.

"Hey," Jade said by way of greeting.

"Good morning!" Callie said from the back seat. She had a jaunty hat on, the kind of newsboy cap Jade always wished she could wear. It looked cute and sweet on Callie, emphasizing her petite features and fine bone structure. The few times Jade had tried one she'd looked like some kind of transvestite. "Ready for shop-o-rama?"

Jade felt her eyebrows rise. "Two hours. Two hours max you said!" She stared accusingly at Henri and then back at Callie.

Henri pulled out of the driveway and started driving. "We'll stop for lunch and coffee if needed."

Jade sagged back in the seat. "Maybe I should've brought my laptop."

"For shopping?" asked Callie.

"No, for leaving you at the mall while I hang out at the food court."

Henri gave an evil cackle. "Now you are in our clutches. There is no escape."

Jade had to laugh at his over-the-top performance. "I should just surrender, shouldn't I?"

"Resistance is futile," Callie said from the backseat.

Despite the dire words, Jade found herself smiling, sliding on her sunglasses against the early morning glare.

"Is your magic still unaffected?" Callie asked.

"You mean from all the hoo-doo going on? Yeah, seems so," answered Jade, turning slightly to see Callie "How about you guys?"

"Ugh, I can't do any of my little spells. I usually have one that takes the frizz out of my hair, because it's super fine. Anyway…" Callie trailed off and pulled off her newsboy cap. Her blonde hair exploded out from under the cap.

"Whoa. I'm amazed that thing stays on," muttered Jade.

"Right?" said Callie forlornly. Her hair was a frizzed mess. It made her look like she had a halo around her head. Callie sighed and started twisting her hair back up again, securing the cap on and tucking in errant strands. "It backfired this morning and now it's twice as bad as normal. I don't dare try to fix it. I'm firmly in a hat-zone until this gets sorted out."

"You want me to try?" Jade asked. "I don't know the spell, but maybe if you teach me?"

Callie turned her cow-eyes on Jade. "I will give you a baby if you can fix this."

Jade shuddered. "Ew, gross. No babies necessary. We can try after we're done shopping."

Callie leaned forward and squeezed Jade's shoulder in thanks. Jade felt proud of herself for not flinching away or grimacing. See, you could teach an old dog new tricks.

"What about you?" Jade asked and then paused, taking in the way Henri was squirming a bit uncomfortably in his seat.

"Um, it's best if you don't ask."

Jade frowned. "Why? What did you do?"

Henri glanced over at her and then back at the road. "It's just that... you know sometimes there are other areas of your body that need grooming and you just-"

"Stop!" Jade exclaimed holding her hands out in front of her, keeping her eyes directed forward. "I really like you and we're friends, but we have not reached that level of intimacy yet. And possibly never."

Henri exhaled in relief. "I wasn't going to bring it up. You asked."

Jade's eyes darted sideways and when it didn't seem like Henri was going to add more, she slowly relaxed her arms. The silence is the car became awkward and stilted. Jade drummed her fingers on the car door.

"But if you're, like, in pain or maybe injured or scarred, I can try to reverse your spell or fix it. But we're never going to talk about it after today. Ever."

Henri chuckled a bit. "No permanent injury. No pain. A metric ton of embarrassment with some humiliation and disgust added in for good measure, but... no pain."

Jade nodded. "Okay. Good." She swallowed hard. "Because I'd help out if you were desperate. But we're totally not there yet. I mean, clearly you guys are in the inner circle." She made a kind of gesture with her hands indicating a large circle in front of her. "But that's some epic blood oath friendship stuff right there."

"Duly noted," Callie said dryly. She sighed. "And as for the rest of the Coven, I think it's about the same. Everyone's having bad reactions and outcomes to their magic."

"So, what do you do? I mean us, I mean 'we,'" Jade made air quotes around the word, meaning the whole Coven. "What do we do?"

Callie shrugged. "I'm not sure. Paris is seriously considering putting a ban on all magic. Personally, I'm not going to try anything else and I know some other witches have already decided to stop using magic too, but there will always be those that won't stop without an official ban, or haven't tried anything yet and haven't seen the repercussions. It makes witches… uncomfortable to be cut off from their magic. It's like losing one of our senses."

Callie's voice was sad and melancholy, the solemn tone of it resonating with Jade. Jade tried to imagine how she would feel if she were suddenly told she couldn't use her magic. She'd be more angry than upset, but maybe that's because she hadn't had it for long. Like a shiny new toy on Christmas morning, she'd be angry she hadn't gotten to play with it for a while, but she'd probably forget about it soon enough. It wasn't as though it were a beloved thing that she'd had her whole life, suddenly unavailable to her.

"But," Callie said, obviously forcing her voice brighter. "I can't do anything about right now. But I *can* help you find a dress. Let shop-o-rama commence!" Jade managed a waning smile.

After three clothing stores and two shoe stores, Callie had found a dress and heels, Henri had a suit and tie and both of them were hounding Jade to try something on.

"No," Jade said emphatically at the dress Henri was holding up for her.

"You can't keep saying no," he whined, shaking the red satin number in front her.

"Yes, I can. Listen. No."

"Why?" he shook the dress again.

She looked it up and down disdainfully. "I just… don't you think it's a little… you know… skimpy?"

Henri looked at the dress hanging on the rack. It was a strapless and fire-engine red - the satin fabric shiny and shimmery in the light. Henri looked honestly befuddled by Jade's description.

"What? This is perfectly respectable! Besides you've got a great body, why not flaunt it?"

She sighed. "I don't want to *flaunt* it," Jade said tightly.

Callie looked up from two racks over where she was rifling through dresses, searching for one for Jade. "Seriously? I'd flaunt it."

Jade pushed an errant hair off her face, wrinkling her nose slightly as the strand tickled her skin. "I just… No. That one's a no."

Henri sighed, putting the dress back on the rack with enough force to make it jiggle. "They've all been 'no's," he said dejectedly. "This isn't nearly as much fun as I hoped. How can we get you to the ball on time, Cinderella, if you don't like anything we pick?"

Jade frowned, looking over the racks of clothing. She spotted a dark navy number off to the side. "That one seems… okay."

Henri stepped over to it nodding and touching the fabric. He and Callie shared a look and Callie clearly wore an expression that indicated Henri should handle this. They'd been picking dresses for Jade for two hours and she'd vetoed all of them. Henri squared his shoulders and turned back to Jade. "You'd probably look lovely in it and you know who else would look lovely in it? My grandmother. She's seventy-four and I'm pretty sure she has the same thing in her closet."

Jade stared the floor length, long-sleeved gown. It was dark, it had a lot of fabric. Jade looked good in navy. "Look, I just don't want to have all my…bits hanging out."

"No one wants to put your bits on display," Henri said. "But you're young! Wear something bright! Something fun!"

Jade looked over the racks of clothing again. She'd never had a really nice, formal evening dress. After seeing the long, gossamer gown Callie had purchased, Jade could admit she was feeling a slight longing for something pretty, something feminine. Callie had looked like a pretty, sexy Tinkerbell in her dress, especially now that Jade had fixed her hair and it was back to its fine, shiny-blonde perfection. Jade ran her hands over some of the fabrics, feeling the different textures under her fingers. She just didn't want to be exposed. Nothing low-cut, nothing strapless, nothing too tight or revealing. She wanted to feel comfortable in what she picked. She didn't want to be pulling and tugging at something all evening.

Callie came up next to her. "I know you said you didn't really have a favorite color, but I think you'd look really nice in jewel tones," she offered. Jade flicked her eyes over to the reds, greens and blues lining one area of the wall. She pursed her lips.

"But you could pull off pastels as well," said Henri, and Jade looked to the other side where the summer fashions were reduced in price, the dregs of the season hanging like discarded toys after Christmas. Looking at the row of clothing, organized by size, she saw something toward the end of the rack, in a couple sizes larger than she normally wore. She took a cautious step forward and tried to ignore Callie and Henri watching her. She pushed the other dresses aside and looked at the sliver fabric. It was shiny and bright, the light grey fabric gilded with silver thread and some random rhinestones. It had a cowl neck, long sleeves and was a little lower cut across the back than she normally liked. Still, since the front neckline was higher than all the other dresses she'd seen, she figured she could live with it. She pulled it off the rack and ignored when she heard the hopeful intake of breath from Callie. The dress was a little shorter than she would've preferred and would probably hit her about mid-thigh, but it wasn't unreasonable.

"I'll try on this one."

Callie clapped a little bit, fingertips touching lightly. Henri grabbed the tag. "You know this is two sizes too big, right? I mean, it's a steal since it's a left over, but it's not gonna fit right."

"Yeah. But I've got magic on my side, don't I?" Jade smirked, feeling a little dangerous and coy.

Henri smiled back. "That you do. Go try on your dress, Cinderella."

Henri had been right, it didn't fit quite right. But, Jade thought turning around in the dressing room and craning her neck over her shoulder, she could take it to a tailor and get it fixed up a bit and it would still cost less than half the dresses Callie and Henri had picked out today. Plus, it wasn't obscenely short, it wasn't uncomfortably tight, it wasn't hideously low-cut and the sleeves came all the way down to her wrist bones. Being tall meant that wasn't always likely when she tried stuff on.

There was a series of sharp, hard knocks on the dressing room door. "Come on out, let's see," called Henri.

Jade was already shimmying out of the dress and back into her jeans. "I'm already done. I'm taking it."

"You can't just take it without me seeing it!" Henri protested. Jade slipped her t-shirt over her head and pulled her ponytail tight as she stuffed her feet back into her shoes. She pulled open the dressing room door.

"Trust me, it's fine."

"Fine? Fine?" Henri said incredulously. "This is your first Coven Ball! You have to look great! You have to look spectacular, you have to look…" he fumbled for a word. "Better than fine."

"Why?" Jade asked, slinging the dress over her arm and heading for the till. "Everyone's already seen me. It's not like half these people haven't seen me covered in sewer sludge or with the shit kicked out of me." She thought specifically of how she looked after she managed to escape from the demon that Matthew had used to try to kill her. "Kind of late to make a first impression." Jade looked around the store. "Where's Callie?"

Henri waved a hand. "Meeting us at the restaurant." He fingered the material of the dress. "At least let me pick out the shoes?"

Jade tossed the dress down on the counter to pay, looking at Henri's face. He looked so hopeful she couldn't say no. "Fine." As his face lit up, she shot out some hasty conditions. "No platforms. They are ridiculous and since I just got my cast off my arm,

I'm not looking to put one on my foot if I trip. And none of those itty bitty heels. The little rubber things always come off and then you're like Bambi on the ice."

"I will find you the best shoes. Shoes you have dreamed about. Shoes you will weep over."

Jade handed over her credit card, wincing a bit as she did. She really needed to cancel her apartment and utilities. Sure she was getting paid by the Coven, but it was just ridiculous to hang onto her place if she wasn't going back. If she went and got the rest of her stuff, she'd probably already have a pair of shoes that would go with her new dress.

"Just find me ones I can still walk in after a couple drinks."

Henri's phone started chirping - a high-pitched grasshopper noise and he pulled it out as he nodded. "Oh! Dex is having lunch with us." He looked back up at her. "What's with the face?"

"What face?" Jade replied back, taking her bag from the salesclerk. "There is no face.

"Yeah, exactly. You look like you just got shot up with enough botox to kill a small child. You have zero expression, which on you? Means it's a 'face.'"

She hesitated a moment and then blurted out. "Why does everyone like him?"

"What are you talking about? Dex is great!"

This time, she could feel the face she was making - all eyebrows and scowling lips. "He's creepy."

"What?" exclaimed Henri, causing three people to turn and look at them as they walked to the restaurant. "He's such a nice guy! He, Paris and Veronica are like the cool kids at a high school, you know? Good at magic, good looking." Henri seemed thoughtful for a moment. "I think people thought Paris and Veronica were going to make a long term go of it. They used to be a couple."

Jade felt something thick and heavy in her stomach. She probably shouldn't have waited so long to eat after breakfast. "I just… I don't like Dex."

"You hardly know him. You met him just the one time, right?"

Jade shrugged. "Yeah, I guess."

"C'mon. Get to know him a bit better and you'll like him."

She felt stubborn, like a child, wanting to stomp her foot in disagreement. "Maybe I don't want to get to know him better. It's not like he lives here or anything."

"Well, no, but he's another Coven Leader and you are one of our most powerful witches. Odds are your paths will keep crossing. Nobody really means for it to happen, but people of a certain power level all tend to end up hanging out together and socializing. That's just the way it is."

"Sounds elitist."

"You say elitist, I say human nature. Like attracts like. I'm not saying it's bad, it's just the way it is." He shrugged. "But Dex is a nice guy. I'd trust him with my mother's china. If she had china. Hell, I'd trust him with her grimoire and she had spells in there that would make you blush."

Jade couldn't say anything more without sounding completely ridiculous and petulant. While she couldn't put her finger on it exactly, even after only meeting Dex the once, something about him set her off. The fact that everyone else seemed to think he was fantastic only made her want to dislike him more.

Walking into the restaurant, Jade spotted Callie and Dex at a table. Callie was sipping on a soda while Dex was talking animatedly with his hands. Callie snorted in laughter and Dex continued whatever story he was relating, even as Callie flapped her hands at him, trying to swallow the mouthful of soda she had in her mouth. She just managed to get it down the hatch by the time Jade and Henri made it to the table.

"Jade!" Dex exclaimed. "So good to see you again."

Jade smiled tightly. "Yeah."

"Shopping for the Coven Ball?" he asked, craning his neck to see her bag.

"Yep," she answered, feeling the need to clutch her bag close. Henri poked her in the back with a finger and she realized she'd been standing still, blocking his way into either of the booth's seats. She slid in next to Callie, even though it meant slightly less room with both of their shopping bags and purses on one side.

"Here, allow me," Dex said, holding his hand out for her things, motioning like he would put them on his seat.

"I got it," Jade said, clutching her stuff tight. She ignored the pointed look Henri gave her, flicking up her menu and reading it. Even though the dress she bought was two sizes too big, the idea of the Coven Ball coming up had her choosing a salad off the menu. Dressing on the side. Yuck.

"Live a little," Dex prodded. "I'm sure you can afford to go a little crazy," he said when she ordered.

The skin on the back of her neck tingled as she met his gaze. He was so obviously fake to her. She looked at Callie and Henri, feeling as though she were caught on some kind of strange reality show - *Spot the Creeper!* Both of them were looking at her quizzically.

"Just the salad," she said, folding the menu closed and handing it back to the server.

"Don't be one of those women who orders a salad and then eats food off other people's plates," Dex teased.

Her jaw made a squeaking sound when she ground her teeth. She'd always meant to see a dentist about it in case it was the early signs of TMJ. From the sounds it was making now as she eyeballed Dex, she should make that dental appointment sooner rather than later.

"I won't," she said coldly. He smiled at her, completely unfazed by her attitude. The rest of the group put in their orders and the server hurried away. Jade sat back in the booth, her spine right up against the cheap pleather fabric. "How's your magic, Dex?" she asked abruptly.

He paused, taking a sip of his iced tea. "Honestly? I'm out of sorts. I don't know that I've ever had any problems with my magic. None that I can remember. And being cut off from my Coven as well… It's been tough."

"Hmm. I bet." Jade crossed her arms over her chest, head tilted sideways. "So you must have been affected as soon as you showed up. Or was it that you showed up and then the Coven became affected?"

He licked his lips a little and smiled, setting his glass down on the table.

"Your Coven is still unaffected, correct?" asked Callie. Dex turned to her and nodded.

"Thankfully, yes. They're not showing any signs of… infection for lack of a better word."

"That's great," Jade deadpanned. "But back to my question. Timeline. You show up. Coven magic goes wonky. Then your magic. Or was it your magic then the Coven's?"

"Jade!" Callie exclaimed. "You sound like you're accusing him."

Jade shrugged. "I just like to know how things happen."

"Yeah, but…" Callie trailed off a bit and eyed her meaningfully. "Dex is another Coven Leader. He's like family."

"Cain and Abel were family. Look how that turned out." Callie's jaw dropped at Jade's words. "What? It's just a question. If he's family, like you say," Jade repeated, forcing the words out slow and careful as she looked at Dex, "then I'm sure he's more than happy to help me figure it all out. I'm only doing it for the good of the Coven."

Okay, so Jade laid the last bit on a little thick - a few extra wide-eyed blinks back toward Callie; a sympathetic eyebrow raise at Henri, and then she pinned Dex with her grey eyes. She knew that if she tilted her head and let them catch the light just right, they always looked a little too pale against her pupils. It tended to make people nervous.

"It's fine, Callie," Dex soothed, reaching out and patting Callie on the hand patronizingly. Jade wanted to rap his knuckles with her butter knife. "I totally understand where Jade is coming from. She doesn't know me like you do." He looked back at Jade. "I don't know for certain when it started. I don't actively practice magic non-stop. I could have been affected for several hours before I noticed, or only several minutes. I also don't know if we can even tell who the first person was that was affected here at the Coven or if several areas were affected at once. It's quite the mystery."

Jade was already wondering if she could pull Counter-Magic's log from yesterday and see if there was any kind of formula or pattern that could be extracted. If there were, she could extrapolate it backward and see if that supported what Dex was saying. "Tough break for the Coven. A lot of unknowns."

Dex nodded sagely. "Yes. Your magic is still unaffected though, correct?" He took a sip of his drink, giving her the same wide-eyed innocent look that she'd given him.

Touché, asshole. Jade smiled, brittle and sharp. "Yep. What is it witches like to say? Touch wood." She knocked on the table once.

"I hear you've also quite the affinity with demon magic."

Jade raised an eyebrow. "Really? Who told you that?"

Dex shrugged. "Word travels. Especially when it's about something so unique and strange. I admit, I'm curious about it. I hear you have some demon grimoires, two of the three."

"Sounds like you know all there is to know already."

"Come now, don't be modest. It's quite a feat. Demon magic can be so… tricky. Generally anathema to the Coven in general."

"I guess I'm just a special snowflake," Jade said, taking a sip of her water and biting down hard on an ice cube.

"It must be difficult to be different from everyone else in the Coven." His tone was sympathetic and out of the corner of her eye, Jade could see Callie's face already morphing into one of empathy and feeling for Jade. Dex's eyes in contrast were sharp and cutting. Jade chanced a quick glance at Henri and Callie - both of them were looking at her sympathetically, almost oblivious to Dex. It had to be magic, didn't it? Jade couldn't be the only one that got a creeper vibe off Dex while everyone else thought he was fantastic. She started pushing her magic out, seeing if she could feel anything around the table that would indicate it was some kind of spell work.

Jade was getting used to keeping her magic mostly coiled up inside her. In some ways, letting it go just now was like taking a bra off after a long day. It was only once the clasp released that she realized how tight the garment had been. Her magic uncurled carefully, stiffly. In her mind, she saw it like long branches of green wood - stiff but bendable. Unhappy at having been folded up for so long. She pushed it out, feeling for other magic at the table, magic coming off Dex.

There was none.

But Dex… his eyes narrowed slightly and he shifted a millimeter back, away from Jade. Away from her magic. Neither Callie nor Henri moved. Was it because they were familiar with Jade's magic? Or could they not feel it because there was something wrong with their own powers?

Dex felt it. He was trying to act like he hadn't, but Jade was sure the way he moved meant he had.

"Jade's part of our family," Callie was saying. Her hand came to rest upon Jade's and Jade pulled her magic back tightly, like the snap of a yo-yo coming home to its owner. "She's not separate from us."

"Of course not," said Dex lowly. His eyes slid away from Jade's and rested on Callie - warm and soft. "I'm sure you've made her feel quite at home. Veronica tells me you always did have a fondness for strays."

Ouch. Jade almost wanted to salute him for that one because Callie just smiled even warmer and Henri started in on how Callie once found a bird with a broken wing and made Gellar x-ray it at the Coven when the local vet couldn't be reached. Both Callie and Henri seemed oblivious to the way Dex said it - as though Jade were some mangy cat that had been found wandering alone and wailing on the side of a road.

Jade was glad she decided on only salad for lunch since the rest of the meal was like the Dex Appreciation Hour. If she'd ordered something heavier, it would be sitting harder than the rock the salad was turning into in her stomach. Dex, Henri and Callie talked about people they knew at the Coven, people who were so happy Dex was back visiting and could he come by a little more often? Would he happen to have his grimoire with him? Oh he just happened to have a spell for stuffy noses and scratchy throats and flu season was coming and he'd be so happy to share it. Did he know that the apple tree outside his old house had the best apples in town?

Moira would only use those apples when she made her turnovers. Dex confessed to trying a spell on the tree when he was in his teens and it was just too bad that he hadn't written it down. God, it was like watching a bad soap opera where you knew who the villain was and everyone else was blindly wandering around.

Doubt niggled at her stomach, though. Maybe it was that she truly wasn't a part of the Coven yet, or never really would be. Maybe she was too cynical, too different to ever be a part of their cozy remembrances and fond tales. Like a foreigner in a strange land, maybe she would always have a heavy accent, no matter how well she spoke the language.

Her phone started vibrating in her pocket and she couldn't reach for it fast enough, glad for the distraction from Dex's overbearing presence. She barely registered Paris' name on the caller-ID before she answered.

"Jade speaking."

"Hello, Jade," he said, and after an hour of listening to Dex's overly warm and friendly voice, Jade had never been so happy to hear Paris' clipped tone and British accent. "I was wondering if you were free this afternoon?"

"Yes." Even to her own ears, her tone was sharp and quick. Her eyes darted over to Callie and Henri and she felt a little bad. "I mean, um… Hang on." She mouthed Paris' name and pointed to a quiet corner where she was going to take the call. She slid out of the booth and once she was sure she was out of earshot, she put the phone back to her ear.

"Sorry, what's up?"

"Is this a bad time?"

"Fuck no," she said emphatically. "I'm just… whatever," she waved her hand, sort of forgetting that he couldn't see her. "I'm free. Totally free. Unless you need someone to go back into the sewers in which case, oh wow, look at the time, gotta go."

"Hardly," he said. From his tone she could picture his expression perfectly - slightly amused. "I know there's a lot going on with the Coven right now and unfortunately that hasn't left me a lot of time to work with you on your magic."

"Oh, you know, it's been okay. The guys in Counter-Magic are fine and Josef has me reading books and going into sewers," she said wryly. "Fun times."

"I'm sure. Still, I've been somewhat remiss in your teachings. Although the Coven magic is affected, yours is not and you shouldn't be penalized for it."

"Uh, thanks," she said for lack of anything else. She picked at a loose piece of ugly wallpaper in the corner, scratching at the dried up glue and ripping a corner off. She glanced around making sure no one saw her and then went back to picking.

"If you're free," Paris continued, "I thought we could work on some circle casting. Of course, I won't be practicing any magic myself, but circle casting is a way to get in touch with your own magic and requires more of a… focused mind. I think I can help you work on that without any magic."

"Um, okay. Where do you want to meet?"

"Where are you right now?"

"The mall." She immediately felt about fourteen years old and rolled her eyes. Jesus. No wonder Dex compared her to a stray. She straightened her spine. "I can grab a cab or take the bus." Fuck, she was never leaving her car when she went anywhere again. She hated being without it.

"No need, I can pick you up. Are you sure you're free? You're not in the middle of something?"

Jade glanced over at the table where Dex was in the middle of gesticulating wildly with a huge grin on his face while Callie and Henri laughed. She felt bad for leaving Callie and Henri. She liked hanging out with them. But ditching Dex totally made up for it.

"Nope. All done."

She arranged to meet Paris at one of the entrances in twenty minutes. Back at the table, Callie quirked her eyebrows when Jade grabbed her purse.

"Paris wants to go over some magic stuff, so…" she trailed off, fishing in her wallet for her portion of the bill. Callie waved her off.

"I can get your part. You can catch me next time."

Jade fingered the bills in her wallet awkwardly. "Thanks. I better head to the exit so I'm not late. See you guys." Standing, she nodded and smiled at Callie and Henri, pausing before she looked at Dex.

"I'll be seeing you around, Jade," he said, smiling with his perfect teeth.

"I'm sure you will," she said, giving him her brightest smile back.

*

Parked outside of one of the mall entrances, Paris read through the latest report from the Coven Department heads on his Smartphone and frowned. He was going to have to ban magic use. He didn't see a way around it. He hated the small keyboard on his phone and instead switched over to voice memo, detailing that all spells and magic use were banned unless approved by a senior Coven member until further notice. He then had to draft a second voice memo for Suki to send out indicating which Coven members would be suitable for approving any attempts at magic. The list was short. Himself, Hannah, Josef from Counter Magic, Marcus from Supernatural Defense and Claire from Research and Development. He was in the middle of memos to Josef, Marcus and Claire when the passenger door of his car opened. He didn't pause in his dictation and Jade immediately seemed to get what he was doing, sliding in quietly and tossing some bags in the back.

Paris wrapped it up, making a note for Suki to add the usual greeting, salutations and ending statements on his correspondence and asked her to send them all out as soon as they were prepared. He quickly sent the voice memos to Suki and then turned to look at Jade.

"Working on a Saturday?" she asked.

"I generally do some work on the weekends, yes, but with something amiss with Coven magic, it seemed prudent to keep at it."

"Sucks to be you," Jade said, buckling her belt. "Did I hear you banning magic use?"

He nodded, pulling the car away from the curb. "Unfortunately, yes. I had hoped we could resolve it, but we're still no closer to identifying it. Until we can determine what the cause is and how to counteract it, it's best if we simply stop using magic. We may very well be making the problem worse by continuing. Based on reports, no one's spells are working anyway, so I may as well make it official and people will stop trying."

"Will they?" Jade asked. "Stop, I mean?"

"Of course. Once they get the alert, all magic use will cease."

"Wow."

He spared a quick glance at her. "Why is that surprising?"

Her shoulders moved up and down in a shrug. "I dunno. You tell me not to push a button and I'm gonna want to push it. You tell me not to use magic and -" she waggled her fingers, little sparks of fire dancing off them as she did.

"I see your magic is still unaffected," he said dryly.

"Yep. So does that mean I'm exempt from the ban?"

"Technically, yes. It doesn't really affect you. But, in a show of support for the Coven, I would appreciate it if you didn't use magic around other witches."

"Best not show my shiny new toys when all the other witches have busted-up old toys, got it."

"Precisely."

Jade looked out the window. "Where are we going?"

"I thought we could stop off at your place first and you can change your clothing. We're headed out to the nature preserve, so you'll want to be in more suitable attire. Like mine." He indicated his denim pants and hiking boots.

She snorted a bit. "You could just say I need to wear my grubbies." She must have interpreted the look on his face correctly because she continued.

"Yoga pants or leggings. Sweatshirt. Outdoorsy things. Runners."

"That is what I said."

"Oh my god, English, never change."

The trip to her small cottage didn't take long and she was already out of the car before he barely had time to shut it off. Paris noticed he could still feel her demon locks, swirling around the house, especially the doorway, but he didn't seem to be blocked anymore. As she had indicated previously, she had managed to reconfigure them to allow him in. With something wrong with the Coven's magic, he hadn't had an opportunity to study his mother's grimoires any further, keeping them under lock and key at his house. If Jade kept on as she was, she would soon surpass him. She may be new to magic in general, but she clearly had an aptitude for the demon spells. Paris found them tricky and… sneaky in a way that he couldn't quite understand nor predict. Jade appeared to have no similar issues that he could tell.

He followed her into her house, finding the space itself in the beginnings of responding to her. Her magic had started to settle into the building, sooner than he thought it would. It generally took witches much longer to 'claim' a space, but this small house clearly resonated with Jade now. She tromped up the stairs with her usually heavy elephant steps, yelling that he could get a drink or snack from the kitchen if he wanted.

Paris was content to wait just inside the foyer, not planning on staying long. He couldn't help but notice as he looked around that while her magic seemed to be permeating the space, she hadn't added any personal touches.

It was then that Paris realized he'd completely forgotten Jade had never returned to her old life to gather her things. She'd come to the Coven with a suitcase and a few things and he'd neglected to make any arrangements to have her things sent or taken care of, or even offered her time off to do it.

He thought he could hear her voice coming from upstairs, but he didn't think she was talking to him. Perhaps she was on the phone? At any rate, she was stampeding back down the stairs in jeans and a sweatshirt he recognized as one she wore regularly. Or rather was forced to wear regularly since she probably didn't have any other clothes.

"Ready!" She jumped down the last three steps at once, landing with a thud.

"It occurs to me that you'll likely be wanting your things from your apartment. Clothing, knick-knacks. Personal items and the like. Your car, I would assume."

Jade fidgeted. "Oh, yeah. I guess." She waved a hand. "I'll head back some weekend and pick all that stuff up."

"Once we take care of this issue, I can go with you. Or not," he added at her expression.

"No, I mean yeah, that's fine. We can… plan that. Once it's all settled down. No rush."

Paris frowned, not sure what she meant. She must want to gather her belongings - move in officially.

Or possibly not?

Watching her shift from one foot to the other, snapping her fingers in a fit of nervous energy, he realized that she was only placating him.

"Do you not want to bring your things here?" Paris asked.

"What?" Jade said sharply, eyes snapping back to him. "Don't be ridiculous. I said I was staying. I'm staying."

"I didn't mean to imply you weren't staying only that… perhaps you want to leave yourself the option of not staying?"

Her eyes narrowed slightly. "You're really good at politician speak, you know that?"

Paris tipped his head in acknowledgement. "It's my job."

"That and teaching me magic. We should get going," she said, neatly sidestepping him and heading out the door. It was an effective way of ending their conversation, he had to give her that.

Back in the car, he drove past the entrance to the nature preserve that was close to Jade's house, watching her crane her neck at the entrance gates as they drove by.

"We're heading a bit further out today to a different area of the preserve that isn't used as much. If we're going to be working on circle casting, I thought we should stay away from more heavily used areas."

"My magic's still good, I know it is," she said defensively.

"I know. I can feel that. But it's still better to be a little bit further away so that there's no interference."

Jade shifted in her seat, facing him a bit. "Hey about feeling my magic, can you feel when I do this?"

Paris felt a surge of magic at him, poking at his own, testing the boundaries. "Yes, why?"

"Would Callie and Henri feel it?" she replied back, ignoring his question.

"Possibly. They aren't as strong as I am and I'm more attune to your magic both as Coven Leader and as your mentor. If you told them to be aware of it, I'm sure they'd notice it."

"Would Dex?"

He took his eyes off the road for a moment to glance at her. "Again, possibly. Why?"

Jade took a slow breath, crossing her arms over her chest. "You know him, right?"

"Yes, as a friend and as a Coven Leader. Why?"

She pursed her lips, staring out the front windshield. "Nothing. Just… curious."

Paris would be a fool to believe that she really meant it when she said, 'nothing,' but it was definitely a clear indicator that whatever it *was*, she wasn't willing to discuss it just yet. He hoped that she would confide in him when she felt ready and until she did, he resolved not to pressure her.

Paris focused instead on the landscape around them. Large maple trees were nearing the end of their fall color change, their fiery red leaves going sallow and yellow, more leaves falling on the ground than staying attached to the trees. Autumn was possibly his favorite season and he found himself sad to see it go. He remembered long walks in the preserve with his mother in autumn as she took him out to gather leaves, branches and other odds and ends for spell casting. Paris pulled the car over at a roadside turnout and stopped the engine.

"We hike from here on in."

CHAPTER 8

Jade's nose wrinkled and she looked into the woods with trepidation. "How far are we going?" she asked.

Paris got out of the car, grabbing a small pack from the backseat and slinging it over his shoulders.

"Part of circle casting is being well grounded. The best way to do that is to be surrounded by nature."

"Yeah, I got that part. But how far away is 'nature'?" she asked using her fingers to fake quotation marks at the word. Jade gestured at the wide expanse of trees and foliage. "Can't we just hang out here?"

"I'm afraid not," he said easily, starting to walk toward a heavily overgrown hiking path.

"Do I get a machete?" Jade called out, scurrying after him.

"We try to leave the forest as we find it," Paris replied, pushing aside a large tree branch as he stepped into the trees. He held it aside for her so it wouldn't come back and smack her soundly in the face. Once they got a little further in, she could more easily make out the pathway he was following. It clearly wasn't used often, but was still defined enough for them to follow. They hiked in relative silence. It wasn't extremely difficult, but it did cause her to breathe deeper and faster; she could hear Paris doing the same in front of her. She liked the silence of the forest, with only the sounds of some birds, the crunching of their boots, and the rhythmic sound of their breathing. She stopped a few times to reach out and touch a tree or some moss, kick a small rock or some branches. The tip of her nose was cold and she sniffed a bit, wondering if Paris had tissues in his backpack.

After about half an hour, Paris paused to pull a bottle of water out, passing it to her before taking one for himself. "You don't do much of this, do you?" he asked, meaning the hiking.

She took a long gulp of water and wiped her mouth with her sleeve. "Nope. I guess I'm more of a city girl." Jade looked upwards into the dense canopy of yellowing leaves, leaving her throat bare and exposed as she gaped. "It's pretty though." The leaves made a strange and dense pattern above her and she wondered at the structure of it. She felt a strange pull at her brain, like a deep, heavy note playing in an orchestra - too quiet for the ear to hear, but heavy enough that you could feel the reverberation in your chest and bones. She didn't like it.

She focused on it and then turned her head sharply east. "Is there water nearby?" she asked suddenly, not sure why she asked.

Paris seemed surprised, eyebrows raising slightly as he nodded. "Yes, there's a small lake about fifteen minutes in that direction." He pointed off where she was looking. "It used to be quite popular for camping and picnicking, but not so much anymore."

She shivered, a tremor running through her body and settling over her shoulders.

"I have an extra sweater if you're cold," Paris said, reaching into the pack.

Jade shook her head, finally turning back to him. She really wasn't all that cold. They'd been moving briskly and she was well dressed. "No, I'm… I'm fine. We should probably keep going."

"We can head to the lake, if you like. Perhaps your magic is trying to lead you there. You do need some work with your water spells."

Jade hesitated, staring off in the direction of the lake. "What about circle casting?"

Paris shrugged, slinging the pack back on. "If your magic is telling you something, we should follow it. There will be time for circle casting later."

He stepped in front of her, taking a quick look at his compass to ensure they were going in the right direction. Jade fell a little behind Paris as they walked, slowing her steps. She couldn't explain how she felt. She didn't want to go where he was leading. She opened her mouth to tell Paris, but couldn't figure out what to say. He was just about to push aside a mass of overgrown branches that were blocking their way when her hand reached out on its own and clutched the back of his shoulder.

"Stop."

Paris turned to face her and she pulled her hand back slowly.

"I don't want to go any farther," Jade said, the words blurting out of her. The sweat that she'd worked up hiking was going cold and clammy on her skin and she swiped at the top of her lip with the sleeve of her sweater. She felt anxious and jittery, like she was expecting something to pop out of the bushes and scare her.

He frowned at her. "Are you sick? Do you not feel well?"

Jade shook her head. "I don't want to work on water today. Can we go back to doing circles?"

"If you're ill we can go back to the car. Can you make it?"

"I'm not sick, I just… I want to go back the other way. The way we were going before." She licked her lips and glanced around a bit. "I don't… I don't like it here. I feel like…" she hesitated a bit, feeling slightly foolish as she spoke. "I feel like something bad happened here."

Paris' face seemed to morph into understanding. "I mentioned this place used to be popular for picnicking?" he asked. When she nodded, he continued, "There was an accident, many years ago and since then, most witches stopped coming here. They say the same thing. Not everyone feels it so I wasn't sure if you would or not."

"Do you?"

Paris tilted his head in a 'maybe-yes-maybe-no' kind of way. "It's difficult to say if I feel it because others in the Coven do and I'm tied to Coven magic or if I feel it on my own. I do get an 'off' sort of feeling from this area, but no one's magic has actually been affected. I thought if you were drawn here then perhaps it would be a good area for you to work on your water skills since not many people use it. But if you're one of the witches that's sensitive to this area, we should move along."

He started heading back the way they came and Jade could feel the pressure that had been building in her lungs decrease with each step they took in the other direction.

They were back on the path they had originally been on, Jade following Paris closely. She wanted to ask what kind of accident, but was afraid to. She wondered what must have happened to leave that kind of lingering presence in the area. Instead, she asked, "How come not everyone feels it?"

She saw Paris' shoulders shift in a shrug, the light backpack he wore moving slightly. "Different levels of magic, different sensitivities. Being sensitive to magic is like your other senses. Some people can pick out scents better than others, some have better than 20/20 vision. Some witches sense things that others don't."

They hiked in silence for almost an hour. The afternoon sun was waning in the trees and Jade did find she was getting cold now, wondering if she could just ask Paris for the sweater he had in the backpack. The pathway broke through to a small clearing and Paris slung the pack off and dropped it to the ground. Looking up, the trees seemed to bow toward the center, so tall they looked like they touched at the middle.

"How do you feel now?" Paris asked.

She shrugged, hands on her hips. "Fine. Let's do this circle thing. I'm good."

He looked around briefly on the ground and, spotting what he wanted, took a few steps away from her. He picked up a branch from the ground and handed it to her, glanced around and found another for himself. When he walked further into the clearing, she followed.

"The circle," he began, "is the most perfect form in geometry in math, in life. It is the basis of all things. The ellipse that planets travel in, the globes of planets, are all circles albeit distorted. A circle has no beginning and no end much like time and nature, our magical parents. The only thing wrong with a circle is our definition of it."

"You mean the number pi," Jade said staring up at him.

He smiled at her. "Correct." She felt a warm rush of pride at being right.

Paris took his stick and dragged it across the ground, turning in a circle himself as he did.

"Is that it?" she asked quickly. "Is your circle… done-ish?"

"Yes and no," Paris said cryptically. "My intent is the biggest piece of the puzzle. At this time, with my magic being affected, I haven't put my intent behind this circle. However, by nature of me being a witch, simply by going through the motions, I have casted a circle. This one would be limited and not likely to do anything great or extraordinary for my magic. But, for all intents and purposes, it is a circle. Now," at his tone, she straightened her shoulders. "I want you to do the same, but since your magic isn't affected, I want you to think about your intent, specifically, that you are casting a circle."

Jade felt foolish as she put her stick on the ground and spun around in a circle, thinking, '*I'm casting a circle*.' She had half a notion that at any moment a camera crew would pop out of the forest and she'd have just been coven-punked, but the woods were silent. As she stepped back to her original position, she felt like she got a small shock - a tingle traveling up her spine.

"Did I do it? Is that it?"

"Very good," Paris said, smiling at her. She grinned back. "If you would, step out of your circle for a moment."

She pursed her lips, trying to figure out where exactly the boundary was since it wasn't marked on the ground. Jade found though as soon as she raised her foot and stretched it out, it was like she could feel where it ended - a strange kind of pushing-popping sensation slid up her leg when she crossed over. Paris stepped away from his own circle.

"See if you can step into mine," he said.

She picked her foot up, feeling reminiscent of childhood hopscotch games with Lily - trying to step over the square with the rock on it to reach the proper one. Like her own circle, she felt as though she could feel a barrier, only this time it was denser, thicker. She had to fight a bit to get into it. Stepping fully into Paris' circle, she wrinkled her nose and curled her shoulders up.

"How do you feel?"

"Like…" Jade looked around surreptitiously. "Like you're around me. Uncomfortably around me. Overshadowing me. Or like you caught me stealing from your bedroom or something weird."

"Unnerving is it not?"

"Yes," Jade breathed with a distasteful look on her face. It felt like there was a cold trickle of water running down her spine, pooling at the base of her back. Looking over at Paris, it seemed like his eyes, normally exceptionally blue on their own, were even brighter and sharper.

"You can step out now."

She leapt out of his circle, happy to be done with it. She gave herself a little shimmy, feeling like she needed to shake-off his presence.

Paris kept his eyes on her and then stepped forward into her circle.

Immediately her scalp started to tingle. It sent a shiver down her neck and across her scapula. She flexed her shoulder blades, trying to work the feeling out. It was different from being in his circle, but no less uncomfortable.

"And now?" he asked.

"It's like you're crowding me. In my personal space bubble. I don't like it. It feels… cloying." Jade curled her fingers into a lose fist and then flattened them out again, repeating the motion as though it could burn off some of the sticky feeling she had from Paris being in her circle. "I want to push you out of my circle."

Paris stepped out of her circle quickly and she took a deep breath. The cloying feeling fading away the longer he was out.

"Creepy," Jade said lowly.

Paris gestured to the ground. "Let's sit."

She sat down cross-legged and then had to tilt at an awkward angle so to remove a painful little branch she had landed on. After tossing it aside she settled herself. Paris sat down in front of her with ease and grace, as though the ground had been waiting for him, ready to make him comfortable.

"As you just learned, casting a circle amplifies our powers. However, it isn't something you can just throw around lightly. Your powers will be stronger, sharper. It's a hard talent to learn."

Jade frowned. "Casting? But I just did it."

"Not just casting your circle, but perhaps recognizing that someone else has cast a circle without feeling them step into it. Or knowing that there's a circle that's been cast somewhere in your vicinity. It's also quite difficult to control your power while you're in a circle. At times it can seem like the circle is casting its own spell, regardless of your will."

She thought about that for a moment, considering. "So I need to learn to sense if someone has cast a circle without waiting to have them step in it and I have to learn how to not let mine get away from me."

"Precisely. It's more important for you to understand it than to learn how to do it. I know you can do it, Jade. I knew you would be able to before I brought you out here. You're quite powerful. But can you control it? Or could you tell if I've been here before today and cast a circle here without seeing me do it?"

"Did you?"

"No," Paris answered and then paused. "Not here."

She narrowed her eyes. "Where?"

"That's part of another lesson," he said with a grin.

Jade felt a rush of warmth for how proud he seemed of himself. "Aw, look at you! All cagey and sly; high five." She held her hand up and he stared at it for a moment, like he was unsure what to do. Slowly his hand came up and he gave hers a solid slap. "Nice," she said. "So, when can I work in my circle?"

"How about right now?"

She rubbed her hands together gleefully, feeling a thrill low down in her stomach at the prospect. She felt like she'd just been given a shiny new toy. "Really?"

"Really," Pars replied, getting to his feet. He held out a hand for her, but she was already up and brushing off her jeans. "I'm… hesitant to let you try fire in a circle just yet. You've shown such an aptitude for it, but you're control is still a bit…"

"Bad?" she filled in.

"Shaky," he amended. "You mentioned at your tarot card reading that you don't like water and then you didn't want to go to the lake to cast any water spells."

"Is this a magic lesson or a therapy lesson?" she asked, shifting back and forth on her feet. She really didn't like working with water. She'd sort of been hoping to avoid it, like a child pretending if they don't look in the closet, there couldn't be anything hiding there.

"Both in a sense, I suppose," answered Paris. "Why don't you like working with water?"

Jade shrugged, feeling uneasy, like a bug under a microscope. "Um, I dunno. I just…" she thought about the few water spells she'd tried - little tiny ones with a pot of water on the stove or some small amounts of mist or liquid. "It makes me feel…" she gestured at her chest, not sure how to explain it. "I just don't like it. When I use a fire spell, I don't really have to think about it, or think about certain words. I can mumble my way through the spell, not even saying stuff right and as long as I know what I want, it happens. But with water…" she licked her lips, feeling the familiar tingle she got when she thought about it, a weight settling across her chest. "I get nervous before I even start. It's like I don't want to? And I know I don't want to and I'm doing it anyway." Jade stole a glance at him finally, having avoided looking at him while she was talking. She'd been afraid he'd be looking at her strangely, like she was some kind of freak, but instead he just looked quietly open and intrigued, paying attention to what she was saying and giving her time to formulate her thoughts. "Sometimes," she said, her words halting and slow, his silence making it easier for her to continue, "sometimes I feel like I can't breathe. I know it's not true, but," she stopped, feeling the need to draw in a deep breath and fill her lungs, just from talking about it. "It's there. Just sitting." She made a swirling motion with her hands over her chest.

Paris let her words hang in the air and she felt better that he didn't try to discount her feelings or tell her that she was being irrational or foolish.

"Your feelings are an important part of your magic. If there's something keeping you from casting water spells, it would be in your best interests to work with it and try to resolve it. However, if you're opposed, I won't force you."

Jade chewed the skin on the inside of her lips, wishing she'd brought some chapstick with her. She looked around the small clearing. It was a pretty little area - the colors of fall on their way out, creeping slowly toward winter, settling over the greens of moss, leaves, weeds and bushes. She still had a lingering sensation in her chest and stomach from the lake area earlier, like a drop of the wrong paint color on a fresh wall, smeared around and pushed in, not truly wiped away. She was stupid for feeling that way, wasn't she? Paris was here, they were in a calm area, daylight surrounded them.

"There's nothing here that can hurt me."

Paris blinked in surprise and Jade wished she hadn't said it out loud. She wasn't sure why she did. It was out of her mouth before the words had fully formed in her brain.

"No, there isn't. But, there's also no rush. If you don't want to do it, we'll work on air or earth. All three are excellent elements to work with here in the preserve.

Jade shook her hands out, trying to get rid of the sticky, cloying nerves thrumming through her veins. "No, I'm good." *Fake it till you make it*, she thought.

"Okay."

She liked that he didn't second-guess her, forcing her to keep iterating that she was fine. He simply nodded and took her at her word. He gestured to the area where her circle was and she thought she could almost see it, a strange, shimmering round spot, waiting for her.

"Your circle, Jade."

Stepping in, Jade felt the difference easier now; it was an increase in her assuredness and her confidence. She looked around and noticed that things were sharper to her. Paris, as he stood to face her, seemed sharper too. More alive; more vivid. It was hard to break her stare from him, but she did and turned around to take in a 360 view. She breathed deeply, feeling the cool air settle into her lungs, crisp and a little damp.

"Do you remember any of your water spells?"

She nodded, worrying the fabric of her jeans slightly. "Yeah, I've read a few and tried them out."

"Ah yes, your memory for printed things," Paris said. "You'll be lucky as you continue on in your lessons." He paused for a moment and she saw him fidget. It was such an odd gesture on him - foreign and strange. "You'll make a fine witch. Not that you aren't already, but, you'll continue to do well."

Jade felt puffed up, like a fat pigeon, at his words and she tried not to stammer and kick at the forest floor like a child. "Um. Thanks."

"So, your water spell." Paris made a 'go-ahead' gesture with his hand.

Jade nodded. "Yeah, I thought about working on it the other night. I wanted to get some mist to dance, like my fire does, but I just ended up playing around with fire instead."

"Try it now."

Jade closed her eyes for a moment and tried to push the heavy feeling in her chest away, focusing instead on the feeling she got when she worked with fire - a warm, fragrant feeling. When she worked with fire, it was like opening an oven while baking a pie - a rush of heat and scent that was surprising and maybe a little scary at first, but always flared out to satisfaction and pleasure as you inhaled. Thinking about that feeling, but trying to focus instead on water, she spread her hands out in front of her, cupping them, and spoke her incantation. Nothing happened at first and she had to open her eyes to check with Paris who gave her a quick nod, indicating she was doing it correctly. She said it twice more, then a small ball of mist began to form in the space between her hands.

"There you are," Paris said lowly. "How does that feel?"

Jade moved her fingertips slightly around the mist, like a potter working clay. "Cold. Sharp." She felt it in her chest as well as in her fingers. A dank pressure, like jello inside her lungs - jiggly and damp. She didn't like it, feeling her lips curl with distaste.

"See if you can shape it. Perhaps a box or a triangle. Something simple."

Jade concentrated, feeling a pressure build up behind her eyes. Fire was quick and deft; it responded to her immediately. The watery mist reminded her more of mud or sludge than liquid - heavy and stagnant. She worked the mist in her hands, trying to stay patient and mostly succeeding. After a few minutes, she had a long cylindrical column of it, the grayness of it turning a more melancholy blue. As Jade realized the color had changed, it changed again to a murky, yellowish-green - like mossy silt churned up.

"What are you thinking of?" she heard Paris ask, his voice seeming far away to her.

"Nothing. Just… water. Mud." Jade stared at the dirty cylinder. "It's so different from fire."

Until Paris stepped into her line of sight, she hadn't realized she'd turned slightly away from him. "How so?"

Jade didn't know what she was going to say until she started speaking. "When I call fire, it's….friendly. Excitable. Like a puppy that wants to play with me."

She pulled her hands away from the column of mist and it hovered in front of her. "When I think about water, it's like… it's waiting for me, like it knows things about me." She felt her power jump up a notch, unbidden and the cylinder flattened out and became a sheet, inverting and then drifting overhead. She felt like a cartoon animal with only one rain cloud above its head.

"I think we'll stop here for today," Paris said.

She felt the deep pulling sensation on her chest and lungs strengthen, tugging at her. It made her feel sick, like she'd eaten too much at a party. She swallowed, feeling the tightness in her throat. Jade couldn't take her eyes off the sheet of mist above her and she flinched when she felt the first drops of rain on her face.

Through the small cloud she'd created in front of her, she could see the rest of the sky darkening - clouds moving in fast, rolling over each other like steam billowing out from an industrial plant.

"You're pulling in too much power, Jade. I need you to focus on only the cloud above you. I'd like you to cast it off, and then step out of your circle."

Jade heard Paris, heard the words and the tone in his voice, but the tugging at her chest was relentless. She had this sudden thought that if she just had enough water, it would go away. Like a compass, she could feel the lake they'd passed by off to her left and further back, in the woods. It rang in her head like a discordant note from a bass instrument, deep and low, making her stomach twist up. There were words on her lips that she didn't know she wanted to say until she spoke them aloud. "Sometimes… sometimes I think it wants me to belong to it."

A crack of thunder barreled out of the sky, rumbling in her bones and she shivered at the sound.

"Jade, I want you to step out of your circle."

She turned to look at him and he reached out, into her circle. A jolt of his power shocked her when his hand crossed over into her space and she jumped when he touched her arm.

Then, just beyond the low, fog-horn note of the lake, she felt something else. Equally discordant, only shrill. It had a strange tempo to it, pulling her attention back into the forest and away from Paris. Rain started to fall - fat, cold drops, splashing onto her face, making her clothes damp immediately.

"Do you hear that?" she asked. Now that she was focused on the new sound, the sound of the lake was relegated to the back of her mind, like the ominous soundtrack of a horror film. All she could hear was the disjointed hum of… something else. Something that didn't belong.

The rain started falling harder, denser. The kind of rain that is relentless against a windshield, clouding out everything else in a pool of liquid glass - blurry and distorted. Another crack of thunder bellowed.

"Focus, Jade. You're losing control."

"Can't you hear that?" she argued. "It doesn't belong here."

"You're using too much power, Jade, and you haven't the skill nor the control for it."

Jade felt like she was stretching, reaching, so close to figuring out what she was hearing, what she was feeling, and she didn't want to stop. It was akin to being on tippy-toes; what she wanted just out of grasp, but within the realm touch - fingers brushing against the edge of *something*.

Paris' hand tightened around her arm and she was surprised at the force of it. She turned slowly, looking first down at his hand, white knuckled on her arm and then at his face. He was sopping wet; his hair black streaks against the side of his face, his eyelashes black spikes framing his eyes. The strange sound from the forest still rang in her ear and she pulled away, tugging mindlessly against him. He tugged her back, forcefully and she frowned.

"I can't use my magic," Paris said. "I shouldn't. You have to stop."

Seeing the expression on his face, hearing the urgency in his eyes, Jade felt like she was waking up from something. She knew it was raining, but looking around she realized it was pouring, sheets of water falling down on them. Now that she was aware of it, she could hear the white noise of the rain and found it drowned out the sound of the lake and whatever else it was that she heard. She blinked up at the sky, rain clouding her vision. The sky was dark with the storm.

"Pull it back," he ordered.

"I'm sorry," Jade said, her words drowned out by another boom of thunder. She tried to feel for the edges of the storm, feel how far it had moved out and how much she'd have to pull it back in. She felt as though she were groping in the dark for a light switch, fingers reaching and pressing out, searching. As if spurred by her mental imagery, one of her hands came up and grasped at the fabric of Paris' sleeve, twisting it in her grasp.

"I don't know. I can't find the end of it." She was like a child poking at something found in a cave, not realizing until too late that she awakened the monster. Jade couldn't find the end of her magic. She had this notion that if she could just find the edge, she could pull it in, bring it back to herself. Every direction she felt in, she just felt *more*. More rain, more water, more power.

Except….

Except for Paris. When she cast her magic out, he was like a rock - edges sharply defined and solid. Jade could feel his power, thrumming underneath her fingertips, and the ferocity of it shocked her. She didn't expect it to be so vicious. She had imagined his power would be like her own - bright and razor-edged, brisk and immense. Instead, his power was fierce like a hurricane - pulsing, pushing and pressing at the edges.

Unlike her own, Paris' power was expertly leashed. Even though she could feel the strength of it almost singing in her bones, it was tampered down, buckled in.

She only wanted a bit of it. Just a little of his power would be all she needed to find the edges of her water spell, she was sure of it. She didn't know exactly what she was doing, but she imagined she was pulling some of his power out, like a siphon. Just a little. Just enough to help her out.

"What are you doing?" he asked quickly, pulling away a bit. Her fingers clenched into his arm hard.

Jade didn't know how to articulate it, she just knew if she had a little bit of his power, of his control, she could do this, she could stop this. The rain was coming down in sheets and she was soaked through, her clothes heavy and gathering a chill. She tugged on Paris' magic with her own.

"My magic's affected," he protested, but he didn't pull further away. Jade pushed at the edges of his power and she could hear where his magic was out of tune. His magic echoed the strange-wrong sound of the forest - like a plucked tuning fork matching the same tones all around it. She tried to push the sound of Paris' power away for a moment and focus on her own and was stunned when she heard it clearly, like a set of wooden wind chimes and burning flames - clear, bright and in tune.

"Mine's good. Can't you hear it?"

Paris frowned, leaning in closer to her, his face almost at the edge of her circle. Jade had this perfect, sudden sense that as long as he filtered his magic through her, it would work. She could almost see the exact moment he realized the same thing. The muscles of his arm flexed under her hand as he straightened himself a bit. His power ebbed back into him, away from her and she opened her mouth to protest, suddenly not sure that he did understand. His eyes met hers and then she *got* it. He was gathering his magic, priming it for use. Jade had about three seconds in which her brain went into overdrive - she wondered if this was such a good idea, if she should have maybe thought this through better, how impossibly blue Paris' eyes were framed by his black, wet eyelashes. Her eardrums popped so painfully she wanted to clap her hands over her ears, but she couldn't unclench her fingers from Paris' arm. She felt pressure all around her, closing in on her and then a surge of his power went into her, went *through* her, barbed and ferocious. There was a sharp, piercing pain in her chest and a deep sucking feeling against her ribs, like her insides were being pulled out of her body through a thin straw.

Jade wanted to tell him to stop, that she didn't like it and to push him away, but she could feel it was working. Paris' power surged over hers, fanned outward and found the edges of her spell easily. He reeled in her magic like a ruler-bearing schoolteacher corralling a truant student. The force of his magic pulling her own power back towards them made her knees want to buckle, but at the same time, raised her up on her toes, curling her body toward him in a harsh arc. Her circle was like an invisible barrier between them. He could reach through it, but she could sense he couldn't actually cross into it, and it didn't seem like he could pull her out. Her feet simply refused to step forward, no matter how much she thought it might be a good idea.

Jade's magic was coming back to her, the wind on its back, bringing a shrill sucking sound to her ears. She winced at the pressure and pain, knowing her face must be contorting in an odd rictus, whereas Paris' remained still - his eyes burning bright blue and hard to look at directly. She turned her head away, needing to gasp at the swelling force in her chest as her magic funneled back into her. The pain wasn't excruciating, but Jade had a fear welling up inside her that if Paris continued, it would be. She wondered if this was how Matthew, the witch who tried to kill her, felt when Paris broke his magic. A sharp coil of fear tightened in her gut and without thought, she pushed her power back outward. There was a loud crack and she and Paris were thrown backward from each other.

She slid across the wet ground - grass scuffing up her hands and mud sliding down the back of her jeans. Jade swiped at the rain in her eyes and saw Paris about five feet away, similarly sprawled on the ground, panting a bit from exertion.

As Jade moved to roll over to push herself to her hands and feet, her body protested, all of her joints locking up. Her ribcage groaned in pain. She lay down on the ground blinking up at the cloudy, but rain free sky, her arms and legs akimbo, star-fished out around her.

"Are you all right?" Paris called out, and she could see him pushing himself to his feet. She gave him her best, 'are you fucking kidding me?' look, but then felt bad about the pained expression on face, so she managed a 'thumbs up' before her arm flopped back down in the mud with a 'thwack.'

Circle Casting 101. She was sure she either aced it or totally flunked out.

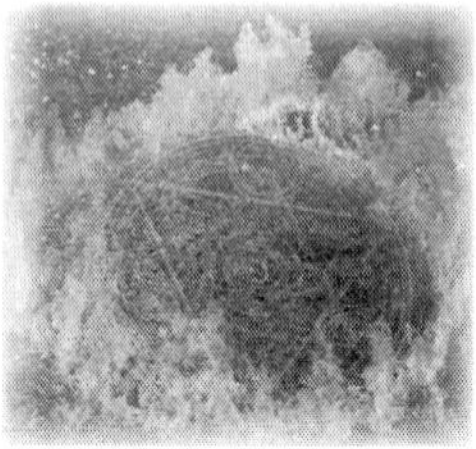

CHAPTER 9

The ground was slick under Paris' feet as he picked his way carefully over to where Jade was stretched out on the ground.

Other than giving him the thumbs-up signal a moment ago, indicating she was okay, she hadn't moved. He stood over her and she squinted up at him. They were both soaking wet and he tried not to loom over her, both to not crowd her and to not drip on her.

"Can you not get up?" he asked, brow furrowing at her motionlessness.

"I'm just gonna…" she waved a hand haphazardly. "I need a minute."

"Are you certain you're all right?"

Jade nodded, closing her eyes for a moment. "Tired."

Paris didn't doubt it. He was quite relieved to see that she didn't seem to be suffering any other ill effects that he could see other than fatigue. She'd used quite a bit of magic and he wasn't sure she realized it.

When she'd started using too much power, when he'd touched her, he'd immediately felt the difference between her magic and his. While his had been getting more discordant over the last couple days, hers rang true and in that moment he felt his power shift back into proper tune with hers. He'd felt relief - like a long, lingering ache you'd gotten used to finally easing up. Her power had been different than what he'd been expecting. Paris had thought given Jade's proficiency with magic and with how powerful she was, that her power would be sharp and quick but it wasn't. He still felt Jade's power and her magic was intense, but also oddly muffled. Paris had the impression that it should be so much more than it was, but somehow, it didn't quite meet its potential. Looking down at Jade now, as she gathered her wits, he recalled how she'd seemed to burn herself out when using large quantities of magic. Dr. Gellar had said it was akin to running too much electricity through a circuit and Paris felt he better understood it now. He'd felt it when their magic merged. Jade's magic was strong, ready to be called forth, but somehow she wasn't quite in sync with it. Somehow, it wasn't as clear as it could be.

For all his feelings on her magic being muted, he'd still known in that moment, by instinct he supposed, that if he removed his hand from her arm, his power would fall back out of tune and be damaged like the rest of the Coven's magic. Paris had managed to channel his power along with Jade's, through Jade herself, and pull back the massive storm she'd created. He wasn't sure what she meant when she talked about her feelings toward water - Jade had seemed lost and very troubled by the element.

Somehow her apprehension or problem with the element had led to her losing control of her spell work and she'd called far too much power and it needed to be reigned back in. He'd done the best he could, but when he pushed out one last little bit to call the last vestiges of her magic back and funnel it into her, something seemed to snap inside Jade and her power had lashed out at him, stronger than it ever had before. It pushed him away from her and threw her right out of her own circle.

Paris glanced around the clearing, at a loss for what to do while Jade gathered herself. His eyes narrowed and he turned in a circle slowly. Every tree surrounding the clearing had a scorch mark etched horizontally across the trunk, a remnant from the power Jade exerted pushing him back.

"Okay, I'm getting up," Jade said with a groan, pulling Paris' attention from the trees. She sat up and then pushed herself slowly to her feet. He hovered somewhat uselessly while she righted herself. He wanted to reach out and assist her, but had realized early on that she was quite sensitive to being touched and having her space invaded. Paris tried to maintain a discrete distance as she got up and wobbled for a moment.

"Still all right?"

Jade pushed back some errant strands that had loosened themselves from her ponytail and nodded slowly. "Yeah." She looked up to the sky, taking in the grey overcast clouds. It wasn't raining, but it wasn't sunny either.

"Still cloudy," she said, looking back at him with a question in her eyes.

"You pushed me back before I was done."

She grimaced slightly. "Oops." She made another face - comically twisted and disgusted and then turned slightly at the waist. "Oh yuck, there's mud all down my pants. I hate nature."

Paris huffed at her tone. "I know a spell that could clean you off and dry you as well, but I dare not use any magic while I'm still affected by the problems of the Coven. Unless I filter it through you."

She took a step backward quickly, holding up a hand. "Uh, no thanks. It's just some mud and water. I'm okay."

He frowned at her immediate reluctance. "Was it unpleasant? Did it hurt you?"

Jade shuffled awkwardly on her feet and he took that to mean 'yes,' but she didn't want to say. "Um. Kinda? Not at first. It was like… You know when your funny bone gets hit, it's not quite pain, but you really don't like it? Or when your foot falls asleep and then wakes up?" Jade waited for him to nod before she continued. "It was sort of like that. It didn't hurt really, but I didn't like it." She shook her head distastefully.

"I apologize. I didn't realize it would feel like that."

"S'okay," she said with a shrug. "My water spell got away from me and you were trying to clean up my mess. I get it."

Paris nodded for lack of anything to say. Jade shivered slightly and he realized she must be cold. "Well," he said finally. "We should head back. I'm sure you're cold."

She smirked. "If the next words out of your mouth are 'let's get you out of those wet things…'"

she said, tone teasing. She stepped past him, heading back the way they came.

She teetered a bit on her feet, but managed a steady pace, seeming to know the way back without him leading her. He could see the mud, sloppy on her back, trailing down into her jeans and he winced in sympathy both for her and for his car, which would be covered as soon as they both got in.

Life without magic was certainly messy.

"Jade," he began as he followed her down the pathway. "What did you mean? You said the water wanted you to belong to it."

Paris could see her shoulders stiffen, the wingspan of her scapula tightening.

"I don't know. It was just a dumb feeling."

He got the impression from her posture it was anything but. He paused and then switched to another thing she said that caught his attention. "What about the sound that didn't belong?"

Jade stopped in front of him and he worried that he'd pushed too far and she was going to snap at him. Instead, she just looked pensive and thoughtful.

"I don't know," she said, but unlike a moment ago when she used the words to push him away, this time he could see she was honestly considering his question. "You know how power hums? Like Callie said she could hear me humming when we first met and I could hear the same thing with you."

Paris nodded, giving her time to think, to continue.

"I hear that with some witches. Not everyone and not all the time. I hear you most of the time. I guess because you're powerful, or maybe 'cause you're Coven Leader. Sometimes if Callie or Henri is using magic I can hear them too. But out there," she gestured with her hand to the expanse of the forest, "I could hear something the same, but not. Like it should have been the same but it wasn't." She frowned and he could tell she was struggling with her words. "I don't know."

"Was it the lake area? As I said, many witches feel something amiss there. It wouldn't just be you."

Jade started shaking her head before he was done talking. "No. That was… It wasn't that." She seemed resolute that the two things were separate and he wanted to press her more on the lake only because she seemed so reluctant to discuss it and that troubled him.

She pursed her lips. "I thought if I could just get closer to it, the weird hum," she clarified, "I could figure it out. But then everything else just went to shit."

Paris barked out a sharp laugh before could stop himself at the rawness in her tone. She had been so thoughtful in her words, so careful about choosing them and then it just unraveled. He supposed she was right, it had all just gone to shit.

Jade shrugged and then started on back down the path and Paris gathered their conversation was over. She was silent the rest of the walk down, the only sound the squelching of their feet in their shoes.

The woods got drier the closer they got to the car and Paris wished he could say the same for Jade and himself. By the time they reached the car, a chill had settled into his bones and he was sorely missing his magic. Jade didn't complain about being cold, but he knew she must be from her pale skin and tightly pressed lips. The heater only blew cold air while the car warmed up and they were well on their way back to the Coven by the time it produced air hot enough to warm them. Jade flipped all the vents on her side of the car toward her, pressing her fingertips, white and stark, against the grills, trying to warm her hands up.

"What a bust."

"I wouldn't say that entirely," Paris replied. "You may have found us something about the Coven's magic problem. I'm going to see what Hannah thinks. Would you be amenable to coming back out?"

Jade paused for a moment and he spared a glance her way. She was worrying her bottom lip between her teeth, still pressing her fingers tightly to the slats of the vents. "We can skip the lake part, right?"

Paris made a note to ask Hannah about that as well. While some witches got a bad feeling about the area, Jade's reaction seemed stronger than most.

"I see no reason why we can't avoid it. Was the strange feeling you got from there?"

"Not the weird hum, no."

"Then it shouldn't be a problem."

Jade made a sort of 'hmph' sound and then rubbed her hands together briskly, probably to warm them. "Ugh, I'm cold, I'm wet, and there's mud in my underwear, which is probably too much information, but it's so hideous it needs to be shared so we both feel as uncomfortable as I do."

"Well, it didn't go exactly as I hoped, but still, it wasn't a total loss."

"Yeah." She stared out the window, her face turned away from him as he drove. He thought about perhaps engaging her in a discussion, but found he couldn't think of anything to say that didn't sound inane or ridiculous. Though they weren't having a conversation, when he finally pulled the car up in front of her little cottage, he was still reluctant to let her go.

She was already tugging on the handle and stepping out before he could think of anything.

"Jade," he started quickly, leaning over toward the passenger side. She was already out of the car and had to bend over to look back in at him.

"What?"

"You did well today. Despite the way it all turned out."

"Uh, thanks." She said it like she wasn't really sure why he was telling her that, but was grateful nonetheless.

"But you do need to work on your control." Paris winced at his words, not sure why he couldn't have just let sleeping dogs lie.

Jade crinkled her nose at him. "Way to ruin the moment, English." She rolled her eyes at him and he got the sense she wasn't really angry or upset, just amused by him. She closed the car door, tapping twice on the roof by way of goodbye. She didn't turn around as she made her way up the steps of her front walk and then inside, shutting the door firmly behind her. It was only when the car transmission cycled down, changing the white background noise that he realized he'd been sitting there staring at her door long after she'd gone in.

*

Jade left little bits of mud as she walked into her cottage and she contemplated taking off her pants in the hallway before heading upstairs, but figured it would just make more of a mess. She trudged up the stairs carefully, doing a strange sort of shuffle where she was trying to move fast and at the same time not trying to move much of her body.

Bruce was at the top of the stairs, his lizard eyes shining in the light, judging her.

"Hey, I found you in a sewer. Lizards that live in glass houses should get undressed in the dark."

Her metaphor didn't even make sense to herself and Bruce's long pink tongue came out, like he was using it to scent the air around her. It made its customary 'pffftt' sound and then he waddled away, back into her room.

"Drama queen," she muttered.

Getting undressed in the shower was the best idea she could come up with and she used the opportunity to rinse most of the mud out of her jeans. Twenty minutes later the wet clothes were in the hamper and she was in warm, *dry* yoga pants and a hoodie, padding downstairs. She used her wet top to clean up stray bits of mud before tossing the whole lot in the washing machine. Bruce toddled along behind her, his sharp, long claws ticky-tacking on the floor.

With the machine started, she turned to face him, hands on her hips. "Right. Coffee time." He blinked at her with owlish eyes, flapping his Elizabethan lizard collar once. "You want some? Maybe in a saucer?" she asked as he followed her to the kitchen.

"Possum."

Jade stopped short at Seth's drawl, Bruce hissing loudly at her feet. Seth was leaning against the jamb of her pantry, feigning casualness. Bruce trotted over, Elizabethan collar fully up and flared out, like a fan.

She supposed it was the equivalent of his hackles being up.

"Ugh." Jade tossed her head back and rolled her eyes a bit at Seth. "Seriously creepy. Are you just hanging out in there waiting for me to show up?" She stalked over to the coffee machine and started brewing a pot.

Seth sighed. "Oh, possum. Time was you were deliciously afraid of me. I miss the good old days." He took a deep sniff and then looked at her pointedly. "Oh good, it's still there. You do well at hiding the look of it, but fear has its own perfume."

Jade tried not to let her spine stiffen too much. She wasn't stupid enough to not be afraid of him, but dammit. She was tired and she still had a strange unsettled feeling in her gut from being out in the forest. The combination of the weird sound she'd tried to chase and the sick tugging feeling she felt from the lake sat in her stomach like a ball of wet yarn - cold, clammy and gross.

"Maybe I would be more afraid of you if you didn't show up so much."

"Touché, possum, touché. Always the most clever of my witches. I came by to see how you were faring."

"With what?" Although she wished she could do it, she simply couldn't bring herself to turn her back on him even as she made her coffee. It would certainly prove to him that she wasn't afraid, but the truth was, she was afraid. Turning her back on Seth would be like lying down next to a lion and saying, 'nice kitty, here you go!'

"I believe I mentioned the last time I was here that there's trickery afoot."

"Yep." Jade leaned against the counter, crossing her arms over her chest.

Seth smiled, his teeth shiny and white. "That's what I love about you, possum. You're quite adept at this back and forth. You'd be amazed at how people often spill their guts at only a few words from me, but not you." He winked at her, his dark eyes glinting. "Bare minimum."

He narrowed his eyes a little and leaned forward slightly, as though daring her to speak a little more. Jade had to admit, it was tempting to ask him questions or just give out information so he would leave quicker. She took a fortifying breath and focused on the sound of the coffee dripping into the pot behind her. Lowly, so quiet she almost didn't hear it, Bruce was making a deep rumbling sound. Lizard growl, she supposed.

Seth leaned back, seemingly pleased. "You do entertain me. So," he said, voice becoming sharper, louder. "How are things at your Coven? Magic all wonky?"

"Is that your technical term for it?"

He grinned like the Cheshire Cat. "Yes, it is. Your magic's still fine though, isn't it?"

"Why do you ask questions you already know the answer to?"

"Answering a question with a question!" he exclaimed. "Ten points, possum. Tell me, does it bother you or relieve you that your magic is unaffected?" Seth raised an eyebrow at her, two of his fingers rubbing together. Sometimes he came across too much like a cartoon villain. If he had a handlebar mustache, he'd be twirling it.

"I'm not dealing with you, Seth," she said baldly. Jade felt the need to put that out there. She had to keep it foremost in her mind at all times: Seth was only here for a deal. It was all he wanted from her.

Well, she hoped it was all he wanted from her.

"Because," Seth continued as though she hadn't spoken, "I have to wonder if you're pleased that your magic is unaffected or feeling rather left out. Like a stray cat in the rain outside a warm and cozy house. Sure," he shrugged, "maybe you didn't want to be in the house anyway, but I bet you wanted to know what it was like first."

Seth was remarkably good at pushing her buttons. Jade wasn't normally good at keeping her impulses under control, but with Seth, losing control of her mouth and spouting off could get her in over her head fast.

"And I bet that brain of yours is just tick-tick-ticking away with ideas. Who's responsible, for what reason, and how to figure it all out. Tick-tick-tick." The last three words were closer to a hiss than to regular speech and the hairs on the back of Jade's neck stood up. Bruce hissed in response, showing his fangs.

"But what would you do even if you *could* figure it out? There's your conundrum, possum. What to do, what to do. Tell me, do you think your gallant English Coven Leader has any idea what to do with a problem like this?"

"He's doing fine," Jade said quickly and cursed herself for being baited. It was one thing for Seth to taunt her but it was another to talk trash about Paris, who wasn't even there to defend himself. Not that Paris would care if Seth talked trash about him. Okay, he'd care that there was a demon in Jade's pantry and that she was standing there talking to it, but other than that he probably gave zero fucks. Or whatever the super-polite, highly-mannered version of a fuck was.

Seth's pressed a hand against his chest, long fingers extended, nails sharp. "Defending his honor. Be still my heart. What's the female equivalent of chivalry?"

"There isn't one," Jade said flatly. "Women didn't feel the need to make up a special term just for being a decent person."

Seth winked at her again and she shuddered. "But come now, possum. Tell me what's going on in that lovely brain of yours. You know who's responsible, don't you?"

Jade fought the urge to shift on her feet and fidget. Okay, so she didn't *know,* but she strongly suspected Dex. She didn't like him. She disliked him the moment she put eyes on him. It was so obvious to Jade that he had something to do with what was wrong with the Coven. He oozed when he walked. He was smarmy. It was the kind of smarmy that tried to hide behind charming, but just fell flat.

And everyone seemed to *love* him. Dex this, Dex that. He's so wonderful, blah, blah, blah. It was weird.

But what could she say about it? *Hey I get a hinky vibe from him and I know you all like him, but still! Take it from the new girl, you know the one that didn't know she was a witch until this year? And the same one that isn't affected by whatever is jacking your magic? Let me tell you, that dude you love is bad news.*

She'd lose whatever good favor she'd managed to gain. Not that she cared about that kind of stuff.

Because she didn't. Not really. Okay fine, Jade cared. She didn't want to be a social pariah. Jade wasn't good at all that social niceties and mingling shit. That had been Lily. Lily would know what to do, what to say and how to say it. People listened to Lily. If Jade said anything right now, she'd probably be lynched.

Pass.

On the bright side, if she did speak up and they wanted to lynch her, it's not like they could use any of their magic to do it.

"I thought as much," Seth said knowingly and she wanted to scowl and reply that she hadn't said anything, but that was part of the problem. She'd been silent too long and it was more than a little obvious that she had her suspicions.

"If you need help-" he started.

"I won't call you," she finished flatly.

"What if I gave you a freebie?"

"First one's free?" she questioned. "I'm sure just about every drug dealer out there has used that one and it never ends well." She eyeballed him carefully. "And I doubt anything with you is free."

"For you, I'd make an exception. I do enjoy our little chats. Although it will be hard to top the one we had when you were about to get your heart torn out. The blood! The excitement!" Seth sighed. "Good times." He clapped his hands together loudly and she flinched at the noise. Bruce flicked up his Elizabethan collar again and hissed. Seth smiled at them both, sharp teeth pristine and shiny. "Well! As sorry as I am to go, I wouldn't want to overstay my welcome.

Ta for now, possum. Keep using that noggin of yours. It's so wonderful to watch you work."

There was a soft sucking sound in the air and Jade's ears popped as Seth shimmered and then vanished.

Bruce spat in the direction of the pantry, his pink tongue flicking out with a crack. He looked up at her accusingly again, like he had the last time Seth had popped by.

"I know!" she exclaimed, feeling the chastisement in Bruce's glare. "Let me tell you, that wasn't even the worst part of my day." The coffee had brewed enough for her to pour a strong cup, the liquid, dark and black with a few stray grinds floating on top. Her hands had been shaky while Seth was there and now she had to live with the result. The day had been a total bust, one of her worst yet. Dress shopping, lunch with Dex, circle casting gone bad, and then Seth. Blergh.

Plus, there was that über creepy feeling she'd gotten in the forest, from the lake. Jade had a lingering sick feeling in her gut and she found the feeling increased just thinking about it. She swallowed hard, trying to will it away.

Mug in hand, she headed back upstairs, crawling into bed. It was still early in the evening, but she felt wiped out. Some internet time or maybe a light read was all she felt up to. The coffee wouldn't keep her up - she was too used to the caffeine at this point - and she liked the ritual of tucking her feet under her sheets and blankets, blowing air across the meniscus of the coffee and seeing it puddle and whirl. Bruce hopped up onto the bed too, making it jiggle and shimmy a bit with his weight. He scratched twice at a spot near the foot of the bed and then flopped over dramatically, making the liquid in her mug almost slosh over.

"Hey! A little delicacy when I've got hot liquids."

He 'pfffft'ed at her, tongue flicking out over his lizard chops and he closed his eyes. Jade pulled out her e-reader and picked something light and easy - no intense plots, no double crosses, no heavy angst. Her eyes were drooping not thirty minutes later and she swirled the last bit of coffee in her mug and then shot-gunned it back quickly. She flicked the light off and settled down, feeling Bruce press up against her hip seconds later - a solid, warm weight along her leg.

Jade dreamed of Lily that night. She ran ahead of Jade, through the forest, dodging past trees and under fat hanging branches. Jade struggled to keep up - her legs feeling heavy and thick. She could see Lily's hair bouncing through the foliage - deep brown and silky - strands getting caught on twigs and branches. Jade ran after her, feeling like she was running with her eyes partially closed. Branches nipped at her face, drawing scratches and she batted at them uselessly.

Jade finally broke free of the forest and found herself staring at a large, smooth-surfaced lake. The forest and sky were reflected back at her from the surface and she found herself dizzy with the image - two skies, two wooden docks, two tires swinging lazily from a long rope, two sets of trees bowing over the lake. She walked out onto the dock, the wood creaking and swaying slightly under her weight. The sick feeling from before churned in her gut, making a cold sweat break out over her upper lip and forehead. At the end of the dock, Jade got down on her hands and knees and peered into the murky green water. It had a strange glow to it, like it was lit from underneath. Her hands curled over the edge of the dock, knuckles white with force. She could see Lily under the water, her body vertical, feet trailing off into nothingness below her and her face turned up toward the surface, toward Jade. Lily's eyes were closed and her face still - a sleeping fairy tale princess, her hair undulating with silent underwater currents. Her arms stretched out above her, buoyed up by the water, reaching for the sky. Jade leaned in closer, her ponytail swinging over her shoulder and dipping into the water, disturbing the pristine surface and causing a slight ripple to cascade outward.

Lily's eyes opened - shockingly green and sharp, even in the murky water, and directed right at Jade. Jade's heart thumped twice out of sync, the off-beat rhythm making her breath catch. Lily smiled and reached her fingers for Jade, uncurling them toward her, stretching out her hands. Jade reached back without hesitation, her hand breaking the surface of the water, feeling icy cold as it submerged beneath, straining to Lily.

Their fingers touched, Lily's skin frozen and soft against Jade's. A loud crack echoed in the space, reverberating in Jade's ears.

Jade startled awake, weight pressing down on her and she struggled to get her arms free, feeling them trapped by something. She instinctively kicked with her legs, finding them equally trapped and she panicked, thrashing about wildly. She hit something soft and dense with her foot and Bruce let out a 'yip' kind of sound. Her hand connected with the closet door, making it rattle.

Closet. She was in the closet. Trapped under her own bedclothes. Bruce was in the closet with her. She stilled and felt Bruce press his lizard muzzle to her shoulder, knocking against her plaintively.

"Sorry, Bruce," she whispered, catching her breath and untangling her arms carefully from the blankets. Now that she wasn't thrashing wildly, it was perfectly simple to break free. Her hair was in her face and she pushed it aside, cracking open the closet door to see the nightstand clock.

It was already morning. She must have slept through her migration to the closet, having no memory of making the move. It was mildly troubling. She would have gotten out of bed and had to drag all her blankets with her, settling herself and Bruce in the dark interior, before managing to get the doors closed. Bruce stuck his triangular muzzle in the crack Jade had opened in the doors and pushed them the rest of the way open, trotting out into her room.

Jade scrubbed her face with her hands and managed to half-shuffle, half-stumble out of the closet, yanking her blankets with her and depositing them on the bed in a big heap. She put her hands on her hips. Bruce scurried under her bed and Jade bent down far enough to ensure he was all right. She had kicked him rather soundly when she'd woken, not realizing where she was. He was curled around her special shoebox - the one she filled with mementoes and knick-knacks, and kept close to her always. Bruce gave her a bit of an indignant look, wrapping his body tighter around the box and Jade sighed. "I'm sorry," she repeated, a little exasperated. "I didn't know it was you." He smacked his tongue a bit and then settled his chin on the ground, closing his eyes to her and feigning sleep. The big faker. She pushed to her feet, hands on hips.

Right. Sunday. Time for a little demon magic studying, laundry and groceries. Maybe some house cleaning. Jade had come across a few spells while she was fielding calls with Counter magic that may be helpful with that. A few of the incidents logged had been cleaning spells gone wrong - ones Jade hadn't even known existed. Since there was nothing wrong with Jade's magic, it looked like she'd just found her project for the day.

*

The spell Jade found for cleaning the shower was a bust. A horrible, hard-water encrusted, soap-scum-film bust. She was totally bringing it up with Paris next time they talked. What was the point of all this power if she still had to get down on her hands and knees and scrub the damn thing?

Being a witch was supposed to be way cooler than this.

At first, when it hadn't worked, she worried that her magic was finally starting to fall apart, like everyone else's in the Coven. Several fire balls later, she had to admit defeat. Her magic was fine, she was just unable to cast the spell.

Fucker. She hated cleaning the bathroom.

Which was how she found herself at the local supermarket chain standing in the cleaning supplies aisle wondering which product would do the most work for her. She needed groceries anyway, so it wasn't a total loss of a day. Jade's cart was already laden with her coffee, fruit and vegetables. God she hated people who said they genuinely liked vegetables. Jade herself did not, but she ate them because that's what adults were supposed to do. Plus, she needed to ensure she would fit into all those clothes she was planning on going back to her apartment to get, packing up and bringing to the Coven.

Someday.

She picked up a canister that promised all Jade had to do was spray it on, and then wipe it off twenty minutes later and presto-chango! No soap scum. She placed it in her cart, next to her hair dye and dishwasher tabs. She was careful about how she packed her cart and it irked her when she unpacked it at the till in a particular manner and the clerk would toss groceries in the bags all willy-nilly. Bread with cleaning supplies. Meat with bananas. Dryer sheets with grapes. Sacrilege. After picking up some diet soda and yogurt, she surveyed her list and finding it complete, headed for the checkout, trying to gauge which of the impossibly young clerks was least likely to toss her cheese in with the hot roasted chicken.

"Jade, fancy running into you here."

There was that clicking sound in her jaw again when she ground her teeth. Jade turned slowly toward the voice. "Dex."

"Getting groceries?" he asked, indicating her cart.

She raised an eyebrow. "Cracked that nut, did you? I can see why they gave you your own coven."

Dex smiled, seemingly unperturbed.

Jade made a move to push her cart past him and he moved in step beside her.

"I tried to stop by and see you the other day, but your house is strangely warded."

"Yep." She got in line at one of the checkouts, waiting for her turn.

"I've never come across warding like that before," Dex prodded. "Demon magic? From the demon grimoircs?"

Standing there looking at the tabloid magazines and the chocolate bars, she decided to go for broke. It wasn't like they were friends. Jade didn't want to be friends. Giving a quick glance around, she didn't see anyone she recognized from the Coven, so if she was going to stir some shit up, at least no one was around to witness it.

"Why do you keep talking to me, Dex?"

His brows furrowed. "What do you mean? I simply want us to be friends."

"But we're not friends. And we don't have to be. I've made it pretty clear I don't want to be and you keep pushing me. Why?"

"Maybe I like you."

"You don't even know me. You probably know a hell of a lot about my power rating and I would take you being interested in that over you pretending to be friends."

He smiled at her and she got the same feeling from it that she got when Seth smiled. It made her cold and a little afraid.

"I had hoped we could be friends, Jade," Dex said, staring off a little ways and she got the impression it was the first honest thing he'd ever said to her.

"Why?" Jade pressed.

"Your powers are extraordinary. Easily a match for Paris or myself. You could lead your own coven. Perhaps you should. And you've got quite the knack with demon magic along with the grimoires."

The idea didn't interest her in the slightest. "I've got nothing invested in being a bureaucrat. Possibly less than nothing."

He turned back to her, his dark eyes intense. "It wouldn't have to be that way. Maybe that's the way Paris runs things, but it can change."

She shifted her weight a bit, cocking out one of her hips. "Really? And how could it be, Dex?"

"You could do so much."

"For you?" she questioned.

He shrugged. "Or for yourself. Anything you wanted. Especially if you have those demon grimoires." He leaned in closer. "What's in those books, Jade?"

She snorted. "You must be certifiable if you think I'll tell you a damn thing about those books." Paris had repeatedly drilled into Jade how dangerous those books were. She wasn't about to share them, or anything about them, with Dex.

His jaw clenched, making a muscle in his cheek twitch. "They're too much magic for a novice like you. They should be with someone who can handle them."

Jade's creep-o-meter had its needle buried again. His voice, his face, his words…. everything about him screamed 'Danger! Danger!' She'd made a mistake once in her past, not trusting that voice inside her and she wasn't about to do it again.

“Were you always a psychopath or did you just become one once you got your own coven?” she asked.

Dex smiled again, leaning forward and plucking a chocolate bar off one of the shelves. He unwrapped it and took a bite, chewing carefully.

“Who will you tell, Jade? Callie? Henri? Paris? Will you go running and tell them I’m a bad, bad man and I’ve got tricks galore up my sleeve?”

She jutted her chin out. “Maybe I will.”

“You let me know how that goes. You know, I remember being seven, playing in a field and I caught a hummingbird using a spell I’d just learned. I broke its neck. My mother found me then, with a dead bird at my feet. I cried as I told her how I found it, wanting to help it and realizing it was already dead. She helped me bury it and even said a few words, resting her hand on my shoulder for comfort. I had to bury my face in my hands so she wouldn’t see me laugh. I imagine she thought I was too sensitive, overcome with emotion.” Dex took a step closer to her and Jade willed herself to stay put, staring up at his eyes. He was using his height to tower over her, physically using his bulk to press in on her. Though she was tall for a woman, Jade was no match for him physically. He was broader in the shoulders, had more lean muscle mass and stronger legs and arms. The way he used his form and his bulk to bully into her space made her heart rabbit-beat. Jade was more than well aware that she wouldn’t win, couldn’t win, a physical fight with a man. Not if it was dependent on outlasting him. She might be able to win in the first few minutes if she played fast and dirty, but after that, a man would simply out last her, waiting until she tired-out.

But, she was in a public place, a crowded place right now. There were people all around her and though they weren't Coven members, they would still likely keep Dex at bay. He couldn't lay a hand on her without causing a scene. All she had to do was keep her cool. If she started yelling at him or lost her temper and hit him, that's what everyone would say - Dex and Jade had been having a lovely, perhaps intimate talk, when she suddenly lost her mind and belted him one.

The whole goddamn Coven seemed to love him after all.

"If I can fool my own mother, what are my chances against Paris, do you think?"

"What did you do to the Coven's magic?" she asked, staring him straight in the eye.

"You decided it was me the moment we met, didn't you?"

"Yes."

"Why?" he asked, eyes narrowing slightly.

Jade ran through a quick list of reasons in her head. He'd been too nice, everyone seemed to like him too much. Maybe it was just that she was jealous - she wished she could elicit that kind of response in the Coven. Or maybe she just had a really good sense of people, one that she learned the hard way not to mistrust. It seemed entirely obvious to her that Dex was responsible. He showed up at the Coven right when things started going bad. It played out like a bad soap opera and Jade felt like the viewer at home, wanting to shout at the television that everyone else was blind. But, when Jade boiled it down and was really honest with herself, painfully honest, it all came back to how Dex had crowded into her space on that first day. He'd been oblivious to how he'd invaded her personal area, and that willful ignorance had set bells off in her psyche instantaneously. Dex ignored how she backed up and puffed up a bit to claim back her territory. He pressed forward, asking Jade for coffee, not taking no for an answer. It reminded Jade too much of another time, another person when Jade ignored the warning signs. At first, Dex was simply paying for the actions of someone in Jade's past, but the more she found out about Dex, the more she realized she was right to be suspicious.

Jade owed him none of her reasons, nor any explanation so she shrugged. "You tell me."

Dex chewed his chocolate bar carefully. "I'll make you a deal, Jade," he said slowly and she felt her skin crawl at the words, so similar to Seth's. "You stay out of my secrets and I'll stay out of yours."

"I don't have any secrets," she lied baldly.

"No? Then why is it when I look into your records, I see you listed for most of your life as Lily and only in the last couple of years as Jade?"

She swallowed in surprise and hoped the gesture could be mistaken for just a natural occurrence and not a response to his words.

Dex leaned in even closer, his face millimeters from hers. "Why is it you don't go by that name anymore?"

The way he worded the question made her realize he was fishing. If he really knew about her and Lily, the question would have been phrased differently. Jade's lips curled in a small smile and she stared back at him.

"Like I said, I don't have any secrets." She was far more comfortable in her bluff this time and she saw that she was right from the flash of annoyance and frustration across his face.

Dex leaned back, popping the rest of the chocolate bar in his mouth and dropping the empty wrapper in her cart. "Fine. Run and tell Paris. I wonder whom he'll believe? His friend of many years, a fellow Coven ruler, or the stray cat he dragged in off the streets who didn't know a curse from a curio when he found her? I wonder how much persuasion it would even take to convince him that you're behind it all."

Goddammit. He may not know fuck-all about her and Lily, but he sure knew where to aim his barbs. It was the exact thing she was afraid of - that she'd tell Paris and not only would he not believe her, but she'd somehow end up implicated herself.

"Are you done? It's my turn at the checkout," she said, feigning a bored tone, jerking her chin toward the bewildered clerk, who was watching them whisper low and intensely to one another.

"See you around, Jade," said Dex, tapping her cart twice with his hand as he left.

Jade looked up at the fresh-faced kid behind the till who flicked his eyes from Dex's retreating back to Jade.

"Um, are you gonna pay for the chocolate bar he ate?" he asked, nerves coloring his voice.

Jade rolled her eyes and gritted her teeth. Son of a bitch.

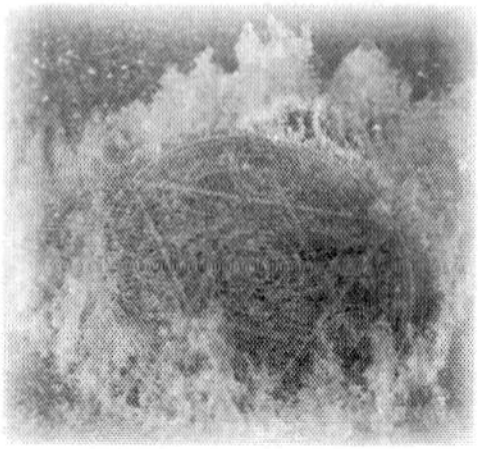

CHAPTER 10

The knock at Paris' office door was completely unexpected. At eight o'clock on a Sunday night, he was certain he had the entire Covenstead to himself. The door creaked open a bit and Veronica poked her head in.

"Knock-knock," she said with a smile.

He blinked in surprise. If he was entirely honest with himself, he expected Jade and not Veronica. Although there was no reason why Jade would stop by so late on a weekend. "What are you doing here so late?"

She entered, carrying a tray with coffee on it in one hand, a brown paper bag from the local bakery in the other. "I'm head of my own coven, Paris. I know what it's like to spend many a late night at the office. I come bearing gifts." She raised the tray of coffee and bag slightly.

Paris gestured her in, pushing his chair back a bit from his desk. She set the tray down on his desk and he saw the familiar scrawl from the coffee baristas down the block, indicating it was his usual drink, with extra syrup, just as he liked it. Veronica had a plain black coffee for herself and as Paris poked into the bag, pulling out a brioche for himself, she kicked off her pumps and sat down in the chair opposite his desk, curling her legs under her like a cat. As usual, not a hair was out of place and she looked impeccable even though it was far closer to the end of the day than the start.

"Still working on your Coven's magic problem?" Veronica asked, sipping at her coffee.

He nodded, taking a bite of the pastry and chewing it a bit first. "Yes. I'm going over some land records for the preserve. I was out there with Jade the other day and she felt something off."

"Really? Off how?"

Paris hedged. "She wasn't able to articulate it well. Her magic's still quite fresh."

Veronica made a low kind of 'hmmm' sound. "You do have your hands full with her, don't you?" She poked at the lid of her coffee with one of her nails, punching half-moon circles in the plastic.

Paris took a drink of his coffee, feeling the sugar run over his tongue. "She's extraordinarily powerful. I'm damn lucky she decided to stay with the Coven. I'm not sure what I would have done otherwise."

"How committed is she to the Coven?"

"What do you mean?" Paris asked, frowning.

Veronica shrugged. "From what I hear, she hasn't officially moved here yet. She still has her old apartment, hasn't brought any of her things here. Her clothing, her car…" Veronica trailed off. "Are you worried?"

"No," said Paris, a bit slower than he expected. "I don't think Jade's had a home for a long time."

"Did she tell you that?"

"No. It's just a sense I get from her. Her introduction to the Coven was shaky at best," Paris said, wincing slightly at the simplification - having a Coven member try to tear out your heart and also finding out that she either had to join the Coven or be stripped of her magic was a bit more than 'shaky.' He hadn't been lying to Veronica when he said he'd been lucky Jade stayed. If she'd decided to leave, Paris would have been the one tasked with breaking her magic. He hadn't thought he could do it without killing her. Now, knowing how strong she was, he was sure of it. She would have died if he'd tried, and he probably would've burnt out his own magic as well.

"You don't think she had anything to do with what's happened to your magic here, do you?"

"Absolutely not." This time Paris answered quickly, firmly. "I trust her."

Veronica took a long drink of her coffee. "I just worry," she said quietly, staring at her cup.

"About Jade?" Paris asked, incredulous. "No, she's not behind this, whatever it is. She hasn't been here long enough to learn something of this magnitude. Granted, at first I wondered if she stumbled across something by accident, with the demon grimoires she's got, but she hasn't done this. I don't think she would have even if she could."

"She's quite familiar with them, is she?"

Paris nodded. "Yes. She picks up demon magic faster than normal magic. Doesn't get headaches or blurred vision. I've yet to crack any of the spells and

I'm quite familiar with my mother's magic. Jade has already figured out how to lock her front door with them."

"Interesting," said Veronica, pushing herself back into the chair, keeping her posture perfect even as she made herself more comfortable. "Do you think it's a good idea for her to have those books?"

"I doubt I could get them away from her if I tried." Paris took a sip of his sweet drink, rolling it around his tongue. "In all honesty, though, despite her newness, I think she's the best person for those books."

Veronica made a low sound of agreement, sipping on her own coffee. "I only met with her briefly, and I thought I maybe overwhelmed her a bit."

Paris held back a wry huff. "She's not easily overwhelmed. I'm sure she was fine."

Veronica eyed him for a moment. "How high did she test for power?"

Paris paused for a moment. "High. Higher than anyone else in the Coven."

"Except you of course."

Paris tipped his head slightly. "For now."

"Are you serious? That high?" Veronica blinked a few times, "It's a wonder she doesn't just blow holes in stone with that much power."

"She doesn't know how to use most of it and she gets these-" he made a motion around his face and head, "headaches and nosebleeds. We don't know why."

"I've never heard of that happening before."

"Neither have I. Nor Hannah." He sat back in his chair, rubbing a hand over his face.

Veronica waved her hand at him. "It's late. You're tired. Pack it up and go home. It will all still be here tomorrow."

"Is that an order or just friendly advice?" he asked, a teasing tone in his voice.

Veronica paused and leveled him with a look, the air suddenly feeling a bit sharper than it had been moments before. "Is that what we are? Friends?"

Paris took a moment to form his thoughts. "I have always considered you a friend. You know that."

Veronica tapped her nail on the top of her cup thoughtfully. "For a while you considered us more."

"For a while," he said slowly, nodding a bit. "But that was a long time ago."

She smiled at him, face warm and soft. "You make it sound like we're eighty. Surely it can't be that long."

He huffed, a dry sound pulled from his lungs. "No. Not at all, but…"

Veronica held a hand up to him, breaking her gaze for a moment and looking away, pausing before looking back. "Let's leave that one unfinished and simply say that sometimes history repeats itself and sometimes it doesn't."

Paris nodded again. "Fair enough."

She stood, pushing her feet daintily back into her pumps and he rushed to stand at the same time, coming around his desk to stand before her. He'd never felt awkward around her until this moment, when she leaned forward to kiss him on the cheek like she normally did. He froze with uncertainty, not sure now how to respond. Paris couldn't remember ever paying attention before, always just accepting the gesture, but now, after the words they had just spoken, he almost wanted to pull back, but felt it would be even more awkward and strange. The politician in him kept his body still, his hand coming up to cup her elbow, while not truly engaging in any motion forward toward her. He felt her lips press against his cheek, felt her casually swipe away at the color she usually left behind and then pull back.

“Good night, Paris.”

He managed a smile. “Good night, Veronica.”

She returned his smile, grabbing her purse from where she’d dropped it on the floor and heading to the door. “Don’t work too much later.”

“I won’t,” he promised.

Paris packed up quickly after Veronica left, sliding his laptop into its carrying bag and pulling in some reports he wanted to read over before he went to bed. He paused while folding up a map of the nature preserve, staring down at it thoughtfully. He’d outlined the path he and Jade had travelled the other day, including the lake area she wanted to avoid. He hoped to visit the area the next day with Hannah and Jade together and see if Jade could narrow down what had caught her attention. It didn’t escape his notice that Jade was the only real lead he had. He’d read reports from department heads, read theories and suggestions, reviewed all the logged reports of magic going awry before he’d banned it from being used and nothing seemed to point to any pattern or known anomaly. So far the only real hope he’d had for solving the problem was when Jade stood in the forest and declared she heard something. Something that Paris himself did not, or could not. Somehow Jade not only remained unaffected, but could possibly find the source of their problems.

It also made him wonder in how many other ways she was different from the rest of the Coven, including himself. From her birth outside a Coven, to her atypical physical reaction to magic and now to her pseudo-immunity from and ability to detect something affecting Coven magic, she was continually being set apart from the Coven at the same time that he was trying to integrate her into their ranks. He'd studied too much about nature, learned too much about it while he was learning his magic skills, to be foolish enough to trust that it was merely happenstance. Nature had a way of showing things it wanted seen, pushing the roots of them through the solid concrete of the world until someone paid attention.

He just wished he knew what it meant.

*

Jade had a plan. Sort of.

Okay, so it wasn't so much of a plan as a half-formed idea, but she'd worked with worse and she was willing to go with it.

While working with the demon grimoires, the ones from Paris' mother, Jade had come across several notes on demon runes. Jade had seen Paris uses runes before when creating a scrying mirror and she'd been intrigued. Their strange shapes and forms had seemed both mystical and knowing. Sure, Paris hadn't gone over runes at all with Jade yet (and certainly not demon runes), but she stuck by her personal motto: How Hard Could It Be?

Jade flipped to the section she recalled seeing a bit about demon runes in one of the grimoires and started reading over it again. While she generally had an excellent memory for printed material, the demon grimoires were not like any other books she'd read. She could read them longer than Paris and didn't suffer headaches as quickly, but she found her mind wandered while she read them. It wasn't like her. Certainly not when she was interested in something. Her brain became unfocused and chaotic while she worked on the books and she often had to take notes to stay on task.

Jade found the rune she remembered, sketching out her thoughts on a small notebook. Deception Detection. She snorted. It made her think of video games or laser tag at the mall. It seemed straightforward. Paris cautioned her against doing any of the demon magic, and especially against doing any without consulting him first, but again, personal motto: How Hard Could It Be? Besides, rune work seemed like small stuff - no big flash bangs, no shiny lights, no smoking…anything.

First step, she needed fir tree ash. Since she wasn't really the outdoorsy type, she had to google what fir trees looked like. It was a pleasant surprise to realize there were several Douglas Fir trees in her neighborhood, assuming she could rely on the pictures from the internet. Ah, internet research! It could all be true or it could be akin to instructions for turning lead into gold. Looking shiftily about in case there was some kind of neighborhood tree watch, she clipped some branches, gathering them tight in her fist. Bruce sniffed at the foliage as she came back inside and she held it out for him to sniff, like a dog. His lizard snout went up one side and down the other before he let out a mighty sneeze, his entire body giving a shimmy. She considered it an approval of sorts.

It was tough not to whip out her power to set the branches ablaze and get the ash she needed, but Callie had once mentioned that burning items using matches kept things 'magic free' and it seemed to Jade that the demon rune was something she didn't want to contaminate with her own magic - if such a thing as demon runes could be contaminated. She wasn't sure and it wasn't like Jade could pick up the phone and ask. The quick-sulfur smell of the match-strike burned her nostrils in an oddly pleasant way. The branches were still a little wet, not yet drying out over the short fall season; in seconds her kitchen was full of dank, grey smoke. She waved a hand in front of her face ineffectually while Bruce coughed plaintively from the corner. Jade got up and opened a window for him and he hobbled over, sticking his face in the screen, breathing in the crisp late autumn air dramatically. She rolled her eyes.

"You big sook," Jade said fondly. He responded with a sharp 'pffffft,' and she went back to the table.

She read over the rune casting three times to ensure she had it correct and then pushed up her sleeves. Right. Rune-making time. Jade dipped her finger into the still-warm ash and then, trying to focus her mind on what she wanted (*Dex is such a liar, a lying liar who LIES and I'm going to prove it)* she sketched out the rune. Once done, she slapped her palm on it.

Nothing.

Jade frowned, looking at the skin of her palm which had a dirty mirror image of the rune she'd drawn, the ash soft and sooty on her hand. She slapped her palm down once more thinking of her intent, willing it to work. Still nothing.

Jade chewed the inside of her cheek, reviewing the instructions, looking for any words she might have missed. It seemed simple - ash from a fir tree, intent, rune drawing and presto-chango! Lie detection rune.

She wiped her hands clean with a small cotton muslin sheet. While she didn't have many magical spell casting items, she had started a small collection. She was now the proud owner of some a few casting bowls, some chalk, several cotton muslin scraps of fabric, and had the beginnings of a small herb collection. The instructions in Sakkara's books were always quite clear - clean up all existing, residual magic and start fresh every time.

Four tries later, she still had nothing. Jade cleaned off her hands, wiped down the table and tossed the cotton cloth down with a little more force than was necessary. This wasn't supposed to be hard. She was supposed to be good at this. Jade eyed her ever-thinning ash pile. If she didn't get this soon, she'd have to go cut more branches. She shook out her arms in a 'jazz-hands' kind of shimmy, shrugged her shoulders and cracked her neck a bit. She spared a glance at Bruce who watched her with lazy eyes from his perch on the counter - judging her with his shifty gaze.

"You know any time you want to help out, feel free," she said sweeping her hands across the table, gesturing at the rune making. He flicked his tongue at her.

Jade rolled her neck in a circle again, hearing it crack in a few places and feeling the relief in the joints. Okay. Maybe a slightly different tactic for her intent. If she understood correctly, her intent was the spark that made the rune possible. So maybe 'I want to catch a liar-liar-pants-on-fire' wasn't specific enough. What did Jade want? She took a deep breath and blew it out slowly.

Jade wanted to find out what was wrong with the Coven and fix it. She dipped her finger in ash and started sketching. Okay, so maybe the Coven wasn't completely her home yet, but it was kind of homey and she had friends here. She didn't want Callie or Henri being taken advantage of. They couldn't use their magic and they were miserable without it. Callie vowed only to wash her hair if Jade could de-frizz it and Henri had sworn off personal grooming of any delicate places until this whole mess was sorted out. They were her friends - new friends, but friends nonetheless and she wanted to help them. If someone was lying to them, Jade wanted to figure it out. Callie and Henri had been welcoming - they'd been friendly and open. They were nice to her. She liked them. She could maybe even love them someday.

Jade stared down at the sketched out rune and held her palm over it, waffling for just a moment. She really wanted this to work. She slapped her hand down, willing it to work and… Felt a tingle?

It was like a feather brushing against her nerve endings. She didn't think it had fully worked, but it was more than she had before. Jade turned her palm up and looked down at the ash marking on it. It shimmered slightly and seemed to dissolve into her skin, sinking under the surface for a moment before rising back up and turning into just ash again.

Close, but no cigar. Yet.

She wiped everything down (again! God she was going to have a serious aversion to cleaning and dusting after this) and started from the beginning. Deep breath in, deep breath out. She could do this. The ash was powdery and fine against Jade's finger as she dipped the tip in and then started tracing over the rune pattern. She thought about Callie and Henri, unable to use their magic. She thought about the calls she'd logged at Counter-Magic - witches unable to practice their spells.

She thought about Paris. He looked tired when she saw him on Saturday, during their walk and circle casting in the woods. Jade got the feeling that the Coven's magic problem weighed on him heavily. He was a standup kind of guy and even though it wasn't his fault there was something wrong with everyone's magic, Jade really got an eau de guilt-and-desperation about him. She wanted to help him. She'd be lying to herself if she didn't admit that she wanted to make him proud too. Could you lie to yourself while trying to cast a lie-detection rune? Was it like a dog chasing its tail?

Focus. Intent. What was her intent? She wanted to find out if Dex was lying - lying to her, lying to the Coven, lying to Paris.

Jade slapped her hand down on the rune and gasped as a sharp, icy pain shot through her palm, into her wrist and coalesced at her elbow. It was like hitting her funny bone really hard at just the right angle - totally not funny at all and painful as fuck. She tried to pull her hand away from the rune and felt stuck - like she was attached to the table. Pushing up from her chair and knocking it over, she stood, pulling back with all her weight. Her hand became 'unstuck' and she went skidding backwards, landing hard on her ass, her teeth snapping shut with a clack. Her fingers were bent in a claw-like formation and she turned her hand over to see the imprint of the rune pulsing on her palm - each pulse a heartbeat of pain up her ulna, settling in her elbow. The rune shimmered and glittered and then sunk into her hand with a burning sensation. She clutched at her wrist as if she could cut off the pain shooting up her arm and keep it from traveling further.

Miraculously, it stopped.

Jade breathed heavily, feeling the weight of Bruce as he sidled along next to her, pressing his flank against her side. She turned and twisted her hand, finding that if the light hit her palm just right, she could still see the rune on her skin, like a faint, worn scar. She turned to Bruce.

"Holy crap, Bruce. I think I did it."

*

Jade went to bed that night with the clear-headed determination that she was going to beat Dex at his own game. She had a plan! She had magic! She had a rune! She'd even found a dress for the Coven Ball! Sure, she didn't know if the rune would work but, no matter. She was a can-do person and she was going to figure it all out, no matter what.

If Jade were a Broadway kind of girl, she'd be singing that things were coming up roses. She settled down to sleep, Bruce curled in a ball at her feet, and thought about how tomorrow she was going to solve the Coven's problems.

When she woke up, her eyes were grainy and gritty reminding her of the time she'd spent the day wearing false eyelashes with too much glue. Her face felt puffy and sore, like she was dehydrated and left out in the sun to bake.

She rolled over and pain shot down her shoulder, to her elbow and then her wrist, making her hand tingle and prickle. The spot where the rune had been was the most painful of all. Jade raised her arm and turned her hand over, checking her palm. She could still see the rune shimmering a bit in the early morning light. A faint pulse of pain worked its way up her arm, continuing to settle in her elbow.

Fuck. She may have made a teeny-tiny mistake.

This totally hadn't been in the grimoire. Jade didn't think she'd messed it up, but she couldn't say for sure.

Her alarm buzzed again and she sent a jolt of power out at it, smashing it into bits. The last thing she needed was that stupid beeping in her ear. She fumbled for her phone and managed to text Daniel that she would *not* be meeting him at the preserve for running. Bruce pressed his serpentine body up against her arm and she hissed at the contact at first, but then sighed when the pain seemed to dissipate at his touch. She didn't know if it was magic or just the comfort of another living creature and she didn't care. He nosed at her rune palm and she rested it on his head, feeling some of the hurt trickle away.

"Thanks, Big Green," she murmured. His tongue snaked out in her direction with his 'pfffft' sound. Her phone buzzed with Daniel texting her back that she was a big sooky baby for bailing on running and he'd give her grief about it when she saw him at the

Coven. She made a face and then worked her way to the shower, hoping the heat would help her arm.

It didn't.

By the time she was at the Coven, about two hours later, she felt a continual pulse of hot pain in her palm. It reverberated up her arm, stopping along at each of her joints and making itself known. She pulled off her sunglasses as she walked into the Covenstead, seeing Henri sitting at his desk, typing away on his computer. He looked up as she approached and made a face.

"You look like shit."

"Thanks," she said dryly.

His face morphed into apology and he leaned forward. "Seriously, are you okay? You don't look good."

Jade waved a hand. Henri didn't like demon magic and Jade didn't have the heart to tell him she was possibly suffering a demon rune hangover. "It's nothing." The rune flared up on her palm, causing a sharp shot of agony through her skin. She grit her teeth. She may be in a bit of a pickle. Jade could suck it up with the best of them and was no stranger to being in pain and pretending she wasn't (hello again, childhood), but at the same time, this might be magic gone bad and she didn't know enough about it to know if it was serious or not.

"Um, is Paris in?"

"I think so?" Henri said, eyebrows coming together. "Let me check." He turned back to his computer, pressing a few buttons. "He's showing as online and in his office."

Jade nodded and started for the stairs, climbing them doggedly. "Thanks, Henri."

This would suck. She had to tell Paris she did demon magic without his knowledge or approval and that she may have fucked it up.

This would suck *huge.*

As she passed by people on her way up the stairs and to Paris' office, her palm flared up a few times - enough that she started trying to pinpoint what was causing it. On the third floor, Jade moved to the side of hallway and paused, not-so-stealthily standing next to a large plant. A duo of witches walked by, one saying that all she'd had for dinner last night was a bowl of popcorn. The rune flared to life and Jade clenched her jaw. Pain throbbed up her arm and settled in her shoulder. She focused on steadying her breathing, staying put. Data collection, at its finest, was all about consistency. She waited it out and a minute later, a trio of male witches walked by, one proclaiming he'd been to the gym four times in four days and was benching some obscene amount. Jade's palm coursed with pain again, sending sparks to her elbow and shoulder.

It was detecting lies. Holy shit, it worked.

Okay, so it was totally more painful than she'd expected and she felt like utter crap, but still, success.

Someone walked by on their phone swearing up and down that they'd been working late that last Tuesday and Jesus, no, they were not having an affair. Her rune practically sang with pain and her knees felt weak. It shimmered on her palm, iridescent and shiny, like a freshwater pearl. Time to head to Paris' office and see if Jade could catch Dex in a lie.

She passed by three more liars on her way to Paris' office - someone promising to call their mother, someone talking about the size of jeans they wore, someone saying they couldn't meet for lunch because they were busy. God almighty, was everyone a lying liar who lied?

Jade felt dizzy and a little sick by the time she arrived. Paris' assistant's desk was once again empty, the ever-elusive Suki still missing. Jade was only grateful this time as it meant she didn't have to check in with anyone before she knocked once on the door and let herself in.

Paris looked up from his desk as Jade came in, frowning. "You look horrid. What's wrong?"

"I'm charmed," Jade said, stumbling in. She made a beeline for the Queen Anne chairs in the corner, flopping down in one. Paris stood from his chair and came over to where she was slouched, legs akimbo out in front of her.

"What's the matter?"

She made a face and kind of grunted a bit. "I think I fucked up."

Paris raised an eyebrow at her. "You think, or..?"

"Fine," she said sharply. "I know I did." She bit the inside of her lip. "Um, so how much do you know about demon runes?"

CHAPTER 11

Paris sighed, pinching the bridge of his nose. His cell phone buzzed in his pocket and he ignored it. "What have you done?"

Jade held out her hand, palm up and the moment she did, he could feel the density of magic around her. It was thick and murky, like a stagnant pool of water. He blinked, staring down at her palm. "I think I'm a human polygraph machine," she said.

Paris frowned, staring at her palm, almost transfixed by the amount of power contained in such a small area. "Pardon?"

"Lie to me."

He was at a loss, his mind going instantly blank. She stared at him wide eyed, blinking once or twice. "C'mon, you must have something. Any kind of lie will do."

Paris shook his head slightly. "Um… I wish you'd never joined the Coven."

He saw a split second of disbelief on her face and then her palm shimmered and sparkled, rune lettering flaring to life. Her face went tight, lips pressing together, jaw muscle flexing slightly and he realized it must hurt her. Paris could feel the magic in her blood, in her bones, writhe up against her skin, like it was trying to push out of her body. She sank back against the chair, taking a shaky breath. "Wow, that really was a lie."

"Of course it was," he said, his tone snappish. He took her proffered hand and turned it over in his own. He touched her palm and thought he could feel a rune beneath the skin, like scar tissue. "What is this? Where did you get this?"

"Er." She looked a bit sheepish. "Your mother's demon grimoires?" Jade said like it was a question.

He pursed his lips together and before he could speak, she was already protesting.

"I know, okay, I know! You said not to and I did and can we both just agree it was really fucking foolish and I'm sorry and I would say it won't happen again, but we both know that would be a lie and I really don't want to go through the whole shooting-pain-in-my-hand-and-up-my-arm-thing again so it's best if I don't make promises I know I won't keep."

They faced off for a moment, both of them unwilling to look away or blink. Paris broke first. "Tell me what you did and how you did."

He listened as she went through the process - burning ash, her intent, her failed tries and then her success.

"I felt okay last night, but this morning I feel like I'm really hung-over. Only there was no fun involved. My arm hurts and people lie. Oh my god they lie. I passed by four liars on the way here."

Paris held up a hand to stem the tide of her speech. She was getting riled up and he suspected it had to do with the amount of power she was channeling to keep the rune working. His cell phone continued to buzz in his pocket, making him feel somewhat assaulted on all fronts. "Hmm, did it say in the book how to stop it?"

Her head tilt and glare spoke volumes. "Would I be here if it did?"

"So you cast a rune, a demon rune, on yourself, having never worked with runes before and not understanding them fully, without knowing if there was a counter-spell in the grimoire? That about sum it up?"

Jade squirmed a bit. "When you put it like that, it sounds dumb."

Paris wasn't sure he'd had enough coffee yet for this. "It was. It was incredibly foolish of you. What on earth would possess you to do such a thing?"

Her shoulders shifted and she jutted her chin out mulishly. "I wanted to find out who broke the Coven's magic," she said, not making eye contact.

"And how was this to help you?"

"Because it was going to prove someone was lying."

"Who? Do you suspect someone?" Paris asked, leaning forward, intent on her. This was the first he'd heard of Jade having any suspicions and he was surprised she didn't just come to him right away. "You must have someone in mind. You can't possibly have thought of just randomly walking around and asking people."

"No," she huffed, as though the very thought of that was ridiculous.

"Then, tell me. Who do you suspect?"

Jade crossed her arms over her chest, wincing slightly when she had to fold her runed arm against her body. "Dex, okay? I think it's Dex."

Paris leaned back a bit, surprised. "Dex?"

"See!" she said, sitting upright and pointing her finger at him. "This is exactly why I needed proof because everyone loves him. And I don't. I really don't. He pushes all my 'No' buttons, but it's like… I'm new. I'm the witch not born in a coven and I'm the one that had demons after her and I'm the one who can use demon magic and no one will care what my opinion is when you're all friends with him."

Paris was flabbergasted. He had no idea Jade felt that strongly about Dex, but also about her opinion lacking any weight with him, or the rest of the Coven. "So instead of coming to me with your suspicions and talking to me about it like a rational being, you decided to practice unknown demon magic on your body."

"Would you have listened to me?" she asked hotly and somewhat rhetorically if her tone was any indication.

"Well, we won't know now, will we?"

Jade rolled her eyes. "Don't use the third person on me, okay?"

Paris pursed his lips. "Fine. *You* won't know now if I would have believed you."

She curled in on herself a bit, her face going blank and solemn, and he felt like a heel. He should perhaps just keep a litter of puppies in his office so he could kick them whenever he wanted to feel just as bad as he did now.

"But you don't, do you?" Jade's voice was flat and quiet. "You're just pissed about the demon magic, but you're not really considering that it's Dex who's doing this to your Coven. To you."

Paris felt trapped. He felt like he had to proceed carefully. She stared at him defiantly and yet a little hopeful. He didn't want to outright crush her feelings, but at the same time, he'd had no idea she didn't trust Dex. "I know you don't trust people easily," he began and she cut him off.

"I knew it. I fucking knew it. Then bring him up here and let's ask him and I'll show you. I'll show you exactly why I cast an unknown demon rune on my hand. I'll prove it."

Paris held back a sigh. He didn't like to give in to ultimatums or demands, but perhaps in this case, it would be for the best if he did simply invite Dex up here and they could settle it. Then he could see what could be done about the demon rune. He opened his mouth to say as such when there was a knock at his door.

"A moment," he said to Jade, hoping his face indicated they weren't done yet. She fell back into the chair with what could only be described as a sulky expression. "Yes?" he called out.

Josef poked his head in. "You aren't answering your cell phone and we've got a bit of a situation."

Paris reached into his pocket and saw four missed calls - two from Josef, one from Callie and one from Suki. "What is it?" he asked, standing.

"Missing child," Josef said without preamble. "He's six, a wanderer, and a bit of a sleepwalker. Tends to toddle off. His mother, Nora, works in HR, can usually locate him with a spell and problem solved, but with the Coven's magic not working…"

"She can't find him," Paris finished. "And neither can we." He immediately turned to look at Jade, sunk back in the cushions. "Although you probably can."

She shrugged. "I can try. I don't know any locator spells."

Paris frowned. The thing with locator spells was they usually required some kind of a connection. If not that, then they needed a great deal of focus and control. Before they'd known who Jade was Paris had used a locator spell to find her. He'd cobbled together bits and pieces of spells into one he knew would work, using his years of magic as a base. Jade didn't have that kind of knowledge nor did she have the kind of focus needed. Hearing the way she felt just now, she certainly didn't have the emotional connection to anyone in the Coven that would be required.

"You've got a face on," she said warily staring up at him.

"Locator spells can be… tricky."

She waved her rune-palm at him. "I think we've established I can do tricky."

Paris grimaced. "That's not quite what I meant." He considered her for a moment, an idea coming to him. "Would you agree to let me filter my magic through you again?"

"Like back in the forest?"

He nodded and she looked thoughtful. Paris wished he knew what was going on in her mind. "I know you said it was unpleasant, but…"

"I got it. Missing kid." She huffed quietly, her lips pursing oddly as she chewed on the inside of her cheek. "It's not like I'm gonna say no and let some kid just be lost or whatever."

"Thank you."

Paris turned back to Josef, who was waiting patiently in the doorway. "I was training with Jade the other day out in the preserve. We discovered that I'm able to filter my magic through her and it doesn't suffer from the same sickness as the rest of the Coven's magic when I do so."

Josef nodded. "We probably have everything you'd need for a number of locator spells down in Counter Magic. You could work from there."

"We'll be along shortly," Paris said and Josef backed out of his office, shutting the door behind him. Jade was already getting to her feet, curling the arm with the rune close to her body.

"Are you up for this?"

Her eyebrows came together in a 'V.' "Yes."

"You mentioned you don't feel well."

She shrugged as though it didn't matter. "I told you, I'm not going to say no. But…" Her eyes went hard. "When we're done, when we find this kid or whatever, I want you to call Dex and make him tell you he had nothing to do with this whole wonky magic thing. In front of me," she clarified. "And my polygraph hand. *After* that, we can figure out how to un-rune it. But not before I get to question him."

"You're convinced it's him."

"Yep."

Paris couldn't help but feel disappointed in both her resolve and that she hadn't even thought of coming to him first without trying to solve the problem on her own. It didn't speak well of how she felt about her position in the Coven, although perhaps she had a point. He wasn't prepared to believe her. He'd known Dex nearly his whole life.

"Very well. We'll get this sorted and then I'll ask Dex to come meet us." Paris paused, looking over Jade, standing there, her body tense, her arm cradled close. "Perhaps after that we can discuss why you felt you couldn't come to me with this."

"Uh, because you don't believe me? Like, not at all. You're not even pretending to believe me." She glanced down at her arm. "Not that it would do any good if you did, because, you know, lie detector." Jade gestured at herself. "But you're not even considering it."

"Jade, I…"

"Can we not?" she interrupted him, her grey eyes sharp and cold. "Let's just go and save Timmy from the well or whatever it is we need to do."

She pushed past him, not turning back as she left his office and was out the door, leaving him only to follow.

*

Jade crossed her arms over her chest and tried to pay attention as Paris gathered the materials he needed for a location spell. Just because she was pissed and maybe feeling a little defensive was no reason not to learn. Or so she told herself.

Counter-Magic had an awesome magic pantry which Jade hadn't gotten a chance to see before now, having been regulated to her 'learning' tasks. Except for the rookie-hazing sewer incident, she'd been logging calls and working her way through old reports and workbooks. As soon as Paris entered the offices of the Counter-Magic department, he'd headed directly to the back rooms - a spot Jade hadn't been privy to yet - and Josef had opened up several locked cabinets. Watching Paris pick his supplies was like watching a master chef go grocery shopping. He chose items, gave them a sniff or a pinch, cradled them in his hands and moved onto the next thing.

After he'd gathered some roots, herbs and a few stones he wanted, he'd asked Josef if they had anything belonging to the young boy who was missing. Josef had handed over a set of game-playing cards, probably carefully inserted into their protective sleeves by his mother since six year olds weren't generally known for how well they kept their stuff. Jade watched and tried to take mental notes as Paris assembled his items, including a mortar and pestle, and then asked for a map of the Coven area.

"Is this how you found me?" Jade asked, head jerking toward the map as Josef set it down on a large table "Before you knew who I was."

Paris' head made a see-saw kind of motion. "Slightly different. I had to create a different kind of spell to find you since I was focusing in on your magic and didn't have anything that belonged to you. It's easier with an object to focus on. This is a fairly standard spell for lost people, but it does rely on having something of theirs."

He set the items down on the table and then looked at Jade.

"Would you mind picking each of them up and focusing on your magic? I'm concerned that whatever's wrong with our magic has perhaps contaminated them a bit by me handling them and I'd like you to touch each item first."

Jade stepped forward, picking up a few satchels of herbs and then some stones. She sort of tossed them back and forth in her hands, finding that they did feel a bit 'off' to her at the start, but once she could feel the 'rightness' of them again, she set them down. The mortar and pestle was the strangest, feeling like they were vibrating at the wrong frequency. She petted it a bit with her fingertips, feeling the grain and texture of the stone under her skin. After a minute or so, she felt like it was warmer, better, and she set it down.

Paris stepped closer to her and she moved back, away from him and the table. He grimaced. "In the forest, I had to be touching you to make my magic filter through yours. I've been trying as we've stood here and I don't think it works unless we're touching."

"Oh," she said flatly, stepping closer to him. She reached out a hand, the one without the rune on it, and hovered it over his shoulder, dropping it down unceremoniously. "Like this okay?"

Paris paused for a second and then Jade felt a rush of his power shoot up her hand. It was hot, contrasting sharply with the cold ache of the rune she had on her other side. She felt as though her body were being neatly divided in half - Paris' magic working on one side, and the demon rune working on the other. Paris wrinkled his nose a bit.

"I can sense the rune." He looked like he'd just bitten into a rotten vegetable gone mushy and sour when he'd been expecting crisp and earthy. "Does it hurt?"

Jade shrugged one shoulder. "It aches a bit. Like I've been using a hammer on a steel beam all day."

He met her eyes and standing this close, with her hand on his shoulder, she wanted to look away. He was too close and she felt a bit trapped. "We've discussed you doing magic without consulting me first."

"We have," she said, her tone a little cool. Two could play the vague-and-unhelpful-statement-game.

Paris pursed his lips together slightly. "What I mean is, you shouldn't try things like this without checking with me first."

Jade took a deep breath, trying to quell her anger at his words. When she inhaled she caught the scent of sandalwood and cedar chips with a bit of laundry detergent and maybe some mint. It was a comforting smell and it hit her hard in the gut when she realized it was Paris - those were all the scents she associated with him. His eyes darted momentarily to his shoulder and her own followed seeing her fingers moving slightly, pressing into the fabric of his shirt and feeling the flesh underneath. She stilled her hand. Then Joseph cleared his throat. She wondered how long they would have stood there staring at each other if Josef hadn't.

Jade had forgotten he was still in the room. She looked away from Paris, focusing instead on the table where the items were gathered. She watched as he meticulously placed some items in the mortar, grinding them up with counter-clockwise strokes. The smell of something sharp and almost lemony hit her nostrils, making her nose twitch a bit. It was followed by a more earthy scent, like moss or dirt. Paris carefully placed the stones in the mortar, using his fingers to mix it a bit, like making chicken and covering it with breadcrumbs. He added a snippet from the protective covering of the trading card. Jade could see in her mind's eye how a young child would turn the brightly colored cards over and over in their hands, eagerly looking to complete a set, trading with friends, getting new additions for birthdays and holidays.

"Where does he live?" asked Paris and Jade was completely stymied for a moment until she realized he was talking to Josef. Josef stepped forward, gesturing to an area on the map, but not touching it.

"He's on the south side of the preserve."

Paris made a low 'hmm' sound and Jade swore she could feel the vibration of his voice through her fingers resting on his shoulder. His magic was finely wound and hummed in its intensity and she found herself slightly swaying a bit, like it was a song or a rhythm. She wondered if it was a consequence of how he was funneling his power or if it was just her. Paris stepped a bit closer to the table with the map and she moved instinctively with him, stretching her arm slightly when he bent over the table to get a closer view of the map. He sprinkled the dust mixture onto the paper and Jade felt a flare of his power, of his intent, rippling through her own magic. It was so structured and clear. At the same time, she could also feel her own magic, sitting up and wanting to participate - like a puppy watching a game of fetch with other dogs and owners. Her demon rune palm throbbed a bit, sending a cold spike to her elbow and then to her shoulder.

Paris flinched slightly. "Focus, Jade," he said, his voice low.

She shook her head a bit, fingers flexing on his shoulder. The map seemed to warble and wobble in front of her. Jade could see the dust Paris had spread out swirling and snaking its way around the map. She could *feel* it trying to find the boy - feel Paris' magic searching him out. The colored dust worked its way into the preserve and Jade thought, what a wonderful place it must be for a young child - all big trees, nooks and crannies to hide in. Birds and animals scurrying about.

But then her eyes were drawn to the bright blue splotch on the map. The lake. Her stomach clenched. She felt her power spike - sending a frisson to both her demon rune palm and to the hand that was resting on Paris' shoulder. Paris twitched.

"Jade," Paris warned, his voice sounding like it was coming from far away. Jade couldn't stop staring at the lake, remembering the feeling she had when she'd been close by and then, the dream she'd had. Lily, her face white and still under the surface of the water.

Cold seeped up her arm, from the demon rune, settling in her shoulder and feeling like it was running through her veins, working toward her chest. The dust on the map, almost coalescing into a small circle, started spreading out again wider, into more of an oblong kidney shape than anything useful.

"Jade, focus on the spell."

She was focusing on the spell. Or at least, she thought she was. She felt Paris' magic flood her veins - hot and sharp. She could feel the strange place in her chest where his magic, her own powers and the demon rune collided - leaving a sick, empty kind of feeling. Her fingers dug into his shoulder and she thought she should apologize or let go, but she couldn't. Her power pushed against his and it felt like knocking her head against a brick wall - resonating, painful, thick and dull.

"Almost there," she heard Josef mutter and when Jade looked at the magic dust on the map, she could see what he meant. It was shrinking down, into a smaller and smaller speck. Paris' power pulsing behind it, focusing the spell and at the same time, forcing Jade's magic back. She wanted to help him, but she couldn't stop staring at the wavy blue blotch of water that represented the lake and feeling sick in her chest. She swallowed, feeling the phantom presence of water in her sinus cavity - sharp and cold.

Paris' hand shot out and grabbed her free one, his fingers clenching painfully around hers. "Christ, Jade. Stop," he gritted out. "I'm almost done."

His fingers were hot against her own - trapping them in a vice-like grip. The demon rune flared ice-cold and she gasped at the pain. Without thinking, she tried to tug her hand away, tried to step back, but his grip didn't release. Her chest burned. Her fingers let go of Paris' shoulder and she started pushing him away, trying to get away from the ache in her hand, the pressure in her chest and the water, o*h god all the water* -

"Jade! Stop!"

She felt Paris' power surge into her and it was like being squeezed - like she was just a bag of bits and bobs and he was taking up all the free space, making her push out at her seams, ready to burst.

Paris crushed her fingers in his and Jade thought hers might snap. She kicked out, mindlessly, catching him in the back of the knee and he buckled a bit, tugging her down with him. Then there were arms around her, moving her back, away from Paris, pulling her, spinning her and she stumbled, facing a collection of Coven witches, staring at her with fear and a little horror in their eyes.

Confused, she looked down at the hands around her and then up at Josef. He set her right on her feet, hands hovering when she wobbled a bit.

"Sorry, dear. But you were like two microphones pointed at one another." His eyes were kind and maybe a little amused as he stared down at her. "You know, if one of those microphones started kicking."

Jade looked over Josef's shoulder and saw Paris, rubbing his knee as he glared at her.

"Oh," she breathed. Her magic felt fuzzy and muddled, like it was buried under piles of felt and fabric - far off with thick layers in between. She shook her head a bit.

"I think you'll find our missing child at these coordinates," Paris said, pointing to a spot on the map that Jade couldn't see from where she stood.

There was a moment of silence and then Josef's voice boomed out. "All right, it's not a spectator sport. Everyone out."

There was a beat when it seemed like no one was going to listen to him and then like a band had snapped, the room started clearing. After a few moments, it was just Jade and Paris. Alone. In awkward silence.

Which was broken when Dex poked his head in the room.

"Wow, what's going on in here?" he said, lips curled in a smile. "Got a hallway full of gossiping witches and…" he sniffed the air. "Smells like magic. A lot of magic. I thought we couldn't use any?"

"You!" Jade said, finger pointing at Dex. This was exactly what she'd been waiting for, what she wanted since this whole mess started - for Dex to poke his perfect nose in and for her to have the opportunity to smash it. "What did you do to the Coven's magic?"

It was fast, so fast she wasn't sure if Paris saw it, but Dex seemed to smirk a bit before he went wide-eyed. Jade was like a violin string pulled tight - waiting for him to speak, to lie, for her demon rune to prove it and then she'd snap.

"Me? Nothing."

Jade opened her mouth to contradict him, to wave her runed hand up like a burning flag when she realized it wasn't reacting. She stared down dumbly at it. No. No, no, no, no. She'd planned this. Feeling off kilter from what had just happened with her magic and Paris, she rushed forward.

"Like hell," she countered. "You did something, I know you did. You and your smarmy face and your creepy charm and your weird grocery store confrontations. You're the one that did something to the Coven's magic and you're going to tell us what it was."

"Jade," Paris' voice said from behind her. Jade whirled around, waving her pointing finger at him now.

"No, you're biased. Everyone in this goddamn coven is biased. He did something and he's going to admit and I'll prove it."

"I really don't know what you mean. I haven't done anything to the Coven's magic."

Again, Jade looked from her runed hand, to Dex and back again. Betrayal coursed through her veins. "No, I know you did it."

"Jade, enough," said Paris, fatigue creeping into his voice.

Jade shook her hand like it was a faulty cell phone or broken flashlight. "No, it's you, I know it's you and if this isn't working, it's because it's broken or the magic we just did fucked it or because he's a psychopath and they can fool polygraphs, you know-"

"Jade!" Paris shouted. "Enough!"

She glared at him mutinously. He may as well have shushed her in a crowd of people. She burned with rage and hurt. "I know it's him."

"All evidence," Paris said, gesturing to her silent demon-runed hand, "would appear to indicate otherwise."

Jade was shaking her head. "This," she said holding up her hand, "is a glitch. I know he did it and none of you want to believe me, but that doesn't mean it's not true!"

Paris looked from her and then to Dex. "Dex, I apologize on Jade's behalf-"

"Don't you fucking dare!" Jade interrupted, moving in front of Paris, going toe-to-toe with him. He was not going to pull this on her. Her face was hot with embarrassment and she felt a little shaky, partially from not knowing why the rune didn't work, but also from the residual magic. "Don't you dare apologize on my behalf. It's goddamn patronizing and it assumes a) that I've done something apology worthy, which I haven't, b) that I can't do it for myself and c) that I'm fucking sorry when I'm not!"

Paris batted away her pointing finger, with a swipe of his hand. “Dex,” he said, never breaking his gaze from Jade. “If you’ll excuse us.”

Jade turned to look at him. “Don’t you move a muscle, pretty boy, I’m not done with you.”

“Yes, you are!” Paris bellowed.

Jade could see Dex trying to fight off a cruel smile before he spoke. “It’s fine, Paris. I’ll catch up with you this afternoon.”

“You fucker,” Jade muttered, crossing her arms over her chest. She felt on fire with anger, her power pulsing under her skin like a bad fever, wanting to break out. She wanted to just… send magic at him, just to see what would happen, if he could or would defend himself. At the thought of it, her magic jumped up against her skin and then Paris’ hand clamped down on her shoulder and she wanted to fall to the ground, feeling his power forcing hers to buckle. He was filtering his magic through her again and using it to prod hers into submission. It was a double-edged cruelty - forcing her magic to bend under his by using her own immunity to the Coven’s magical taint so she could be a filter. Dex slipped back out the door, shutting it firmly behind him and Jade kicked out again, her foot coming down hard on Paris’ instep.

“Might is right, hey? Classy,” she bit out, jerking away from him.

Paris glanced at the doorway, in thought for a moment and Jade took the opportunity to take another step away from him. Her movement away seemed to galvanize his focus back to her. She heard Paris take a long, deep breath as though he was steeling himself for something. When he spoke, his voice was soft and low.

"At first, I believed your lack of control and focus, coupled with your impetuousness and complete disregard for authority were only minor hindrances. You would learn. You would mature. However, it's becoming abundantly clear that these are real barriers with your magic. Not your limits, not your lack of knowledge, not even your sass."

"Hey, that's uncalled for," she said.

He slammed his fist down on the table and she jumped a bit.

"I wasn't finished!"

Jade stared at his fist on the table. "Don't bully me."

"I'm not," Paris said, voice deadly calm.

She cocked an eyebrow at him. "Really? Because years of growing up with my dad would beg to differ," she replied, eyeing where he'd slammed his fist into the table.

Paris seemed to blanch at that and she felt bad for all of thirty milliseconds before he spoke again.

"You need to listen to me."

That tone, that authoritative tone made her spine feel prickly. She opened her mouth to argue back, but he cut her off, beating her to it.

"I'm telling you this as your mentor, as an expert, and as your Coven Leader. No more magic. Not until you learn better control."

She glowered at him. "You can't do that."

"Yes, I can."

"No, I mean you really can't do that. What are you going to do to stop me? Your magic is broken."

"Don't force my hand on this, Jade. My magic may not be working to spec, but I still have abilities and talents in my arsenal that you know nothing about."

Okay, so that was probably true. Jade swallowed, wondering if he was bluffing. She felt hot tears of frustration and indignation prickling at her eyes but she wasn't going to cry, not in public.

"I'm trying to help," she protested hotly. "It's not my fault if you can't see the truth."

As convincing arguments went, it was shitty - browbeating the opposition with their weaknesses. Fuck. She wasn't good at this. She needed Lily for these kinds of things. Lily would know what to say, would know how to smooth over Jade's mistakes and placate Paris' feelings.

"No more magic," he repeated.

Jade ground her teeth together. She hated losing. Because that's what it felt like. Losing. It wasn't listening to reason, it wasn't seeing the other side - right now, from where she stood, it just felt a whole lot like they'd been having a fight and she just lost.

"Fine."

"I mean it."

"I said fine!" Jade shouted back. She blinked several times in a row and swallowed hard around the tightness in her throat, muscles aching. She avoided looking at Paris, turning her face sideways. She knew with her complexion it was totally obvious she was trying not to cry and even though it wasn't remotely his fault that she was fair-skinned, she somehow hated *him* for it.

The room was silent, and she didn't know if Paris was waiting to say something more to her or if she was supposed to say something back to him. All she knew was she wanted to go home. But she didn't quite know where that was. Was it the cottage where Bruce was probably curled up on a heating vent? Or was it her apartment, back in the city, where most of her things were?

"Jade," Paris said, his voice quieter, softer than it had been before. "I know things have been difficult-"

She shook her head. He didn't know. He didn't know about Lily and he didn't want to know about Dex. "I'm really not in the mood for the warm-fuzzy part of today's tyranny."

"I'm not a tyrant," he said, a tired edge in his voice.

Jade finally looked back and met his eyes. He looked more tired than he had this morning, more wrung out. The flash of sympathy she normally would have felt for him was too buried under the continual effort it took to keep from crying. "Could've fooled me."

She turned away and tried to make her steps as even and solid as she could, focusing on the way they reverberated on the tile instead of on his harsh exhale as she left.

*

The worst thing about trying not to cry in front of a bunch of people was the feeling that everyone knew you were about to cry, knew you were trying to stop it and knew you couldn't. It was the strange combination of averted gazes, sympathetic looks and pure disinterest from some people. Jade grabbed her purse and coat from her desk at Counter Magic and managed to make it to one of the ladies' washrooms where she promptly shut the door and then kicked the wall a few times. She tried to focus on the pain in her toes so she could stop thinking about how she felt.

Angry, frustrated, and embarrassed. Stupid feelings. She kicked the wall a few more times, going for more rhythmic and even strikes - not really hard enough to hurt anymore. More for something to do, something to focus on while she calmed down.

Fucking stupid. So fucking stupid. She should have known better. She should have known it wasn't going to work and that Paris wouldn't believe her. Despite the fact that Dex passed the lie detection rune, Jade was still wholly convinced he was responsible. She just didn't know why the rune didn't work.

Jade inhaled deeply a few times, getting her feelings under control. She looked in the mirror and cursed. She hated her pale skin. She was all flushed and blotchy, her grey eyes standing out sharply. Fuck it. It couldn't be helped. She wanted out. She was going home.

Or rather, to her cottage. The jury was still out on if it was home or not.

She successfully managed to avoid looking up at anyone, keeping her steps forceful and brisk - imagining herself like a Mack Truck at a constant speed - unstoppable. It worked pretty well till she got to the bus stop and had to stand there, feeling like a loser waiting for her bus. There was a slight wind in the air, cold and sharp on her face. She pretended that it was strong enough to account for the tears still pricking at her eyes.

Goddamn public transportation. She needed her car.

Back at her little cottage, Jade slammed the door as she entered, kicking off her shoes viciously. Bruce came around the corner and made an inquiring sort of 'pffftt' sound, glaring at her shoes, lying carless on the floor.

"Sorry, Bruce," she said lowly. He padded to the stairs and then loped up them with an easy grace she wouldn't have expected from him.

Jade made a direct beeline for the kitchen, flipping open the book with the demon rune and not even bothering to sit down as she read it - hunched over the table, chewing on one of her ragged cuticles. She tasted blood and only then managed to pull her hand away from her mouth, fisting it in the fabric of her pants.

She felt the tingle of Seth's arrival seconds before he appeared in the pantry. She spoke before he even had the chance to, without turning around.

"I'm not in the mood, Seth. Get lost."

"Rough day at the office, possum? I could feel you vibrating from the other side."

Jade turned and glared at him. "Creeper. Do you spy on me from over there?"

He smirked. "Wouldn't I love to." He snapped his teeth together with a loud clack and then sighed. "Unfortunately, no. But this portal does afford me a certain connection to your emotional state and you're all fired up about something." He sniffed the air a bit. "Is that betrayal I smell?"

"Hardly," she said, wondering if that was the crux of how she really felt. Betrayed. By Paris for not believing her, by the Coven for not accepting her the way she wanted to be accepted and by her magic for failing her.

"What have you got there?" Seth asked, neck craning slightly to see what she was bent over reading. "Ah, demon runes. Clever. You know a lot of people can't use them. Too subtle."

Jade paused. Seth could probably tell her why her rune hadn't worked, but she couldn't just ask him. That would be asking him for a favor, and would tip their neutral scale. She'd owe him.

"Really?" she said, feigning disinterest, wondering if he would keep talking.

She heard a tick-tick-tick sound and looked up to see Seth tapping his finger against the doorjamb of her pantry. "You know, possum, if you have a question, you've only to ask."

Damn, she must be as transparent as an underage kid trying to buy liquor. She hesitated. She wondered how much the knowledge was worth - to both her and Seth. It could be all for nothing - it could be that the information Seth could potentially give her wasn't even useful. Or it could be that it was worth way more than she was willing to bargain.

Bargain. That was the key word. That's what it all came down to. Was she willing to deal with Seth? It was only a short time ago, a *very short* time ago, that Jade had declared to Paris that she'd have to be pretty stupid to get into a demon deal, even if she was new. Now here she was, contemplating it.

Seth grinned, teeth glistening and pearlescent. "I can see those little hamster wheels spinning away, Jade." The sound of her name from him was a jolt - he never called her by her name - always referring to her as 'possum.' She wondered if it meant something in the demon world.

"You're thinking: Is it worth it? What does he know? What will he tell me? And, how much will it cost?"

"Yes," she replied. At this point, she felt well and truly out of her comfort zone and into his. He'd probably made thousands of deals - knew all the ins and outs. Jade was just one more human to him - another worm on his hook.

"The thing is, Jade, I've no interest to have you beholden to me for such a trinket. Little bit of demon rune knowledge is hardly in my league. I'm a higher-class demon. I've got enough other deals with witches to keep me busy. Light rune magic, minor spell work, little charms and tiny incantations are all a bit beneath me. I prefer weightier things."

"Unbelievable," she said, metering out the syllables slowly and harshly. "I'm finally in a place where I'm considering this and you're telling me it's too much like slumming for you?" Jade shook her head. "Forget this. I'm sealing off the pantry. You can go fuck yourself."

"Now, now, now, possum. Why so hasty?" Seth back-peddled, holding up his hands defensively. "I'm sorry if I hurt your little human emotions." Jade ground her teeth and tried to stay silent at his tone. "Although truth be told, I think they were more than a little bruised already when you showed up, is that right?"

When she didn't answer, Seth waved his hand. "No need to reply. I can smell it all in the air. Betrayal, anger, hurt," he sniffed again. "Disappointment." He sighed. "It smells wonderful.

Not as good as fear, but quite lovely. I do want to deal with you, Jade. I just want it to be a bit more memorable. Worthy. Of both of us."

"Again, you're saying you won't help."

"I didn't say that," Seth replied. "Only that I wouldn't deal."

Jade frowned, suspicion curling in her gut. "What's that mean?"

Seth sighed, put upon. "It means, dear possum, I actually want to help you. Out of the goodness of my heart."

She raised an eyebrow at him.

"Okay, so to be truthful, there's no goodness in my heart. But I would like to give you a nugget and have your… gratitude." The way he said the word made Jade feel dirty and a little slimy. "Maybe that will help our little fledging relationship along. Maybe you'll see how useful I can be."

"Is this wooing?" Jade asked. "Am I being wooed by you?"

Seth's eyes glittered and Jade could almost see a tail behind him, swishing in glee. The illusion was gone when she looked directly for it, but when she focused on his face, she could see it out of the sides of her eyes - back and forth, back and forth.

"I suppose it is. Are you feeling wooed?"

"I'm feeling something, but it's more along the lines of distaste and mistrust."

Seth sighed again. "Ah, the course of true demon deals never did run smooth." He clapped his hands suddenly and she started, jumping a bit at the loud sound. "All right, let's get down to the nitty-gritty. What's your problem?"

"Wait, to be clear, I owe you nothing after this. We are not making a deal, there is no deal between us. No future deal is being agreed to, nor implied by this transaction."

"The fine print. Clever to bring that up. You are correct. No deal, you're not implying nor inferring a future deal. This transaction is one-sided. I am giving you information. But," he said sharply and she stilled, waiting for the shoe to drop, "that means I decide when this transaction is over. I stop giving you information when I feel like it. Not when you're done asking."

Jade went over Seth's words carefully in her head, feeling the urge to write them down so she could double-check them. She didn't think there was anything fishy about it. Other than that he was a demon. She couldn't see anywhere that the words had been duplicitous or double-edged. So the last question was this: was this a rabbit hole she was willing to jump down? How much was this worth to her? She wanted to help the Coven, but, if she was honest with herself, she kind of also wanted to stick it to them. Not in a painful way, but more of a 'See, I fucking TOLD YOU SO,' kind of way. Yeah, it was petty and it was small, but she really wanted to show them she was right. She was a talented witch, an important asset. They could have trusted her.

Paris could have trusted her.

She may not have the history with him that he had with Dex, but Paris didn't even *listen* to her. Maybe Jade was foolish to have thought that he should, but it was how she felt.

"Okay," she said, her voice coming out quiet. She knew Seth would hear her, even if she whispered.

"Now, come closer, possum and tell me all your troubles."

Jade picked up Sakkara's grimoire and moved closer to the pantry, clutching it in front of her like a shield. As she got closer, Seth seemed to pause for a moment and then look her up and down. It wasn't sexual or carnal. It was more like he was seeing something he hadn't noticed before, something that had him confused.

"My, things have been busy, haven't they," Seth murmured. "Got quite a bit going on in that noggin of yours. Getting a little crowded."

Jade held the grimoire closer, tighter to her chest. "What do you mean?"

He made a 'tsk' kind of sound. "Sorry, possum. That's a whole other vat of bones, as we demons say. Now, tell me about your rune work."

"I wanted to catch a liar," she said, holding the book up in front of her so he could see it, like an altar sever holding a bible for a priest. She pointed at the rune she'd done, tapping it with her finger. "I thought it worked, but then when I asked him, Dex, it didn't flare up like it had for other lies."

Seth tapped his finger on his upper lip. He made a motion like he wanted to reach out and touch the book, but then he glanced at the overall doorway of the pantry, as if sensing the barrier there.

"Hold up your hand," he said.

"I don't think it's working now," Jade said.

"Hand, possum."

Jade juggled the book into one hand and held up the demon rune hand. It still ached slightly. Seth squinted at it and then 'hmm'd. He held his own hand up and then hissed, "*aperio*," at her. She flinched, her hand burning under his word. The rune flared to life, lighting up on her hand like a floodlight. He nodded sagely as though he expected this.

"A little warning, next time." Her jaw was clenched tight as she spoke. Seth waved his hand again, and the burning subsided, the rune dimming out.

"Oh, I can't wait for next time," Seth replied. "Well, you certainly have the rune correct, and it was still functioning."

"Was?"

He grinned. "Getting it to show burned it out." He shrugged. "Side effect."

"If it was still working then why didn't it, you know, work?"

"What did you say to your errant liar? Your words exactly."

Jade huffed, breathing out long and slow as she thought. "I asked… um… What did you do to the Coven's magic?"

"And his reply?"

"He said nothing. He said he hadn't done anything to the Coven's magic."

Seth leaned back a bit, steepling his fingers under his chin.

"Did you ask him if he was involved?"

Jade frowned. "I thought that's what I just said?"

"No, you asked if he did anything. As I mentioned, demon runes are subtle. If this man, this Dex, didn't actively do something, didn't actively cast the spell himself, then he wasn't lying when he answered your question."

Jade considered this. "Are you fucking with me? I had my shot and I got tripped up on semantics?" She felt hot and cold. She couldn't believe she'd been so stupid.

Seth shrugged. "Demon magic is specific. We like to take advantage of humans and their tendency to be non-specific. You rely a lot on implied meanings or intents. We do not."

"I don't know whether I'm more mad at you or myself." Jade made a disgusted sound. "Can you tell me if he really did do it and what he did?"

"Sorry. Can't."

Jade snapped the grimoire shut. "Fine. Be that way. I'll figure it out on my own. I'll cast the rune again and this time, I'll nail him to the wall."

"Oooh," Seth shivered. "I get all tingly when you talk like that."

She slammed the pantry door in his face.

CHAPTER 12

Paris found it increasingly difficult to focus on his work. He found his mind kept drifting back to his argument with Jade and her stubborn assertion that Dex was responsible for the Coven's magic problems.

But it wasn't just his argument with Jade bothering him. It was one moment, the moment he'd still been wholly wrapped up in Jade's magic, feeling his own power starting to resonate correctly. Everything felt clearer, sharper - like he hadn't realized he'd been viewing things through a veil of murky water. Suddenly things had felt right again. Paris' spell to find the boy had worked and even though Josef had to separate Paris and Jade, Paris felt like his magic was fixed - better.

At that moment, Dex walked into the room - and Paris hadn't known who he was.

It ended like a light bulb popping - sharp, fast and quick. Jade started accusing Dex, and Paris felt the rest of her magic sluice out of him, like water down a drainpipe. Paris was resolutely on Dex's side just as quickly. Of course Dex wasn't responsible. Dex was a friend to the Coven, a friend to Paris.

But that moment when his magic had run true, when Paris had looked at Dex and thought, 'Who is that?', stuck in his mind, like a thorn in the soft fleshy part of his hand.

He felt strange even thinking about it now. It felt as though he were remembering something else, some other time, some story that was told to him in passing. It was ridiculous. Dex was his friend. He'd known Dex for years.

Hadn't he?

He couldn't explain it. Part of him wanted to be able to completely discount what Jade said. Part of him felt like a betrayer for even considering it. It felt wrong and strange to think that Dex had anything at all to do with the problems they were having. He certainly had the evidence to disregard Jade's accusation. She'd asked Dex if he'd done anything to the Coven magic and Dex had said no. Jade's rune hadn't lit up. End of story.

But there was still that split second, when Dex walked in and he was a stranger.

A knock sounded at his office door and Callie's head poked itself around the door, her blond hair fanning out and curling a bit around the wood.

"Got a sec?" Before he could answer, she was stepping in and shutting the door behind her. "I hear you and Jade had… words."

"If we ever manage to bottle and market the speed at which Coven gossip spreads, we'll make millions."

Callie snorted in agreement, pulling up one of the chairs opposite Paris' desk, setting it a bit closer than he normally had it. "So. What happened?"

"You tell me. I'm sure you heard all the details."

She made an apologetic face. "Yeah. I heard Jade accused Dex of having something to do with our magic problems and then you and she got into a bit of a yelling match."

Paris reluctantly nodded. "That's about the sum of it. She's convinced that Dex has something to do with it."

"She doesn't like him. I don't know why. He's… Dex. As far as I know, he's never been anything but nice to her."

"Hmmm. She hasn't liked him since he's arrived?" he asked.

Callie shook her head. "No. To say the very least."

Paris pushed away from his desk a bit. "Jade cast some kind of demon rune on her hand, a lie detector, and then accused Dex of having done something to our magic."

Callie looked at him expectantly. "And?"

"And nothing. Her rune appeared to be functioning fine but it didn't indicate that Dex was lying."

"You've a 'but' face on." Callie frowned. "You seem… I don't know. Uncertain?"

Paris moved his head in a considering manner. "I'm not sure how to phrase it. This whole situation has me unsettled."

"You don't really think Dex has anything to do with this, do you?"

He opened his mouth to say, 'no.' that was the word on his lips and in his mind. But what came out was, "I don't know."

Callie's eyebrows went up. "So do you believe Jade then? What proof does she have?"

"I don't think she has any."

Callie started chewing on her thumb. "I don't know, Paris. I really like Jade. I do. But Dex… I've known him for forever."

"I know," Paris said automatically. He hadn't even meant to say it; it had just come out. It was strange feeling his own sentiments echoed in Callie's words, but also at the same time feeling frustrated and uneasy. "But something about Jade's conviction…" he trailed off, not sure where he wanted to go with his words. He thought about Dex, about his friendship with Dex and felt odd. He felt as though…

"It's like I'm remembering something I wasn't there for," he said out loud.

"What?"

Something felt more solid in him, more steady as soon as he voiced the words. He looked up at Callie. "When you think about Dex, how do you feel?"

Callie shrugged. "I don't know. I guess I feel… like I always feel when I think of him. I like him. He's my friend."

"Is he?"

Callie squinted at Paris. "What? Of course he is. He's been our friend for years."

Something cold and thick was settling in Paris' gut at her words, at the expression on her face. She looked utterly convinced but also, somehow blank. Like a fanatic.

"When was the last time you saw Dex before he came to the Coven?"

"Oh, I just saw him… well. I mean it couldn't have been too long ago," Callie mused. She shook her head a bit as she thought. "Uh, you know, it was um. Well, before Jade came to the Coven. Definitely."

"But when exactly?" he pressed.

Callie fidgeted a bit. "I don't…" she met his gaze, looking a little lost. "I can't remember."

The cold, thick feeling in his stomach settled like a heavy stone. "Nor I."

"What does that mean, Paris?" Callie asked, but he could see in her face she already suspected what it meant.

Paris pushed back his chair, rising to his feet. "It means I need to go see Jade, probably apologize, and find out if she suspects anything else about what's wrong with the Coven's magic. Something's been affecting us from the start. We thought it was just our magic, but…"

"It's us too," Callie said, her voice wavering slightly. "It's not just our magic that's wrong, it's us." Callie shook her head. "This feels weird. I feel wrong when I talk about it. Like…"

"Like you need to stop and apologize," Paris finished for her.

"Yeah." She nodded, her large brown eyes focused on him. "And Jade thinks he did this to us."

"Well, she thinks he's responsible for the Coven's magic problems."

"But her hand thing, her demon rune, it didn't work."

Paris paused "No. It didn't. But she was upset. I was upset. We had words. And now I think I should try to apologize and see if she's still willing to help."

Callie's head tipped forward and she rubbed her temples a bit. "I'm so confused. I'm trying to focus on what we're talking about and it's like bits and pieces are getting snatched away from me."

"Whatever has been done is powerful. I find it hard to focus on our conversation as well," Paris admitted. As he sat there, talking to Callie, he found he kept wanting to soothe over what he'd said, take back his words and deny he thought anything was untoward about Dex. He stood up. "I'm going to see Hannah first and then Jade. Hannah's the strongest of us and was the first to detect that something was wrong with our magic. Perhaps with this new information she can learn more. With Jade, I've been able to filter my magic through her and it… clears it somehow. I don't know if she'll let me do it again, but at the very least, she doesn't appear affected by anything that's happening to the Coven's magic or to us."

Callie nodded. "Okay. I can try searching the library database for memory spells or deception or…" she shook her head again, trying to clear it. She grabbed a pad of sticky notes off Paris' desk and snatched a pen, scribbling furiously. "God, I've got to write this down, I feel like as soon as I leave I'm going to forget." She tore her notes off the pad and folded them carefully, tucking them in her pocket. Paris came around the corner of his desk and as he did, Callie surged forward and hugged him tightly. "You better still be real."

Paris hugged her back, easily remembering Callie - their friendship stretching back all the way back, as far as he could remember. "I am."

"Good luck with Jade."

He grimaced. "Thank you. I fear I'll need it."

*

Paris knocked at Hannah's door, tucking his hands into his pocket. There was a nip in the air, his breath visible on each exhale. He couldn't pretend it was autumn much longer with the weather going frigid and cold.

"Paris," Hannah said as she opened the door. She gestured him in quickly with her usual familiarity. "I wasn't expecting you."

"Sorry to barge in. I've got more information on what's happening to Coven magic and I needed to talk to you about it."

She made a kind of 'ah' sound, nodding in that sage way of hers. "Come to the sitting room. I've got some tea on."

He knew better than to start talking before he was seated, mug in hand. She plopped two sugar cubes into his drink and then eyeballed him for a moment before plunking in a third. "You look like you need that today. What can I do for you?"

"It's about Dex."

Hannah sat, looking regal and poised in her chair. She took a sip of her tea, slurping it a little due to the temperature of the water. "Hmm. Dex."

"You don't seem too surprised."

Hannah looked as though she were considering her words carefully. "I'm not. Not exactly."

Paris set his cup down on the side table, without taking a sip. "Hannah, do you know something about him?"

"No. I don't think so. Why don't you tell me why you are asking," she said, sitting back in her seat a bit.

"I don't think I know him," Paris confessed, feeling a sharp burn of *wrong* as he mouthed the words. He pushed through it, knowing he needed to get this out. "I don't know if anyone in the coven does." He told Hannah about what happened, how he was filtering his magic through Jade and directly after, when his magic still felt like it was working, Dex had arrived and Paris hadn't recognized him.

Hannah looked at him, nodding slightly. She hesitated, her teacup trembling slightly. Paris waited for her to speak. After a moment, she appeared ready. "When he arrived, it was as though I had to make myself remember him." She smiled faintly and he felt such a rush of profound relief at her words. "I admit, until just now, I thought it was the just the beginnings of my age finally showing itself. I often lose things here and there - a key, a stone I meant to use in a spell, a packet of herbs I picked up." Hannah had a sad, wistful look on her face and Paris' heart lurched at it. He often forgot how old she was. In his mind, she was eternal - always there. She'd joked about her age before, but she'd never spoken so frankly about it. "This was the first time I'd felt like I'd lost a person."

"You didn't really remember him, did you?"

"No," she said quietly. "And now I see that keeping that information to myself was wrong. I thought it was just me." She looked sheepish and frail for a moment and Paris reached forward, taking one of her hands. She clutched it tightly. "What a mistake."

"You couldn't have known."

Her fingers tightened around his for a moment, her eyes shiny with moisture. She let his hand go, flapping her fingers at him, brushing at her eyes a bit. "Well, we can discuss my aging at another date. A much, much later date," Hannah said, picking up her teacup again. "So, what are you going to do about this?"

"I admit, I was hoping you'd tell me."

"There's a reason you are Coven Leader and I am not. I've no interest in making grand decisions and plans. Something tells me you've already got an idea in your head."

Paris sighed. "I need to go see Jade. I think she's suspected Dex all along and today she tried to prove it was him and something went wrong." He paused thinking about how Jade's demon rune didn't work. "I'm not sure what. At any rate, she's the only person that seems to be truly unaffected by it. She tried to help the Coven today, help me," Paris continued, "and I managed to tear a strip off her a mile wide."

"Well, she's tough. She can take it."

"Let's hope she feels the same way," Paris said ruefully. He picked up his teacup and saucer, taking a sip of the hot sweet liquid. "Hannah, how much power would a spell like this take? To change our memories and to affect our magic."

Hannah tapped a fingertip against her china cup. "Quite a bit, though I'm sure you guessed that. I would say likely demon magic." She paused and tipped her head a bit. "Or possibly blood magic."

Paris grimaced feeling a bit sick. "I've been letting a sociopath walk around the Coven freely and all the while I've been calling him a friend, haven't I?" he asked rhetorically. He was glad when Hannah chose to stay silent, simply drinking her tea. "What kind of magic am I going to have to do to break blood magic? Is it even possible?"

Hannah considered his question. "If I'm gauging his power correctly, you're still more powerful than he is."

"But will it be enough? I know next to nothing about demon magic and I've never used blood magic myself, let alone tried to break it. I know some spells but I've not used them."

"You've got your mother's grimoires."

Paris felt the weight of those grimoires on his shoulders. "You think my mother's books would have something strong enough in them to break magic this powerful?"

"I think if anyone could do it, your mother would have been the one. Plus, you've got Jade."

"Do I?" he asked. "I wonder. I was quite hard on her."

"The Coven is her home. We're her home."

"I don't think she feels that." Paris rubbed a hand across his jaw. "I suppose I'll find out. I'm half afraid I'll get to her door and she'll sock me one."

"Your best bet is to roll with it. If she hits you, she'll pack a wallop. Be grateful her cast is off."

As always, Hannah managed to bring a smile to his face, no matter how grim it was. "Thank you," Paris answered dryly, pushing to his feet. "Perhaps, if you don't mind, you could assist Callie in her searches in the library? I would feel better if you were looking into it as well."

"Of course."

"I can take you there."

"I'll take myself. Stop stalling and go see Jade."

*

It wasn't working.

Jade had been trying to recreate the demon rune for an hour and she couldn't get it to work. Bruce, interested in the activity she supposed, had padded downstairs and into the kitchen. He lay with his belly pressed against the floor, watching her with his reflective eyes.

"Ugh, I know!" she said as she failed again and he lazily flicked his tongue at her. Jade knew exactly what the problem was. She couldn't get the feeling back she'd had the first time she'd cast the rune - the certainty she'd felt about helping the Coven, helping Paris. When she tried, she found she just felt angry and hurt all over again. She took a deep breath and shook out her hands, trying to start over. She wiped down the table with her cotton cloth, imagining it was cleaning the surface of all magic and bad mojo. Jade circled the rag over the surface counter-clockwise, trying to calm her brain.

It had always been a problem for her. She'd only ever really been able to be calm and centered when she was with Lily.

There was a deep tug of melancholy at the thought of her. Everything was off lately. Jade thought about the dream she'd had recently; Lily in the lake, her hair fanned out around her, arms stretched up to the surface. A ghostly stalagmite under the water, swaying almost imperceptibly to a hidden current. The feeling she got when she thought of that lake - sick and heavy. The look on Paris' face when he yelled at her. Coming back to the cottage and wondering if she should even stay.

Instead of focusing on the Coven and Paris, as she did the last time she made the rune, she tried to focus on Lily instead. She closed her eyes and tried to remember the calm, almost sleep-like feeling she would get when Lily was around.

She heard Bruce shift to his feet and then heard his nails on the floor as he waddled over to her. Ticky-tacky, ticky-tacky. She felt him press his serpentine body against her calf, a warm heavy weight against her muscle. It reminded her of Lily too in a way - a grounding weight, pulling her emotions down deep, coiling them low and dense where they couldn't spring up and confuse things. Like her fingers were one end of a magnet and her pile of ash another, she dipped her fingertips in the burned soot unerringly, and started sketching out the rune on the table. She kept her eyes closed, feeling… something. She wasn't sure what. It was calm and heavy - like a pot of hot stew sitting on a stove on a cold day. It made her feel safe and bound. Jade opened her eyes and stared down at the rune she'd traced. It was a little lopsided and slanted and when she placed her palm on it, she was met with the all too familiar sensation of absolutely nothing happening.

She pushed herself away from the table a bit in disgust. She couldn't get it to work. Bruce made his 'pfffft' sound and she looked down at him.

"I don't know," she said plaintively. "It's just not working." She could feel the ball of mistrust still sitting behind her sternum; an uncomfortable weight and she knew it was keeping her from casting the rune.

Bruce made a kind of wistful sound in return and Jade rolled her eyes, petting his scaly head. He blinked up at her sadly. "I don't know why you're so sooky. I'm the one that got yelled at today." He curled his tail around her ankle as she wiped down the table again.

"This isn't going to work," she muttered out loud. "I can't..." she took a deep breath. "Okay. Plan B. What else do we know, Bruce?" Jade crossed her arms over her chest, sitting back in her chair, thinking. The lie detection rune was a bust until she could get over her feelings about the Coven and Paris. She could try to track Dex down, but she didn't really know what she would do with him if she found him. Plus he kind of gave her the creeps. Maybe she should focus on what was actually wrong with the Coven's magic instead of who she knew was behind it. She remembered being in the forest with Paris, feeling the bad-wrong sensation just out of reach of her magic. Not the lake (she shuddered a bit - she still didn't like the lake), but the feeling just beyond it. Discordant and strange, it had tugged at her and grabbed her attention, like a sliver under her skin. Paris had said they'd go back with Hannah. Maybe he already had. It wasn't like Jade was privy to everything he did.

It wasn't like she was about to call him up and ask him either.

Maybe she could go back out there, to the preserve, and see what she could find. Jade tapped her fingers on the table. There was the distinct lack of a car that stood in her way and she didn't think that public transportation would get her out far enough. Although, Jade lived close to one of the preserves entrances, where she ran with Daniel. Maybe she could try to approach it from the other direction - going in from her running path and focusing on the weird mojo from there. It might be closer than she thought.

"Plan, Bruce!" Jade exclaimed, standing up. He skittered backwards and his Elizabethan collar flapped a bit in response to her excited tone. "We're going to need our running gear and to pack a bag. Field trip to the forest."

Ten minutes later she had her running shoes on, was dressed in several layers and was stuffing her laptop backpack with what she considered to be 'outdoors-y survival things.' She had a bottle of water, an afghan from the back of her sofa and two boxes of crackers from the kitchen.

"It's not like I'm planning on being out there forever," she said to Bruce conversationally. He was stretched out on the sofa watching her. He'd looked a little shifty-eyed ever since she took the afghan. Jade suspected he'd been using it for naps and was put out that she'd confiscated it. "I'm just going to check a few things out. Recon. And then come back here." She zipped the bag shut and slung it over her shoulder. "It's not like anyone's gonna even notice I'm gone."

Okay, the talking to herself thing was getting a little out of hand. Sure, Bruce was looking at her while she spoke, but it wasn't like he understood her. Probably. Jade hadn't realized how lonely she'd been until she started talking aloud to him. While she'd never had close friends at work, she'd been social - saying hello to people, grabbing a coffee with them, discussing the latest quarter's results. At the Coven, she'd sort of made friends with Callie and Henri, but she was still on her own a lot of the time.

Bruce flicked his tongue at her lazily, stretching out on the sofa. He never took his eyes off her as she bent down to put on her shoes, tying the laces tight.

"So. Be a good lizard," Jade said awkwardly. "And if I'm not back in a day…" she trailed off staring at him and then made a disgusted sound at herself. "I've got to stop talking to you like you're a person."

She pulled the door shut behind her as she left, hopping down the steps. She slowed down when she saw a car in front of her house.

"There you are!" Veronica said, coming out of the driver's side. She stood, leaning over the top of the car casually, as though it wasn't the end of fall outside, the weather turning cold and sharp.

"Uh, hey. Can I help you?"

"I wanted to come by and chat with you, but I can't seem to make it up your walkway."

"Oh, sorry about that," Jade answered. "I've got it spelled. You know, for a lock."

Veronica smiled and Jade frowned. Her smile was strange, but Jade couldn't put her finger on why.

"So I figured. I don't know if I've ever felt one like it."

"It's demon magic," said Jade, wanting to cut the conversation short. If there was one thing that usually did it at the Coven, it was the mention of demon magic.

But, that only made Veronica's smile seem brighter. "Really? How intriguing."

Jade shrugged, hitching the backpack up on her shoulders. "Sure. Uh listen, I'm on my way out."

"You look like you're going hiking," Veronica said, looking up and down Jade's outfit.

Jade narrowed her eyes. The hinky vibe she was getting from Veronica was growing exponentially. "What do you want?"

"I think a better question is, what do *you* want?"

Jade was pretty sure her face made that screwed up expression she got when she didn't understand something.

Veronica jerked her head a bit toward the passenger seat of the car and started sliding back into the driver's side. "We should talk. Just us girls."

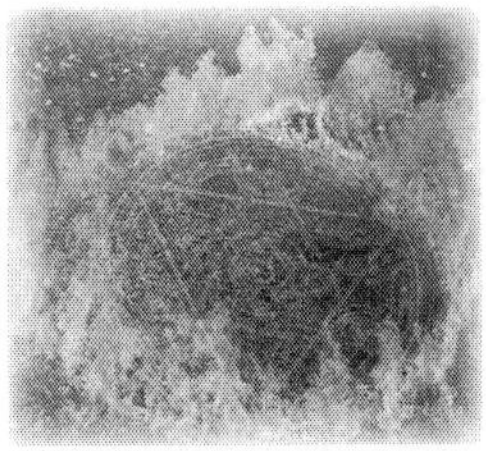

CHAPTER 13

Jade was intrigued by Veronica. She could admit it. She drummed her fingers against her leg for a moment, deciding, watching Veronica smile as she got behind the wheel, pausing to check her lipstick in the mirror. She leaned over and unlocked the door to the passenger side, looking up at Jade expectantly. Jade took slow steps forward, pausing as she opened the door.

"Is this the part in the horror film where the audience is screaming at me to not get in this car?"

"I don't know, Jade. What is it you think I'm going to do to you? You've still got all your magic, don't you?"

Jade pulled open the back door and tossed her bag in the back. As she got in the front seat, Veronica took out a compact and touched up her makeup.

"So that's how you stay looking so perfect all day long," Jade said, eyeing Veronica as she touched up her makeup.

"It's a pain in the ass, but necessary. People like you much better when you're pretty. Shallow but true." Veronica tucked her compact and lipstick back in her purse, smoothing her hair. "Don't you agree?"

Jade half shrugged, half nodded. "I guess. People do tend to like and trust good looking people."

"So, where are you going?"

Jade decided just to put her cards all out on the table and not dance around the issue. "I am going to the preserve to see what Dex has done to Coven magic. But," Jade said, pausing as she saw Veronica's expression change from one of interest to one of knowing, "I'm getting the feeling you already know what he did, don't you?"

Veronica apparently felt the same urge to address Jade frankly and responded back in kind, not even trying to tiptoe around. "Dex," groused Veronica. "His problem is he pushes. He pushes and pushes and pushes and doesn't know when to stop." She shoulder checked and pulled out into the street. "You were the wild card in this, Jade. You were the piece we couldn't predict. We thought the spell would work on everyone."

"The spell on the Coven's magic?" Jade asked, feeling the need to clarify. She was completely taken aback. Of all the things she expected when she walked out the front door to find out what was happening, getting into a car with Veronica and having it all dumped into her lap was not one of them. She didn't feel in danger or threatened, but she was still ready to toss out some fireballs if it all went south.

"That and the spell to make everyone remember Dex."

"Whoa, what?"

"There's a reason everyone likes him so much and it's not his sparkling personality," Veronica said wryly.

"That's a magic spell?"

"Yes, another one that didn't work on you."

"Wait, so everyone likes him because of the spell?"

"Yes, and remembers always liking him because of the spell."

Jade blinked a few times, staring at the street signs as they went by. "That actually makes me feel a lot better about all this. Because he gives off serious creeper vibes."

Veronica turned the car down the road toward the preserve, the same road that Paris had taken her on the other day, when they went to work on her circle magic. "Tell me about it. That's part of the problem with Dex. He doesn't know when to quit."

"So are you and he…?" Jade asked, eyebrow going up.

"No. Not for his lack of trying." Veronica sounded a little disgusted and affronted.

"When I asked Dex what he did to Coven magic, he said nothing. I was testing him with magic of my own, to see if he was lying and he passed," Jade continued, thoughtful. "But if you're working with him, then was it you?"

Veronica seemed tense. "I cast the spell that shifted Coven magic out of balance, yes. It's tied to Dex, for as long as he's here."

"Why?"

"So no one would feel Dex's memory spell. Changing someone's memory is… big. Changing an entire Coven's worth… it wouldn't have gone unnoticed."

"Unless everyone's magic was broken," Jade finished.

"Yes. They would be completely focused on fixing it and nothing else."

"What's your deal? Why are you telling me all this?"

"Because we had a plan and it's not working. It's not working because of Dex and because of you and because of Paris."

"Paris," Jade said. "What did he do?"

"It's what he won't do," Veronica said hotly, slapping a hand on the steering wheel. "I'm attractive and even though Dex had to do a spell to make the Coven remember him, I actually *do* have a history with Paris and it should have been simple enough to get what I wanted. Unfortunately, he's got a goddamn noble streak and the Coven always comes first with him. The Coven and now you."

"Me?"

"You," Veronica affirmed.

"I'm not… he's… We're not," Jade sputtered.

"Stop before you hurt yourself."

"Well, we're not," Jade replied firmly. "If he's not playing slap and tickle with you it's not because of me."

Veronica made a sort of 'mm-hmm' sound and Jade resisted the urge to keep protesting. She smoothed her ponytail out, giving herself some time to find her words.

"What *do* you want anyway? What's all this for?"

Veronica turned her head to look at Jade and ground her jaw. "I suppose I may as well tell you, I'm telling you everything else. Sakkara's books. The one's you found."

"The demon grimoires?"

"I need them. Paris' mother was…" she sighed, staring out the windshield. "There was no one like her. She had so much power, so much control and when I heard that she'd written demon grimoires… I need them."

"How do you know about them? It's not exactly common knowledge."

Veronica waved a hand, turning into the preserve with a one-handed grip on the wheel. "You'd be surprised what gets around." The car jerked to a stop and she put it in park, turning to face Jade. "I know you have at least two, and Paris has one. But I can't figure out where he's keeping his. You must have yours at your house, but no one can even get close."

"Because of my spell. My demon locks," Jade murmured.

"Exactly. It's not like we haven't tried." She leaned in a little closer to Jade. "What's in there about demon deals? Is there a way to break them? Can it be done?"

"I don't know. I haven't read them all the way through yet," Jade replied.

Veronica huffed. "You were in a coven all of two minutes before you found out about demon magic and started using it. And, I hear you're a natural. Better at it than regular magic."

"Seriously, does everyone just gossip all day long?" Jade asked, a little outraged. "Aren't people supposed to be working?"

"Idle hands," Veronica mused. "Not just the devil's playground."

"And now you've gone turncoat against Dex. Why? Why did you agree to drive me out here?" Jade looked around, seeing the forest spread out in front of her. If she focused closely, she could feel the same thing from before - the strange wrong feeling deep in the woods.

Veronica's fingers flexed, her knuckles white, the tips of her perfectly manicured nails glinting in the light. "I want out. It was supposed to be fast. Cast the spells and get in. With everyone's magic broken, no one would notice the spell on their memories. Find the grimoires, get them and get out. But it all went to shit with you in the mix. Neither spell worked on you and you hated him from the get go. Paris wouldn't tell me about the grimoires, and we couldn't get near your house."

"Why both you and Dex together? Why didn't you just come on your own? You said you have a history here," Jade argued.

"I do. I did manage to convince Dex to at least let me try with Paris first but…" Veronica sighed and then laughed. It wasn't a pleasant sound. It was harsh and brittle. "Paris talks to me like a colleague, nothing more, despite my efforts."

Jade blinked at the statement wondering how much 'effort' Veronica had tried to use on Paris.

"I hoped I could woo those books out of him. Dex was all over me, pushing me. I guess there's no honor among thieves. He probably trusted me to get the grimoires on my own about as much as I would have trusted him. Dex has always had big ideas. He wants power and he found out I wanted those books. I was supposed to go in and see if I could get them, or at least get Paris to tell me where they were. But Dex didn't give me enough time." She huffed. "Or maybe it doesn't matter. Paris didn't seem to be at all susceptible to my flirting. I did manage to find out you had two of the grimoires and then Dex and I tried to break into you house but you had this… lizard thing. It came out of your house and attacked. What the hell is that thing anyway?"

"Bruce?" Jade questioned. She remembered the first night he stayed he'd gone outside, hissing at something in the bushes. "That was you?" Jade felt like a colossal idiot. She hadn't even realized there's been someone there.

"That was us. After that, Dex wanted to try it his way - all flash-bang. He was convinced it would work and we could snatch the grimoires. But then you," Veronica continued, shaking her head slightly. "You didn't like Dex from the start and you somehow knew he was responsible, even if you didn't know how or why. It should have been done by now. We should have gotten those grimoires and gotten out. Now Dex wants to use more power and try the memory spell again. He thinks he can get it to work on you this time." Veronica shook her head. "But there's something… off about you." Despite the fact that Veronica was kind of a sociopath, her words stung Jade a bit. "I don't think the spell will work. I don't know what it is, but you don't react to magic like you should. I want to cut our losses, but Dex isn't giving up, and I need you to stop him. It's too much now."

"You want me to clean up your mess," Jade said. "Why aren't you telling Paris this? He's Coven Leader. He's got all the good mojo. If you guys have a history and if you turn on some of your 'charm,'" Jade made air quotes around the word, "he'd help you."

"He would," Veronica murmured and then gave a wry laugh. "But then I'd have to look him in the face and tell him what I did." She gazed out into the forest, her eyes going a bit glassy. "And I don't know if he's brutish enough to go up against Dex." She looked Jade up and down. "You are though."

"Gee, thanks."

"I mean it as a compliment," Veronica said with a shrug. She jerked her chin toward the forest. "He's in there now, trying to alter the spell, trying to get you in it, or pull it apart and reshape it. I don't think it can be done and when he figures that out, he'll go for something else."

"This is your plan?" Jade asked incredulous. "Drive me into the woods and set me loose like some kind of sniffer dog? You're not even going to help?"

Veronica at least had the decency to look away, ashamed. "I can't. Dex… knows things about me. He knows where to push." She rubbed at her lips and jaw with her hand, smearing her makeup and not seeming to notice. Her hands fluttered slightly. "He and I are like junkyard dogs that huddle together for warmth, but also circle each other, waiting for a weak spot, both hungry for a scrap of steak. He's a bigger dog than me, and I've got to be smart about this. I don't have the power to go up against him. But you do."

Jade wanted to laugh at the absurdity. Sure, she had power. She had lots of power apparently. She was also green like a ten-dollar ring and according to Paris, and wasn't supposed to use any magic until she learned better control.

"What exactly is it you think I can do, Veronica?"

"You'll do whatever you have to do. And you won't balk at it."

Well, she wasn't wrong about that. Jade wasn't above fighting dirty. Jade drummed her fingers on her thighs, deciding. Without realizing she was going to speak, she started asking Veronica questions.

"What kind of magic does Dex like?"

Veronica thought about it for a moment. "Showy. Even if no one's around, it's got to be showy. He'll always go for a trickier spell than necessary."

"How good is he?"

"He's good. His emotions don't get in the way."

"And his elements?"

Veronica made a so-so motion with her hand. "He doesn't go for much elemental magic. He likes the spells and the incantations. Blood magic, wet work." At Jade's expression Veronica paused. "Has Paris taught you about blood magic yet?"

Jade shook her head. "No. There were some things in the grimoires, but I thought…" Jade had thought it was strictly a demon magic tool. "What's it like, blood magic?"

Veronica grimaced. "Messy. Thick. Cuts deep. I'm not making puns here or anything, that's what it feels like. That's how it works."

"What kind of blood are we talking about here? Animal, human?"

"Depends on what he wants." Veronica pulled up her sleeve showing a white strip of gauze wrapped around her inner elbow. "We used our own for the spell on the Coven. I guess since he doesn't have me, he'll have to double up on his own blood to invoke it again."

Jade stared out into the woods, narrowing her eyes, trying to find the feeling she'd found before - the *strange-wrong-bad* feeling in the forest. She was quick to find it this time or maybe it found her, she wasn't sure. Was she getting better at this or was the feeling worse because Dex was out there right now casting spells he had no right to? Jade turned back and looked at Veronica, who was watching her intently, waiting. She studied Veronica up and down. Jade didn't think she was lying - she didn't give off a weird or creepy vibe like Dex did. If there was one thing Jade thought herself good at, it was reading people. She hadn't liked Dex from the start and clearly, she was right. But Veronica….

"You're not really evil, are you?" Jade mused.

Veronica huffed. "Not sure if that's a statement or a question but no, I'm not. I just need those books."

"Why?"

"I'm smart, Jade. I'm damn smart," she said without a hint of artifice. "Smart enough to get my own coven even though I don't quite have the power for it. People have overlooked it so far probably because I'm damn good looking too." Jade shrugged and nodded along. Veronica was probably right. "But I knew I wasn't going to be young and good looking forever and I needed more power."

"What did you do?" asked Jade, already getting a sneaking suspicion.

"I made a deal. A demon deal for more power. At first…" she sighed. "It must be so easy for witches like you, having this power all the time. I could do any spell I wanted. My Coven ran more smoothly, I could fix things that were broken, and it was like people knew, they could sense I had more power. And then…"

"Then what?"

"Then the demon started showing up all the time. Wanting small favors - a witch spell that demons can't cast, or for me to make a phone call for him or spy on someone or get information but now I just want out. I don't care about the power anymore. I just want out." Veronica laughed, thin and tight. "I thought… I thought that all demons were the same and surely I could outsmart one. How hard could it be? But I went and made a demon deal with a former Egyptian god. I'm so screwed."

Veronica's words made the hair on the back of Jade's neck rise up. "Are you talking about Seth?" Jade asked, incredulous.

Veronica fixed her wide, green eyes on Jade. "Do you know of him? Is he in the books? Does it say how I can break my deal?"

"I haven't seen him in the books but he shows up all the time in my pantry. He's been hanging around me since I showed up at the Coven."

"What? Have you made a deal?"

"No."

Veronica seemed deflated by this, as though she were hoping that she and Jade could have something in common. Seth, that rat-bastard. He'd known all along what was going on with the Coven's magic.

"Did he know about the spell on the Coven? Did he help you with it?"

"More or less," Veronica said. "He knows when I call on the power gained from our deal. I wouldn't have had the power to do it without my deal with him."

Jade huffed. Seth had essentially helped Veronica with her spell and then ran to tattle about it to Jade, playing both sides. What a fucker.

"I need out of that deal," Veronica said, her voice thin. "Are you sure you haven't read anything in Sakkara's grimoires?"

Jade shrugged with one shoulder. "Not about breaking deals, no."

Veronica slumped a bit in her seat and swore under her breath.

"And Dex?" Jade questioned. "Does he have a deal too?"

Veronica's fingers flexed. "No. It's not like we stayed up at night and braiding each other's hair and sharing secrets but if I had to guess, I'd say one coven isn't good enough for him."

"So, what, he wants more?"

"I think he wants them all," Veronica said flatly. "I think he wants all of us under him, under his thumb. He'd like all our magic at his beck and call."

"But that's not how Coven Leaders work," Jade protested.

"That's not how Paris works," Veronica clarified. "Paris has more than enough of his own power and has no interest in anyone else's. But as Coven Leader, he could take it if he wanted. He could warp it, siphon it, turn it. He wouldn't. Dex would. Dex wants to."

Jade sighed, leaning her head against the window. Everything Veronica said jived with what Jade felt about Dex and now, getting it all confirmed, Jade almost felt a little trapped. Now that she knew all of this, there was no way she could walk away. She had to do something.

"Well, fuck," she muttered. The interior of the car was silent for a moment, Jade staring out the window.

"Look, I don't mean to be pushy, but you kind of need to get going," Veronica said, making a shoo-ing motion with her fingers. "Tick-tock."

"Hey, when you're asking for my help, you don't get to tell me how to help you," Jade said hotly.

"He's out there right now, casting spells. Blood work. This isn't the time for dilly-dallying."

"Well, maybe you should have thought of that before you made a demon deal and then had to join 'maniacal forces' with Dex," Jade said, making air quotes around the words. "I hate to be judgy-mcjudgypants," okay so that wasn't exactly true. Jade kind of liked putting her judgypants on, "but where was all this concern before?"

Veronica pursed her lips together tightly. "Are you helping or not?"

"I'm helping," Jade said, tossing her hands up in exasperations. She wrenched the door handle open and got out of the car in a huff. Before she slammed the door shut, she bent down to talk to Veronica one more time. "But seriously if this doesn't work out, will you at least tell Paris where to find my body?" She asked, eyebrow raised.

Veronica rolled her eyes. "I wouldn't have driven you out here if I didn't think you could do it."

"Is that supposed to be a pep talk? Ugh, just… if you can't face him in person, drop him a text at least. If you're so sure I'll survive then you have to know

I'll tell him all about your involvement. He's going to find out anyway."

Veronica inhaled deep, jaw working as she stared at Jade. "Fine."

"Fine." Jade repeated back, shrugging with one shoulder.

"Good luck."

"Good riddance," Jade said, slamming the door shut and turning toward the forest.

*

Paris sat in his car outside Jade's cottage and told himself he wasn't afraid to climb the steps. He was simply working out exactly what he wanted to say. Something apologetic and tasteful. Something calm and diplomatic. Something that wouldn't get the door slammed in his face. After he realized he'd been parked outside Jade's house for ten minutes and still had no clue how to start, he resolved to get out of the car and just do it. Something would come to him. Probably.

He felt the twinge of demon magic as he crossed over the spell she used to lock her house. He'd forgotten completely about it and was glad she'd spelled it to let him in or he'd be making an embarrassing phone call asking her to please come outside and speak to him. It would probably be easier for her to hang up on him than slam the door in his face, so he'd rather not take that chance.

Paris knocked sharply on the door, three times and waited.

And waited.

He frowned and knocked again. Well, this was a little cringe worthy. If she wasn't home, he honestly had no idea where to start looking for her. He'd just assumed she would be here.

"Jade," he called out. "If you're in there fuming at me, I've come to apologize." There. That sounded proper and calm. Surely if she was sulking behind the door, it would generate some good will.

Nothing.

He knocked once more, calling out her name. On a whim, he reached out, tried the handle and found the door unlocked. Paris supposed she didn't really need a lock if she had her demon wards. Hoping he wasn't digging himself a deeper hole by entering her house uninvited, he stepped cautiously in.

A quiet hiss-growl stopped him half way through the door. "Jade?" he questioned lowly, fearing something had happened to her. He heard a strange clacking sound - claws on tile - and fought the urge to bolt out of the house. If Jade was here, in trouble, he would not leave without helping her.

Paris could admit the sound he made when the strange lizard creature stepped into the hallway was not altogether one of his most dignified, nor was the entire thing one of his finer moments. Without thinking, without remembering his magic wasn't working, he shot off a bafflement spell, meant to daze the animal, and then cursed when all that happened was a rain of glitter fell from the sky, lazily falling around the lizard-thing like flakes in a snow globe.

A long pink tongue flecked out and caught some of the glitter and it rolled it over in its mouth, like it was tasting it.

"Christ on a cracker, you're the thing from the sewer," Paris breathed. "How long have you been here?"

It made a strange 'pfffft' sound, coming forward as though challenging Paris. Its eyes were cross and it had a scaly Elizabethan collar raised, like hackles on a dog. Paris held up his hands and then turned them over, palm up in a gesture of friendliness. His eyes darted around, looking for clues. He saw a small pot of water on the floor by the sofa, a pillow next to it with what looked like one of Jade's t-shirts lying on top. He took a step closer, shutting the front door behind him. The lizard thing sniffed the air, its snout moving back and forth. Whatever it found, it seemed to like because the collar went down and it backed up a little before turning around and then trotting over to the pot, having a quick drink of water, and then lying down on the pillow and t-shirt.

"I bet you've been here the whole time," Paris said, his voice low. He entered the room, watching the creature carefully. "Ever since you disappeared from the Coven."

It made another 'pffft' sound, as if in agreement and Paris inclined his head a bit, watching the strange eyes of the thing as they tracked his every movement.

"I think you might even understand me a bit."

It made a clicking sound, tongue coming out again in a fast lick of the air. Paris felt a quick bolt of magic and was stunned when he realized it came from the lizard and felt exactly like Jade's magic.

"You're her familiar," Paris said, incredulous. He hunkered down, dropping to his knees to get a better look. The lizard blinked lazily up at him, now completely at ease. Familiars were incredibly rare.

While most animals had the loyalty, devotion and benevolent spirit required to be a familiar, they lacked the required intelligence. A familiar needed to be able to understand a witch beyond simple commands like 'sit' or 'stay.' They needed to be able to contain or channel magic without any animal instincts overriding the spell work. An ordinary dog, cat or other household pet would never do. Familiars tended to be magical creatures themselves, which were quite scarce.

Somehow, this strange lizard thing had found its way to Jade and she'd managed to bind it to her. It was connected to her in a rather fond manner if the way it slept on her worn t-shirt was any indication.

Paris reached out and touched it on the head, feeling its warm, dry, and strangely supple skin. It blinked its eyes lazily, preening a bit under the touch. "Where is she? Is she here?"

"Pffffft," it hissed, its eyes darting to the doorway in a way that made Paris think it wasn't just happenstance.

"Gone out, hm?" Paris said lowly, using the same tone he would when talking to a cat or dog. It settled its head back down on the t-shirt and pillow, tongue darting out quickly once before it relaxed. Paris found the odd creature mesmerizing in a way - it seemed so domesticated and relaxed - a far cry from how it had been described to Paris when it had first been discovered. It exuded a faint trace of magic identical in feeling to Jade's and he found himself drawn to the way the magic vibrated, his own still feeling woefully out of tune and broken.

He was shaken out of his reverie by his phone ringing. The creature blinked up at him, irritated, eyes slitting open to glare at the interruption.

"Sorry," Paris said quietly, pulling his phone out. "Paris here."

There was a slight pause before the person on the other end spoke. "Hello, Paris."

The tone of her voice, almost grudging and slow, made him blink in surprise. "Veronica, are you all right?"

There was another pause on the phone and if he listened carefully, he could hear the sounds of a car traveling. Veronica sighed. "Look, I'm sorry."

"All right," Paris said, not sure what Veronica meant. He pulled his hand away from the creature and stood upright. "For?"

"I never meant for things to go this far, but they did and… You have to understand, I'm not like you. You've had extraordinary power your whole life and you just… fit in your Coven. I've always had the drive and the intellect, but not the aptitude and it's like seeing the world I want to be part of from behind a glass wall and I'm always pushing my nose against it, unable to get through."

Paris was bewildered. "What on earth are you talking about?"

There was another firm exhalation of air and Paris felt his stomach drop a bit. "I've just dropped Jade off in the preserve. To stop him. To stop Dex."

Sometimes, when the pressure changed suddenly because of the weather, or he was inside a plane that dropped quickly, Paris' would feel like his ears were hollow and tinny. It was as though he was hearing things from the bottom of a long, thin tube made out of metal. The same thing happened now and it was as though Veronica was talking from far away.

"I only wanted the grimoires, your mother's books. I just… I made a deal, Paris. A demon deal and I needed to know if your mother had a way to break it. I needed more power. I don't have it on my own and I can't keep my Coven forever without it. But Dex is… I knew he was dangerous when I threw my lot in with him, but I thought I could handle it." She laughed wryly; a dry sound that echoed slightly. "I guess that's the problems with sociopaths. They don't always do what you'd expect."

Paris felt a nudge against his foot and looked down to see the creature's tail curled around his ankle, squeezing it slightly. He blinked, feeling his hearing re-align and come back to normal. He'd only just now started suspecting Dex and he'd not even had an inkling that Veronica was involved. He felt a little sick for a moment, flipping through his memories, remembering their friendship and a time when they were more than friends. He wondered if it was just more magic - more memory manipulation. He had to ask, "Do I even know you?"

"Well, I suppose I deserved that," she said in his ear, her voice quiet and low. "I guess that depends on what you mean. I'm not part of the memory hex that Dex used. You do know me. But I suppose… maybe you never really knew me at all." She sounded sad and melancholy and anything he would have normally felt for her was trampled when his mind flickered back through what she'd said.

"What did you mean, you dropped Jade off in the preserve to stop Dex?"

"He's going to try the spell again. The hex he used. It didn't work on Jade. There's something different about her, but I guess you know that already."

"Why did you … how could… how long…" Paris' couldn't form a proper sentence. He wasn't sure what he wanted to ask or if there was any question to which Veronica would respond that would make him feel better about any of this. He finally settled on, "Where in the preserve?"

"The south-east entrance. It's not like I kidnapped her and tossed her out the side of the car. She knows what she's getting into."

Paris wanted to crush his phone in his hand and throw it against a wall. His other hand, the one not holding the phone clenched into a fist. "I cannot listen to you try to pardon your actions right now."

There was a heavy silence on the phone; only the sound of wheels on pavement let him know she hadn't hung up. "I'm sorry," she said finally. "For everything."

The silence when she did hang up was pristine and powerful. He realized he'd not even gotten the chance to ask her any really important questions - who was Dex? How powerful was he? What did she know about him?

Although he wasn't sure he could have trusted her answers if he had asked. Paris stared at his phone feeling the weight of betrayal.

"Pfffft." He felt something against his leg again and saw the lizard creature had gotten to its feet and was butting its head against Paris. He was momentarily confused until its serpentine eyes flicked to the door and then back to him meaningfully.

Paris shook himself a bit. He had to get to the preserve. While his magic was faulty, he still knew incredibly more magic than Jade. She was powerful, but lacked knowledge and experience. He couldn't even imagine what she might know that could be of use, other than brute force spells. As he rushed out of Jade's house, he heard the creature follow him. When Paris got to his car, it leapt in front of him, pushing him a bit to the side and, after some scrabbling, settled itself in the back seat, looking at him expectantly. If it could have talked, Paris got the distinct impression it would have said, '*Well? Hurry up.*' Paris slid into the driver's seat and heard the crunch of gravel spit up off his tires as he pushed the accelerator a little too hard - the car jumping with a lurch as the frictional force finally caught and shot them forward. The creature hissed in displeasure. The sound was sharp and hard in Paris' ear and he wanted to laugh a little hysterically at the situation.

Maybe he would. Later.

*

After getting out of Veronica's car, Jade squared her shoulders and cracked her neck before setting off into the woods. It wasn't until she heard the car drive away that she realized she'd left her bag with all her stuff inside.

Well, a blanket and a couple boxes of crackers weren't going to help her anyway.

Probably.

The path was easy enough to follow, but she was still glad she'd already been here once with Paris. It helped take the edge off the 'W*hat the hell are you* *doing?*' feeling. The truth was, she wasn't totally sure what she was doing. She wasn't sure why she didn't just hunker down and wait for Paris to show up. Of course, that assumed that Veronica would contact him. But when Jade thought about stopping, thought about huddling down in the forest and waiting, something inside her chest lurched. She didn't know if it was magic or if it was just her own sense of 'let's get this shit done,' but something kept her moving forward.

When she stretched out her magic, she could sense the one-two punch that she knew now to be Dex and Veronica's spell, as well as the eerie feeling from the lake. It seemed like the feeling was closer now than it had been before, and she wondered if Dex had moved closer to the lake. The forest was quiet as she walked - too late in the year for birds, and she was probably scaring all the woodland life away with her stomping and tromping footfalls. Jade wasn't exactly light on her feet, certainly not while hiking. She'd never really been one to 'commune' with nature. She focused on the steady sound of her own breath - in and out - and the tugging, pulling sensation of both the lake and Dex's magic.

Jade twisted and turned with the path, sometimes veering off it for a few steps, just to make sure the strange tugging sensation was still there. She could feel it when she passed by the lake; its cold, deep water off to her right. She paused and closed her eyes, leaning against a tree. She had an inexplicable desire to turn then, head to the lake and … do something. She wasn't sure what.

A shock went through her chest suddenly and she lurched forward a bit, feeling sick and a little strange.

It was Dex's magic. She didn't know how she knew, but she did. Blood magic. She could feel it in the air - almost taste it. It was like Veronica had said - thick and heavy. Cloying. It tried to settle on top of her own magic, like a beetle-infested blanket. Jade pushed power out of herself, imagining it like a plastic bubble - protecting her from the creepy-crawly feeling pressing in on her. Leveraging herself off the tree she leaned against, she moved forward again, deeper into the forest.

She was glad it wasn't dark. The sky was overcast - the almost-winter sun painting everything grey and sharp with its light. Despite the brightness, though, she still didn't see Dex through the trees until she stumbled out of the forest, slipped down a muddy hill and skidded to a stop in a small clearing.

"Fuck," she said sharply, nearly slipping and landing on her butt. An elegant and awe-inspiring entrance it was not.

Dex didn't look surprised to see her, even as she got her feet under her. There was a dead stag in front of him - glassy eyed and horrible. It looked like it hadn't gone down easy. It was messy; the fur matted with blood and dirt, its long, powerful legs twisted at weird angles. Dex was covered in blood from the tips of his fingers to his elbows and Jade could feel her lips curling back in disgust. He stared at her intently and Jade got the feeling he was waiting for something from her, some kind of sign.

"Gross." She hoped her expression contained the full revulsion she felt.

Dex smiled, bending over the stag and drawing runes on its body with its own blood. "You say that now, but in thirty seconds, once the new spell takes hold, we'll be best friends. What is it they say? BFF? I can't wait for you to tell me all your little secrets. I've got a feeling you've got quite a few."

Jade felt her skin go cold at his words, a slight sweat breaking out on top of her lip. Without thinking, she shot her power out, pushing fire toward the stag, hoping that if it burned before he finished, it would ruin his spell.

Dex waved a hand, sending her fire spell off into the trees where it sputtered and spat, winking out. "No finesse. You just push power around with no real intent or spell-work behind it." He pointed a finger at her. "It's all about knowledge."

Jade was stunned at how quickly he tossed her magic aside. She knew she was raw - untested - and that her magic was still simple compared to other magic at the Coven, but she'd hoped that her power level would make up for it. Dex ignored her, going back to his rune work. He pulled out a small satchel of something and started sprinkling it around the stag - herbs, ash of some kind - Jade didn't know what. He was standing there doing magic right in front of her and she didn't know how to stop him.

She thought back to the demon grimoires, to the spells she'd read. Jade concentrated and started casting one of the fire ones she'd learned from them. She thought of the scrawled handwriting of Sakkara's grimoires, the amount of knowledge and magic Paris' mother must have had. This spell took more time, more concentration. Jade flicked her fingers out and this time, when Dex made a motion to shoo her spell away, it didn't work and the stag's fur caught fire. The smell of burning hair and skin filled her nostrils immediately and she stumbled backwards, falling over something on the ground, landing hard on her butt.

Dex made a strangled sound of fury and Jade had a moment to think, '*oh shit*' before he rounded on her and shouted some kind of hex or curse. She threw her hands up and could only think, '*No, don't want*' in defense. She felt something hit up against her magic, her body - painful and sharp and she shuddered from the pain. Dex's magic slid against her but didn't sink in. He collected himself for another volley and Jade thought about how when she'd been in the forest last, how Paris couldn't cross her circle. She saw the perfect shape in her mind and even though she didn't have anything to draw it with, she imagined she did - imagined she traced out the shape, round and perfect. The grass and dirt flared up around her, a perfect circle of flame and smoke, surrounding her.

"You think that can protect you? From blood magic?" Dex sneered. Heedless of the flames rising from the burning carcass of the stag, he stepped toward it, chanted something Jade didn't understand and then slammed his palm down on top of the burning flesh, his eyes wide and vicious.

Jade felt more than saw a shockwave of magic flare out from the stag, like a sun gone supernova. She winced and braced for some kind of impact.

Nothing happened. She blinked up at Dex, watching his face as it turned from expectant to furious. She had seen the wave of magic, saw it spark out, but she didn't feel any different. From the look on Dex's face, he knew it too.

"How?" he seethed. "How is it that you are immune to this spell?" His fists were clenched, the stag corpse burning in front of him. The smell still crossed over her circle and she cringed backward when it filled her nostrils - sharp and acrid. Jade had the urge to skitter back, to move further away, but she didn't want to leave her circle. She didn't know if her circle would or could move with her. Dex took a step closer and Jade hunched in. "I killed for this spell, I bled for this spell. A spell to work on every witch tied to the Coven. You should be just as vacant-eyed and malleable as the rest of them."

Jade had an awful thought. If Dex had just re-worked his spell, then Paris, wherever he was, would be affected. Even if Veronica contacted him, would he even realize Jade was in trouble? That she needed help?

"You know, maybe the problem is you don't really belong in the Coven," Dex said, his voice going low and mean. "Maybe a witch born outside can never really belong. Or maybe it's just you. Maybe they don't feel you're tied to them. Maybe you're just too different, Jade." The way he said her name was like a curse - he spat it out like it made his mouth taste foul. "Maybe you'll never belong here. Maybe," he said, eyes thoughtful. "Maybe you should think about joining up with me."

It was essentially everything she'd been telling herself since she got to the Coven, everything she'd been afraid of, everything she pretended wasn't true or didn't matter. Hearing it come from Dex was like being slapped in the face. She'd be dammed if she'd give him the satisfaction of knowing it though. She wasn't about to buckle under some two-bit pop psychology spouted off by the villain. Jade hated when that happened in the movies.

"Or maybe you're just shit for brains at casting this spell," she said with a casual shrug, feigning arrogance she didn't feel. "Or maybe I'd rather be on the outside of this Coven looking in than ever consider cozying up with a sociopath like you."

Dex came closer, eyes wide with rage. He finally matched her feelings about him. It was as though his outward persona was now in tune with what she'd thought of him all along. Jade hadn't been able to articulate it before, but this is how she felt when she saw him. Like he should have always been wide-eyed, manic, anger and rage his right and left hands - both of them ready to do battle at his side. Jade thought her words might have angered him a bit more than she'd intended as he raged forward shouting, "You think your circle can protect you? Your pitiful little circle? You don't even know what you're capable of. You have all this power, demon grimoires at your disposal and this is what you protect yourself with?" Dex gestured madly at Jade as she sat on her ass in the forest, cowering from him.

That stung. She was doing the best she could. Her pride took a hit at Dex's words and in response, her circle flared up around her. She felt better seeing the blue-orange flame surrounding her. She felt… almost safe. Centered. It wasn't a feeling she'd had in a long time. Not since Lily. Thinking of her was distracting. It turned her attention from Dex and his contorted face and focused instead on the feeling inside her. The peculiar sleepy feeling she would get around Lily. It helped her think. It kept her from shooting her mouth off. It made her reason through her actions. It was the sort of clarity she needed right now. Jade needed to think past Dex's rage and his words, and focus on what she knew. On figuring out a way to stop him. Stop Dex or kill him.

*

As Paris stopped the car in the preserve and got out, the lizard right on his heels, he could feel magic in the air - dank and syrupy. It wasn't Jade; Paris knew the way her power felt. It must be Dex. The lizard hissed and its Elizabethan collar came up, fanning out around its face like a strange, green halo. It didn't like the magic either, which made the hairs on Paris' neck stand upright. It gave a hoarse bark and scampered off into the forest line, its tail leaving a zigzag trail behind it.

"Wait!" Paris called ineffectually before starting to hustle after it. It didn't move fast, probably due to its short, stumpy legs. Its belly was low to the ground, dragging over protruding tree roots and low shrubs. It stuck to the path and instead of sniffing the ground like a dog or wolf might do, Paris found it stopped every few feet and then flared up its Elizabethan collar - like it was a satellite searching for a signal. It would pause and then continue on. At one point, it stopped and seemed torn. It looked off the path, deeper into the forest, toward where the lake was and Paris stepped closer to it and spoke without realizing he intended to.

"I don't think that's her. That's just the lake."

It blinked up at him; its iridescent eyes glowing slightly and then turned away from the direction of the lake and back on the path.

Not two minutes later, it stopped again and hissed - a loud, thick wet sound and Paris was sure that if he'd been in front of the creature when it happened, he would have been covered in some kind of spit and foam. Gooseflesh rose on Paris' arms and he took a step back as he felt a wave of magic out there, in the forest, coming for him. It was strong and dark. He blinked as he realized it wasn't just coming for him, it was coming for the entire Coven - blood magic. The taint on the air was thick and coppery. Paris patted himself down wildly, hoping he had something sharp enough on himself to draw his own blood for a counter-hex. Not knowing what was coming made it damn near impossible, but he had to at least try. As his hand closed around the car keys, he could hear his mother's voice in his head, '*blood to commence, blood for defense,*' - one of her old-witch sayings to remind him that to fight blood magic, you needed blood magic. He was just about to jab his hand with a key and hope it would be sharp enough to break the skin, when the lizard-creature swept its tail up and over its own body, swirling it, almost swinging it like a bat. Paris thought he saw something - a bolt of light or a strobe of power - ricochet off the lizard's tail and blast off to the left. The lizard made a horrible screeching sound and fell to its side.

Paris was stunned to find himself unharmed. He moved closer to where the lizard lay on the ground panting quietly, eyes blinking, forked pink tongue lolling out of its mouth. It had just saved him from whatever magic had come for him in the forest. Paris was fairly certain it hadn't stopped the magic from affecting the rest of the Coven, but it had certainly stopped it from hitting him. He put a hand on the creature's side finding the skin a little rough and warm to the touch. The smell of the blood magic was gone, replaced by a more familiar feeling - that of Jade's magic. It carried a faint floral scent he couldn't quite place and also a spicy undertone - cloves, he thought. The creature panted, its eyes rolling around in their sockets until they met Paris' own.

"Thank you," Paris said quietly. He'd never heard of anyone defended by a familiar before. It must be quite an extraordinary creature. The clove scent became stronger and as the creature's breathing slowed down, Paris had the sense that it wasn't going to die, but it did need to rest after such a feat. Its eyes darted up the trail and then back at Paris and he swore he could feel the creature urging him on.

"We'll come back for you," Paris said lowly, feeling like he owed this strange animal that at the very least.

He set off again into the forest to find Jade, to find Dex.

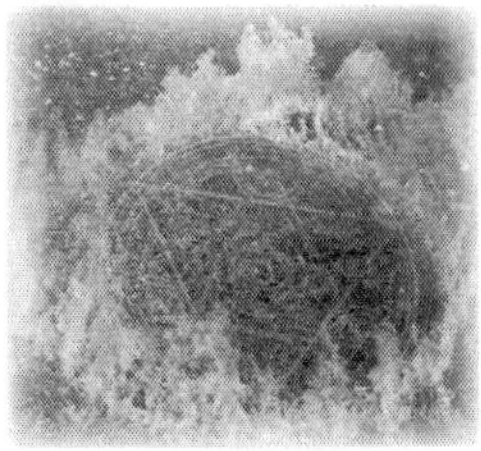

CHAPTER 14

Jade watched, trapped in her own circle, as Dex pulled a small knife from his pocket and slashed open his palm, making a fist, letting blood drip onto the forest floor. "If you won't bend under a Coven spell, then I'll cast another, just for you. A blood spell, a spell by name. Have you ever even heard one, Jade?"

She hadn't. She didn't know if she should be afraid or not. She got the bit about the blood magic - pretty sure it was bad news - but she had no idea what was so different about a blood spell by name. What did it matter? Jade slunk backwards another inch, feeling the barrier of her circle against her back, hot and tingly.

"Not even your circle can protect you," Dex murmured. Jade's circle flared in front of her, as though sensing his menace. "Not from a named blood spell. There's a reason they're so rare. Bastardized and twisted as they're handed down, not every caster can survive one. Only a handful of witches have the chops to make it work." When he grinned, he reminded Jade of a jackal, glittering eyes and sharp teeth. "You have to be strong enough, cruel enough. You'll hand over those grimoires like they belong to me; like you never even realized they shouldn't be mine. We'll be best friends," he said with a leer. "Maybe even more than that."

Jade felt sick as he started murmuring something and she thought she could almost recognize it. Like hearing a German telecast, she felt she was so close to understanding what Dex was saying, if only she could concentrate enough. It sounded harsh - all consonants - t's, k's, and some f's. She felt cold as she listened to the syllables - a bone deep chill that made her marrow ache. She could feel the power of his words, the age of them, pressing down against her circle. His spell was like predatory barbed fingers, pushing against the edge, looking for soft spots in her magic. Holding her circle against it was like holding a heavy weight, high above her. She could feel the strain building in her head, in her chest. His magic clawed against hers - sharp and venomous. If she had to put a word to it, it would be 'toxic.' It made her skin feel grimy and dirty. The flames of her circle lit up against it, burning blue and purple against the onslaught of his spell.

Jade didn't have to know the language to know when he was getting close to the end. The way he ogled her, eyes alight and a slight smile on his face, was the only clue she needed. Her heart rabbit-beat, thumping in her chest. She couldn't move - she was using all her power to hold her circle, hoping it would be enough. She didn't want to know what would happen if it wasn't. Would she be like a prisoner in her own mind? Would she end up like a soulless automaton? Would she know she was under a spell? Marching under Dex's orders, doing what he said, all the while screaming inside? Jade only understood the last word he said - the one he hissed even as he stepped closer - a word she would always hold close to her heart.

"Lily."

Jade couldn't be sure if the jolt she felt was from the spell or from him saying her name, Lily's name. She flinched, her flames spurting like they'd been sprayed by a shot of premium tequila. Jade blinked, feeling the strange heat from her fire - hot, but not burning - lapping at her face. She looked up at Dex, expecting something - maybe for him to seem benevolent or for her to feel something different toward him, something fond or kind. He seemed so sure his spell would work and to be honest, she feared it would too. The way it had pressed against her own magic - scratching at the door - she thought it would find a way in. But nothing seemed to be happening. Jade stayed where she was, leaning away from him, still within the confines of her circle. He was still a megalomaniac; she still disliked him, maybe hated him. He was just as ugly and wrong to her as he'd ever been.

Dex frowned, eyes narrowing on her. "No." He shook his head. "That's your name, your real name. I read your file. Your name used to be Lily."

"It was never *my* name," Jade said, not sure why she felt the need to make the distinction to him of all people. The words just slipped from her lips.

His eyebrows came together in a sharp 'V' and as he stared, Jade got the feeling he was trying to figure her out, like a puzzle or a lock. She shifted on the ground, inside her circle, her feet getting tangled in some desiccating vines and debris. Looking at them, Jade felt a nudging at her brain, like a tapping on her grey matter, and she focused on the vines. She shifted her feet a bit, noting how they were somehow caught by the organic matter.

Not caught, a voice whispered in her head. *Bound.*

Jade shivered in response. She wasn't sure if she'd really heard the words or if she'd imagined them. They might have been her own words or they might have been… someone else's. She wanted them to be someone else's. The voice in her head sounded just like-

Focus. Bound.

The words were soft, smooth. They felt like cold water on a fever or burn, chasing away the sting and pain with a soothing touch. Jade hadn't had that feeling in a long time. Not since she'd lost Lily. Jade tried to focus. She thought about the word and what it could mean.

Then she remembered. In Sakkara's grimoire, with all her demon magic, there'd been a spell. A spell to bind a witch's power, keep him or her from using magic. Jade didn't know for how long, or if it would even work. But she didn't need it to be forever. She only needed it to be enough to stop Dex *now*. Maybe she could get away, get Paris and he could break Dex's magic, like he'd done with the witch that tried to kill her. If Dex's magic was bound, he wouldn't be able to fight back against Paris - sort of the magical equivalent of Jade holding Dex's arms behind his back.

Her memory for printed material enabled her to see the words in her head, Sakkara's odd handwriting in her mind's eye. Dex slashed open another slit on his palm and started saying his strange words again - the blood name spell. Presumably this time he'd try it with Jade's name. At the same time, Jade started stumbling through the demon-binding spell. Her words overlapped with his hard clacking sounds and she felt his magic mash up against hers, like two waves smashing together in the ocean. He stumbled back a bit, surprised and then started speaking louder, fisting his hand tighter and dripping more blood. Jade pushed herself to her feet, pulling her magic away from the protective barrier of her circle and trying to funnel it more into the demon spell. She could feel the spell trying to catch, like tires on a slippery surface. She pushed at it, feeling it skitter way from under her control. Jade had to stop, refocus her thoughts and start again. Dex's magic was against hers, a frantic, mindless beast clawing at her power. He was rage and fury against her circle. Bits of his magic broke through as Jade pulled more of her focus into the demon spell. She felt sharp licks of pain like tiny teeth nipping at her skin. Her tongue tripped over the bizarre demon language of the binding spell, forcing her to speak slower than she wanted, slower than she needed. Her flames were turning a deep black-purple - whether in response to Dex's spell or her own, she wasn't sure. The flames went darker and turned cold as they continued. The comforting warmth they had brought Jade before turned to a hollow chill. The binding spell was so close to snapping into place. Jade could feel bits of it coalescing around her, swirling like a massive jigsaw puzzle. She tried to focus, tried to control it. She was losing power. It was taking too much and her head felt thick and sluggish. Dex grinned as he got to the end of his spell and spat out her name this time. Jade.

There was no jolt. There was nothing. Maybe because she was expecting it or maybe, given the incredulous look Dex was sporting, because it simply didn't work. Jade didn't know what it meant, but it gave her more time to work while Dex stopped - incredulous and enraged. Jade needed more power. Her own was getting weak and noodle-like. It felt soft in places in her mind. Press too hard and she'd fall through the holes. She knew she was bleeding out too much energy, using brute force when she should be funneling controlled bursts to the spell, but she didn't know how.

Jade felt Paris before she saw him. She felt the brittle, cold fury of his power seconds before he stepped out of the forest. Jade could see the force of Paris' magic - tactile and tangible in front of her as Dex was pushed back, off his feet and knocked into a tree.

"I need more power," Jade said, her voice clipped and harsh. She was worried that Paris would want her to explain, would ask her why, but instead, he simply stepped up to her, his hand coming through her circle easily. When Paris touched her, Jade felt a surge of his power slip alongside hers, like a shot of gasoline to a motor. He pushed his magic into her, vicious and stark. The power spiraled out of her wildly, a kaleidoscope of crazed magic.

"You have to focus, Jade. I can feel the spell you're doing, but I don't know it. I can't manage it."

He was shouting at her and until then, she didn't realize that she'd kicked up a wind storm in the forest. Branches, leaves, dirt, pine needles swirled around them fiercely, but Paris and Jade were both protected, her circle growing wide enough to encompass him. Bits of debris burned away as they met her circle, creating grey and black smoke that spun out from the edges, powered by the force of her magic.

There was too much going on. Paris' power surging through her, Dex getting to his feet and pushing his magic against hers, debris flying around, the sound of charring as bits spun off her circle, Paris yelling at her to focus, Dex screaming, the binding spell dancing just outside of her reach. The spell caught her mind. It was so close, *so close,* to being perfect, to locking into place, but it felt like she was trying to shore a mud house up in the rain - getting one side ready and stable only to have to let go and grab another side as it slid down and out of reach. An intense pain shot stabbed into her brain, slicing through the soft tissue, spongy and wet. She felt her magic wobble, felt it falter. She couldn't do this much longer. Pressure built behind Jade's sinuses, feeling like her insides were growing larger than her outsides. She pulled more power from Paris and it felt like grinding glass into her grey matter. Something warm and wet poured out of her ear and Paris was still yelling at her, maybe telling her to stop, maybe telling her to do something else, Jade couldn't tell. All she could feel was the spell, starting to become more powerful than she was. It was pulling her in, pulling her down. It was a gravity well sucking her in as it tried to fix itself, pulling her apart with its force.

Let me help you.

The voice inside her head draped over her like a thin, filmy tablecloth, covering her senses from the outside, muting the noise, the smells, the sights. Calming, soothing. The pain receded, lessened to a dull, distant ache. Jade saw everything through a long, dark tunnel now, the spell at the end. It was crisp and clear and she could easily see the broken bit. Only the one spot needed fixing - a crux point that needed an extra burst of power. But just there. Just that one spot.

That's it, there it is. You can do it.

She wanted to cry. She felt so safe with that voice in her ear and it was so easy in that moment to reach out and snap the spot into place. One last burst of power gushed through her, sucked in by the power of the spell itself and Jade saw it surge toward Dex. Just before it hit him, he shouted something, and a resounding crack of power shot out of him. He blinked out of view - a burst of smoke and light where he should have been.

With a loud sucking sound, Jade's power died. Like a ruptured sore, it burst with a feeling of pain and relief. She pitched face forward, felt Paris' grip on her arm, strong and sure, and it kept her from landing directly on her face. Paris lowered her to the ground, rolling her on her back. She felt far away, like the dream of Lily, when Lily had been underwater in the lake. This time, Jade was the one underwater - gallons of water between her and the surface - only foggy bits of light filtering through. Paris was talking to her and his voice was muffled and murky. He shook her a bit, or rather, shook her body. It was a separate entity - distinct and apart from her. Jade could see the way he moved, and her vision blurred a bit from the motion of her body, but she didn't feel it. From a distance, she saw her hand reach up and touch Paris' arm, fingering the material of his jacket and she didn't feel that either. She only sensed a casual curiosity at the sensation of touch. It too was far away and distant. Jade felt heavy, weighed down by something pressing in on her. Water pressing in on her. Everything was muddled and indistinct. Her eyelids closed, without any input from her, like curtains coming down on a stage.

Her ears popped and the world came rushing back: taste, smell, sound, touch and when she finally opened her eyes, sight.

"Jade? Can you hear me?"

She blinked at Paris and tried to push herself up a bit. One of his arms came around the back of her shoulders, helping her into a reclined position. There was a cold wet spot on each ear, running down her neck and she reached up to touch one side, seeing blood on her fingers. She looked past Paris' worried face to where Dex had been standing when he disappeared.

"Where did he go?"

Paris' fingers tightened on her shoulder. "I don't know. Teleportation spell. They're… nasty. Tricky. I didn't think anyone would be fool enough to try one. He'll be lucky to still be in one piece." He grimaced. "I'm sorry to ask, but I need you to do some magic. Anything."

Jade looked at him, not understanding the request. "I don't… what?"

"When Dex disappeared, Coven magic was released from the spell it was under, but it's still out of sorts. Like being out of tune. I need to feel your magic so I can reset the Coven's magic."

"Oh," she said, still feeling far away and confused. She thought about it and sent a puff of fire out in front of her. The spell was easy and came quick, the heat of it flaring against her skin. She let the fireball roll and twist, staring at the flickering lights, feeling drowsy. Paris' hand tightened on her own and she turned to look at him. His face was pale and a chalky in the firelight. He was moving his lips slightly and she could feel the tension in his body, hear the hum of his magic like a deep bass instrument.

Something snapped in place around her like a rubber band being plucked. A shiver worked its way through her body and when she took her next breath, she found it felt easy and light - as though she'd been breathing thin air for a long time and finally had enough oxygen.

"Did it work? Did you do it?" she asked.

He nodded grimly, his face pinched and tight. Jade had a coworker back in her other life, before the Coven, that got migraines. They would come on suddenly and sometimes her coworker, Francis, had to leave for the rest of the day. He would get the same pinched look on his face that Paris had now - as though his skin could crack at the edges of his eyes and lips. Jade wondered if what he'd just done had been painful. It seemed like it had been tiring. Paris shifted a bit, coming behind her. "Can you stand? We should get you out of here."

"Yeah. Okay," she said half-heartedly and then made absolutely no effort to move.

"Jade," prompted Paris, getting his arms under hers and prodding her a bit. "Stand up."

She looked down, still feeling disconnected from her body. Jade wiggled her feet a bit, taking in the sensation of sending the signal to her feet and having them answer. "Oh, yeah." She pushed her heels into the ground and Paris hefted her up, steadying her when she wobbled.

"Are you okay to walk?" he asked and she thought it was kind of late to be inquiring about that now since she was on her feet and moving. He gave her an odd look and she realized she'd said it out loud.

"I think so," Jade added. She still felt fuzzy and distant. "I'd like to go home now."

Paris nodded slowly and then set off into the forest. Jade reached out and snagged the back of his jacket, feeling odd and disconnected until she had something to hang on to. Paris didn't say anything so she guessed it was okay. She focused on the ground beneath her feet, the snap of twigs and leaves as she walked, the smell of the forest air in her nose.

She tried not to think at all about the voice she'd heard in her head. The presence she'd felt in her body. It was a presence and voice so familiar and well-known to her that it was unmistakable.

Lily.

*

Paris led the way through the forest, working back toward where he'd left the lizard creature. He sincerely hoped the strange animal was doing better than when Paris had left him - he didn't think he had it in him to carry it back. As soon as Dex disappeared, Paris felt the Coven's magic released from whatever spell it had been under, but instead of rebounding back to how it should be, it continued to wobble out of sync. Paris knew he had a short window of opportunity to reset it while it was still freshly freed, before it found a bad frequency or a tainted ley line and became twisted. He hadn't wanted to push Jade to use magic, but she was there and he knew her magic was good. He hadn't had any other reference point, and given the other spell that Dex had cast, the one on their memories, Paris hadn't quite trusted his own memory on how Coven Magic should feel. Once Jade had cast her small fire spell, he'd brought the Coven magic in line with her - effectively tuning them all to Jade. He didn't look forward to explaining that at the next Department Head meeting.

The control and precision it took left him with a piercing migraine - it throbbed in time with his pulse, making his eyes water and squint against the light poking through the trees.

Jade was wobbly on her feet behind Paris - her hand fisted in his coat - trudging along behind him with heavy footsteps. Paris felt like Orpheus leading Eurydice out from the Underworld. He had to keep resisting the urge to turn around and ask if Jade was all right. She was keeping up, so he assumed she was. She would tell him if she needed to stop.

Paris also wasn't sure, if he turned around, if he could keep from asking her about what had happened back at the clearing.

He recalled, as he'd followed the air of magic to where she and Dex were, hearing Dex casting a spell.

He'd arrived just as Dex was proclaiming that he'd read Jade's file and he knew her real name was Lily.

Jade had answered back that Lily had never been her name.

Paris distinctly remembered asking Jade about it once. He'd seen a picture of a young girl; a girl who looked like Jade and he'd asked why the name on the back of the photo said Lily. Jade told Paris she'd changed her name, and Paris had seen documentation to that effect. A name change had been filed when Jade was twenty-one, changing her official first name from Lily to Jade. But in the clearing, he remembered her exact words when Dex had confronted her.

It was never my name.

Then, there had been the moment, right after Dex had disappeared, when Jade had fallen. A surge of magic burned in the air and she pitched forward. Paris managed to keep her from landing on her face and breaking her nose. She'd been disoriented, looking around as though she didn't know where she was. He'd shaken her a bit, trying to snap her out of whatever reverie she'd become stuck in. When she looked at Paris, he'd gotten the sudden, stark feeling she didn't know who he was. She'd looked at him as though he was a complete stranger - her eyebrows frowning, her lips slightly pursed, her eyes crinkled at the corners. When he looked at her, he didn't see the usual cold grey of her irises.

Her eyes had been green. A bright, vibrant green he'd never seen before.

She'd reached up and touched his coat as though testing the material to see if it were real. Then her eyes had closed and she jolted like she'd been shot;

her fingers clamping around his arm like a claw. When she opened her eyes, they'd gone back to grey.

Paris wondered if what he saw was real. If it was the left over magic coursing through the area. Or if it were something else.

"Bruce!"

The sound of Jade's voice broke him out of his thoughts as she pushed past him. The lizard creature he'd left on the ground was waddling toward them awkwardly, its loping gait off-kilter and bizarre.

Jade hunkered down in front of it and it leapt forward an inch, its pink tongue darting out and kissing Jade on the nose.

"What are you doing here?" Jade asked it, rubbing her hand over its head and then scratching underneath the flap that was its Elizabethan collar.

"I was at your house looking for you when Veronica called."

"So she did call you," Jade said quietly, settling her knees on the ground. The lizard put one clawed foot up on Jade's thigh, claiming her.

Paris nodded grimly. "She did and explained some… things. When I left to come here, it followed me. It was sleeping on one of your t-shirts in your living room."

Jade glanced down, pursing her lips, looking like a kid who'd been caught stealing cookies. "Yeah, he came by after he escaped and… well…"

"You didn't say anything."

"I felt bad for him!" she said, looking up at him with wide eyes. Paris looked from her to the lizard and then back again - the two of them giving him large, sympathy-inducing cow eyes. He couldn't help but check that Jade's were still firmly grey. Not a trace of green in sight.

Paris sighed. "Did you know you'd made him a familiar?"

Jade frowned. "I don't even know what that is."

Paris' head hurt way too much to continue having this discussion in the middle of the forest. "Right. Well. We can discuss it later."

They continued their trek through the forest, Paris leading again, Jade behind him and behind Jade, the lizard. Who was apparently named Bruce, if Paris heard correctly. Paris wondered why Jade had called it - him- that. He wondered why she felt the need to keep it a secret.

He wondered why her eyes had turned green. He wondered why she had told Dex that Lily was never her name. He wondered why she hadn't yet gone back and gotten her things from her other apartment. He wondered a lot of things about her. He'd realized previously that after he brought her to the Coven, he hadn't investigated anything about her or her past at all and he'd neglected it since. To be honest, he hadn't even thought of it. Paris knew the history of most witches in his Coven, or rather, he knew they had grown up in the Coven and he was sure if he had any questions, with only a slight bit of work, he could get any answers he wanted.

With Jade it was an entirely different story. If he wanted answers, he was going to have to dig.

They made it to his car without further incident, Jade opening up the back door and gesturing for Bruce to hop in, which he did, surprisingly agile for his size.

"We should go to the Covenstead and have you examined by Dr. Gellar," Paris said lowly, turning the engine over.

"Yeah," Jade replied, absently rubbing at the dried blood under one of her ear canals, staring out the window at the forest. "I feel okay though."

He gave her a pointed look and she turned to face him, sensing his gaze on her.

"What? I mean I'm not going to go run a marathon and I'm pretty sure Gellar will say I just pushed too hard and used too much magic. I've got a headache. I'll likely get told to take two aspirin and call her in the morning. Unless..." Jade trailed off looking closer at him. "Unless you need to go? You look a little rough around the edges."

Paris sighed. He was squinting against the light, his migraine getting more sensitive. Resetting Coven magic hadn't been something he'd ever thought he'd have to do. He also felt the push-pull of his own magic as it struggled to find a new norm, tuned to Jade's magic instead of what it had been used to for his entire life. It was like breaking in a new brand of running shoes after mile-ing out an old favorite - he felt confined and chafed in some places, but was marveling at the better fit in others. It didn't mean it was entirely comfortable.

"Uh, do you need me to drive?" Jade asked. Paris realized he'd been silent for a couple minutes and hadn't answered her question. He looked out at the dirt road and his eyes narrowed even more when he looked up at the bright sky.

"Yep," Jade said quickly, unbuckling her seat belt. "Let's swap."

He managed to get out and trudge to the other side of the car, sliding into the passenger seat gratefully as Jade got behind the wheel. Paris rested his head against the seat watching her as she cracked her neck a bit and adjusted the seat and mirrors. He noticed the trail of blood trickling from her ear. It was slighter than it was on the other ear and he had a surge of guilt for making her drive. She didn't feel well either.

Jade turned to him and while her eyes were still solidly grey, they did seem somewhat brighter than usual, framed by tiny red veins in their whites. "You can sleep if you want. I know the way back to the Covenstead."

Paris thought he may have managed a slight nod, but couldn't be sure. He felt a nudge against his elbow and looked down to see the yellow-green muzzle of Bruce, Jade's familiar, prodding against his arm. Bruce looked up at Paris and his eyes flickered reflectively for a moment. Paris patted him twice on the head and Bruce let out a low 'pffft' sound. Paris lasted long enough to feel the rough road beneath them transition to pavement as they exited the preserve parking area and made it back on the main drag before he drifted to sleep.

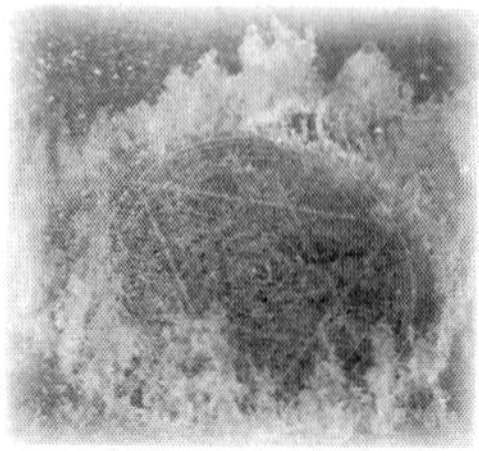

CHAPTER 15

"I see an empty glass!" Henri called, pointing at Jade as she finished off her red wine.

Callie came out of her kitchen waving an open bottle of red. "I'm here! Crisis averted!"

Jade smiled as she held her glass out for Callie to slosh wine into it. Jade's eyes went wide as Callie kept pouring well past the point where the glass was comfortably full.

"Whoa!" Jade exclaimed, as Callie finally finished pouring, the glass precariously full. "I haven't eaten since lunch!"

"It's the Coven Ball pre-party party!" Callie said with a flourish, brandishing the wine bottle like it wasn't as full as it still was.

"To be followed by the actual party and then the post-party party," Henri said helpfully, sipping from his own glass.

Callie invited Jade and Henri to get ready at her house before the Coven Ball and truth be told, Jade had been glad for the invite. She'd never been to a big party like the ball and she was happy for the company as she figured out her hair and makeup. Time and tide wait for no one, and never had that been clearer than when Jade realized the day after she stopped Dex, the Coven Ball was still that weekend and she hadn't managed to get her dress to the tailor. She originally worried that it wouldn't be ready in time for the dance but the tailor, the husband of a Coven witch, had said he would be happy to have it ready for the event, especially given how she'd managed to restore their magic. Jade had mumbled some kind of thanks, not really sure how the tailor knew what had happened, and then left. By the time she got to the coffee shop, she'd been stopped twice more. Once to thank her for her work and once to ask her how she managed to run with her magic all off kilter 'like this' the witch had said, gesturing wildly.

Confused, Jade had made her way directly to Paris and he'd explained that when he'd reset Coven magic, he'd set it to match Jade's magic - the only magic he knew to be fully functional at the time. Jade found out even more about it when she arrived in Counter-Magic later on that day. Though Coven magic had been reset, the incident log was still as long as it had been during the time when it was broken. Although spells didn't seem to be malfunctioning completely now, they were slightly off as people worked on reconfiguring their magic to the new norm. Jade found she was the focus of a lot of sideways stares and some hushed words, but it didn't seem as ostracizing as it had before.

She was looking forward to the big gala. She carefully sipped from her glass, watching the meniscus in case it tipped over the edge. Damn,

Callie had gotten it full. Jade was tempted to ask if she'd used magic to pour like that. Setting her glass down, Jade picked up a few more bobby pins and secured a couple of places in her hair that felt wobbly. Callie persuaded Jade to wear her hair down for the Coven Ball and Jade lasted about an hour until the tenth time she had to push her hair out of her face and it got caught in her lip gloss. She'd managed some kind of messy half bun, half pony-tail that she would likely never be able to replicate. Callie worked on curling some bits and pieces that fell out. Jade ducked out of the way of the hot-iron three times as Callie waved it while she regaled them with stories from last year's ball before Jade declared her hair done and Callie blessedly set the curling iron down. Henri smirked at Jade over his own wine glass as Jade breathed a sigh of relief.

"Your shoes!" Henri said suddenly, getting up from the dining room table and heading for his bag at the front door. "You will cry when you see them."

Jade turned to Callie. "Is that a good thing or bad thing? Good like 'they're so pretty' I'll cry or bad like, 'you'll need thirty-six bandages and a partial skin graft after you wear these for two hours.'"

Callie laughed. "The former I hope."

"You hope?" Jade repeated sharply, faking a smile as Henri came back waving a bag.

Jade didn't exactly cry, but she could admit she was moved by the shoes. They were so pretty. Shiny, sparkly and dainty, they also had a slightly wider heel that meant she wouldn't be falling on her ass all night. They looked like Cinderella shoes and Jade felt her girlish heart melt at the sight of them.

She slid her feet in and felt a slight pinch at the toes. Okay, there may be some crying and bandages later, but these shoes would be worth it. She turned her feet to the left and right, then pointed and flexed them, checking her feet out in the shoes.

"See?" Henri said.

"If I die, bury me in these shoes."

Callie swooped her wine glass down and clinked it against Jade's, making Jade's slosh a bit and spill wine on the table. Callie automatically spat out a spell, one that was presumably supposed to take the stain away, but instead turned it a deeper shade of purple. She murmured, "Your magic's so different," under her breath and then made a 'pish' sound and declared she would worry about things like wine stains tomorrow.

The sound of a car horn from outside made them all turn their heads like meerkats toward the door, each realizing that at some point, Nick and Daniel (Callie and Henri's boyfriends respectively) had turned off the sports channel and snuck outside to get the car. Jade grabbed her coat and purse and was at the door, swinging it open while Henri was still shrugging into his suit jacket and Callie valiantly finished off her glass of wine.

Jade was seriously impressed. She didn't think you could drink wine like that without some kind of side effect. Was there a wine equivalent of brain freeze? From the way Callie polished off her glass, there mustn't be.

Daniel was waiting at the door to hustle them along, giving Callie a hand as she stumbled out, pausing to lock the door behind them. Nick, Callie's partner, leaned out the driver's side window and cat-called at them, honking his horn a few more times for good measure. Daniel escorted them down the steps and toward the car where Callie, with her slighter build, got sandwiched between Jade and Henri in the backseat, Daniel and Nick up front. The car was full of chatter and excitement and Jade was swept up in the noise, letting it wash over her.

The few days since Dex and Veronica had disappeared had been tiring. Jade had been careful to keep herself as busy as she could. Immediately after they'd left the preserve, Jade'd taken Paris to the Covenstead and both of them submitted to a cursory exam by Gellar. Jade received her prescription of 'take two aspirin, drink plenty of fluids and get some rest' and promptly ignored it. She'd gone home and done a load of laundry, showered and then gone out, gotten a coffee and then eyed her garden shed. It seemed like forever ago that Paris had told her to look at her little shed and find the tools she needed for her lawn. Indeed, once inside, she found a wide-toothed rake and she used it to pull the fallen leaves on her front yard into three piles, focusing on making the piles even and resolutely not thinking about anything that had happened in the preserve. Only at that point, when she felt like if she lay down she would sleep as soon as her head hit the pillow, did she call the day over.

Despite her fatigue, she must have woken up long enough in the middle of the night to move to the closet. She woke up there with no memory of moving. Bruce had been tucked up against her back, the two of them jammed into the closet like stuffed animals in a shipping box - limbs all over, pressed up against the wall, blankets mashed up.

Jade tried not to think about it.

She didn't think about the voice she'd heard in her mind when she'd been in the forest fighting Dex. It was hard. It was like sticking a sliver of wood under the soft skin of her finger and then trying not to touch it. She kept busy. Jade went to work early in the morning and stayed a little later at night than she needed to. Josef said she was really good at logging incidents and since the Coven's magic was tuned to Jade's now, he was letting her take some of the easier cases. Jade found she was quickly able to figure out where spells or hex work had gone wrong and was faster than the more experienced agents at resetting the magic. The other agents were catching up as they became more accustomed to her magic's frequency, but Jade finally felt like she was making inroads, learning magic faster than before.

In the evenings, she hung out with Callie or Henri or both. She switched her running time with Daniel for a couple days to have it after work instead of before. She did a remarkable job of keeping herself totally occupied, all the while knowing exactly from what she was keeping herself occupied, or rather, from whom.

Jade didn't know if she was ready to think about Lily; or since there was never really a day when she didn't think about Lily, maybe she just wasn't ready to think about what happened in the forest.

She'd heard Lily. She'd felt Lily. Or had she? Jade started doubting herself. She started doubting that she'd felt anything in the forest other than a part of herself that missed Lily. At that moment, trying to fight against Dex, Jade had desperately needed help.

Maybe she just imagined Lily's presence. Maybe it had been nothing but the power of Jade's mind.

"Jade, we're here."

Henri's hand on her forearm jolted her out of her wool-gathering and she forced her best fake smile and let him help her out of the car, leaning on him a little as she got her feet underneath her, still adjusting to the new shoes.

Yep. Definitely going to need some of those bandages by the night's end.

They ditched their coats behind Henri's desk in the front foyer, leaving them in a big pile on his chair. The cafeteria lights had been dimmed and the room had been decorated tastefully with things that Jade had only ever seen on Pinterest or the cover of magazines. She didn't even know what they were called - except for the flowers and trees. She could at least recognize them. The large, filmy drapes and bows however were beyond her vocabulary. The entire room looked like a cold winter fairyland with everything dusted with light snow.

"Oh wow," she said. "It's like Frosty the Snowman threw up in here."

Callie snorted, which set everyone else off on a bit of a laughing jag and Jade felt a little gauche and out of place until Callie placed a hand on her arm and said, "Oh my god it does! Like it's nice, but it can be a bit much, right?" Nick draped his free arm over Callie's petite shoulder and she tucked in a little closer. They seemed to fit so easily together that Jade felt a momentary pang of something she couldn't identify. Callie nodded to someone over Jade's shoulder and Jade turned to see Paris walking toward them. Unlike the last few times Jade had seen him around the Coven when he looked tired and worn, tonight he looked more relaxed. He was in a dark suit with a brilliant blue kerchief tucked in his pocket. He was holding a drink, a short, squat glass of amber liquid, and Jade cast her eyes around looking for a bar or a place where she could get one, suddenly worried she forgot her wallet. Stupid tiny purse. She knew she put her debit and credit cards in as well as some cash and her ID, but she felt the sudden urge to check. By the time Paris joined them, Jade had her nose in her purse, counting through her stuff and feeling better now that she knew things were where they should be. The greetings everyone was exchanging felt weird and stiff so when it came time for Jade to say hello to Paris she just jerked her chin at him and said, "Hey, what's up?"

It took her a moment to realize that Callie, Henri, Nick and Daniel were pulling away, leaving her with Paris and goddamn, she still didn't know where to get a drink from.

"I like your hanky," Jade said, gesturing with her finger at the blue scrap of fabric.

Paris inclined his head in thanks. "I'll be sure to mention it to Hannah, it was a gift from her."

"Ah, that explains it," Jade said with a nod. It matched his eyes and he didn't seem like the kind of guy that would pick it out for himself. It was totally something a mom or someone like Hannah would do.

"Explains what?"

"It, um, matches-" Jade stammered a bit feeling silly saying it out loud. "You, I mean, eyeball, I mean - it matches your eyes." She felt a little hot and flustered. "Where did you get that drink?"

"There's an open bar over where the coffee creamers usually are."

"Open bar? Seriously? I thought the whole point of the pre-party party Callie had was to get us tipsy enough so we wouldn't go broke here."

Paris smirked. "No, Callie just likes to drink."

"I'll say. Man, her liver must take up her entire torso. She can put it away."

He smiled more fully, his eyes crinkling at the corners. "Come, let's get you a drink."

*

Paris gestured off to the side and Jade blinked few times and then fell in step beside him. They walked in a companionable silence to the bar where a young man in standard waiter uniform looked up expectantly at them.

"Whatever he's having," Jade said with a wave and Paris raised an eyebrow, wondering if she even knew what he was drinking. The bartender nodded once and then set out a glass and poured two fingers worth of liquor. As he returned the bottle to the shelf, Jade turned to Paris quickly. "Do I tip? Is that the thing to do here?" she asked sotto voice. He gave her a curt nod and Jade fished around in her purse for a tip and then plunked it in a jar off to the side. She took a sip of her drink and coughed.

"God almighty, what is this?" she said, her eyes watering.

"Canadian whiskey," Paris answered with a small smile, taking a drink of his own.

Jade fanned herself a bit, coughing. "Holy god. That's. Wow."

"It'll put hair on your chest."

She gave him a look. "Let's hope not." She took a tentative second sip, seemingly more careful this time. "Nope, I'm gonna have to cut that." She turned to the bartender. "I need a tall glass and some ginger ale."

After being provided both, Jade mixed her drink and chewed a bit on the stir stick absently, looking Paris over.

"So, how's Coven business?" she asked without preamble, leaning up a bit against the bar. Paris gave the bartender a glance and the young man made himself busy elsewhere.

"It's been… trying."

"You looked tired," Jade blurted and then continued, "I mean not now, now you look… good, you know, the suit and the hanky and all, but… whatever, I'm just saying… are things better now?"

Paris inclined his head slightly. Things were slightly better now. He'd spent the most of the week trying to figure out suitable replacements for both Dex and Veronica's Covens. Neither of them had been seen since the incident. Dex, Paris understood. He wasn't the sort to face up to his actions and there was also the possibility that his teleportation spell had gone badly. They weren't known for being the most stable spells and could lead to disfigurement, dementia or a combination of both. Veronica, Paris had hoped, would turn herself back over to either Paris or to her Coven, but she hadn't been heard from. Paris, along with his senior leaders, was still trying to vet the remaining members of both Dex and Veronica's Covens. While it appeared that both of them were acting independently of their Covens, Paris wasn't willing to take the chance. Fool him once and all that. It also meant that all the decisions that would normally have been left to Dex and Veronica were coming to Paris' Coven now. While Paris always felt he had good people, he wasn't exactly in a trusting mood at the moment. He'd finally gotten a handle on both of their Covens, at least administratively, and there were some good candidates for Coven Leaders. Until they could be fully vetted, Josef from Counter-Magic agreed to temporarily act as Coven Leader for Dex's Coven and Claire from R & D agreed to look after Veronica's.

"Things are settling down," he said finally, taking another sip of his drink.

Jade chewed on her lip for a moment and then said, "Hey, I'm sorry, you know. Veronica said you guys were… well, close and it must really suck to find out that she was," Jade waved her fingers about, "a turncoat or whatever you guys call witches gone bad. I mean, she helped out in the end, so that was good but, it's shitty for you. And your history with her. Of stuff. You know, together."

"Thank you," he said quietly. She looked like she wanted to add more, but ended up taking another sip of her drink, only grimacing slightly as she swallowed.

"Good evening, everyone."

Jade and Paris both turned their heads toward the back of the room where Hannah was standing with a microphone.

"I didn't even know pants were an option," Jade hissed lowly. Hannah was in a smart darkly colored pantsuit and Jade looked at Paris like he'd betrayed her.

"I'm sorry?" he said, not quite sure what she was talking about.

"You should be," Jade replied just before Hannah spoke again.

"Paris was gracious enough to let me handle our blessing tonight," Hannah continued and Paris grimaced slightly. By being 'gracious' Hannah meant, 'called her close to midnight the day before and nearly begged her to take over since he hadn't had time to prepare anything.' He was damn lucky she was always there for him. "This has been a trying time and I speak on behalf of the entire Coven Leadership when I thank you for your continued support and understanding, especially as we transition our magic." Ah, there it was - the slight grumble of the crowd as Hannah addressed the change in their magic. Paris watched carefully to see if there was anyone bitter or upset. There seemed to be a general sense of discontent, but it didn't appear to be onerous. Hannah gave the entire room a formidable stare - the stare of an older woman who would not be trifled with. It was quite the look and Paris saw a few people cast their eyes down and away in deference. "Please use the resources at your disposal if you have any issues. We do best when we act together. Blessed be."

The sentiment was echoed by the room at large, Paris included, and he saw Jade glance around quickly, from the corner of his eye and it occurred to him he hadn't had a chance to let her know there would be a small speech tonight. He only had a brief moment to think, 'Oh shit,' before Hannah went on and he realized how well and truly screwed he was. "We are very fortunate tonight to formally welcome Jade to our Coven." Hannah paused, her gaze directed toward Jade. Every eye in the room turned around to look at Paris and Jade as they stood at the back by the bar.

Jade turned to him, possibly the calmest he'd ever seen her and said in a cool tone, "I'm going to kill you while you sleep."

"I mentioned this part of the evening," he replied, fighting the urge to pull at his tie.

"Yeah, a week ago and I got the distinct impression it was optional."

It may have been optional if Paris was leading the speeches, but it was clearly not when Hannah was in charge.

"It will be a lovely gesture both from the Coven and you."

"Jade, why don't you come up here, dear?" Hannah called.

Jade grit her teeth. "I've got a lovely gesture for you," she said to Paris.

"Bring Paris with you," Hannah added. She was using an overly sunny tone and Paris was sure she knew very well what was going on at the back of the room.

Paris could see in Jade's eyes she was contemplating saying, 'no' and not budging from where she was. He saw the moment Jade caught sight of Callie and Henri making enthusiastic 'come on up here' motions with their hands - faces wide with smiles. Jade looked sideways at Paris and kind of jerked her head at him in a resigned 'shall we go?' gesture and she led the way over to Hannah.

Hannah had to tilt her head to look up at Jade, who stood quite tall in her heels. She came forward to grab one of Jade's hands and clasp it between her own. Jade slouched a bit as though adjusting her height to compensate for Hannah's stature.

"Jade," said Hannah. "I hope you know how welcome you are to the Coven, though I fear you do not yet believe it." Hannah searched Jade's eyes for a moment, seemingly looking for something and patted Jade's hand. "Being part of the Coven means you will have the protection of our number and the affection of our hearts. I hope that you continue to remember this as you remain with us. Being part of a family means that you won't always like everyone and they won't always like you." Jade snorted a bit at that, a wry smile curling her lips. "But," Hannah continued, her voice firm, "you always have a place here. We are all separate and yet we are one. Now, I believe Paris has something for you."

Hannah raised one eyebrow at Paris as if daring him to contradict her and he was bloody grateful that even in the chaos of the past week, he'd not forgotten Jade's talisman. He reached into the inner pocket of his jacket and pulled out the long silver chain with the charm at the end. He stepped forward and spoke lowly, knowing however that the entire Coven would be craning their ears to hear what he'd chosen and why.

"I've chosen a salamander for your talisman, Jade. The salamander is traditionally associated with fire, which you've shown to wield spectacularly. It's also a symbol of courage, enduring faith and loyalty, which I hope will all be synonymous with your time at the Coven."

Jade's eyes had zeroed in on the small, curved lizard at the bottom of the chain and she reached out and pinched it between her fingers, turning it over and examining it. He had a rush of nerves that she wouldn't like it, but she grinned and said, "It kinda looks like Bruce."

Paris felt his nerves dissipate at her fond look. "That too." He handed the necklace over to Hannah who clasped it in her hands. Paris felt a rush of magic as Hannah's power poked at the talisman checking Paris magic. Hannah gave a satisfied nod and Paris was man enough to admit he breathed a small sigh of relief.

"I bind this talisman to the one we call Jade, for her security and guidance. May it be a source of power and protection for as long as she wears it." Hannah spoke loud enough for the Coven to hear her, her voice ringing out in the room with surprising volume for a woman so slight.

In her heels, Jade had to bend down quite far for Hannah to be able to place the necklace over her head and around her neck. Before Jade could straighten back up fully, Hannah clasped her shoulders and pulled her in for a hug. "Welcome to the Coven, Jade," Hannah said. Their embrace was made all the more awkward by the difference in their heights. Hannah kissed her on the cheek in a motherly fashion and Jade stumbled slightly to balance in her heels. Hannah finally released her and Jade wobbled back upright. Paris had to bite his lip to keep from laughing at the look of surprise on Jade's face. He looked a little closer at her.

"Are you blushing?" he asked incredulously.

"Shut up. I am not," Jade said back. She was indeed blushing slightly, tugging a bit at the hem of her dress with one hand as if she could make it longer. He resolved not to tease her about it further and instead turned to the last thing he had left to do for tonight. He began in a clear voice that could be heard at least by those in the front row. He was sure with Coven gossip being what it was, his words would make it to the back row by the time they sat down to eat.

"I apologize, Jade."

Jade looked a little confused, glancing sideways at the crowd watching them and then back to him. "Uh, for what?"

"You tried to warn me, warn the Coven about Dex and I didn't listen to you. It's another reason I chose the salamander for your charm. As I mentioned, it's a symbol of loyalty and courage, both of which you showed when you defended our Coven from an outside influence that meant us harm."

She swallowed and looked a little like a deer in headlights, her eyes darting again to the crowd and back to him, like she thought she might be the only one that realized they were in front of a crowd of people. Paris meant to apologize to Jade the day she stopped Dex, and he meant to do it every day since, but then realized that in order to make it as meaningful as possible, he really should do it in front of the Coven. He'd come to the realization that he hadn't made Jade's transition to Coven life as easy as he could have and hoped this would start to make amends.

"On behalf of the Coven, I thank you. For myself, I apologize for not treating your suspicions and accusations with the care and attention they deserved."

"Uh, well, you were kind of under a spell. All of you. But, um, apology accepted. And you're welcome," she finished, her voice halting and somewhat stilted.

On a whim, he leaned over in a parody of Hannah, to kiss her on the cheek. He told himself that if Jade moved away, he would respect her distance but instead, she froze, as still as a field rabbit seeing movement on the plain. He kept his kiss polite and perfunctory - nearly indistinguishable from Hannah's, but as he pulled back, he saw she was blushing even more, watching him carefully. She looked like she wanted to ask him a question, but instead, she pulled back, putting distance between them again.

Paris offered her a small smile and then turned to the rest of the coven at large. "And now if you will all take your seats, dinner will be served."

*

As predicted, Jade needed several bandages on her feet. She waved goodbye at Callie and Henri, both of them hanging out opposite sides of the back of Nick's car, with Callie blowing Jade one last kiss before Nick pulled away. Back in her little cottage, Jade took off her Cinderella shoes and surveyed the damage to her feet. Bruce padded down the stairs and flicked his tongue at her.

"The price of beauty, Bruce. High and painful," Jade said, as she wiggled her toes into the rug at the front door.

Washing off her makeup and brushing her teeth were always tiresome chores she wished she could skip, but with the amount of extra makeup she was wearing tonight, it wasn't optional. She wobbled a bit as she continued her nighttime routine. Damn

Canadian whiskey. She'd had two more after the first one and she wasn't even sure why. It tasted awful, but there was definitely something about it.

Back in her bedroom, she paused, seeing Bruce's tail poking out from under the bed. "Is that your spot tonight, buddy?" she asked, crouching down low and peeking at him under the bed. He was curled around something, his reflective eyes blinking at her. It took Jade a moment to realize it was her shoebox, the one she lugged with her everywhere she went. "Be careful with that," she said, only half teasing. "It's got all my important things."

Bruce shifted a bit, like he was getting comfortable, curling closer around the box. Relatively certain he meant it no harm, Jade crawled into bed, hoping that by tomorrow the two glasses of water she downed while washing her face would stave off any hangovers.

She woke in the closet again, Bruce pressed up against her, his tail curled underneath one of her armpits. She fought with the blankets until her arms were free, pushing up against the wall, the dim light coming from underneath the door crack enough for her to see Bruce on the other side of the closet, staring at her. Her back was killing her and part of her left foot was asleep and waking up, sending pins and needles through her nerve endings.

"This has got to stop," she said, running a hand through her sleep-tangled hair. "Maybe I should lock the closet door. Maybe handcuff myself to the bed." Jade sighed. It wasn't so much the sleeping in the closet that bothered her. What bothered her was not remembering going in. All her blankets were with her and pillows too. She obviously woke up enough to grab things, but not enough to remember. She didn't like it.

With a sigh, Jade pushed open the closet door, squinting at the change of light. Though it still wasn't too bright outside, the winter morning not yet bursting forth, it was still brighter than in the closet. She groaned as she got to her feet, feeling every joint protest the movement. Something on the bed caught her eye and she stilled, staring dumbly.

On top of her bed was her shoebox, the one Bruce had been curled around, the one she kept underneath the bed. All of her things had been taken out, sorted into neat little piles in a semi-circle, like someone had been sitting on the bed, spreading them out to view them.

Jade felt sick seeing the pristine arrangement. It wasn't the haphazard format of someone half-asleep, someone with their eyes partially closed and still on the verge of dreaming. It was the careful organization of someone looking through items and sorting them. There was the small collection of rocks she kept, some writing instruments, a deck of well-worn playing cards, some odd bits - a shoelace, a report card, a broken necklace. And then photographs. Jade moved toward the bed slowly, seeing the photographs fanned out, like a hand of cards in a poker game. She touched them, pushing them farther apart from each other, seeing them sorted neatly in chronological order. Bruce pressed against her leg and she looked down at him briefly before gathering all the things on the bed and putting them back in the shoebox, methodically placing them back in the same order in which they were always kept. She closed the lid firmly and shoved the box back under the bed.

Jade walked slowly, carefully to the bathroom, keeping her eyes downcast as she went. She turned on the light and then placed her hands on the vanity, staring at her white knuckles and red fingertips as she pressed against the cool tile. Bruce came in beside her and she flicked her eyes over to him, seeing his own eyes solemn and dark. She took a deep breath and let it out slowly.

"Lily," she said quietly, her voice low and even. "Are you there?"

She raised her eyes to the mirror, meeting her own gaze and watching carefully. She waited for the calm, collected feeling she'd felt in the clearing when she was trying to bind Dex. She waited for her world to get a little muted and fuzzy at the edges, like it did before Lily would show up. Staring at her grey irises, she didn't know if she was relieved or devastated. Her eyes were a little bloodshot and Jade pretended it was from drinking last night and not because she thought she might cry.

"If you're there, I need you to show me."

Jade felt something then; a tickle at the corner of her brain. It felt like someone was behind her, just over her shoulder, hiding in her blind spot. If she moved too quickly, or looked too fast, she would lose them. She took another deep breath and exhaled through her mouth, her lips pursing slightly as she breathed. Then, she saw it. One of her irises, the left one, turned green at the edges, the color bleeding inward until it touched the pupil, spreading out like osmosis, turning the entire torus green. It took less than a second before she blinked and it was grey again. Jade leaned in closer and turned her head slightly to get a better look. Her own eye blinked back at her - only grey. But for a moment it had been there. Green. The bright apple green of Lily's eyes. Jade laughed shakily and backed away from the mirror until her back hit the wall, one of her hands coming up to cover her mouth. Bruce pressed against her leg and she crouched down.

"Bruce, I think she's back."

Margarita Gakis loves the art, creativity and romanticism of storytelling. Sometimes, however, the act of putting pen to paper proves challenging, elusive. She develops genuine, relatable characters who grow in the hearts of her readers. From that foundation, the stories flourish into a warm friend.

She enjoys pursuits which blur the lines between the analytical and creative sides of her brain. This includes her day job in electronic data management, where she uses her creativity to solve logical problems, and also her lessons learning to play the cello, where she finds beauty in the structure of music and the instrument. She believes there is a place for both logic and imagination to work together. When they do, the results are magical.

Margarita has a special spot in her heart for dogs and lives with three of them. It can be a little overwhelming but the quality snuggle time makes up for it.

She lives in Calgary, Alberta with her family. You can keep up with her at: http://margaritagakis.wordpress.com or at FablePress.com.

Check out these other great speculative fiction titles from Fable Press:

The Hidden Icon
by Jillian Kuhlmann

Available on Amazon.com

A gentle storyteller who has always been able to sense the thoughts and feelings of others, Eiren discovers that the source of her power stems from an incredible darkness. To save her family and her land from further strife, she surrenders to her kingdom's mortal enemy - unwittingly embracing that darkness and her own surprising capacity for fury and vengeance.

Demon Jack
by Patrick Donovan

Available on Amazon.com

Fifteen years ago, Jack died and chose to sell his soul. Now, a few years out of prison and living on the streets of Boston, Jack is perfectly content to keep a low profile and avoid his turbulent past.

It's working out until the only person he considers a friend turns on him, possessed by something far worse than the demon holding the contract to Jack's soul. Now, he's been recruited (some might say blackmailed) by an ancient order with roots in the Inquisition to hunt down whatever malevolent force is responsible for turning Boston's homeless into ravenous killers.

… These great stories and more at FablePress.com/books.html

11651236R00213

Made in the USA
San Bernardino, CA
23 May 2014